Martian Biosphere:

A World of

Cybernetic Beasts

Matthew Anderson

Published February 2022 by

Morris Publishing Australia

www.morrispublishingaustralia.com

Martian Biosphere:
A World of
Cybernetic Beasts

Matthew Anderson

ISBN: 978-0-6453719-3-2

 A catalogue record for this book is available from the National Library of Australia

Dedication

To my dear Nana for her enduring love and support.

*To my beloved dog Max and in loving memory of his brother
Milo who sadly passed away shortly before publication,
both of whom patiently kept me company
over the years while I was writing this book.*

Acknowledgments

To Elaine Ouston and Ron Day of Gondor Writers' Centre for their very patient and professional endeavours to edit this book to publishing standard and for their ongoing encouragement of me as an author.

To Mr Les Ward of Ward Legal for his very professional and genuine advice.

Prologue:

Tonight's Executions

Numerous animals passed by the cages to see the carnivores that had tormented them. Animals they had feared when they still roamed free. Yet most of them did not express hate; though a few angry individuals pounded on the bars demanding to know what happened to their family members or friends.

One group of animals walking back and forwards, were students from a nearby school. They had come on a night-time excursion. A larger male long-tailed monkey carried the load of eight baby animals including a tamarin, two opossums, a peacock, and several rodents. One of the group – a baby tamarin – clambered onto the bars to look inside. The mangabey urged the baby monkey back to him, so it clambered onto his tail. The monkey proceeded to Ryan's pen.

The puma stopped pacing and moved to the back of the cage when the baby animals started gawking.

'It's a puma!' one of the baby monkeys exclaimed.

'So that is what they look like,' the opossum said peering in.

'Did you eat my dad?' the baby peafowl asked sombrely as he also peered in.

The last comment caused Ryan to flinch, pulling his ears back with guilt. The cat hunched over with his head hanging. He had yet to harden himself to hunting. He was consoled by the knowledge that the baby peacock could never know which of the many males was his dad. Neither did his siblings, such was the curious nature of fertilisation of the eggs.

He was a murderer, plain and simple. The cat knew that. They all did; but what choice did they have. Kill or be killed was the lore. Without eating, he would starve. The population needed to be kept in check, though that was a pragmatic way of looking at it.

1

However, unlike on earth, if you had the cybernetic brain and died here, you could simply live again as another animal. Here, death was not the end of all things. Sure, you never got to see your loved ones again. You had to leave your entire life behind, but at least there was always going to be a new life. Many of these herbivores were killers in their last lives. They had faced the same dilemmas and had chosen the only logical option. The entire wild system ran on a carousel of life, death and suffering known as the food web.

These thoughts were running through Ryan's head as he tried to justify his killing. His human morals still fought with the need to kill.

Outside, beyond the Zoo, an execution ceremony area was being set up. A crowd was already gathering to watch the events unfold. For Ryan and the others, it was evident something bad was going to happen tonight. Most likely, it would involve their death.

The voice of one of the apes came over the broadcasting system, 'The executions will begin shortly.'

Chapter 1

Initiating Neural Installation

Ryan

First, there was blackness, followed by an intense uncomfortable pins and needles sensation. As the nerves became more functional, he felt his limbs for the first time. His arms, legs, and tail began to come to life. His ear swivelled as he opened his eyes. Awake for the first time.

A female voice came over a loudspeaker. 'Ryan, can you hear me?' His ears pricked up and swivelled to hear the sound. His new body was coming to life.

'Yes, I can hear you. My ears are working just fine. I'm not deaf!' He thought he spoke, and his mouth tried to move, but it did not match his words. He was confused when she replied.

'Good, that means your neural thought to radio wave transmitter is working, along with your sense of hearing.'

The light came in and he saw the world again for the first time in years. The bright white lights were fuzzy as they filtered into his eyes. He was still restrained with synthetic rubber straps that kept his paws and torso tied down to the table. He could see the other side of the mirror. A woman stood there. So, the voice wasn't a robotic voice as he expected. She wore a white lab coat. Her long brown hair was tied up into a ponytail. She had a distinctive tan complexion. Her brown eyes stared at him as she pulled out a colour chart.

'Ryan, what colour is my hair, and what colours do you see on the colour chart.' The chart appeared as she said it, projected onto the white wall next to the glass.

He focused and responded, 'Blues, yellows and browns on the chart, white and black too. Your hair is brown and wavy. Why did you have to make me red-green colour blind?' he complained while the woman typed the data into a pad-like electronic device in front of her.

'You have red-green colour blindness as per normal of your species. To ensure the closest to your species original genetic makeup, we have excluded the genes for red colour cones. This is normal in most mammals, excluding primates and marsupials. Adding red colour cones would significantly modify the structure of the back of your eyes. Now we will have to test smell and touch.' She pressed a button so that a feather duster like object came to his paws. The object began moving back and forwards, testing to see if his paws could sense the feeling.

'It tickles, alright,' he snorted then asked, 'Now, how are you going to test taste and smell?' He purred in amusement from his paws getting tickled.

Another robotic arm with a strange series of objects appeared. It contained a piece of fish, a flower, a piece of dung, chunks of other animal's fur, scent gland secretions, rotten meat, and urine from his species, among others. He responded to each: indifference to the flowers, salivating to the fresh meat and fish. He reacted with mostly disgust to the rest – except one that was of the scent of another of his kind on heat. He lifted his head, raising his nose to get a better sniff of that scent.

'Most smell like poop, but the last one, quite literally,' he responded in a snarky manner.

'Good, all of your senses work. Now we need to check if your nervous system is working properly. Can you move your tail and claws?' As she asked him to move, the restraints on his tail and paws loosened, allowing him to whack his tail around a few times and to extend and retract his claws.

'Your neural/machine connection is working. Now we are going to have to test your reaction to pain.' The woman pressed several buttons causing an unexpected robot to administer a sharp needle prick on his forelimb. He winced. The straps had been specifically placed to stop him from reacting negatively. A droplet of blood came from the tiny hole. After all of this, the restrained animal just wanted to get up and get going out of there.

'One last sensory test is left; light perception. We will however be monitoring your hormonal responses in the virtual brain before you leave the terminal. If we do not make sure you properly react to your hormones, then you may not be able to feel hunger, thirst, and emotions. Considering you have a computer for a brain, the organic/synthetic interaction point is essential to healthy body and mental functioning. You need to be able to properly react to adrenaline, testosterone, and other important body chemicals. As you are not dead from oxygen deprivation and not paralysed from unsuccessful spinal cord neural cable conjunction, it is confirmed that the most basic functions work properly. We will turn the light up and down, to dim and brighten it to see if you can see these letters.'

He looked at the alphabet of letters as the light brightened and dimmed. He could still see the letters for most of the different lighting settings; even the black letters when the lights were turned to a fraction of their brightness.

It was time to leave this chamber. The straps loosened enough for him to stand. He had a good look at himself. He had big brown paws, and a brown fur coat with a paler whitish cream of fluffy fur under his body. He knew he was a puma. He had chosen to be this. It was one of the first thirty of the thousands of species available for selection.

He took his first steps, then did a mighty stretch and let out a loud yawn. He looked sheepishly at the glass door where the next animal was waiting to come in.

'Hey, testing-lab lady, this is actually really awesome – besides being partly colour-blind. What's next? Which way do I go?'

'You now must leave this room through the door to your right, take another right turn and follow the directions towards the Hovership animal distribution terminal.'

He went towards the exit, walking on the cool, tiled floors. Before going through the door, he turned back to the woman, still visible through the glass window, and said, 'Thank you, I'll be on my way.'

The woman nodded slightly. As he walked through, the metallic door closed behind him.

This was not the beginnings of his existence; his mind was whirling with the thoughts of his old life. In truth, he had hardly ever seen any animals in the flesh. He used to live light-years away from here. The only animals he saw were in the zoo way back in his home colony, which had nothing bigger than a large dog.

He now had a flesh and blood animal body around a cybernetic brain and upper spinal cord from the human form he once had.

A radio and a speaker in the back of his throat allowed proper speech. Billions had gone into making sure the technology worked properly for the hundreds of thousands that have been through this process before him. He knew he was far from the only one. In other words, the greater world beyond Mars was complicated. The facility was famed for the incredible work into animal/human transitions.

Outside of the room, the corridor began. If it weren't for the massive, five-metre-high, glass tunnel beside him, it would have been a white and sterile corridor, deprived of organic matter – except for animals and what came out of them. The glass wall was holding back a river's worth of water. The wall itself was seventy-five centimetres thick plexiglass. Through the clear wall, he could see that the tunnel was a second way for the aquatic creatures to make their way to the terminal after being awoken.

The water inside the tunnel was completely clear against the white background, causing the various animals passing to stand out. A green peacock bass stuck out prominently as it swam by.

A shoal of jungle perch made their way, swimming above his head in the higher reaches of the tunnel, just below the water's surface. Below them a group of giant otters swam by – surfacing for air as they went. A Chinese softshell turtle passed near the bottom of the tank. Down there, another fish moved along – a slow catfish sweeping its tail from side to side. Its dull patterns and large fins made it look like a piece of seaweed or a rock. He was still gawking at the fish and other marine animals when the other doors further up the tunnel began to open.

He had never seen the animal species that appeared. In fact, he could not attach names to them. He was speechless. This was too much. He heard how the different species were endless, but wow! He gawked at the size of the tank – the largest fish tank in the solar system with cubic kilometres of water and kilometres of walls.

'Wait, are those sea cows!' he said in wonder and astonishment as a trio of African manatees came swimming slowly down the corridor. Their massive eyes stared at him, as they moved up to the top of the tank. They took huge breaths before descending again.

Another animal that had just come out of the Chamber of Awakening stopped. Sitting right beside him, the coyote had been too awestruck by the aquatic movement path to speak much, or to notice the much bigger carnivorous predator right beside her. She looked up towards his face then jumped back a metre and loudly barked. He merely turned his head to look. 'Didn't see you there – sorry,' he said to the terrified coyote.

'I just was too distracted to see you, that's all. Good thing that they banned eating each other in the terminal,' the coyote replied.

The brownish coloured canine looked up at the African manatee that swam along the tunnel next to them. Its immense tail moved up and down as it swam to near the bottom of the tank. This one looked him right in the eye. Its massive eyeball tracked him as it swam further towards the release ship. Another shoal of fish passed around him. A school of African toothed catfish clung together as they swam along.

He turned his head back to the corridor to see the doors to other chambers open. A flock of Military macaws came out of one, accompanied by a bush turkey. The turkey dropped some of its black feathers whilst running around the hallway. The noisy, big, strange looking birds flew in his direction. He ducked and looked up in surprise as they flew and ran around him. They flew back when they realised that they were going the wrong way. A small mob of wallabies was released next, including pademelons and some agile wallabies. They too bounded around him, many staying well clear. He turned to see the animals emerging further up the hall.

A group of Grevey's Zebra emerged from another gate. He thought it was probably several people being reincarnated simultaneously as the same species. Further down still, a polar bear emerged from another gate. This hallway, hundreds of metres long was quickly filling with many random animals.

He approached the bear. 'Hey, Mr Polar Bear, what is going on? So much is happening that I am a bit confused as to what to do!'

'I'm just as confused as you are. I suppose the elevator at the end of the hall offers the way out to the terminal.' The bear on all fours was easily over a head taller than Ryan. The larger animal was evidently uncomfortable with the increased temperature, panting from the heat and the exertion from running in the air-conditioned interior. 'Seriously, these halls go for miles and miles. I think the end is somewhere over this way.' The bear pointed his nose.

At the end of the hall, Ryan could see the elevator opening. Its large, steel doors slid along the tracks to open, while the inner door was being wound back as well. The lift was filling up with animals.

More came quickly as a feminine voice coming from the lift said, 'Attention please, the elevator to the departure level will be leaving in one-minute's time. Please proceed to the lift or wait in line for the next lift.'

One of the zebras broke into a gallop around the bear and Ryan. 'The lift's going. I don't want to be late!' The rest of the herd soon followed.

The puma heard their loud shouting as he broke into a sprint for the first time.

'That's our way up to the departure platform. Out of the way!' the polar bear roared at the crowd ahead that was going to try and illogically cram themselves into the lift.

The work-out of Ryan's legs felt strange but he was easily capable of keeping up. The polar bear set off in a loping gait, which developed into a sprint. The bear's legs strode far and pulled back in as Ryan caught up with him. The coyote also sprinted as fast as her little legs could carry her.

The three pushed their way past the other animals in the hallway. In fright, many cleared the way. But their appearance caused some to nervously break into a run. In front of them, an Indian rhinoceros pushed into the crowd. A sambar stag joined those ahead with his tall head and antlers above the crowd, as the different animals proceeded towards the elevator.

Ryan joined the other animals gathering in the lift at the end of the hall where the underwater tunnel also turned upwards. The spiral tunnel was carefully designed to prevent crushing water pressures.

He leapt into the elevator, landing on the behind of one of the zebras, who panicked and reared upwards to get him off.

'Get it off, get it off me!' The zebra brayed as it tried to buck him off. Ryan jumped backwards off it, only to smack shoulder-first into the floor.

'Watch it. It's not the time to eat others yet!' the irritated equine said to him.

Now the security camera on the ceiling focussed on him and practically every animal in the room stared at him with incredible scorn. It was going to be a very unusual and awkward elevator ride.

The crowd of different animals crammed in. The zebra pushed in together with the bear and the bush turkeys. A white tiger came last.

The door closed, and the lift began to move up to the floors above. More animals came in on higher levels. These were mainly monkeys and more birds. They leapt and fluttered onto the other animal's backs.

Soon the elevator was packed with a multitude of different creatures trying to fit in – all complaining about being packed in together.

Beside the elevator, the bright blue glow of the underwater shaft that led to the top, shone into the gloom in the lift, silhouetting the animals in light blue and black. A manatee swam upwards. The animals emerging from the underwater tunnels included a wide variety of species. Turtles came from some and many kinds of freshwater fish swam out from other areas.

A group of giant otters passed, turning, and moving upwards with beats of their hind flippers and tails. The brown mammals had to occasionally detour to reach the air pocket supplied at the side of the shaft to help them breathe on their way up.

While the lift was ascending, a feminine voice announced, 'Welcome, creatures. You are all new to Mars. We have come from all nations, cultures, races, sexes, religions, philosophies, and political leanings. We have come from far corners of human known space. Some of us died in human form hundreds of years ago, others only recently. Others volunteered to come here; others were forced. Many wanted to avoid the inevitability of death. Here on Mars, your past is behind you, in your new forms you can begin again. You can go to wherever you want, do what you want, that is, after you leave the terminal.'

As the voice spoke, the other animals and Ryan listened. Their minds began to go into overdrive with the implications of their pasts and potential futures here.

The lift continued upwards through its cycles of stopping and moving until it was packed on many levels. More birds flew in – an eagle, owl, and amazon parrots among them. They landed upon the backs and horns of the other animals. Many other birds packed the perches at the back of the lift. A shoal of shearwaters, argued among themselves as they sat next to the lorikeet parrots, of which there were many colours.

By the end of the lift ride, three hundred animals crammed into the fifteen by fifteen-metre area. A loud ruckus, unable to be tolerated by some of the sound sensitive animals, filled the space.

A group of bush babies had to put their paws over their massive ears as they huddled in one corner trying to block out the sound.

Near them, the few jack rabbits and bush dogs that were in the lift were cringing from the racket, and other small mammals were likewise trying to block the noise.

One pademelon buried his head into the thick fur of a nearby deer. The deer barely noticed the brown marsupial doing so.

When the journey seemed unbearable, the lift came to the end of the many floors that they had to ascend. The mechanisms for the door on the far side began to move. The giant metal doors opened into the interior of the terminal, revealing the Martian sun to the awe inspired animals for the first time.

Chapter 2

A Lion in the Lobby

Ryan

The bright sunlight flooded in on the animals and exposed the terminal in its splendour. Dozens of other animals were already moving around in the terminal.

'Can't see anything – nope nothing,' Ryan grumbled from the back as they begun to exit, spilling out onto the terminal floor.

Sights they had never seen before took several creatures' breath away. The concrete of the airstrip outside stretched out for a kilometre and ended at the ocean that surrounded the airport. Tall shimmering steel towers of the greatest city on Mars were visible. The fact that there was such an easily observable ocean showed a taste of the ecological splendour found across the planet. This section of the ocean was one of the most polluted stretches on the planet. Still, the water was a deep blue.

Self-cleaning tiles and hygienic water-repellent carpet covered the space between the thick windows and the lift. Robots frequently cleaned it. One was going over the terminal floor at that very moment, vacuuming away any debris left on the floor. It was trying to avoid sucking up small animals while doing so. The machines rolled along on treads, ignoring most of the animals going around them in the interior of the terminal. Dozens of different animals trod on the pale green carpet. Throughout the enormous building were many departure gates from the various terminals.

In the waiting lounge was a cinema screen with the image of a timer counting down for the next playing of a video titled, The History of Mars. Other animals were beginning to gather on the many sofas, in preparation for watching the film.

Ryan went to sit amidst the crowd, leaping up onto the sofa before seating. He had a question nagging at the front of his mind.

Searching his memory for what he knew about the planet, the puma quietly asked the creature next to him, 'So why are we not choking whenever we go outside, or freezing to death?'

The animal shrugged. 'I guess we are about to find out.' They sat upon the couch, awaiting the beginning of the twenty-minute-long video that was to tell them how the planet was transformed.

The mixed crowd packed around the screen. Some were sitting on the floor, others like Ryan were up upon the sofa. An owl, perched near where the puma was sitting, turned briefly towards him before looking back at the screen.

The presentation began with the screen's usual showing of flight times then changed to the beginning of the video. All the other screens in that part of the terminal however retained their usual flight times.

The title, The History of the Terraforming of the Martian Biosphere appeared in white text on top of a picture showing a barren desert.

A woman's voice began to speak, 'Mars was once a completely barren and dead planet. Although there was water, atmosphere and even bacteria at some point over 540 million years before humans came into existence. When the first Rovers crossed the planet in the late 20th and early 21st centuries, the planet was a barren dead ball of rock and ice. It was still dead when the first manned expedition reached the planet in 2035.'

The first two minutes of the video showed footage of the barren and dead Mars' surface from space, and the Mars' Rovers, and footage of the first manned expedition to the red planet.

'By 2050 the first mining operations had begun, robotic in nature, the start of the great plundering of the planet's resources. A full-blown expansion into space was beginning at this time. The first manned colony was built by 2060.'

At this point, the footage changed to show mines and factories rising across the Martian surface, pulling huge quantities of ore, mineral and metals out of the ground.

'However, whilst this was occurring, there was a biological catastrophic event taking place on earth. The increasing industrialisation, climate change, invasive species, pollution, and a range of other environmental disasters were ripping through the earth's biodiversity. Already 60% of species were extinct by the 2070s. All the coral reefs and naturally occurring cloud forests were gone by 2120.

'Starting from the late 1990s the genetics and seeds from hundreds of thousands of species were collected from living specimens, dead subfossils, carcasses, black market seized wildlife trade items, zoo animals, botanical gardens, frozen zoos, the pet trade, museums and aquariums. They were stored in the Ararat initiative to preserve earth's rapidly diminishing biosphere.'

This was spoken over a montage of rainforest burning, coral reefs bleaching, various wild animals being poached to incredibly desperate degrees, even zoos were being broken into and their endangered animals were being stolen in pieces. Horrified zookeepers found their rhinos faces torn off, their elephants shot, aviaries broken into, tigers flayed, or their facilities burned to the ground.

Several creatures in the crowd recoiled. A white tigress sitting closer to the screen was amongst them; she pulled her ears back against her head.

Then the footage changed to scientists working in a lab extracting DNA from the various living and dead animal specimens, compiling them into nitrogen chilled freezers for later use.

The voice then continued. The video showed the still barren planet, Mars, from space.

'Then in 2065 it happened – what has since been termed the "Demon Core", an extremely dense black sphere of unknown material struck Mars' surface with enough force to send chunks of rock into orbit and trigger quakes across the planet.

'This core sank its extremely dense gravity into the planet. When combined with Mars' pre-existing gravity, the planet's gravity became similar to that of earth.'

The video showed this process filmed from an orbiting satellite, which was being rapidly flung off course by the sudden change in gravity. It showed massive sandstorms across the planet as sand was being dragged towards the massive dense object. As the sphere entered the ground, quickly sinking, a hole was dug and filled by gravel and rubble.

The video then changed to that of an animated clip showing the exact same core inside the planet, spinning extremely fast and gradually melting the rocks around it.

'The core also began spinning. It mimicked the same spinning of the earth's core to produce the magnetic field around the planet. With this event, terraforming became possible for the first time.' The voice continued over the clip. The image on screen then changed to a boardroom with numerous people, and two robots sitting around a table, talking among themselves.

'The first society of the Terraformers, created by scientist and experts from a range of fields, was designed with the goal of forming a new home for humanity and the biosphere that we were wrecking. There was one more factor to consider, however.'

The people in the boardroom were gesturing with a laser pointed to a PowerPoint demonstrating the early process of attempted terraforming.

'The discovery of the first brain uploading technology allowed for human consciousness to be transferred, along with the entire rest of the mind, to a computer system. This was then placed in a mechanical robot. This created sapient machines and allowed a second life after death.'

Some of the crowd scratched their heads in thought; some showed they were disturbed.

'Whilst most uses were benevolent, more concerning uses began to appear when some found ways to control these sentient, but sometimes mentally controlled machines. Then the same technology was attempted for the creation of a new human body to allow the same process – a mechanical brain in a flesh suit.

'To do this, an enormous amount of work needed to be done. In laboratories on earth and the Martian colonies, experiments were conducted to see if the mind machines could be genetically and cybernetically edited into vertebrate animals. At first, anything smaller than roughly the size of a rat was unfeasible in terms of storage power, setting a lower limit on the size of the testing bodies.'

This information was spoken over a montage of various animals being tested – a sanitised depiction but it still made some of the audience members squeamish. Several of the clips showed the animals in discomfort, pain, and agony, or taking part in various behavioural experiments while the testing was undertaken.

'The early part of the terraforming was underway by this point, hydrogen and oxygen were reacted together to create water, comets were pulled in to help fill the oceans, underground water supplies were bought up through drilling. The first rains washed the alkaline salts out of the sands. Greenhouse gasses like carbon dioxide were joined with a small amount of oxygen and an unimaginable amount of nitrogen to begin forming the new atmosphere.

'Eventually, the first oceans formed in the Valles Marineris and Hellas Planitia. Later, the great northern ocean started to form near the planet's north pole. This ocean was seeded with green, red, and brown algae, zoo plankton and small planktivorous fish. The temperature inland however was still frequently below zero, the algae was already beginning to pump oxygen into the air at this point.'

The voiceover continued, showing rivers and streams flowing over the Martian sands. 'Eventually, mighty rivers were flowing into the rapidly forming oceans.' This was changed to footage of small herbs and grasses sprouting out of the sands. A clip of a long highway of vegetation across a gradually greening landscape was also shown.

'The atmosphere began to move gradually over time. The highest atmospheric constitution was in the Valles Marineris. The high canyon walls helped entrap a breathable pocket of gas. This habitable pocket, however, was quickly going underwater from the continuously rising sea levels. The first land plants were fast breeding from wind dispersing alpine and tundra plant species. Trees would not be released outside of the biodomes and Valles Marineris for at least several decades.

'We, meanwhile, were still experimenting upon the animals. Almost all of the species we created back then still roam the planet today. Many are thousands of kilometres away from where they lived back then.'

The footage changed to a montage of different animals being experimented upon in various painful ways; evidently testing the system of mental uploading.

'Eventually, the breakthrough happened by 2150. The first success was a dog, followed by a rat, then a common raven, a cat, and a grey laboratory opossum. About twenty species were experimented upon in the early days. Through many faults and issues back then, many of the early animals died. Their sacrifice was not in vain. Those brave human volunteers were reincarnated in better and better bodies over time. Different species were completed at diverse times. The first herbivores were sheep, then goats. Eventually, a yak had the brain of a scientist who had died in an accident, uploaded. The very first test subjects were rewarded with new bodies and eventually released into an experimental biodome to begin the ecological testing stage.

'A snow leopard, of all things, was one of the first extinct wild animals to be successfully resurrected and mentally inhabited by a human consciousness. The first fully extinct animal to have this done was a Javan rhinoceros, an animal that had died out in the 2040s; a stupendous achievement in beginning to undo humanities damage to the natural world.'

Footage of both these animals being released into their respective habitats was played next, showing the rhino and snow leopard exploring the interior of the biodomes representing alpine and rainforest climates, respectively.

'The next several biodomes were built in various locations across the planet. Already the rough mapping of where the current Martian climate would end up were made. As a result, most of the domes were constructed in places unlikely to end up underwater from the rapidly rising sea levels. They rose at 4 metres per earth year – 8 per Martian year – and required an enormous input of water, salt, and organic compounds.

Eventually, the rising sea levels and increasingly dense atmosphere came to a barely breathable layer just above the rising sea, which was still the equivalent of being four kilometres above sea level on earth. This layer became suitable for the first intelligent animal released into the wild. The first released animal was a bar-shouldered goose named Heidi. Others of her kind were released shortly after. Most of the first animals were native to the high-altitude peaks of the Andes and Himalayas.

'As the climate warmed, eventually coniferous forests, even temperate grassland and temperate coniferous forests were planted and spread. Some cloud forest and tropical alpine tundra was seeded around the Vales Marinas as well. This spread to many regions near the equator before the sea levels and advancing conifer forest met the rainforest. The alpine flora had then retreated to mountain tops in the more temperate latitudes. The Hellas Platina pockets eventually populated the plains of the southern hemisphere. Soon more and more species were released, however, there was a catch.'

This was spoken over footage of the geese flying over seemingly barren alpine tundras, before forests were shown creeping in, with other fauna inhabiting them over time.

'The rising sea levels were pushing the ecosystems uphill at a relentless speed. Any permanent structures such as early colonies or lower altitude mining operations had to be abandoned to the rising sea levels. The early deciduous forests were barely ahead of the rising sea level, often being submerged beneath the increasing oceans.' The voiceover continued with a montage of the planet's changing sea level over centuries.

'Then disaster struck. Amidst the departing human migration beyond the solar system and the earth's continued environmental degradation, the annihilation happened. We are still not sure what occurred, but within 24 hours, the majority of earth's cities were turned into nuclear hellfire. All outgoing radio communication had been blocked. Something caused the earth to be enveloped in a dark cloud of an unknown material. And then it transpired; the earth's inner core abruptly ripped itself out of the planet. The consequences were severe, the entire of the Eurasian continental plate was shattered – parts of it are still drifting through space. Every species on earth including humanity was wiped out.'

This was spoken over a horrific montage of what could only be described as madness, slaughter, and the collapse of the entire planet within the span of two minutes. Some audience members slumped to the sofa, their hands over their face in horror, others sat wide-eyed staring at the screen with mouths open in shock. The white tigress moaned pitifully in despair while hunched over.

'So, since then we have been trying to turn Mars into a second home. Over eighty percent of the planet's surface is reserved for creatures like you. You are free to do almost anything you want out there. When you die, you will be reborn as a baby of another species on the first thirty list. After your first 30 lifespans, you will be a different species – mostly chosen at random.

'Halfway through the planet's terraformed history, the process was finished. The domes were opened, and the animals could move completely freely, instead of coming and leaving through the airlock gates and having to brave unsuitable habitats to get from place to place.'

The footage now changed to a more hopeful clip, filmed from an airborne drone, of the dome opening and the numerous animals being released into the partially vegetated landscape. The ground was still orange from the morning sunrise. Evidently, this had been filmed a millennium ago, but the point still stood, there was a hopeful chance of the world existing anew here on Mars.

'It has been over 3000 years since the annihilation. The year is 5534. Welcome to Mars everybody.'

There were several shocked and surprised gasps from the crowd. Even Ryan blinked, taken aback by how much time had passed.

The voice continued, 'Your different drop-ships will be at the various gates. The list of accepted and prohibited species for that location will be noted there. However, the ID scanner will tell you if this location is or is not a suitable habitat for your species. It must be noted that many species are only released from one, or a few gates. If this is the case, the scanner will direct you to the precise gate you will be leaving from.

'Now, out there, as you know, there are almost no rules. The only one is not destroying, damaging, or threatening our staff, structures, and vehicles that we are still using – abandoned equipment notwithstanding.

'The other major rule is that nobody tries killing one another until you have left the release site perimeter. You can do all that stuff out there.'

The video finished with a final clip of the lowering of the door of a craft and different animals of many species being released out into the planet beyond.

'Now go, find your gate. Adventure and destiny await all of you out there. Once you are released, you can decide where you go, do what you want to do, and make a destiny and life for yourself; experience freedom.'

Shortly after the end of this video, the remaining creatures picked themselves up off the floor, looking around in various degrees of confusion, anticipation and in some cases, shock.

Ryan was feeling uneasy. The sheer amount of time he had spent ignorant of the actual year they were in was probably the second most disturbing thing, beside the annihilation of earth.

It was time to find his departure gate. Other animals were heading in every direction through the terminal. A white tigress and a dingo caught his attention in the crowd, heading towards a series of gates purported to be leading to tropical destinations.

He stood up with a degree of concern over what he was getting into.

An owl that was sitting on the couch next to him spoke. 'And I didn't even have any choice in signing up to any of this.'

Ryan flattened his ears and stared in concern at the similarly disturbed great grey owl before he trotted off towards the gates.

Many animals were swerving and wandering around in confusion. They finally found the departure times' screens that showed where the flights were going and from what gate in the terminal they were leaving. The destinations of the hundreds of release sites across the planet were advertised on different screens.

The birds took flight and streamed around the terminal. Metal poles and cables extended across the ceiling for the monkeys and other arboreal animals to clamber onto to make their way toward the gates. Large numbers of mammals were walking around looking for their gates– the giraffes, the zebras, the deer, the coyotes, and rabbits.

The polar bear walked towards the windows, raising his head before rearing onto his hind legs, staring out in amazement at the view beyond the terminal. The zebras moved about together in a small herd, looking at each of the gates to decide which one they should use.

Ryan padded forward to find his gate. He had to stop for a second when an immense blonde woolly mammoth walked by. It could have stomped him flat had he not stopped. He didn't even know that blond mammoths still existed.

'I guess that is not something you see every day,' he muttered. He stepped back as the blonde pachyderm stopped and looked him in the eye.

'What are you looking at? You look like you've never seen one like me. Then again you probably have not.' The mammoth looked at the new crowd before turning towards the terminals and walking off towards the windows – its cream fur shaking with every step.

The birds flew overhead. Brightly coloured birds of paradise flew along with albatrosses and eagles in different directions. Crowds were quickly gathering around the gates. Some of them had to be turned away from the wrong gates that led to incompatible habitats – such as a gorilla nearly travelling to a desert. He knew he would not be able to survive and thrive in the habitats where that Hovership went. The selection was to ensure that the species were released to appropriate locations.

It was time for Ryan to make an important decision. Where was he going to live? He had only a small amount of knowledge about his species. Of the other animals around, he knew even less. He had lumped the lorikeets and amazon parrots as both parrots when they were in the lift. The polar bear, something he had only seen on film before, was a familiar species in appearance, but the physical presence and scent like an enormous wet dog was something completely different from what he expected.

The many gates led to different habitats. The deserts showing on some screens at gate 57 would be sparse in prey. Both hot and cold, the plains had no trees for miles. The taiga forest on other screens would get incredibly cold. The swamps would run a gaunt of infections and diseases, not to mention they may have carnivorous water creatures.

He also had to consider the topic of what to eat and if it was ethical to eat other animals. Finally, the rainforest sign stood out to him the most. It had its own separate launch pad.

'Jungle it is – rather not boil to death, or freeze, or drown. I may get eaten alive by everything else in there though. Should just double check the others first before I choose to leave – after all this is a very important decision,' he muttered to himself whilst trotting over there.

One gate had cold pine forests covered in snow on their video, alternating with other shots of a frozen river and snow-covered peaks and tundras. Many other screens throughout the terminal were playing videos of the region around the release sites. Yet another showed a tiny island in the middle of the ocean. He was turned away when he tried to ask the machine if he could go there, evidently, the island would be far too small to have many large land predators.

The next one over showed a cold mountain top covered in various shrubs and grass, with patches of water and cold mists rolling in over the hills. Not for him either. There has to be a suitable one for me somewhere amongst them, he thought. Another was located deep in the dark where no stars shone. The video light shone on dark waters that lapped at a shore that had never seen the sun. A huge, strange beast rippled the water in the camera's shot of the location.

Eventually, after quite some time searching, he came to a gate that might just suit him. It showed a thick rainforest and red sandy beaches. A meadow in front of the release site had deer moving peacefully amidst the thick grasses that were green from recent rains. Other images showed the thick jungles, bright, clear, blue water, and a thick inland river with a distinctive shade of brown, as if it was wash-off from the land.

Ryan walked up between the two entrances to that gate. A tree kangaroo, a fossa, a dingo, even the white tiger and an elephant were among others that were waiting outside the gate. In all, this resulted in a long queue. On the screen, a different image appeared in large white letters on the black background. It said, 'GATE 59 - DEPARTURE: 4:59'. The clock was quickly counting down the minutes and seconds until the flying ship would leave for the wilds beyond. If time is wasted in this queue, I could very well miss this flight, he thought. The voice over the speakers stated that the dropship would be stopping in a desert as well as the jungle. Other creatures would be streamed off at their independent locations, on the way to his drop off zone. This time, he was careful not to smack into anyone else while hurrying to the ships take-off zone.

The doors in front of him began to open, revealing massive crates and boxes of shiny metal with a foam padding on their floors. At the end of the hallway that went down to the Hoverships, the animals of various sizes had their head computers scanned. One of the many functions that they had was a tracking device that told the Terraformers where they were going. They were their lenient overlords after all.

The boxes soon became clearly visible, with a distinct unsettling aspect about them. He stopped to have the head computer scanned again before proceeding into the first of the crates. The doors closed behind him – sealed shut for the time being. This created an uncertain feeling of claustrophobia. He could make out the insides of the dark box. Ryan's keen sight meant he could see the light from the air holes that let some air in and out.

Behind him, the terminal gates continued to accept more animals. The stainless-steel crate door closed off the view of the terminal that he would not see again. The crate was barely big enough for him to turn around in. The hissing of hydraulic robots came from outside of the crate. They clamped around the box and their engines whirred as they moved to carry him into the Hovership.

'Great! Claustrophobic boxes, I thought that I could watch what was passing outside and below us. Not be locked up in an oppressive box for hours on end,' he muttered.

Ryan could hear the crates for the other animals close behind them, locking the animals in darkness. He kneaded his paws on the soft crate floor before beginning to pace back and forwards. The caged puma turned around and around in anticipation. Even his head was starting to feel giddy as the growing realisation of what was to come sank in. He finally sat down in his little dark box and readied himself for the next part of the journey.

He heard the other animals in nearby crates – their various hisses, honks, chirps, and bellows. Their movement could be felt through the floor and the sides of his box.

'Is anybody else here pumped? Any plans on what you guys are going to do when released?' Ryan asked to try to break the boredom and answer a curious question of his own.

'Sort of, frightened mostly, please don't eat me when we are released,' the small voice of the fox said from one of the boxes next to his. He could feel him trembling as he leant against the side of the crate.

'Oh, it's probably not going to be the most exciting experience when there is the threat of death,' Ryan said. Then a sudden realisation hit him. Wait, what am I going to eat? The prey animals are intelligent as well. Am I going to be a murderer? Please tell me that's not the case. He quickly came to the horrifying realisation about the carnivorous body that he now inhabited.

Another voice within a box elsewhere on the ship spoke. 'You must eat meat to survive if you are a carnivore. It is inevitable. Animals will curse your name and kind on their dying breath when you rip them to shreds as you kill them.'

A second voice from another crate positioned elsewhere on the ship, said, 'The creatures out there expire wherever you go. No one likes the ones that have to eat innocents. There will be grieving families of those you devour, and their final cries for help and mercy will haunt you for many lives to come.'

Ryan was looking at his clawed front paws in mild revulsion and horror.

'Okay, Mr Cynical, can you stop droning negatively. Thanks for the advice though,' said another voice from another crate.

While his mind came to terms with what was happening, the various robots moved the last of the crates. He watched through the holes in his cage as they carried and wheeled them inside, stacking them on top of each other and tying them all down with the care and diligence needed for a safe flight. It was not long before the sound of the Hovership could be heard roaring near him. He felt the aircraft beginning to wheel itself out onto the runway, taxing its way out onto the open bitumen. As the ship moved, his crate collided with another crate with a bang.

'Apologies, it's just that my head has an itch I need to scratch, kind of underestimated my own strength.' The animal in the crate that shook his crate snorted the apology as she continued to rub the sides of the crate, disappointed in not finding anything with which she could settle the itch. Eventually, she righted herself and rubbed her head with her huge paws. The sounds of other animals moving about restlessly in their boxes could easily be heard. The thunderous roaring sound of the huge thrusters on the underside of the aircraft beginning to rev up finally drowned out all other noise.

'Aircraft lift-off commencing,' the speaker broadcasted when the aircraft turned on its thrusters. He could feel the Hovership rocket up on the huge fiery downward plumes of flame. He was familiar with this kind of craft and knew what to expect. He could imagine the bitumen slightly melting below the ship. The crates erupted in loud raucous calls from the various surprised and startled animals, some of which banged around in their crates. The ship erupted upwards to a high altitude within several minutes. The sudden movement pushed them all into the floor. He could hear the small animals struggling to get up. They were at greater risk from higher gravity injuries.

The whole plane-like craft shook and trembled from the dramatic increase in altitude. After rising sufficiently, the Hovership moved to the other form of flight, the less explosive kind. A smaller set of jet engines propelled the ship forwards. Gliding on the massive wings along the high upper atmosphere, it was above the storm clouds, and out of the wind and weather below. The aircraft began to move forwards slowly over the top of the atmosphere. The movement was quiet and soft to help against any buffering and winds.

The feeling of the craft lifting had gone through Ryan's bones. The floor was uncomfortable to lie on as the foam had evidently been used numerous times before. It had then occurred to him that this would be a long, uncomfortable flight – probably one with occasional bouts of travel sickness. It would take many hours for him to reach his destination.

He was right. The flight to the release area was long and tiresome. Some of the animals had fallen asleep for a nap by the end of the first hour of flying. In his boredom, he began to listen into the conversations of the animals in the other parts of the ship.

'You're excited for this, are you?' a small possum curled in his carry crate asked another animal.

'Sort of. It will be dangerous out there. Anything could happen. It's going to be difficult to fit into the new neighbourhood, though it should not be impossible to do so,' the other creature, a tree kangaroo, responded.

The possum arrogantly expressed his expectations. 'Haven't you seen the ads? It's going to be easy – all the food you need, lots of nature, wide open spaces, no responsibilities or jobs, just the ability to do whatever you like, and a kind of immortality to go with it.'

Dennis the dingo shook his head. Evidently, he is naïve of the wilds. 'Fool, it's not going to be a walk in the park,' he rebutted,

'There is a reason why they put desperate people from all walks of life here. Some like me were forced. It is not a new heaven that we are being put into. Heaven doesn't have constant murder, disease, death, misery, fear and the other factors that make surviving in the wild a living hell.'

'I personally object. We could be vegetarian despite being traditionally carnivorous; working to help the lives of all species, breaking from the dietary stereotypes of our type,' another voice boasted.

Dennis continued to grumble, bringing concerned murmurs from some of the other animals there. 'This will be more like a battle for survival. If they wanted peace, they would not have put us carnivores out there. What are we going to do when we get hungry, eat berries and shrubs until we shrivel up and starve?' Someone began to object before Dennis continued, 'No there will be murder, lots of it. All of us carnivores will have had blood on our teeth by the end of the week, probably yours.'

'That's horrifying. This suddenly doesn't seem like such a good idea after all, ending up as someone else's dinner and all that.' The tree kangaroo was now curled up, afraid, in the corner of the crate.

The dingo looked off in their general direction in the blackness.

'Hey, Mister Doomsayer, what are you going to do about this grim inevitability that you are freaking everyone out about? Shouldn't there be some rules out there anyway,' Ryan said, trying to instil empathy in Dennis the dingo.

'There are practically no rules. It's what you make of it. There is no true direction in this new life, just all the time on Mars to enjoy it and complete freedom to do whatever you want. I'm going to be on a walkabout until I find somewhere where I can settle down without starving and probably have a family – if I don't get killed before all that happens,' Dennis said.

A few other creatures in surrounding boxes made noises of agreement. 'In the face of adversity without a point in life, I personally think that you should just take life as it comes. Living day by day and not having higher responsibilities – unless we happen to find ourselves wanting to. Enjoy the little things and don't overthink everyone. It is like this paradise you want, except that it is trying to kill you,' the dog said as he explained his philosophy on surviving in the wild.

'Can I totally join up with you? We two wandering the landscape together having the time of our lives as we hunt, live, explore and thrive together,' Ryan asked.

'Sadly, I do believe that we are being offloaded at separate drop sites, many kilometres apart. We may be lucky enough to meet each other in the wild,' Dennis said.

The white tiger interrupted them to join the discussion. 'We may be getting off at the same location – though I might choose to go my own way.'

'Sorry for you if you don't join me. What animal are you?' Ryan asked.

'I'm Natashia. A white tiger,' she responded, nearly bumping her head on the roof when she straightened herself.

'White might not be the best colour for surviving in a green jungle. You might stick out too much when stalking prey.'

'I did make the mistake of specifically picking this colour of coat when it ultimately came down to deciding what I might be. I guess I will have to manage with this handicap,' Natashia responded.

'It will be vital to maintain optimism while out there. Running out of hope must be devastating for the many creatures that experience those situations,' Ryan said as he realised that a lack of morale could be fatal.

Chapter 3

Into the wild

Ryan

Hours passed. The desert release came and went. Dennis's crate had been wheeled out with the other crates for that destination. The interior of the hovercraft became much more spacious. Ryan was still feeling claustrophobic in his carry crate. The craft lifted again, continuing to the north.

After some time of travelling at a lower altitude in the Hovership, the synthetic voice said, 'Animals, please prepare for disembarking and release through landing site 59C.'

The craft continued its path over the land, flying above many biomes on its way there. These included more deserts, savanna, a mountain, and finally a coastal belt of rainforest.

The individual shapes would have been hard to see as the ship flew overhead. The trees would blend into each other and the brown coloured river flash underneath them from this height. They were finally closer to their destination. The ship had crossed the savanna and rainforest stretch in mere minutes before turning itself more acutely and slowing down by a considerable amount as it came closer to the landing site.

The bottom thrusters began to level out the ship's position and lower itself carefully towards the release site.

The Hovership landed, flames spreading out from the landing gear as it came to a stop. It gently met the ground and the engines gradually decreased in power. After a short while, the sound of pistons indicating the release of air from the bottom of the ship came to him clearly. Later, he heard the opening of the large door. It would soon be his turn to be released.

The first release stage began. Robotic arms picked up and moved the crates closest to the exit so that they could be opened easily. Herbivores went first.

The robots downstairs prepared to release the first group of animals. According to a predetermined program, the small animals were released first. The larger herbivores followed.

'Is it our turn?' Ryan asked as the robotic arms picked up and moved his crate.

'Yes, it will be releasing time soon.' Natashia's voice came from another crate somewhere further back.

Nearly half an hour passed. The elephant was yet to be let loose, following the last of the deer. Before they went, the robots picked up Natashia and Ryan's crate and transported them to their individual release zones. After being set down, the door to his cage slipped open and revealed the outside.

The light flooded into the release crate. Ryan drew back, taking several seconds to adjust to the increased late afternoon light levels. It appeared as an almost heavenly glow. When the light subsided, he gawked at what lay beyond the concrete.

This was where the grass began. The setting light to the west lit up a small field. Pinks, reds and yellows of various flowers and bushes poked above, creating a gorgeous freckling of warm colours in the daytime sun.

In the clearing, the land dipped to a low depression filled with tall grasses that obscured the true depth of the ditch. Flowers and pools of water, surrounded by cattails, dotted the depression in the surface. The land rose beyond to a grove of trees that led to the forest beyond. Palms and pandanus raised their heads above the broad-leafed jungle trees that included rare hardwoods like African mahogany. Norfolk Island pines, sticking up above the trees, occasionally interrupted this canopy. The coppiced stems of a cheese fruit tree grew by the pool near tea trees.

Beside him, the white tigress padded out into the light, her paws lightly touching the grass for the first time. She scraped at the grassy ground with her right forepaw, her claws partly extended to get a feel of the outside before continuing. She began kneading the grassy turf then walked across the field, staring around her in wonder. With a sudden spurt, she increased her speed to leap, tumble and splash

28

muddily into a puddle, soaking the white fur of her underbelly in the blackish mud and tea tree oil. The maroon stain in the water came from the melaleuca shrub next to the pond. Lifting her head, she stared in wonder at the blue sky before playfully roaring as if to announce herself to the world.

Ryan had not yet left the release station. He watched in awe as a flock of cockatoos flew over the setting sun. The calls of many bird species and monkeys raucously filled the air. The ponds were alive with a wide variety of frog calls. He heard the drone of cicadas coming from the jungle trees beyond.

Other animals were leaving the release site to move into the wilds beyond. To his left, a fossa, a cat like Madagascan mongoose, looking like a miniature version of him, left the crate, dashing to meet the outside and rolling around in the grass.

Ryan left the gate and stood still taking in the green grass and colourful flowers that contrasted with the deep dark green of the jungle beyond. There was so much to explore in this new world. Dennis's words of warning had mostly left his mind for the moment, replaced by a desire to explore.

The soft grass flattened under his paws as he flexed his toes to take in the new sensations. Ryan headed towards the forest beyond, as inquisitive as a kitten. The puma ran to a patch of grassy marshy ground, leaping into the air and doing a half summersault so he would splash into the mud. He slid along on his back some distance before coming to a stop, then stopped to look up at the clear blue sky and the clouds. He was trying to imitate the tiger that had just lifted herself out of the pond. As she shook off the mud, it splattered him.

'Enjoying the natural beauty, I see, Ryan,' the tigress commented agreeably as she headed towards the jungle.

'It is lovely,' he said gazing around in awe.

He looked back towards the Hovership from the bottom of the depression. He could see the last of the doors lowered to reveal the cages at the back of the release area. An elephant squinted in the light when suddenly exposed to the outside. As the last robot released her, she moved forward. Beside her, a large sambar stag came bounding out. They were visible next to the cage's chain link mesh that kept the animals away from the valuable electronics of the release base.

Ryan decided to continue across the grass. He knew it would be foolhardy to follow the animals that were initially released, looking for a meal. He decided it would be better for him to wait. *What now?* he thought.

He saw the other released animals making their way into the woods. The jungle beyond the meadow was abuzz with the new arrivals.

A flock of pelicans flapped up into the orange sky, their huge wings making shadows.

He suddenly realised he was hungry. He had not eaten during the Hovership ride. He had been too nauseous for most of the flight. He had not eaten for the entirety of this new life as a puma. Hunting this close to the release site however was foolhardy. A pair of robotic mini guns decorated the roof of the Hovership, ready to shoot any released predators that attacked before the creatures had time to get into the jungle. To allow them to kill as the prey was released would make the releases useless.

Despite the risks, Philippine eagles circled over the woods, peering into the trees near the release site. Monkeys retreated from the emergent branches of the various jungle trees fleeing when the sinister shape of an eagle came swooping over the treetops. The edge of the forest was beyond the safe zone. The far reaches of the meadow were also outside of it.

Metallic wires, a few metres from the ground, reached out from the release site to the trees to provide a way for the various arboreal animals to make their way safely to the forest. The fossa and tree kangaroos tried using the wires to make their way into the forest. But the larger, clumsier tree kangaroos could not balance on the tightrope like wires. Their claws slipped as they struggled to force their nine-kilogram frames to shuffle sideways on feet too widely spaced to walk on the wire. Eventually they all dropped, crashing to the grass below. Realising their exposed location made them vulnerable, the marsupials began to hop as fast as their short limbs allowed. They hopped across the open ground with more urgency than speed. Occasionally, they fell onto all fours before pulling themselves up again for another couple of hops. They were winded by the time they reached the tree line.

The tigress was disappearing into the forest, her pelt still visible until the foliage obscured the white and brown stripes.

Ryan turned left to find something to eat beyond the boundaries of the clearing and explore his new world. Trotting off the grass, scents flooded his nostrils. A confusing mix of animal scents, flowers, trees, and the smell of salt amidst a slight smell of decay from the rotting layer of wet leaves on the ground. He could hear the splashing of small waves through the trees beyond. He moved into a trot, brushing aside the foliage that got in his way, including the palmetto palms and the small number of low shrubs.

Thirty metres further, he came to the edge of a cliff. It had suddenly materialised shortly after he had entered the thick green forest. The cliff was five metres tall and surrounded a calm cove, sheltering it from the sea. A gentle sloshing sound occasionally came from the little wave momentum that made it through a tunnel and into the cove.

The bed of seagrass covering the bottom painted the water green. Peering down, he could see small dark figures covering patches of the grass. On closer inspection, he saw they were marine iguanas coming for a feed. They grabbed what they could before scrambling back onto land again to warm up. Most scaled the cliff and hid in the trees when he came near.

Some of the lizards stayed on the rocky cliff side nearby. When he considered eating the iguanas, guilt consumed him. 'Prey... possibly. I do need to hunt, but they seem defenceless. No, not yet. The poor guys are just minding their own business and are out of my reach.' The iguanas hiding right above him would have heard this. He guessed it gave them relief.

Looking down from the cliff top, he saw something large moving vigorously in the water. The iguanas also noticed this. They realised there was another carnivore in their midst. They scattered – some diving into the water while others paddled towards the beach, clambered out, or climbed the cliffs and trees. A patch of red appeared at one side of the cove.

Shadows of surrounding trees falling onto the red and turquoise water below partly hid the larger figure that graced the waters. Ryan could now see that there were four animals down there. Three large crocodiles were using their strong tails to move quickly through the water towards their prey and the immense splatter of red that had spread across the water. The source of the blood was only now visible. The body of an animal floated on the water. An awful snapping and splashing reached Ryan's ears as flesh and bone were ripped apart. These sounds could be heard across the cove.

Above the cliff, another animal that was a part of the same release as him, stared down at the water, speechless and horrified. She was trembling in shock and fear. This deer was a small one, chocolate brown with white spots on its flanks that helped her to blend into the surroundings. She swivelled her ears and turned her head to face him. He went to greet her, but as soon as she realised what she was looking at, she turned and leapt into the undergrowth and disappeared.

He looked down to see what had disturbed the deer so much. Below him in the water was the cause of this commotion and her shock; the animal was a dead deer of the same species as the one he had just seen. The blue anti-tick spray was still there, colouring a part of the animal's flank.

This unfortunate doe had accidentally sped off a cliff minutes after being released, never getting the chance to experience her new life. Instead, she plunged feet first into a crocodile infested inlet. This area was out of reach of the mini-guns and thus beyond the areas where the Terraformers could guarantee the animal's safety.

The American crocodiles continued to butcher the carcass. One spun, dislocating the hip joint and tearing at the ligaments and muscles while tearing off a leg. Ryan was both hungry at the sight of the meat and disgusted at the same time. He shouted to the crocodiles, 'What kind of butchery is this?'

The crocodile that was ripping the offal out and chewing down on the soft organs, swallowed a bloody chunk of offal, including most of the liver and attaching tissues. He responded, 'This is our dinner in the real jungle, not that pretty garden they tell you about. You will have to get used to it to survive.' He wolfed down another chunk of bloodied meat.

The second crocodile shook a hunk of meat. Ryan shuddered when he realised this was the small intestine, still attached to the stomach. Another crocodile joined in. He ripped the head off from the neck. The skull crunched sickly when he applied several hundred pounds of pressure to it. The other continued to rip into the shoulder of the deer.

'You're new here, and still sensitive to blood and gore, but you will get used to it. All the carnivores have to adjust to this life. If they don't get accustomed to it, then they are no predator at all. Here, have a snack to get your first taste of the life you will have to live,' one of the crocodiles said.

A strong head shake threw the bloodied chunk of guts in Ryan's direction. The hunk of meat tumbled around in the air.

He swung his left forepaw in its direction and caught the meat with his claws, raking the rope-like guts up to his position. He pulled the chunk closer to him.

He fought the revulsion that he felt at eating raw meat and let his new animal instincts take over. Chewing noise followed the soft splat of the meat landing on the ground as his premolars sheared the venison into smaller shreds. He tucked into the dirty flesh that had been rolling in the surrounding soil. This gave it an overall dirt-like taste and hid some of the gore. Being so new to this environment, this deer was free of digesting vegetation and internal parasites that were so common here.

He hungrily chewed into the piece of flesh and finished it with a gulp. His thoughts were already contemplating how messed up this place could be, while painfully admitting to doing a horrid thing. He gulped down the next mouthful and shook his head to clear his thoughts.

'Everyone says I will have to kill perfectly innocent animals just to live. How can anyone justify that to themselves?' he asked a nearby crocodile.

'You have to stalk them, then chase them down and kill them before they scream at you too much. The herbivores know this is how it works. It's how our whole world works, *Survival of the fittest*. Some herbivores can kill you just out of malice if you're not cautious. A crazy bunch of them think they have a better solution to the carnivore problem, to the detriment of us. I would avoid them if I were you,' the crocodile said before swallowing another hunk of tissue. Ryan grimaced as the crocodile ripped the lungs out of the chest with a dreadful snap of ribs, taking the pectoral muscles with it.

33

'But how will I tell what herbivores to avoid?' he asked while thinking how stupid that question sounded. The croc responded as he finished his meal, his hunger sated for the next month.

'The big ones of course – the big deer and huge antelope, elephants, giant forest hogs and the giant sloths. They will either run at you, away from you or stand their ground. Even the fleeing ones can be dangerous,' the crocodile warned.

'Are there any especially dangerous herbivores.'

'Beware of the ones from the towns that come in big groups hunting predators that they hate. They have weapons of stone and bone, steel, iron and obsidian and other implements of murder. They own boats and entire towns,' he warned him, 'As for you, I have some advice – stay on the coast. There is little competition here for territory from the town animals. They don't frequent that area often and avoid us crocodiles. The deer meat was just a taste to get you started on your way. It must have been your first meal. I wish you luck out there and a long life.'

Ryan sat stunned. *Was he telling me the truth? Animals using weapons? That is absurd. I will believe that when I see it.*

The crocodiles finished their meal then swam out of the cove towards a series of tunnels and passages to the ocean. The end of the cove was partly obscured by mangroves clinging onto the side of the cliff. The high tide submerged the tops of their roots.

Ryan sunk onto his stomach, muttering to himself, 'This is a lot to take in at once.'

A high tide was particularly unusual on a planet such as this. The two moons were so small that they had little effect on the overall high tide level. He was even more surprised when a three-metre-long tawny nurse shark emerged into the lagoon from a tunnel from the sea. Connected to the sea near the entrances was an underwater grotto, lined with colourful corals. The cliff and vegetation above were obscuring part of the inlet. The fish followed the scent of the blood through the water. The marine iguanas clinging on the sides of the cliff watched the shark. The yellow shark shadowed the sea grass and the small outcroppings of soft corals and tropical algae at the bottom of the lagoon.

The various small reef fish hid in the sand and the rocks as a third American crocodile dragged the remnants of the deer underwater.

The shark tussled with it ripping off a large chunk from the neck, before swimming away with its large piece of flesh. The shark's leathery tail flicked high above the water, sending a splash of water high into the air.

The croc grabbed the carcass. He shook it so violently that he tore a chuck off, the rest scattering in the water. A part of the carcass came up against the rocks. A foolish sense of courage consumed Ryan. Without thinking, he went around to the edge of the cliff, then clambered down onto the mangrove bushes that surrounded the underwater entrance of the cove, to avoid the third crocodile and the shark.

He ran towards the cliff and grabbed the fallen tree at the far end of the cove. The branches were rotting in the water past the edge of the cliff. He pushed himself away from the tree and paddled out to the carcass. The third crocodile had finished eating and brushed past him as he dived to reach the carcass.

The salt stung his eyes and his ears filled with water. He struggled to overcome his buoyancy, paddled downwards, and grabbed the dead body with his claws. He swam up again as the air in his lungs was diminishing. He finally broke the surface, gasped for air, and swam back to the tree.

He grabbed the tree with his three free paws and sank his teeth into the spine. But when he started moving up the branch, things went wrong.

The nurse shark swam up from the bottom and latched onto the carcass, trying to tear off the other half of the remains. The puma continued hauling it up, over the rocks and the tree branches. The shark let go of the limb she had just removed and slipped back into the water, grabbing the limb again as she dived.

Ryan pulled his section of the remains up onto the top of the cliff, much to the surprise of the marine iguanas watching from the trees. He backed into the forest clearing with the mutilated carcass in his mouth. Here he could at least enjoy a whole meal in peace. He chewed into the carcass contentedly. He would not go hungry this evening. The sense of horror that he had just mutilated someone's corpse crept back into his mind. He spent twenty minutes eating meat off the carcass, gnawing at the bones and flesh, satisfying his hunger, but feeding his disgust at the same time.

He soon went to sleep on the leaf litter and red sand forest floor. He dozed for about half an hour on the ground next to the kill before awakening again. After finishing his first meal, he continued through the jungle, following cliffs, caves, and coves to the mangroves by the sea.

The jungle continued onwards, wrapping itself around the shores of the coves and high ground the closer he got to this inland channel of water. He kept following it until a part of the beach levelled out and ran below a cliff. At one end, a partly submerged forest of mangroves blocked the beach.

Chapter 4

The Red Sands of Mars

Dennis

Dennis had been in the desert for over an hour. He thought back to his release from the Hovership. He had risen when he heard, 'All release zone 59A animals, prepare for disembarking,' over the loudspeakers. He had propped himself up, his hind legs still numb from the cramped sleeping area. His tail had begun thumping from side to side in excitement. Sure enough, the robotic arms clamped around his crate and carried it to the other end of the ship.

The dropship reached the first of its destinations, the desert, and landed on the roof of the release site. The machines moved the herbivore crates to the release zone. The smaller herbivores were going first – let loose long before the carnivores to save them from being eaten.

Surprisingly, they didn't open his crate immediately when it came time for the carnivores to begin. The smaller carnivores were let out onto the planet first. This group included coyotes, desert monitors, and three black-footed cats.

Evidently, this meant that there were some minutes to wait before he would be released. He picked himself up. In front of him, he could hear the other crates being moved outwards and untied from the straps that held them. Many of the other crates behind them were also flung open. Dennis's cage was still shut, as were those of the other animals that shared the same problematic predicament. The roars, snorts, and grunts of various animals came from the area in front of him.

From the loud noises of the other animals moving out into the desert he knew that the machines had already opened their crates.

The robots moved to his cage, removing it from its previously tightly screwed door lid. They opened the doors and the sunlight flooded in. Dennis turned to see the outside world for the first time.

He could not see the desert sand at first, because other animals, including a white addax antelope, were moving in front of him. The antelope was one of several that grouped and continued out as part of a herd. The strength of the herd instinct in these uplifted animals was not known to him. Once they departed, he could see his surroundings. The sand was extremely bright from the reflection of the sunlight that shone from the pale fur of the antelopes.

Early released birds had flown far out into the desert. Of the land animals, the herbivores had a head start. The herd moved out with a couple of oryx, a few more addax and three gazelles. A flock of birds came after them, having missed the earlier release. Some species he didn't recognise included pigeon-like sandgrouse and immense bustards, whose wings hit the roof as they left.

Outside on the red sand the antelopes looked around. Between the red sand dunes and empty desert, they could see a river in the near distance with a very green bank of vegetation. Various kinds of grasses and papyrus grew there, causing the river to have a small strip of wetlands with the water and some of the food the animals needed. The group continued to exit the ship while the dingo watched. When all the animals, including the last of the carnivores had been released, the doors of the ship closed. The legs retracted as it rose into the air and turned for the jungle.

Dennis stood and looked around. What should he do? Saliva dripped from his hot panting tongue, indicating his need of both food and water. It was only mid-afternoon. The sun was still boiling hot. *No running for now*, he thought. He turned and trotted down to the desert river. He followed the long trail of tracks from the dozens of other animals that led to the river. No doubt, after a drink they would move in different directions.

Chapter 5

Ignorant of the Law of the land

Ryan

The tide was high, and the mangroves were currently half-submerged. Evening had come to the jungle as the last of the afternoon light disappeared. The mangroves' air breathing roots punctured the sands below the waterline. Before he reached them, he had to cross a narrow strip of salt marsh. Several species of salt tolerant grasses, bushes, and young mangroves inhabited the marsh. Coarse in constitution, the sand was very salty from a one-off typhoon which inhibited trees here. Coconuts, casuarinas, and pandanus trees dominated the forest in this area. Large green fruit hung from the pandanus branches, toxic without special cooking.

Ryan continued walking along the side of the cliff above the coastal strip following this sandy forest edge. There would be many kilometres of walking before he could find a place where he could settle down. In this land, others of his kind and competing predators had likely claimed most hunting territories.

The longer he spent in this forest, the stranger it seemed. The air was cool and humid, split by starlight illuminating the forest floor with a dim glow. This was enough light to observe the forest under darkness. Minimum illumination meant the outlines of the animals and plants were just noticeable with Ryan's sensitive eyes. A barely visible black flying squirrel scrambled back into its hollow, when he gazed into the canopy of the trees to look at the unfamiliar constellations of stars.

Further along the coast, a red forest duiker broke into a leaping run when he passed. The cat only noticed the small reddish antelope when the undergrowth it brushed aside rustled. It was gone before he could even begin to approach. Now a night-time chorus of mosquitos and flying foxes added to the ambience.

Giant bats occasionally revealed themselves through the gaps between the tops of the palms and the African corkwood trees.

Ryan stopped when he reached the end of the cliff. One coconut palm stood out to him. He noticed a strange scent coming from the palm. The scent marking was from another big cat, a species he didn't recognise by scent alone. The black urine marking at the base of the tree had a strange, buttered popcorn smell, mixed with the horrid stench of urea and the smell that would come from a dirty litterbox. This didn't point to one species. At least two species in this jungle smelt like popcorn, though Ryan did not know which two. The scent made him cautious. The puma continued warily knowing he was invading someone else's territory, in his search for a new home.

He knew that with at least two species of big cat in this area, competition would be fierce. At least the mangroves were likely to be empty of overgrown cats, excluding tigers, but instead, they would be inhabited by crocodiles that would love to eat him. To live around here long term, he would have to find a patch of territory that he could claim as his own. He would have to wander the land until he could find a place free from other competitors, ally himself with an already existing territory holder, or steal an area by defeating the previous occupant in battle.

Curiously, the scent trail led towards the river beyond and not to the jungle inland. He was amazed to find massive paw prints that dwarfed his own in a line along the cliff. He proceeded cautiously, ready to flee if chased by a larger carnivore.

Soon he felt the need for sleep. He didn't want to continue stumbling in the dark. The puma found a spot among the leaf litter, scraped a depression — kicking out beetles, cockroaches, a legless lizard, a skink, and an unsightly whip scorpion in the process. He lay down for his first sleep in the forest. As he drifted into dreamtime, he decided that he would have to develop the skill of sleeping up in trees for greater safety.

Hours later Ryan awoke and continued his exploration, now turning inland to search for fresh water to quench his thirst.

By mid-morning he had left the coastal pocket and was heading into the forest. He decided to avoid the paw tracks in case he found their owner.

The interior rainforest was different from the coastal strip, tall immense hundred-year-old kauri pines and kapoks as well as short figs grew in the forests.

In places, strangler figs smothered entire trees. The multitude of different tree species towered over his head. The terraforming machines planted them hundreds of years ago and their descendants spread from those seeds. Massive kapoks, African teaks, and tola trees reached up for the light. Many understory bushes and shrubs filled the gaps between the tall trees. The purple flowers of the jacarandas could sometimes be seen flowering out of season above the immense ancient Hope's cycads. The occasional palm stood up in places reaching for the canopy, joining the floristic chaos of the understory struggling for sunlight, all linked together by rattan palms and lianas.

By now, the sun had risen further into the sky, beating down on the emergent layers where military macaws squabbled with each other over a bunch of branches fifty metres up a tola tree. The floor was still as dark as the night that had fled the upper reaches of the forest. Strange scents filled the air.

The plants, fungi and animal scents all flowed with the breeze into Ryan's nose, and he tried to remember and distinguish the sensory bombardment that the forest had to offer him. The leaves sunk slightly as he padded his feet into the ground stirring up small insects, at least one shrew, and a mouse, as he continued further into the jungle carelessly. He trundled over a large mushroom, its spores flying into the air as a foul cloud, causing him to sneeze when the spores reached his face.

In the mass of tree trunks, it was easy to get lost. They seemed so similar, covered in lichen, moss, and bracket fungi. Ryan nearly forgot he was on Mars and not in a remnant jungle on earth, like that which grew over the Congo, Amazon, Papua, and elsewhere before the Annihilation decimated them so long ago.

Ryan could climb them if he wanted, but it was easier to walk across the ground. Travelling in the trees needed far more caution and balance. He spied a small, weird tamarin that gazed that him. Its brown eyes observed him with curiosity from thirty metres up. It scratched itself before scampering straight up the trunk with two babies. Other members of the small troop of four came to look at him from the safety of the canopy.

Despite being his natural habitat, it felt both confusing and monotonous. As he continued, he met a straight track through the forest that headed towards a river. It appeared to have been carved by a large mammal. Ryan could still not see the end of the trail in either direction. He noticed an animal ahead staring at him. An antelope or deer darted off the trail, too skittish for him to catch. With its big head start, it was another missed hunting opportunity. Ryan decided to turn away and head for the river.

This track was well-worn, rutted, and trampled into the undergrowth. He had to avoid the buttress roots, fungi, and a red and black crocodile newt on the way to the river. Logs that had fallen over the tracks had been moved out of the way to clear the track, pushed by something large and strong into the undergrowth with considerable force.

Other tracks cut through it leading in other directions. Most of these were smaller than the main trail where different creatures walked. Ryan came upon a porcupine, without as many quills as expected. It looked like a rat with a long prickly tail. It took one look at the cat on the trail, then turned and scampered back into the undergrowth.

'Didn't mean to scare you, little fella,' the puma apologised.

By the time he reached the river, there was something far bigger blocking his way. The new beast could have been the one that made this track. Its large rump was as high as Ryan himself at the shoulder. The creature made a snuffling noise as it continued ignoring Ryan.

Possible prey, he thought. After all, he was just behind it within pouncing distance. But it was big. *Probably not a good idea*, he decided. *I won't talk. I'll just see how far I can follow this animal down the trail towards the river.*

He knew he needed to practise his skills for future hunts. But this animal was too big. If he were to pounce, he guessed he would invoke the animal's wrath, and lose the fight.

Overhead something was watching; a camouflaged bird hid in the trees. A tiny brown nightjar was clamped onto one of the branches up ahead. Its massive eye focused on the cat – peering inquisitively at him before fluttering off. It was a very strange time of day for such a nocturnal creature to be spying on him.

Finally, the last of the forest disappeared and the river came into view. The large animal he had followed veered towards the red sand and mud beach.

As it turned, Ryan looked at its large rectangular body with short legs, large toes, short black fur, and a bizarre short trunked face. Ryan was not familiar with the animal, though he thought he had seen its image before.

'Exactly what species are you?' The puma asked, cancelling any plans for eating the larger animal that was considerably heavier than he was.

'A Brazilian tapir. Try me if you want. If you are too stupid or new here to know what I am, then perhaps you would learn a lesson or two if you tried. Good thing you're not stupid enough just to rush in and attack like another idiotic new creature did last year.' The tapir stopped and turned to the puma, 'You followed me to this river. You had many chances to attack. Why didn't you?'

Ryan could see the anger building in this strange animal. 'I didn't want to.'

'At least you figured out how to sneak. That saved you from being ripped apart.' As he spoke, the tapir lifted his trunk to show a large pair of canine teeth, not quite as big as Ryan's but equally as dangerous. Then, much to the cat's relief, the large animal turned and continued walking along the river.

The beach of red sand was swept from inland, intermixed with large amounts of sediment washed from fields, jungles, and grasslands upriver. Small saplings dotted the shore on the upper reach gripping a foothold here and there. Evidently, this sand had been dumped by a flood several months previous.

Ryan suddenly realised that nightfall was coming again. The last of the sun's rays were sinking below the trees. Their bright colours dimmed, and stars began appearing in the night's sky.

The twinkle of stars and an oddly shaped moon soon lit the sky. This looked similar to another star in the sky, Phobos, one of the two asteroid moons that orbited Mars. They were too small to cause the tides to change the way other moons did – such as the one shining on Earth.

Ryan noticed that the jungle continued on the other side of the river. He could hear the loud chirping of crickets and the calls of nocturnal birds. The dark shadow of a crocodile lay on the opposite riverbank, possibly asleep. Fruit bats graced the sky, creating holes in the Milky Way above, as their skin clad wings created shadows against the lights of the night sky. Ryan gasped as he looked at the beauty, both above and below the dark jungle trees that were silhouetted by the low light of evening. He could see surprisingly well with his sensitive vision.

He slipped down to the river, looking out for danger in the shallow clear water. It was too shallow to hide a crocodile. He crouched down to lap up water that tasted of mud and tannin.

Having quenched his thirst, he decided that today had been long enough. A nocturnal animal like himself would normally use the night for hunting and travelling, but he was just too tired after such a long day. This was still his first week in the biosphere. Today he had merely been exploring the environment. He had travelled several kilometres but hadn't found a proper home.

Stretching and yawning, the cat padded to the base of a tamarind tree perched on the edge of the beach. He decided to climb and sleep in this tree. He leapt through the understory, feet leaving the ground and flicking up grains of sand as he moved upwards. His claws dug in, gripping the bark. Hauling himself up to a branch, he flopped on the soft lichen and mosses before his heavy eyelids closed in this new jungle home.

Chapter 6

Counting the Howls

Dennis

The red sand was an unfamiliar feeling on Dennis's paws at first. However, by the end of a day in the desert he had become used to it. He had reached the cooler riverside bank, which was far more pleasant than the hot sun-baked desert. This barren expanse still looked truly timeless, just like it had for countless millennia.

Now he had no supervision, and he was free to do whatever he wanted. The herds of antelope that had come out of the Hovership had stayed in the riverside marshes and decided not to head into the desert, a very wise choice that the canine also made. However, he knew not to associate with them too closely because they could kill him easily. Smaller animals were going to have to do for his food. He had managed to deal with the moral quandary about killing and come to the realisation that it was necessary to get by. So far, he hadn't eaten anything other than a dead bloated fish that floated to the shore on his second day. The rotting condition of its flesh disgusted him, but he had to satisfy his hunger.

Now he was hunting for small prey in the reeds and papyrus. Frogs hopping through the cattails caught his eye. They were burrowing frogs that come out for the rare rains, thriving while the water lasted.

The dingo lunged at the small amphibians, sinking his forepaws into the mud, and snapping at a hapless frog with his mouth. He grabbed a leg and it squeaked loudly.

'It hurts. You've hurt my leg. You broke it! You bas...'

Dennis opened his mouth again and snapped, consuming the bite-sized morsel. He felt slightly uneasy about it, but he needed food.

45

'No hard feelings. I needed to eat, and you were food,' Dennis said to the empty space in front of him.

Now he looked for another. A larger one hopped away into the reeds. The dingo lunged, grabbed its legs, and threw it up into the air. As it came down, he dodged. That was not a burrowing frog. The angry Sonoran toad limped back into the reeds, frothing, white, toxic bubbles of bufo toxin forming on his shoulders.

Such a close brush with poisoning made Dennis pull his ears back in apprehension. Frogs could very well be off the menu. Plenty of other small animals lived in this swamp, after all. Like small marsh birds, rails, and jacanas. And rats were everywhere. Slinking along in the mud he accidentally stumbled into the water. Blundering through the one and a half metre tall reeds, he came upon a patch of water lilies. An African jacana was sitting on a small nest among the large floating leaves. The male looked off to the side as his mate came over to lay another egg in his nest. She had mated with several males and needed to move the eggs to the different nests. The dingo decided that such a sitting target could be worth it, but he would have to be sneaky.

He stalked below the lily pad leaves, popping up only to check his position in comparison to the target. Before long, he had located the nest, and waited for the female to distract the male. He was about to launch above the water, when a Yaqui catfish got to the delicate nest first, upsetting it, and tipping the eggs into the water. The pair frantically tried to get their eggs back above water. As the catfish scoffed one of the eggs, the dingo snapped. He clamped down on the surprised catfish. It writhed around in his jaws. 'What, what, ouch it hurts a lot, like … oh crap I'm done for,' the surprised catfish said as it flapped around in his jaws.

'Sorry about your nest.' Dennis dropped the catfish on bank and apologised to the jacana couple, his paw resting on the struggling fish.

'You should be! Go ahead and eat those drowned eggs. You've ruined our family!' the birds angrily squawked at the dingo. They failed to notice the two eggs that had rolled onto the lily pad that was still unturned and above water.

He gestured to the eggs. 'Over there, those eggs can be saved. Oh… and the other three you managed to save could still be alive.'

'Go and finish that fish and leave us alone. We've lost three.' The jacanas moved to save the last eggs and Dennis decided to return later to devour the now ruined ones.

He finished the catfish and continued inland, away from the river and up onto a rocky outcrop overlooking the stream. Several aloes clung to the base of a rock; their brownish leaves difficult to see against the red rocks at dusk. The bright starlight of the night's sky outlined the phoenix palm that he found. It was here he decided to spend the beginning of his first evening out in the biosphere. He dangled his paws over the edge of a large rock while he lay down on his underside. He swung his head back into the night sky and let out a long low-pitched howl. The lone voice rang out its haunting echo across the river and the surrounding landscape.

What he had not expected were replies. Many howls, mostly angry ones, came from a clustered area about two hundred metres away – closer than he expected. The resident pack of dingoes was announcing themselves. The coarse uneven roaring of a jaguar joined their evening melody, partly ruining the music of their voices.

He waited for more. He needed to know about anyone else in this region that could be a problem to him living here. Sure enough, a good thirty seconds later, several different howls and one throaty roar spilled into the night sky from the same group. This time much closer. The predators were closing faster than Dennis liked.

A pack of dingoes with what could have possibly been a jaguar in tow meant that this place was already truly occupied. Dennis left the rock in a hurry. The first dingoes spilled out of the trees and desert bushes to confront him.

'Out of here intruder, wrong territory mate,' one of the dingoes snarled at him. Others grouped ready to chase.

'Chase that lackwit out of our territory, pack – chase him out!' shouted their leader. Dennis quickly turned and leapt off the boulder, running into the dark. His pursuers followed with excited howls and yips.

Dennis took note of the much fitter wild dingoes catching up across the dunes. They were running parallel to him at first. Then two dingoes that looked similar and a third black and tan dingo quickly gained on him. The two orange dogs came from the front and the black one came from the back. Their ears were erect, and their mouths snarling. 'We will give you a choice. Join us at the bottom of the pack hierarchy. If you try to leave you will die!' one of the orange-furred canines snarled.

Looking ahead, Dennis saw a potential way out. 'Screw you. I don't want any of this submitted servitude bullshit. I'm going my own way,' Dennis barked, urging them on while sprinting further away.

They charged from three directions. He sprinted towards the pair in front of him. A small patch of stony ground lay among the red sand. Spying the stone under the starlight, Dennis hit it with his back paws, then with all his back-leg strength, leapt up off the rocks. Being on sand the other dingoes could not jump as far. One of the orange dingoes reared as Dennis flew over their heads. He came crashing down into a dune, righted himself, and ran off into a spinifex clump filled plain.

He had seen this small patch of grass from the rocky outcrop earlier, beyond it was a patch of thicker grass where a herd of Arabian oryx and gazelles grazed. A group of large lumbering beasts that Dennis could not identify were among them.

As the dingo dashed and dodged his way through the grass clumps, he quickly discovered the unforgettable prickling sensation of the spinifex. The other dingoes followed, sniffing for his scent trail. One of the pack's members picked it up and they started after him.

Dennis came to the edge of the spinifex. He was next to one of the shaggy beasts eating an acacia seedling, when a jaguar came around.

The beast was a diprotodon. It was an angry bear-like, gigantic wombat relative. Spinning around to face Dennis, it snorted inside its bulbous nose in surprise. The multi tonne wombat exposed its yellow incisors to both predators. This was the only thing preventing the jaguar from pouncing on Dennis. The fleeing dingo moved away as the oryx and other gazelles broke into a sprint across the grassland. The dingo pack, still looking for the intruder, raced in amongst the animals.

The jaguar pounced. Dennis rolled into a spiky tussock of spinifex, wincing as he did so. The jaguar landed short. The angry diprotodon stepped up and swiped the jaguar with its paws. Dennis ran out onto the plains leaving the jaguar to its fate. It yelped as it crashed into the spinifex.

As Dennis sprinted onto the plains beyond, he saw that the black and tan dingo had grabbed one of the gazelles. As they were struggling, a massive, winged creature flapped its wings and snapped at the dingo. Dennis saw the huge bill lifting both animals off the ground. The dingo yelped as the beaked animal dropped the gazelle and continued to shake the dingo in its jaws. The beast had no feathers but had wings and a large beak. It flew off carrying the unfortunate canine into the dark sky. Shadows against the distant mountain and its foothills outlined the flying creature and the dingo.

The sudden loss of their pack-mate caused the pursuing predators to flee back towards the river.

Dennis sprinted across the now deserted grassland to the dunes again. Glancing back, he saw the dingoes that had been pursuing him turn back to the river. It was time for him to leave for the mountain beyond. The volcano could have better opportunities for him.

Chapter 7

Territorial Transgressions

Ryan and Dennis

Dawn broke through the leafy city, piecing the canopy in a golden glow as the flying foxes returned from their nightly foraging. Their raucous screeching awakened the puma. He stretched, and was preparing to descend, when he lost his balance.

'Whoa, whoa, whoa, wake up, Ryan!' he said, clutching at the branch. He was halfway under the limb with his hind legs dangling below. His claws raked at the lichen and mosses around the tree's trunk in an effort to steady himself. However, from his position it was easier to let go and fall to the ground. The cat spun around as he fell. He hit the forest floor with a solid thud, back paws landing together first. He brushed himself off, picked himself up and headed towards the river.

The creatures of the night had retreated to their holes in the trunks and soil by the time the sun rose above the trees. The dawn chorus providing an unmelodious song between the branches died away as the forest began to light up. A small herd of deer graced the red sand further up the river, nervously waiting to see if the crocodiles were present before stampeding across. The herd of chital kicked up water in giant white splashes before paddling across silently and hauling themselves out on the other side. They knew they had to be quick to avoid the crocodiles, and whatever else could grab them. They were close enough to the ocean for bull sharks to be present. Few land animals swam here due to the risk, but Ryan still wanted to cross the river.

The puma walked towards the water's edge and jogged along the shore looking for a more suitable crossing location. As he continued along the banks of the river, he knew he would have to cross the river sooner or later if he was to find a new territory. He thought that most areas behind him were most likely occupied.

The cat stopped at a likely crossing place. He placed his front paws into the water and set off from the shore. The water sloshed over him, and he began kicking to cross quickly; to avoid any of the crocodiles. As he continued, he took a glance underwater. It was too murky for him to see his paws clearly. The sensation of leaving the sand completely left him with an odd sense of discomfort and fear of attack from below. He stared at the far shore hoping it would come quickly.

As he approached the far bank, the water became cleaner than the puma expected. When he submerged his head again, he could see the ridges and ditches in the sandy bottom of the river. A shoal of rainbow fish dashed out of the way as he passed over. Further along, he saw something in a circular shape, swim into the sand. Easily 30 centimetres wide, it moved over the dark seagrass. The puma jerked his head above water again, spluttering out water, surprised by what he had seen.

The mangroves on the far shore were evidence he was still close to the ocean and the unusual forces of the tide still had an effect this far inland. He finally reached the other side. He dug into the sandy bottom with his feet. The sand swallowed his feet making it difficult to walk. As he pulled himself onto the bank, pockets of water fell from his fur in rivulets. A final shake of his pelt removed the rest and his fur dried quickly.

He moved back in the trees, stopping to sniff another scent marker sprayed high up on a trunk. This one had the same faint popcorn smell he had found before, but it was more intense, and far more ammonia was emanating from it. He stumbled back, snorting and coughing. It belonged to another big cat. He was about to trespass into another cat's territory.

He looked back up to a cliff some distance behind the trees. The puma had smelt the same scent the day before. He was still standing under the tree when he saw a form appear on top of a boulder nearby. He leapt back three metres in surprise.

'Well, hello there. Nice to meet you… I guess…' Ryan nervously mewed. His ears flattened back against his head. The marker of the territory was not far away.

She bared her teeth and snarled at him. Ryan was rapidly considering bolting back to the water.

'What are you doing here? You're trespassing in my territory. There is only enough room for one of us. Get out!' she roared.

She slowly climbed down the boulder, landing on the dirt with a soft thump and the scrunching of leaf litter. The tiger continued to walk towards him with her ears flattened against her skull and her snarl exposing her large yellow tipped canine teeth. 'Seriously, you should not be here, pest. I don't let any pumas or tigers in on my watch.' She continued to snarl, advancing to pouncing distance.

Ryan moved backwards. The tiger circled the tree.

'I'm so sorry. I didn't mean to intrude. I was simply moving along looking for my own patch of land to live on. I only just found out that you live here. I'll just be leaving back across the river,' the puma mewed. He knew this could easily end in a fight unless he managed to flee or smooth-talk his way out of this. He tried to be subtle with his negotiation and not anger the tiger.

Ryan nervously stammered, 'I am very new here, only been here a few days. I'm trying to find territory of my own. I am still searching and do not mean to stay here. I did not mean to intrude. I will move on if you will just let me pass.'

The tigress leaned back onto her haunches as she considered what he had said. Ryan began to shrink in fear, his fur prickled, and his tail went under him, sweeping side to side.

The tiger continued her advance. 'You should be running by now. Prey isn't supposed to sit there like that offering itself like an appetising snack. I have heard the beach is a great spot for smashing your skull between my jaws.'

Ryan barely had time to think about the implications of those comments. He leapt away, twisting in the air, and running back to the river. A massive weight slammed on his back. The two cats tumbled. The huge paws clamping around his shoulders pinned Ryan.

The larger cat slammed him into the red sand. She moved her jaws to his neck. Ryan squirmed furiously to flip himself into an upside-down position. He began to rake her underside with his hind legs and scratch furiously with his front paws. His claws were streaked red from the gashes in her pelt. She responded by lunging her fanged maw at his head. He lost his grip as he squirmed to shift his face out of the way. His hind limbs had let go and so had one of his arms.

Big mistake. She proceeded to slam him with her forepaws. She pushed him into the sand over and over, bludgeoning his head with her leathery pads.

If he had been a normal unmodified puma, this could have caused considerable injury to the brain. As it was, this was just causing him considerable pain from the blunt impacts and whiplash. He struggled to avoid having his eyes gored out by her teeth. At the same time, he continued to kick with his hind legs inflicting more wounds on her.

The two continued to force themselves at each other's throats. As they slipped and loosened their grips, they began tumbling and twisting in a violent fury, both trying their hardest to inflict injury on the other. Their tails whipped wildly as they snarled and roared. For a moment, Ryan managed to roll her over and be on top. She slapped him again and rolled back.

Her paws left him for a second and Ryan rolled to the side. He was wincing in pain, but adrenaline overrode that for now. The tigress reared to avoid further injury before pouncing. Ryan pumped his legs with all his strength. He leapt towards the river. The tigress pursued, making bigger strides than his. She flew over the ground in a rampaging fury. She was gaining on him. As he fled, Ryan thought, *I'm so very screwed. My life is over*. He launched himself into the air, sailing six metres off the sandy shore and crashing into the water with a massive splash.

The tigress thundered into the water behind him, spraying up white splashes that scared away the fish.

A shallow stretch of water lay in front of them. They pounded through the shallow water generating massive splashes. Something was moving across the bottom. Ryan caught a glance of the round fish again. As the puma leapt towards a submerged sandbank, he felt an uncomfortable zap short circuit through the water. Yowling in pain, he came to a standstill on the sandbank. He stood trying to recover from the electric shock and mewling from that and the numerous bloody wounds over him.

He turned to see the fierce charging tiger getting closer. She was only about four metres away. Slamming her paw on the concealed round fish below the water, she reared up in pain and surprise. She convulsed, roaring, and falling into a fit in the water.

The round creature put its head out of the water near Ryan. 'Saved you cat, that's the first time I've managed to electrocute a tiger by accident. Feel sorry for her though,' said the torpedo ray as it swam away into deeper water.

The tiger was stunned, out cold in the water, barely moving. Ryan was temporally baffled by what had happened.

He sighed relief that the fight was over but concern for the tiger plagued him. His mind was in turmoil. The shock had knocked her out and would probably lead to her drowning. Killing and eating her was not an option. He could run away, but that thought made him feel guilty. What if she died from drowning? It would be his fault. What if he left her to the crocodiles? Perhaps he could then take over her territory. Or... perhaps he could save her. Maybe even befriend her and live with her in her territory. How could he save her? These thoughts ran through Ryan's mind rapidly. His altruism won out.

He ran back along the bank to where the stunned tiger floated. The puma waded out to retrieve her, cautiously avoiding the ray that had knocked her out cold. Ryan gripped the scruff of her neck with his teeth and pulled her back to shore ignoring the pain from his own wounds. Her buoyancy made pulling her through the water so much easier. Dragging her onto dry land was much harder.

He managed to get her body onto the bank, but her tail still floated in the bloodied water. Using his human CPR knowledge, he pounded her chest with his paws to resuscitate her. He realised that no one had done CPR on a tiger before. At that moment, he didn't consider that pumping the chest of a tiger and blowing into her mouth was a dangerous and bizarre proposition.

After three thumps, she woke, not from the oxygen but from the stunning wearing off. In surprise, she spun around, growling, to swipe him. Ryan dodged, leaping back four feet. Her paw slammed into the sand.

When she finally realised what had happened, she said, 'Why did you do that? You could have gotten yourself killed? Honour like that is rare for most wild beasts. Why didn't you leave me to drown?' She panted and gasped, taking air back into her lungs. Ryan continued to look on in a mix of confusion and surprise. 'Anyway, what is your name? I apologise for swiping at you. Saving my life deserves some respect from me.'

Ryan, still shocked by her paw slam, responded. 'My name is Ryan. I don't know who you are. I tried saving you because I thought it was the right thing to do. I hoped that you might forgive me for trespassing, maybe even take me as a friend of sorts. I'm new here. I'm yet to spend even a week in this world.'

'No, I don't feel like raising a cub like you. I guess you could have stumbled into my territory by mistake. Thank you for saving me. But you should not be kind to your prey, or you will be going hungry from a lot of missed opportunities. I'll tell one of the vultures to inform a friend on the coast to look for you to arrive. She may be welcoming of a new pack mate. You just need to follow the river to the estuary, turn left, and walk along the coast. She will find you eventually. You should be off.'

Ryan still had other questions to ask. 'Three more things. What was it that almost killed you? What is your name? And what does the animal I am looking for look like?'

The tigress began pulling herself to her feet, forelimbs first then the back half. 'Torpedo rays, they're like underwater landmines electrocuting any who tread on them. Many of us are more fearful of the crocodiles than them though. The animal you are looking for is a black and tan furred dingo. My name is Anthia. You should get going.'

Ryan nodded before breaking into a trot along the riverbank.

***

Dennis hauled himself to group of the lowest of the pines on the south side of the mountain. He panted heavily, heaving his ribs in and out, as he limped into the shade. Utterly exhausted, he collapsed in a heap at the base of a tree, not even bothering to make a bed. This was the first shade in several hours.

Setting out the night that the other dingoes found him, he had trekked across the dunes to leave them all behind. This forest was the first decent vegetation he had seen. He collapsed, folded his legs beneath him, rolled over, and settled onto the sand, narrowly avoiding getting sand in his eyes. Under the hot noonday sun, he drifted into sleep.

The sky was dim when he stirred. He hauled himself onto his feet and scanned the dunes to the south. Nothing of interest back there. He doubted there was anything south of the river, but perhaps there was. The dingo decided it was better to try his luck up here.

Turning around, he set out into the dry coniferous woods of pine and cedar. He panted. The moisture seemed to have left the back of his throat. His last meal was from the wounded gazelle the other dingo injured. He had killed it, as he had to eat.

He sniffed for water. He detected various trails from volcano rabbits, hyraxes, wallabies, mice, rats, and others all going about their business. No animals were around. Although he didn't know who left them, he would remember these new and alien scents for future use. He trotted through the boulder fields and short cactus clumps – the needles and loamy sand breaking under his paws.

After a while, he finally found a watering hole – or what was left of one. It was just a tiny pool surrounded by dry mossy boulders in the shade of ancient Lebanese cedars. A few terrified rock hyraxes, volcano rabbits, and wallabies moved away quickly.

'Run, hide! It's a predator. It will kill us!' the panicking small mammals squealed as they scattered and hid themselves among the boulders. The brown guineapig look-alike, the hyraxes, were brave enough to watch from cracks and crevices where Dennis could not reach. It was only then he noticed the chuckwalla wedging itself into the rock crevice, inflating itself to make it harder to remove.

'Well, that is quite a welcome,' Dennis growled sarcastically as he bent to drink the cool mineral-laced mountain water. He could smell dead meat, a new odour coming from somewhere close by. He turned and stared in surprise at the chewed-up spur-winged goose carcass. The green feathered wings, head, and feet were the only remains of another predator's meal. The dog turned back to the rocks to see the chuckwalla still stuck in the rocks.

'Indeed so, you surprised all of us, hence you are missing a potential meal. At least you can quench your thirst here,' the chuckwalla said.

Dennis glanced at it again as he drank.

'We are a lot calmer than our larger friends that were here just few minutes ago. One is still here with us.'

Dennis turned to his left, and then withdrew himself, stumbling in surprise. He had failed to see the metaphorical elephant in the room. An Arabian oryx stood just one and a half metres from him. The white antelope pointed its long horns in his direction.

Dennis backed nervously from the antelope. 'You surprised me, big fella. I was pushing into your personal space. I'd rather not end up as a kebab.' The oryx only huffed in response.

Suddenly, something unexpected happened. Dennis felt vibrations through his feet. The sensation moved up into the tall pines that begun to shake. Black-headed grosbeaks flew out of the trees, their tiny wings fluttering rapidly, chirping in alarm. It continued through the entire forest as the eucalypts and cactus trees joined in the dance.

The dingo looked up to the mountain side. There was a loud crack, followed by a thunderous boom that echoed up the slope. A large cloud of rocks and dust emerged from the side of the mountain.

The hyraxes and lizards panicked again, scrambling out of their rock cracks as it began to split. The boulders above him were beginning to crumble, as were the rocks beneath their feet.

'Run, you bastard, run like the wind!' the antelope urged him. They both sprinted in panic down the mountain slope. The hyraxes and lizards scrambled away as the rocks around the pool all came loose, crumbled apart, and began to slide.

The two larger animals ran down together, the dog bounded from boulder to boulder and the antelope ran through the gaps between. They met the other antelopes who were nervously forming into a protective circle.

The bull oryx bellowed in anger and frustration, 'Run, you fools! There is a landslide behind us!'

The herd of oryx broke formation and sprinted together down the slope.

Thankfully, the volcano itself was not erupting, but the mountain side had begun to loosen. Boulders of varying sizes begun rolling downhill, gathering speed as they travelled. The shaking continued. The canopies of the trees shook as their trunks swayed, yet only the most rotten of dead trunks broke off. The healthy trees took the force of the quake in their stride.

Dennis hunched close to the ground as he continued to sprint along, ducking falling branches as the shaking rattled the forest to its core. The birds had already fled up from the floor. The woodpeckers wheeled over his head in confusion. More panicked animals came running down.

Now the sides of the mountain moved and crumbled. Trees moved on either side at uneven rates, some seemed to be moving along with them. It was only when he looked back that he panicked. Between the occasional rolling boulders came a steep cloud of dust and debris.

'Behind us! It's coming!' the dingo howled to the antelopes ahead.

Between the boulders and trunks came bellows and snorts as the herd of white antelopes passed between the rocks. The fleeing canine darted back and forth between the boulders as the landslide came rushing around them. Now entire trees were being felled and added to the tumbling pile above them.

One of the oryxes tripped over a rolling boulder that hurtled down the slope. The animal went tumbling. As its massive horns turned up, a second oryx failed to stop in time and was impaled. The horn ruptured his heart. The linked pair kept tumbling, careering down the hills.

The oryx herd stared in horror as the pair flew towards them. The other antelopes and Dennis moved aside. By now, the rocks were right behind them, and they needed a way out of this situation in a hurry.

The herd continued to stampede as entire chunks of mountainside became dislodged.

The shaking had stopped but the hillside was still moving. The herd continued to run to where the rocks connected back to the cliff. Here the antelopes jumped from the slope to flat ground. Dennis jumped up onto the now moving and disconnecting boulders. He then leapt and scampered along the falling tree trunks, as the leading edge of the rockslide created a dust cloud and consumed hundreds of trees when it went further downhill.

The dingo continued his sprint along the side of the mountain slope panting in fright, knowing he was in great danger. He leapt from boulder to boulder, adjusting how his paws landed on each of the rocks. He ran alongside, through and around the antelopes, snapping at their heels to make them clear room as he ducked and weaved. The tiny volcano rabbits and rock hyrax darted to their holes and crevices as they initially sensed the vibrations. Now only the bigger animals were left above ground. They were quickly running downhill. The gathering cloud of dust surrounded them. Trees, boulders, rocks, and dirt were flooding downhill right behind them.

The herd of oryx followed the dingo, jumping and bounding between the different rocks as the smaller boulders crashed into the valley.

Ahead, a larger boulder, sitting at the edge of the valley, soon came into view. It was a solid six-metres-high and looked like it may provide some shelter from the approaching torrent of sand, dirt, and rock. The two-impaled antelopes were still rolling down the hill together as the other oryx swerved around and hid behind the larger boulder.

Dennis came skidding down the steep hillside and eventually ended up beside them. He found himself among a not happy herd of antelope. He stopped right next to the white antelopes. They pointed their horns at him as the rocks and dirt came flying past. Entire trees had ridden the larger sections of rocks down. They were being mixed together as if in a horrific blender.

The predator and prey briefly tolerated each other's presence as the dirt and rocks flew over their heads, showering them with pebbles as the rest of the mountainside came tumbling and crashing around them.

Looking further into the forest, he noticed the still shaking trees seemed to slow before coming to a stop with the rocks. The shaking had stopped, the dirt and rocks finished flying over them and the dust started to settle.

Dennis nervously looked back over his shoulder at the antelopes that were still treating him with a great deal of suspicion. As soon as he could move without dust in his eyes, he turned his back to the antelopes and without a word, moved up the slopes. He needed to see something before he left this mountain.

Further up the slopes, something was wrong. Sure enough, he came to a breach in the mountain side where the rocks had once been. A large cavity had been blown out of the slopes, and water was pouring down from above. What looked like old volcanic tunnels were filling a deep pool on the floor of the chamber. Strange blue, translucent fish-like creatures swam into the waters whilst crab-like creatures came from the walls and ceilings. They scuttled back wherever the sun hit the water, flapping about on the land as they poured in and scattered into the pool.

A noxious set of fumes was bubbling and steaming up from the water below. He wisely decided to draw back as the steam and mists were now streaming down over the outside. Before he left, he turned inwards to see further inside the mountain. He saw a twisted and broken tunnel of stainless steel. The clean metal contrasted with the broken basalt and hinted at wonders within the ground. He turned away. He climbed a rocky outcrop, turned west, and dropped his jaw.

A huge concrete and metal construction lay broken and shattered over many miles to the west.

The crumbled and broken ruins led to other rocky outcrops out in the desert with a few parts still standing. It had been a giant bridge connected with the mountains far to the west. In the distance, a couple of pillars near the horizon still had clumps of rainforest trees growing on the top. Across the plains, he could see birds flying from one pillared island to the next. Stunned by the revelation, he looked away from the view and headed back downhill.

Chapter 8

Enter the Mentor

Melissa and Ryan

Another long, hot summer dragged on. Here in the rainforest, there was little difference between seasons, unlike further inland. The summer heat continued to beat down in another grove of coconuts and pandanus, their frayed leaves providing dappled shade on the sandy forest floor.

A short figure of a dingo slinked between the trees. The dark figure was no more than 56 centimetres high at the shoulder. Melissa sniffed her way between the trees, not hunting for now. It was simply too hot, and she had eaten yesterday. The scent of a duiker filled her nostrils. A loud noise made her turn her head. The creature with a black and orange pelt was sitting in the palm's shade. A vulture landed above her.

'Greetings, Melissa, Anthia has some news for you,' the vulture said to the dingo.

Melissa looked at the bald black bird that had an orange face and a black feathered body.

'Hello again, old friend. Bernie, is it not?' Melissa responded, turning her black and tan head to face the vulture. Her tail was beginning to wag.

'A new puma, a tiger, and some other animals may be in the area. They released a shipment of new creatures this week. The puma is a potential opportunity for you. He is not very skilled at hunting and needs someone to train him. You did say you wanted someone to assist you. Your possible new pack mate is intelligent and willing to learn but a bit naive. His name is Ryan, and he may be in the coastal forests somewhere close now. Please keep a look out for him and see if he wants to join you. A pack of one must be difficult and lonely for you,' he added. 'It's been a while since I've been at a kill of yours. You never really catch much big game. It's hard, isn't it? Perhaps your new friend can help provide better hunting opportunities. Bye now.'

The vulture flapped his large wings and rose up beyond the canopy.

'See you later, friend,' Melissa called as the bird ascended into the sky.

The dingo thought about the message. *If I'm going to make him a friend, I will of course need to find him first. "In the coastal forest" is a bit vague but at least it is a start.'*

She knew her keen nose would pick up the scent and find him quickly. But first she smelt giraffe. Peering through the undergrowth, she could see a giraffe staring at something, before jerking back between the palms. *There could only be one thing that would make them act like this,* she thought, *someone being very stupid.*

Cautiously, she investigated. As the giraffes ran around her, she broke into a run. She dashed between the willow and pine-like casuarina trees. Her paws came skidding to a halt to avoid a huge giraffe that flung its feet over her head. She ducked as it passed. Up ahead she could see the moving legs of the cat.

***

Ryan found himself in an interesting situation. This morning he had woken when the sun shone into the canopy of the tamarind tree where he rested. Beyond here, the forest changed back to the rainforest, leaving the mangroves behind. The red sand could be easily seen once the beach spinifex was brushed away. The coast had to be near and so he continued his journey towards it.

By this time, it was starting to get hot. He had passed another scent marker, this time of a wolf like canine. He couldn't tell the subspecies from the scent alone, but again he was trespassing on another's territory. Focused on finding the end of the trees, he had ignored the various beach flowers, and not seen the massive giraffes that he had unwittingly stumbled among.

Pinned between several giraffes, he was snarling and whipping his tail back and forwards. He was terrified of the massive Maasai giraffes that were surrounding him. They kicked their massive legs towards him every time he tried to go to the edge of the group. The puma was too inexperienced to attempt to play chicken with the giraffe's legs, and so they conveniently blocked off his escape. The immense giants were as startled as he was.

'You shouldn't have come here, cat,' one of the giraffes condescendingly scolded.

'Get lost, murderer,' another snorted.

'I just need to get away from here without being clubbed to death,' Ryan tried to explain. The giraffe closest to him reared, lifting her front legs a short distance off the ground, then stamping them down again right where Ryan had been before he jumped back. He tried to get to the trees, but the animals blocked him and anyway, he was not game enough to try and climb any of them.

Then he glimpsed something sneaking around the backs of the giraffes. One of the giraffes spun when it felt the pain of fangs biting into its feet. A small black animal darted back as the giraffe ran after it. Ryan saw his opportunity and ran. Two of the giraffes gave chase. A third went around to the front of the animals. They chased the two carnivores towards the water until Ryan spun and ducked then jumped at one of the giraffes.

The puma found himself grabbing onto the backside of the giraffe, slipping as he dug his claws into its spotted hide.

'Get off, idiot cat!' the dingo barked as the running giraffe flung Ryan around.

Another giraffe aimed for him to protect his mate. He let go of the spinning mammal. He landed awkwardly, tumbling, and twirling in the sand. The other giraffe couldn't stop in time and whacked into its mate headfirst. The first giraffe ran off, yelling angry obscenities at the clumsy second giraffe.

Ryan stood to shake sand out of his pelt.

'Saved your ass, Ryan,' the dingo commented as the giraffes walked back into the forest.

'How did you know my name, and why did you try to save me?' the puma asked.

'My name is Melissa. A vulture informed me you were coming, and so I sought you out. I reached you just in time. Perhaps you should be off. By the way, I can see Anthia tried to kill you. You are still carrying the wounds of that encounter. I'm surprised you have no infections yet.'

He walked up to Melissa, wincing again. The unmistakable tiger claw marks still made his back feel raw. Elsewhere on his body, other injuries sustained in that fight were beginning to heal.

Melissa peered at his back. 'They could very well be infected. You tore some of those scabs open in that encounter and they're bleeding. Saltwater might help sterilise those wounds. If we are going to get to know each other, then doing it at the beach would be a good place,' said Melissa initiating their metaphorical ice breaking.

The ocean lapped at his paws as Ryan made himself comfortable in the sand and rolled around in the surf. He was glad to be out of the forest and the dangers it contained. He just wanted to relax so he pushed off into the sea for a short swim. He remembered what the croc had told him but ignored that advice.

The cool water penetrated his fur, coolly sucking the heat off his skin. The salt stung his eyes when he tried to dive under a wave. Attempts to catch the waves didn't work very well. The current pulled him under. When his head came above the water again, he turned to the shore. He could see Melissa standing near the trees.

Just then, a massive wave slammed him into the sand. Ryan pushed off the bottom. Swishing his paws around, he finally broke the surface with a gasp. He took a quick breath of fresh air.

He winced from the salt entering his wounds, flushing the stale blood out. He began paddling back to shore. The waves caused further discomfort as they slammed into his behind. He continued to paddle until his paws reached the bottom. Dashing onto the beach, he looked left and right for the canine. She was not visible.

Eventually she emerged from the trees. He took his first good look at her. He saw her black and tan fur, black upper parts, and orange underparts with a tiny amount of white around the belly. She looked like a miniature wolf with sleek fur that her grooming kept in good nick. She appeared to be in good condition despite roughing it in the wild for years. Coming closer, he noticed a flare of wildness in her eyes that would not be seen in a domesticated dog.

She approached him, head held high, and tail wagging slightly. She displayed a confident pose but not outright aggressive. 'Feel better now?' She looked him up and down as he stood there with dripping fur. 'So, you're the newbie klutz that I've been told about. I've heard that you may want some help.'

Ryan nodded to Melissa. 'Yes. I know it's an incredible inconvenience to ask you to help train me, but can you still do it please? It can be to both of our benefits.'

The dingo hesitated for a second before answering. 'Yes, but I will eat first unless you catch your own prey. Also, you need to listen and follow my instructions until you are competent enough to survive without me. Now come along, you have much to learn, and we have much to discuss. My den is in the coastal forest.'

Ryan came trotting along beside her, pleased to have found a friend who could help him.

Melissa looked at him head tilted to one side. 'This had better not be some ruse to get me eaten.'

'I won't eat you. This is too good of an opportunity. I need to learn survival skills. I would like to learn from you. Thank you very much for offering to help me,' Ryan added as they vanished into the forest.

Chapter 9

Morality of Murder

Ryan

The den was not too extravagant. It was a simple sand hollow dug under a fallen Casuarina tree, fifty metres away from the river. Its leaves had withered away long ago. Melissa had taken the time to snap other casuarina branches to provide a roof to her den. The interior of the den was nothing fancy, just a tree needle covered hollow with the scent of dog.

'Home sweet home. It's not the most elaborate den, but a home never-the-less,' the dingo said to Ryan as she entered the hole under the fallen tree. 'I have several dens in my territory but it's rather hot now and travelling to other dens may not be a good use of energy.'

She settled down on the leaf littered floor. 'So, we should discuss some things before the real training begins tonight.' She had invited Ryan into her den, but he stayed outside in the sun.

'You're new here, inexperienced, you could say,' Melissa started.

'Yeah, I guess and clueless at that. I still have problems eating creatures that scream at you and beg for their lives when you try to kill them.'

'Well then, we'd best start discussing how we carnivores do things around here. I have much to teach you. But I must address your concerns about the morals of hunting. It is difficult to bring yourself to do the killing and to justify it to yourself, but if you are to survive you must do so.' Melissa spoke calmly and waited for Ryan to reply.

'What can I do to justify what I have to do to survive,' Ryan responded with concern on his voice.

'I see there are many lessons I must teach you. This is one of the first. There is an informal unwritten code of ethics that some of us follow.

You don't have to, but it makes justifying your actions to yourself much easier, unless you have already gone completely bonkers.'

'Completely bonkers? That's not a phrase I would ever use to describe my mental state,' Ryan replied.

'Completely bonkers is something that would take multiple lifetimes to reach even for the already mentally unhinged carnivores. Thankfully, lives we have in between as herbivores give us a break from the killing. Going into madness only happens if you completely let yourself go and let the darker corners of your mind overwhelm you. I have only known a few carnivores like this. One of my aunts was one of those. The crazy bitch ate her mate alive and was exiled from the clan. She should have been killed for that,' Melissa snarled as she looked back in disgust.

'Wait, you said you grew up in a clan. I thought dingoes lived in packs not clans, yet you live alone. Did you leave, and do they still live around here?' Ryan asked.

'Long story. I was adopted. The Mountain's Foot Clan, about fifteen kilometres inland from here used to be my home. I'll tell you about that another day.' She continued, 'You however are much better than many of the others here. You are different because you still have an air of innocence, a compassion that can be saved. I believe you can still be a decent moral creature even if you must eat newborn kittens to stay alive. I have done that once before,' Melissa admitted.

'Wait, you ate newborn kittens? That's monstrous.' Ryan rose to his feet, his fur rising on his back.

'Okay, it was years ago at a time when I was starving. We had not eaten for several days and the pregnant lynx we caught, and her kittens, had to be shared with everybody. The thing is that sometimes to survive you have to do horrible things,' she tried to reassure her feline friend.

'I understand, but I'm still horribly uncomfortable and slightly disgusted. Go on,' the cat responded before sitting back down again.

'The first and the most important rule is to kill only what you need. The only justifiable reasons for lethal violence are if you are hunting enough to eat, defending yourself or your family, friends, pack, group, or anyone else. And finally, if you are proactive in preventing a future problem by attacking the not so obvious foes and prey,' she stated.

'And why would you need to attack the not so obvious foes and prey,' Ryan asked, tilting his head in interest.

'To chase intruders that will compete for prey in your territory. The other reasons civilised creatures use includes fighting in war, both attacking and defending as well as mercenary work. The honour of different tribes and civilisations vary, yet so many dishonourable cowards that should be attacked exist,' she explained.

'This rule means that you will not kill creatures out of boredom, barbaric cruelty, and possibly accidental surplus killing. The predatory instincts can sometimes make slaughter entertaining, while such acts would horrify our morality. All killing must have purpose. There should always be a benefit for yourself or for others. An honourable, brave, foolish carnivore often ends up as someone's fur coat or in their stomach,' Melissa continued.

Ryan turned his ears towards her, listening intently as the sun went below the horizon.

'The second rule is that the death should be quick. With the exception of Komodo dragons, hyenas and several others, most other animals try to kill their prey as quickly as possible. Hyena chases can go on for hours, but they finish the hunt by tearing their victim's organs out of their bodies, devouring them while they are still moving. Painted dogs do likewise. Most animals cannot survive long after that. It's an excruciating but quick death.'

'God, that's an awful way to kill someone. Do you hunt in such a barbaric manner?' Ryan was looking fearfully with his eyes wide, and ears tucked back as he sat upright.

'I have morals to prevent that. I only tackle prey I can kill myself. With your help we can catch bigger prey. Your attack method involves pouncing on the prey, wrestling it down and biting out the spinal column, throat, or skull. Nevertheless, prey will escape many times. To let a prey animal go is a decision that will come down to you.

'You are the one who will decide if that stag is too quick; if that bird has retreated into impassable terrain; if it is not justified eating an entire clutch of turtle eggs; or if that baby tapir isn't worth risking an angry adult mauling you to death. And bare-paw shark fishing never ends well.' She chuckled to herself, thinking of acts of idiocy she knew from the past.

Smiling at her amusement, Ryan said, 'I take it there are stories for another time about these most entertaining hunts?'

'There are many critical choices that need to be made before a hunt to ensure success. So be reasonable. For an animal like you, a hunt should not drag on for more than three hours, two of which consist of stalking time. You should never let your prey know you're coming until you begin the pursuit, otherwise you must fight it paw to paw.'

'As for battles for territory or to defend yourself – meagre territory squabbles and carcass stealing should not lead to death unless the scavenger or opponent is the only meal available. For example, don't attack a coyote in the desert to take the bone it is eating. The dog is more edible than what is being fought over,' she continued.

'I heard that some animals use weapons, to even the odds. How is that possible?' Ryan said.

'There are some herbivore packs with human intelligence like yours that do use weapons to protect themselves from predators like us. Battles with them can be extremely dangerous. Your opponents want you dead. You must use your wits, skills at fighting and your strength to win your battles and to avoid death or other consequences. In these battles, be quick about killing or maiming. A maimed enemy cannot kill you and can be finished off later or scared off. In these situations, your survival is your highest priority, no matter what mission your pack sent you on.

'Talking about packs, you should try to remain loyal to them since you may not make many other friends. The weapons they use are particularly lethal; knives and swords, bows and arrows and weapons of every kind. They often use tiny knives, attach the weapon to a saddle, or tie them to their bodies with the help of more dexterous creatures, before battle.

'There are large weapons that creatures can't competently wield by themselves. Guns are another weapon that they find hard to use. They make bulletproof armour from the web of giant spiders but have trouble getting enough. Fighting them is a lesson I cannot teach you without help.'

Ryan interrupted her. 'Whoa, hold it there, lady. This is too much for me to take in. Since when did giant spiders come into this? Are there any other big rules I need to follow?'

'Okay, one last thing; vultures are our friends so don't waste meat, let them finish it off when you have filled yourself. Tonight, I will show you more of my territory, but you should probably make yourself comfortable and rest before we leave. You will need to hunt for the first time, or at least I will teach you how to do so.'

As she finished, Ryan settled into the sand nervously.

The sun had set by the time the pair finished talking. Ryan wanted something to keep the sun off his head the next day, so, using his paws and mouth, he wedged fallen casuarina branches between other limbs of the tree and covered the top with more of them. He then napped for a couple of hours until Melissa woke him. Ryan stretched to prepare himself for hunting.

The two trotted down to the riverbank. The light of the asteroid moon was providing slight illumination, enough for their exceptional vision to work. Arriving at the riverbank, they stopped on the sand, much to Ryan's surprise.

'Now, I will begin your hunting lessons. It may take many months before you become competent. First, you need to show me what you already know about hunting.'

Ryan was listening intently.

'Find a prey animal and catch it, kill it and bring it back to me. Go on, go and hunt,' ordered Melissa.

Ryan was surprised by this order. He thought she was going to show him how it was done. Nervously, he left her to go out on the hunt.

It took him hours to catch anything. A squirrel ran up to a high branch when it saw him. A duiker bounded into the undergrowth when he appeared. The tortoise sealed itself in its fortress. He knew little about how to hunt having been a city slicker in his human days and so needed to learn the subtle nuances of stealth. He crept silently into the undergrowth, crouching to make himself less visible to any prey. He then snuck around searching for scent trails. Soon he found the scent of a peafowl.

He followed this aroma, keeping a watch in the trees above him. It was not long before he saw the immense brilliant green train of the peacock hanging from the bird as it perched on the branch of a drooping casuarina tree.

The cat stalked to the base of the tree, making sure he approached from behind. He clambered up the trunk to the branch, but before he could reach out and grab the bird, he placed too much of his weight on the limb. It collapsed under him with a loud crack, sending the cat tumbling down.

The loud call of the bird echoed through the forest. The surprised animal began to fly downwards since peacocks are not good flyers.

The puma thudded onto the red sand and immediately leapt sideways to continue the pursuit.

The bird hit the ground and ran to compensate for its poor flying skills. The cat continued to follow as the bird weaved and ducked through the undergrowth, avoiding his every move.

The peacock finally took to the air. It flew over the river, fluttering with all its strength but it failed to make the fifty-metre-wide river, landing in the middle.

Both desperate and stupid the big cat launched himself off a small sand cliff into the wide estuary. He paddled hard against the current towards the unfortunate bird, his head high above the salty water.

The bird was still struggling. When he saw the cat coming towards him, he said, 'You're not going to save me from drowning are you? I'm going to drown anyway so just be quick about it. I expect nothing better of you.' The peacock dropped his head with a defeated look.

The puma caught up, grasped the bird with his teeth, and quickly severed its spine, before swimming back like a 17th century gundog with a downed partridge.

Partway through swimming across the river, something grabbed at his prize, Ryan tugged back, staring down at the water with fear. The creature ripped an entire wing off and dragged it down into the water below. Ryan paddled faster in surprise. The trail of blood flowed through the water.

As he heaved himself onto the shore, Melissa came running up to him, looking at his prize.

'I didn't expect you to catch anything tonight, well done.' She then tucked into the meal. He turned away to leave her with the bird, walking a few metres into the undergrowth before collapsing with guilt. He had just murdered an innocent creature for his own gain and to impress his mentor. It even realised its fate and surrendered itself. *Why do I have to do this? Can't I live on fruit or something less gut-wrenching than innocents?* Turning around he walked back for his meal, with his head hung low.

Melissa stopped eating to comfort him. She lifted her head up from the kill. 'I know this must be difficult for you, it is always hard doing it the first time. I sulked for hours after my first couple of kills, so I know what you must be feeling. Eating innocents is the only way you can stay alive. You're an obligatory carnivore, and you should know that. That means that you can only eat meat. Without meat, you will starve. If you eat only plants, you will become sick.

'Come sit, I will tell you of some of the things I have had to do to save myself. You will need to make a lot of hard choices out here. I'll snuggle and even lick you while you eat and tell you stories of my previous lives. I have gone on many adventures in other lives in far off and distant lands and seas.'

'I also made the vows of respect to the prey's soul while you were away. The soul that is about to move to another life always hears it, comforting them that their death was not in vain. However, I should probably tell you this and more tomorrow.'

That said, she went to sleep, head resting on Ryan's back while he finished the bird.

Chapter 10

Adventurous Allies

Dennis

Beyond the edge of the pines, Dennis was hunting among the grove of prickly pears. The cactus trees would make a clumsy failure a very painful mistake. Nevertheless, it was worth investigating. He strode into the dark tangled maze of the cactus, looking for any prey.

In places, strange purple cactus-like plants stood up high, surrounding bizarre bogs containing weird glowing plants. He stopped to sniff the water here. He tried to drink it, only to jump back when he tasted its odd alkaline taste. *Evidently,* he thought, *this is not healthy to drink.*

The lingering scent of a mole rat caught his nose. It led him to a hole that looked as if it had not been used recently, at the base of a cactus. He drew his snout out of the burrow, snorting out the dry dust from his nose. As he pulled his head out, a dead skink hit his head.

He looked up and spied the culprit. A tiny bushbaby stared down at him. The small primate resembled a squirrel but had dexterous hands in the place of paws and a large head with huge eyes and ears.

'Hello there, sir, you look famished and friendless.'

These words piqued the dingo's interest.

'Go ahead, the skink is yours.'

The friendly primate hopped down to the main trunk of the cactus from the large swollen prickly stem that formed part of the canopy. Down the grey-black trunk, the primate scrambled, leaping off the tree and onto the ground before scurrying over the dirt towards the dingo.

'Why are you doing this, little furball?' Dennis asked as he swallowed down the large skink.

'I'm lonely and want to leave this place. I am meant to be heading towards the Principalities, but the bird I was riding on got eaten. It's dangerous out here. An owl could snatch me up any minute. There is somewhere else I need to be,' she explained.

Dennis sighed. 'And how is this my concern?'

'There are forests in a nearby river swamp. Beyond that, is the nation of the Equatorial Principalities in the landlocked river's delta. I had been as far as the edge of the forest but could never cross the desert safely,' she explained.

'What? You want me to carry you right into the path of danger for the both of us?'

'I want someone who is willing to carry me to the swamp, or at least closer to it. Most are too sensible to cross the desert or are too interested in eating me, hence the skink. Could you please take me with you, as long as you don't eat me?'

Dennis considered the request. 'Okay, if you want me to. You're too bony and after that skink, I'm not hungry enough for you to be a second snack for me, so I won't eat you. Besides those big brown eyes staring at me while I eat you might tickle my conscience. It's too crowded for me by the river, but I may not be going over the desert straight away. There is the whole crossing a great big desert and not wanting to dehydrate to death problem that has to be considered.'

The little primate nodded in understanding.

'I'm going hunting in this cactus forest, but you can climb aboard.' Dennis spoke as the small primate retrieved a cloth bag, which seemed to be of importance to her.

She leapt onto his foreleg and climbed up onto his back.

Chapter 11

Are Fish Food?

Ryan

The next morning, the sun had already begun to heat up the forest canopy when Ryan awoke. The last of the previous morning's moisture evaporated from the leaves. The dawn chorus of birds was missing the voice of one peacock.

'So why did you first come to the biosphere all those years ago,' Ryan asked.

Melissa considered the question for a moment. 'I have trouble remembering that far back. It must have been about 80 years ago when I first awoke here, centuries after I died. At least six lives back before that I was a human. I died when I was eighteen. My soul was collected and moved here. A life as an overworked, underpaid sweat shop girl was never going to get me anywhere. If anything, here on Mars I have had a far more interesting series of lives than where I came from.

'Asia was a polluted wreck by that time, the Himalayas hemmed in the smog, nothing much grew but weeds and GMO crops. I had worked since I was twelve. One day, an industrial fire from the welding area set the place ablaze. When the fire started, they activated an automatic soul collection machine to collect any valuable fatalities. My last memories of that life were of being stuck in a smoke-filled chaotic factory followed by the absolute agony of burning alive. I can still smell the burning flesh and the smoke.'

Ryan said, 'I'm sorry if I upset you by asking that question. That didn't sound like an enjoyable past.'

'Don't worry. I'm thankful I got out of that. During the long journey here, I suffered from stir-craziness. In my first life, I was a tropical bird set on a remote volcanic island in the far north. An overzealous frigate bird tore my organs open one day while I was returning to my nest to lay eggs. Then I had the great misfortune of falling into the water in a hungry tiger shark's zone. I was a rat in another life and a stag over a decade ago. It was a bit odd being male though, really puts things into perspective. The sun is getting a bit hot now for stories so I should probably take you out hunting.'

She rose to her feet and gestured towards the river. 'I will check for crocs before entering. We will continue to practise hunting on the other shore.'

The pair set out across the river. To try to hide their presence from crocodiles, they swam quickly without creating many ripples. Dragging themselves out on the other side of the river, Ryan plonked himself on the sand for a quick second before turning to the sky. Above them white seabirds, with black speckled wing tops and long brightly coloured red tail feathers whirled over the estuary. One dived in with a massive splash looking for fish.

'Old friends,' said Melissa, 'though that is only as a species. I don't know any of them personally. I generally don't eat animals I know – unless they are my enemy. Otherwise, it gets incredibly difficult for me to bring myself to do so.' She looked at the tropical birds wheeling above.

'What do you mean? 'Ryan asked with confused curiosity.

'Everybody here reincarnates after they die. Last lifetime I was one of those, until that damn tiger shark got me.'

She pointed to the basalt rocks near the seashore. 'Now if you come to the rocks by the ocean, you may want to see the sea creatures there. You can also practise your swimming. You already know something about that since you successfully crossed the river. Considering that this is your first life, you probably don't know how diverse and downright fascinating the planet's oceans are. There is another entire world down there,' she said as she waded a short distance into the ocean. 'Come over to the rock-pools and I will show you what I mean.'

The pair bounded over to a rocky outcrop directly next to the sea. They were not real rock pools, but rather a calm crevasse protected from the wind. This area was away from the sediment-spewing river mouth. Ryan waded out into the sea on the small beach next to the rocks. He closed his nictitating membranes, also called third eyelids, a feature only vestigial in humans. When his eyes were protected by them, he took a deep gasp of air and dived in.

Paddling, and fighting his buoyancy for a view of the underwater world, he had a glimpse before surfacing for another breath. Diving again, he had a better look. Diverse multicoloured corals encrusted the boulders. Swarms of small fish and various invertebrates swam in the crevices between the rocks. He saw the fish flee when he came close, coming out again as he moved on. Different species, including angelfish, butterfly fish, wrasses, and parrot fish hid among the rocks. Closer looks revealed something abnormal about them. The visibility was poor however, only five metres ahead of him was visible. Just far enough to see the sand. Mud and silt from the river partly covered the coral.

The currents and a nearby sandbar directed much of the sediment away from the reef. Here, the fish had organised themselves into a civilised order. He vaguely saw a large silhouette out in the deep, which unnerved him. The coral was exquisite. He couldn't see the red, due to his eye cones, but the blues and yellows contrasted each other.

The fish swam in and out minding their own business. Surprisingly, most of them were sentient. He could hear their reactions to seeing him staring down at them. The land predator had to quickly pull his head back above water for air, before putting it back down beneath the surface to properly look at them again. The smallest of the sea creatures he could see were non-sentient, being too small for mind machines. This only applied to tiny creatures like insects, most fish, mice, and many other tiny critters.

While staring further out to sea, he took another breath, then put his head back underwater again. It was then he saw, out of the corner of his eye, a silhouette coming slightly closer. It came from a rocky reef attached to the boulders on the seafloor beyond the cliff. The shadow came close enough to be identified as a groper, an immense cod-like spotted fish, big enough to eat a rabbit whole. This was a sentient fish, unlike the tiny gobies further below that darted from the rocks and back.

The fish resembled a sack of potatoes. Its white scales were occasionally interspersed with black spots, and it had an oversized head, small beady eyes, thin rayed fins, and a powerful tail. He stared at the fish, and it looked back before turning to the reef.

Paddling back to shore, he hauled himself out of the water. As he shook the water from his pelt, Melissa came running down from the rocks to meet him.

'Why did you make me go swimming in the ocean like that?' Ryan asked. He blinked quickly because of the salt around his third eyelids.

'You needed to appreciate that there was another world out there in the ocean. Amazing isn't it,' she asked as the cat shook the water out of his fur.

'It's not so much fun, though, when you are stuck in the maddening expanse of endless open water. I met some dolphins that had spent all their lives out there. The endless openness drove them mad,' Melissa said.

'What's next,' Ryan asked.

'We should practise animal hunting on land. First, there are somethings I need to tell you. However, you have proven effective at stalking. Show me how you do it.'

Ryan dropped onto his haunches, creeping along, keeping his underside near the ground. He brushed through the undergrowth, weaving between trees until Melissa told him to stop.

'Good, I barely saw you. The thick undergrowth also partly obscured your scent. Now let's find some prey to try your hunting skills on.'

Within half an hour, they found a duiker browsing in the shade of the bushes. Between eating the leaves on the bush, it checked around constantly to see if anyone was coming. Ryan dropped into a crouch as he pushed his way through the brush, undetected until he was within leaping distance.

As the cat leapt at him, the small antelope flung its head up and twisted away from him. It had already leapt over the first bush by the time the cat hit the ground. He quickly swung his paws into position to bound again after the small antelope. In the next bound, he turned to pursue the prey, leaping further into bushes until he lost track of the duiker altogether. The predator stopped when it had blended its scent with the undergrowth. The small antelope could still be heard further ahead.

Melissa joined him. 'I'm still learning, okay,' Ryan said. He was frustrated with his lack of hunting skills.

'Don't worry,' said Melissa. 'It will take you a long time to learn. We practise and train and we still fail to catch our prey most of the time. Anyway, you are learning very well. In coming days, you will improve as you learn more survival skills. We may even be able to find you a mate and make you a competent hunter someday.'

Her words made Ryan nod before scowling. He began to reply but stopped when he heard something else move through the undergrowth. Ryan stretched his head up to see the new creature. It soon came into partial view. Too big for a meal he decided. A low growl rumbled from the bushes.

Both their hackles raised. Ryan detected the scent of tiger. This time however instead of the orange and black pelt of Anthia, it was a far more familiar brown and white striped individual.

The white tigress, Natashia, was staring at them. Melissa jumped back, tensed up, and snarled defensively. After initially crouching and raising his hackles, Ryan relaxed. He had flipped his ears and growled for about 3 seconds before recognising the tigress. She was chuffing. The puma raised his posture and slightly twisted the tip of his tail. His ears were erect.

'I'm surprised to see you again. You're still alive. How have you been going in the last few days?' Ryan asked the tigress.

'Badly. Hunting has been hard. I hate having to kill. I would have eaten that wolf if she hadn't backed away.' She licked her chops. Ryan snarled in response. Natashia stepped back in surprise.

Melissa whimpered from behind Ryan. 'I'm not a wolf.'

'She's my friend, not lunch. She has been teaching me how to hunt and survive and is my pack mate. Also, you got the species wrong. She's a dingo, not a wolf,' Ryan explained.

'Anyway, I'm not really hungry now. Luckily, I did manage to catch a tapir. It took me a quarter of an hour to kill the poor guy, but I couldn't waste an opportunity when he was there,' Natashia commented.

Ryan was still tense.

'I'll continue until I find a territory of my own. It is great to see that you are still alive. I hope to see you again in the future, Ryan, both of you – you and your dingo friend.' She stood watching them.

Melissa came cautiously forward to stand near Ryan.

'Why does she scare you so much?' he asked her.

'Simple, many of the tigers here prey on dingoes,' she responded quietly. 'I don't like being tiger chow. You're less of a prey animal than me. I don't trust lone tigers. We should leave now so there is no repeat of what happened with you and Anthia.'

'Apologies, Natashia,' said Ryan, 'but we kind of have an issue with tigers. Another tiger tried to kill me only a few days ago. Hunting has been tough, so if you really have a fresh tapir kill, there should be enough meat for us all to share.'

'All right then.' Natashia smirked as she turned tail to walk off into the jungle.

'And one thing, if you dare try harming my friend, I will not hesitate to rip your face into a new shape.' Ryan snarled, adding a serious note to the exchange.

Natashia flinched at the sudden hostility.

Melissa came behind Ryan, still with her ears flicked back, her teeth showing in a silent growl.

'Ryan, this is a frankly stupid idea, being so trusting could get us both killed. If anything goes bad, we better have an escape route.'

Chapter 12

The Kingdom Army

Walking in the shade of the trees the three animals heard cicadas chirping noisily over the forests in the late morning sun. The tip of the cat's tail twitched slightly. Ryan was thinking of the nearby ocean he had seen earlier that day, wondering what lay further out in its depths.

Within a few minutes, Natashia arrived at her kill. A male tapir lay brutally ripped on the riverbank. The rump had already been eaten and a large segment of the abdomen had been ripped open. The brown coat was stained with blood.

There was a problem with eating this, however. There were crocodiles … crocodiles everywhere. Four crocodiles had emerged out of the river to have a taste of the carcass.

Natashia did not like what she saw. She roared loudly before mock charging the crocodiles.

'That's my kill. Wait your turn you thieves!' She roared and snarled as she watched the crocodiles fleeing back into the water.

Ryan moved to the kill and began eating the neck, using his rough tongue to rasp off the neck fur. He lifted his head as he saw movement on the water down river. 'Natashia, you may want to stay quiet,' Ryan said. He watched the subject of interest intently.

A boat was not something he expected to see this morning. It was only a comparatively small boat. The sail was down, as the boat was riding the current downstream. On board, he could see a pair of large brown deer and a gorilla, along with a few cockatoos. Mellissa sped off into the forest at the sight of these creatures and Natashia bounded along the beach as fast as she could. Curious, Ryan snuck back to the edge of the trees to see what was going on.

The gorilla climbed out of the boat when it hit the beach, followed by the two deer who were lightly armoured in hardened cotton and wooden armour. An image of a castle overlaid with a hoofprint was stamped on the armour.

The cockatoos took off in different directions, scouting the nearby landscape. The deer came walking around the perimeter, looking for any trouble. A crocodile was basking on the beach further down the river.

The gorilla, who wore armour interlaced with crocodile leather and wooden plates and wielded a steel tipped spear, had placed a flag on the end of a carved wooden pole into the sand, thumping it in repeatedly. Ryan and the crocodile looked on curiously.

Then the two deer saw the crocodile and came bounding over in his direction. The reptile turned to go into the water. The deer caught up and the crocodile turned around to bite him. The deer dodged and bounded from side to side, playing with him. Then the gorilla came over. Instead of the spear, the gorilla brought a different pole with a noose on one end into the fray.

The crocodile backed away. Its mouth open, ready to bite. The gorilla thrust the branch at him, and he snapped at its end. He tried to roll away, but he noticed too late that well-placed loops of rope were now over the end of his snout, and he was unable to free himself. The noose quickly tightened, sealing his jaw shut.

Then the deer advanced, sharp steel knives were tied to their hooves and iron blades to their antlers. As the crocodile spun, the sambar deer kicked again and again into the belly of the crocodile, quickly marking its underside with its own blood, waiting for the chance to flip the reptile over and gore it with its blades.

Ryan watched in amazement. *These are the animals I was told about. I can't believe what I'm seeing.* He would have interfered if it were not for the gorilla, an animal clearly capable of killing him in a single punch.

The crocodile fought for its life. Shaking violently, it whacked its tail from side to side, trying to hit the deer. The deer jumped over and dodged his tail. As the reptile lifted his head, the deer lowered his bladed antlers and caught his jaw, piercing the skin under the lower jaw. The antlers lifted him his body height off the sand, his tail still dragging on the ground. The stag briefly held the crocodile; the blades, narrowly missing the jugular, had already pierced the windpipe.

82

As the crocodile struggled to be free, the iron blades on the deer's antlers lacerated the crocodile's throat. His body slumped. The sambar stag tossed the crocodile aside.

The reptile spasmed from side to side, blood spurting from slashed arteries. The sambar stag called the gorilla. She had released the noosed branch that they would need again.

The flag flew high above the estuary sand. The gorilla took out a steel knife to begin skinning the crocodile. As he was about to put the knife into the croc, the pair of deer came closer to the water, looking for anyone else to kill.

A second crocodile exploded from the water, grabbing one of the deer, tripping him over and hauling the startled stag back into the water. The deer screamed in panic. The gorilla immediately ran over but by the time he got there, the crocodile was twirling and tearing up the deer under the surface. Maroon blood was floating to the surface. The stag struggled to get above the water trying to move back to the sandy shore, dragging the crocodile with him.

'Help me, you idiots! Get these things off me!' the stag bellowed in pain as another crocodile began to bite into his flank. The gorilla threw his spear at the crocodile's head, cutting its muzzle but it glanced off without penetrating the bone beneath. His differently proportion shoulder to a human made him a poor thrower. The ape dared not enter the water.

Bellowing at the pain, the deer continued kicking and trying to drag himself back onto land again. The reptile hauled him into the deep water, dragging the deer further down. The stag's previously pierced and torn open flank had the intestines grabbed from within and pulled out by the other crocodile. Another came to take the hind legs. They rolled the animal, then tore chunks out of it.

Shocked and trembling at the fate that had befallen its friend, the other deer turned with the gorilla to head back to the land.

The gorilla made himself busy hauling the first dead croc up for skinning. He ripped the head off and tore the bones apart from the muscles. The fat was taken for lamp oil and the skin with osteoderms was taken for fine leather and armour making. By the time they packed what they wanted on the boat, only internal organs and immense strips of muscle were left – enough to have a very handsome meal.

Ryan had watched the whole scene with a sense of horror. He stared at the flag standing in the sand. His lack of colour vision distorted the colours. A white crescent in a green background filled the left side.

Next to it was the shape of the castle and the hoof prints that he saw on the armour. A red triangle lay on a background of black in the centre and a white rectangle, with what looked to be an axe above it on a green background, completed the right side. *Obviously, the flag of the Kingdom army of herbivores I heard about.*

As the crocodile skin and head were taken back onto the boat, Ryan listened to what the gorilla and remaining deer were saying. He gasped in horror at what he heard.

The gorilla said, 'We need to come back here this evening. Suleiman, the mammoth king, wants a forward base here, perhaps a camp in future. We need to secure the area and drive out all the carnivores. Then we will have to deal with those fish cities on the reefs. Let's get out of here before any more of us get devoured by crocodiles, tigers – or pumas for that matter.' The gorilla then turned to stare at Ryan who spun and skulked back into the jungle in shock.

'What puma and tiger?' The deer looked around in surprise.

'The puma that was watching us from the trees the entire time, idiot! There is a dingo, a tiger, and more crocodiles down the river too. The cockatoos already found them all. We'll need back up to deal with them later. Now we need to get out of here and bring in the hunt tonight to clear this stretch of beach. Perhaps that tiger will make a nice coat. White furred tigers are almost unheard of around here. Talking about unheard, why are we talking so loudly. They can probably hear us.'

The deer and gorilla hopped back into the boat. The gorilla began to row back upstream, then threw vines over the side of the ship. They were tied around a manatee that was waiting. It began to paddle its huge tail to pull the boat upstream.

Ryan turned tail and ran back into the forest searching for his canine friend. Her scent quickly led him upstream but further inland.

He dashed through the undergrowth, over and under logs, and around the bases of various trees. Prey scattered as he ran through the forest. Several fruit doves crashed through the vegetation as they flew off. A macaw took off from the lower cover. A duiker went bounding away into the woods. At the end of this treacherous stretch of forest, he spotted Melissa heading towards the water for a drink.

The boat had passed, going upriver with the cockatoos following. The dingo had come down to drink the water at a spot above the tidemark.

Here the water was fresher than lower parts of the river during the day. Melissa let her paws sink into the sand at the edge of the stream. She lapped the flowing water discharged from the river. There was enough rainwater to displace the saltwater from the ocean at this point. She went to place her head down again to drink before yelping in surprise.

The dingo flew back, letting out a high-pitched yelp, tumbling and rolling on her back several times before righting herself. Her ears tucked back, she growled at the crocodile that had launched itself out of the water like a missile.

Ryan came rushing in, teeth bared, and claws extended as he hit the crocodile's back with his left paw. The reptile whirled its jaws towards him, snapping them shut, and missing the feline. His quick reaction saved his life. Melissa had run inland a few metres. The crocodile landed on sand and decided it was not worth the chase.

'How dare you, she's my friend, you monster,' Ryan snarled as he angrily lashed his paw at the crocodile.

'Look who's talking, hypocrite,' the crocodile responded, looking the cat in the eye. Ryan's tail still lashed.

Melissa ran up to support Ryan snarling at the crocodile.

'You both kill innocents like me. All we predators do, except for the vultures of course. It's nothing personal. It's just we all have to eat someone, and that dingo was being a stupid bitch in the wrong spot.'

Melissa snapped her jaws at him at that insult, still snarling at the crocodile.

'Well, it's true. You are a bitch. Anyway, I will be on my way,' the crocodile said. 'The vultures appear to have found something downstream.' The crocodile withdrew into the water and swam downriver.

Back on the bank where all the action had taken place, Natashia had returned to feed on the tapir carcass. Hearing Melissa's yelping she came running up stream just as the crocodile disappeared underwater.

'Well, that was close. Good to see you're okay, Melissa,' Natashia said.

The dingo was still whining and trembling from the shock of the encounter.

'Melissa, you alright?' Ryan asked.

'I'm fine. I'm still in shock, I just had a narrow brush with death. Second big predator this month,' Melissa responded while keeping an eye on the water.

Twenty minutes later, they walked down the river towards the blood-soaked beach. A huge flock of vultures had set upon what was left of the dead crocodile. The deer's carcass was still being torn up between the crocodiles.

'What happened here? Why is this crocodile in pieces?' a vulture asked as it soared downwards over the beach.

Ryan looked towards the flag planted in the beach. 'Look at the flag. I guess it was the Kingdom army. I wanted to help but didn't want to get myself killed.'

The flag waved proudly, but now was tilted and pooped over by vultures. Somehow, it could not be torn normally despite their attempts.

Melissa nodded. 'Yes, that is their flag.' She howled, getting the attention of some of the vultures. 'Old friends of mine have come here, Ryan. I need to introduce you to them.' A few squawked, hissed, or called out greetings. Among them were Indian white-rumped vultures, yellow-headed vultures, several crows, and ravens, and most importantly, one massive white king vulture. Those and black kites, buzzards and other birds were trying to grab scraps off the carcass. 'You will need to tell the vultures what you saw and heard. But first, let's eat.'

They ran to the carcass. Crows, magpies, vultures, and seagulls scattered, wings noisily flapping as they squawked out of the way.

The vulture's beaks had already ripped and pecked the kill. The crocodile's carcass was a bloody mess. The bone was showing through the flesh.

Natashia and Melissa began to chew on the carcass, tearing into the chest cavity. The tiger buried her head into the hollow, munching on the lungs and heart. Melissa had begun eating the crocodile offal that she dragged out and dumped onto the sand. As Natashia pulled her blood drenched head out of the hole they had created, Ryan shrunk back in disgust and horror at his friends being so blood thirsty. He chose something less bloody. As he was chewing on a part of the crocodile's tail, the king vulture approached.

'I see you found your new friend, Melissa. How do you find Ryan? Is he a help, or a nuisance? What does he think about killing for food so far?'

'He's all right. Still somewhat incompetent though. Killing other sentients for food still disgusts and horrifies him. I am more worried about what happened with the boat that came over today.'

'And that is?' the vulture asked. Other vultures returning to the kill interrupted them. He raised his multi-coloured head that was splattered with blood as another vulture dragged out the crocodile liver through a hole in the other side. The smaller yellow-headed vulture began to argue with other vultures on how to rip the organs apart.

The king vulture watched them. 'The good thing about crocodile meat is it rarely contains parasites. It makes for safer eating, unlike that of the tapir. They both taste delicious, from my limited sense of taste anyway. What was I saying? Oh yeah, what did you see earlier?' The vulture paused to listen as he shaved off another section of meat.

'Animals came in a boat,' said Ryan. 'They planted the flag, killed a crocodile and spoke of coming back to claim this area for themselves tonight. They talked about killing all the carnivorous animals in this area. We will need to leave soon.'

'Ah yes, the Kingdom is getting up to no good again, thanks for telling us of this most recent sighting. We should move further into the jungle to avoid the hunting parties. Even we vultures are not safe. Hell. They might have spies with us now.'

Ryan swallowed. He glanced around at the large number of birds around the carcass.

'Don't worry,' said the vulture, 'it's mostly the crows, ravens, and magpies around the edge. I never trusted those corvids much, though.'

At that moment, a group of crocodiles came onto the beach to see what had happened.

'Poor Marty. Another of our friends killed by those Kingdom bastards,' one of the crocodiles grumbled as he sat down on the sand. Melissa could see tears streaming from his eyes.

She, Natashia and Ryan continued to chew into the crocodile meat. The crocodiles were eating what was left of the stag. A few minutes later, they decided to begin to eat the flesh of one of their own kind. Out here, meat is meat.

Soon more of the vultures circled overhead. The sight of the unusually butchered carcass had drawn about a dozen more. They landed to get a closer look before eating.

Some were vultures that Melissa had seen in the past. She knew many of these birds by name. Each area had several different vulture species that would drop down to enjoy the feasts of carrion. The ones who had arrived included black turkey vultures with bald orange heads, big griffin vultures that looked like a brown eagle with a snake for a head, and another strange, scavenging, flying creature.

Ryan struggled to put a name to the beaked, leathery-winged, hairy, quadrupedal creature that came with them.

The new arrivals began to land, their massive wings still open as they touched the ground and pecked at the carcass. The crocodiles had made off with some of their friend's parts. The carnivores recited a funeral speech that they invented years ago.

Ryan and Melissa finished eating, leaving the carcass buried under hungry vultures that were stripping and ripping at the meat. Melissa wanted to talk some more to their leader.

The king vulture, with a white set of wings and body, and a bald multi-coloured head was nearby, slightly separate from the others. Ryan was glad just to have finished his meal. Fighting for a place among all those vultures would have been uncomfortable and perhaps even dangerous.

When the king vulture had finished his meal, he hopped around, flapping over the rest of the vultures telling them to come to where Melissa and Ryan were sitting.

One of the birds settled next to Melissa. 'Looks like you have a new mate; or friend if you're not into that?' the vulture Melissa knew said as he gestured at Ryan. Melissa replied, with a slight growl, 'That's Ryan. He's new here and not yet knowledgeable of our ways. He almost gets himself killed in at least three different ways in a week. He's gradually learning how to hunt. But we have just had a bit of a banquet thanks to those civilised imperialists and our tiger acquaintance.'

'Tell the others what happened here?' the head vulture said looking at the flag.

'Some of the Kingdom's animals came and put this flag here and killed a crocodile, interrupting our lunch of tapir,' Melissa replied.

'They are always a strange bunch, prancing around like they own the whole jungle, and expecting everyone should bend to their will, like a bunch of peasants,' the king vulture said flapping his wings in anger. 'Ryan says the Kingdom animals are coming back to hunt tonight, so we should move further into the jungle. I suggest you both do the same thing.' The king vulture said his goodbyes and turned to fly off. The rest of his flock followed.

'He's another friend of ours, though I don't really have many friends,' Melissa said to Ryan.

Chapter 13

Vultures; Friend or Foe?

Dennis

Dennis stared out at the heat mirage. The desert seemed to stretch to the southern horizon. Crossing it was certain death, as it stretched for thousands of kilometres until the temperate steppes of the southern Taiga expanse. He could only comfortably go east, west, or north. The greenish river wound its way to the east towards the mountainside forests that stretched from the riverbank. Desert-growing phoenix palms and massive prickly pear trees interrupted the mix of conifer and eucalypt forest. What he wanted to head towards was down there somewhere. The mountains could provide a home if there was nowhere else to live. For the time being, he wanted to explore the world where he was.

The recent earthquake had shaken up his life. His new bushbaby friend was trying to follow, though she was currently sleeping in a nearby hollow in a tree to avoid the heat of the day.

This would not be an easy place to live. Apart from the river and the various mountainside ponds, there were no sources of open water on this side of the mountain. He would need to be closer to either the river or the mountain pool if he wished to stay here longer. The dunes and rocks extended all the way to the cold steppes over one thousand kilometres south. Whatever he did, Dennis had to remember not to turn too far south, or he would surely be lost in the desert.

Several days after he picked up Felicia, the bushbaby, he proceeded down the mountain side. He had decided he just had to walk down to the river and follow its course to the swamp in the east. Not so hard he thought.

On reaching the river, he set off at dusk and began his trek under the cover of darkness. The chill of the evening winds penetrated his coat as he sprinted to cover the distance as quickly as he could. He had decided that a long and fast sprint at night could be maintained. He carried the primate on his back. She would not be left behind. The run felt exhilarating, and he howled into the night sky, not looking for prey. He hurtled across the dunes, racing up and over the sandy peaks before running along the dusty and dirt covered desert floor.

The stars were his guide – though they seemed to shift and change the further they went. Under the black night sky, different creatures moved. Golden moles tunnelled under the sand, jerboas and gerbils hopped and scurried over the dunes where spiders searched for sleeping insects.

Few birds flew of an evening, most roosted on the occasional dead tree poking through the dunes. Small clumps of grasses grew here and there, but for the most part, this stretch of dunes moved and shifted with the wind. The cries of other animals came into the night sky occasionally, some familiar, others less so.

Eventually the open plains gave way to more vegetated dunes. By this time, he was exhausted. He panted heavily, and heat radiated off his body. Felicia, the bushbaby had to try to stand higher off his back to avoid being roasted.

Beyond the dunes, he weaved around the aloes, cacti, and spinifex grass clumps until he came to the stretch of trees and large bushes marking the river. The dwarf date palms stood over a similar rock to where he had fled the dingoes last time. Cautiously, he slunk into the shade of the acacia trees at the river's edge. Felicia leapt off his back and clambered up into the trees, disappearing into the canopy.

The dingo crept down to the edge of the papyrus and reeds where he found a clear open patch of water. He drank deeply, to make up for the water he had lost during the run, then peered at the far side of the river, considering how to swim across.

Felicia had run around the trees, jumping from branch to branch. A few dates and some desert grasshoppers counted as a meal and a drink.

'All done, Dennis. Should we cross the river?' the primate asked.

'Why? I mean we could walk to the swamp on this side. I was considering it, but what could be on the other side? I'd rather not get lost any further in the dunes or run into that pack of dingoes that tried to kill me earlier.' He stood staring over the river for a moment then said, 'I guess it is worth a look. Let's go.'

The dog pushed off from the shore, paddling with one foreleg kicking after the other as he instinctively doggy paddled his way across. The bushbaby rode on his head, her tail dipping in the water. He looked out for crocodiles or other dangerous creatures hiding in the stream but thankfully found none.

He hauled himself out of the river and shook his coat free of the moisture, shaking the droplets over the grass and trees nearby. He faced the desert beyond. He still had to get that little primate to where she wanted to go.

Sighing, he set off again. The further he wandered into the hot desert dunes, the more he regretted his promise. The primate was clinging to his underside now, still wide-eyed and growing increasingly hungry.

The sun rose above the horizon. It continued climbing higher and higher into the sky, eventually becoming a burning menace. The river streams they followed narrowed into trickles then dry riverbeds.

Traveling further into the desert, they became horribly lost in a sea of shifting dunes.

Several hours passed. Dennis had decided to veer to the south to cut a shorter route to the wetlands. This plan went awry, and he became lost further into the desert. The little bushbaby was fast asleep now, clinging to his narrow triangular chest to avoid overheating in the hot morning sun.

The sun bore down on the shifting red dunes that were becoming burning hot under his feet. Strange rumblings came through the sand from where there were no visible animals, save for a far-off condor. The tell-tail trails of golden moles and something else, indicated who moved below the dunes.

He stopped, looked around and realised he had made no real progress in many hours. He growled in frustration. 'If you have led me astray, I will eat you, little bag of fleas! Hear me!' he snapped at the bushbaby. She woke up immediately and leapt onto the dunes in surprise.

'Where are we?' Felicia looked around wide eyed.

'Lost, completely and utterly lost in the middle of the desert and dying of thirst. We have to find water, food, and shade before we overheat to death. And if I do overheat and it looks like I will die, I will eat you first for suggesting we get into this mess.'

The dingo turned and retraced his path until the desert winds obscured his tracks. There was scarcely any fauna or flora to be seen. The sandfish disappeared under the sand as soon as they saw him. The desert spiders cartwheeled down the dunes when they sensed him. The only flora he could see was a dormant tumbling Jericho rose, flinging its isolated seeds into the desert.

There was nothing to eat out here and scarcely any water left for him to drink. Even the shallow former pond he found between a parallel set of dunes had completely dried up. Strange bones surrounded it. The only animal out there was a golden mole that he found through its scent. Even this tasty morsel was enough to catch Dennis's attention.

There was a slight furrow heading up the dune side. The sand fell slightly on the other side of the dune as the small underground tenrec continued its way across the dunes. The dingo quickly followed the trail up to the top of the mound. As he ran down the face of the dune after the small mammal, he lost his footing and skidded. He lunged at the ground; his sharp teeth aimed directly at the innocent blind animal hiding below the sand. Before his jaws entered the sand, something large whacked him on the head.

He jumped aside, shaking his head in pain and annoyance, and then realised that it was a hunk of meat. He stared at it, puzzled. *Where did that come from?* he wondered, looking around him.

He eventually righted himself in the sliding sand that threatened to bury him. After regaining his senses, he sniffed the fallen piece of carrion. It had a slight smell of decay, but it was still fresh enough for him to eat. Carefully sitting down and waking the tiny primate on his underside he chewed on the hunk of meat.

'What happened? Where are we?' the tiny bushbaby asked as she crawled up the side of Dennis's chest and moved onto his back.

'We are still lost in this desert. Evidently, I took a wrong turn somewhere on the way here. I have retraced my steps but now the tracks have disappeared. You do know that we could both die of thirst or hunger out here, I've already told you.'

'Where did that meat come from?'

'It dropped from the sky and hit me on the head. Someone must have dropped it, but I didn't see who.'

The bushbaby studied the meat, her face scrunched in disgust. 'I need to eat every day, and this slab of flesh is not suitable food for me. Half-rotten meat contains bacteria that could kill me. This meat will sustain you for the next few days, but we better find some insect food for me and water to avoid dying of thirst.'

Dennis scanned the open desert gully between the next two dunes and saw a dead ironwood tree half buried by another advancing dune. In the tree perched a huge bird.

The dingo trotted down the dune to investigate with Felicia close behind. As the dingo approached the dead tree, the bird stretched his immense 280-centimetre wind span, exposing two large white triangles on the underside of the wing. The vulture's red head came forward from the black feathered body.

'Did you drop that hunk of meat on my head? If you did, thanks for that. I was getting peckish, and prey is sparse in this big desert. What is your name, and what are you?'

'My name is Akash and I'm a condor. I wish to prevent unnecessary death and pain. You are evidently lost and thirsty and probably don't know of the rotting mammoth less than a mile from here. Come and join me there if you wish. I will guide you from the air.' The condor stared at the canine as he spoke to him, checking him and his companion out.

'I'm not so sure about eating maggot bait myself, Akash, but I'm happy to follow you. Thank you for the offer,' Dennis said.

The condor lifted off the perch and flapped into the air, circling, and rising higher and higher. Within a few minutes, he was flying about one hundred metres above the desert floor. He had used the thermal winds to rise so high.

As the massive black shape circled higher and higher into the sky, Dennis called, 'Ever coming down, condor. I'm kind of tired of waiting.'

The vulture began to glide in a straight line over the dune. The dingo followed the bird over more dunes towards a rocky ridge that broke the monotony of the endless sand. Dennis found a sandstone cliff with a scraggly set of mesquite and iron wood trees clinging to gaps between the boulders.

There might be insects for Felicia around here, he thought.

The dingo climbed up the rocks, scrambling and leaping up the walls that were a good thirty metres high. He clambered over the sandstone boulders with no slowing of pace. Small skinks living upon the rocks were scared away. He avoided the small prickly cacti that dotted the cliff face and took care along the steep precipice to avoid falling onto the jumble of rocks below.

When he finally reached the top of the boulders, he could see into the crater. It was mostly empty of life. The far interior of the pit was white with salt. Scattered trees and cacti were the main large plants, though a few desert-adapted acacias, eucalypts, conifers, and at least three welwitschia plants scattered across the gibber flat that marked the sides of the crater.

However, there was life. A monitor lizard scooted off the hot rock bed when he saw the dingo. Birds flew between the trees. Other animals were hiding under the rocks.

'This is the limit for most animals out here.' Akash gestured to the dry gullies and cracked lands with his wings. 'A poor land for any herbivores. A hapless Columbian mammoth bull died here a few days ago. A subtropical species, unlike their woolly relatives, his death is why I'm here. There is a lot of meat and strange carnivores and scavengers from all around have come to eat a section.'

The dog slowly scampered down the rocky cliff face, trying not to cause a landslide or rockslide in one form or another. He trotted out to the carcass. It was rank. The guts had exploded outwards, spreading over the desert sand. Hundreds of vultures had come and gone from the carcass, tearing off much of the meat. Some good meat remained on the underside, buried in the sand, but he would have to dig for it.

He searched for water. The rest of the crater was barren and dry, no water here, any blood and juices would have to sustain him until they could make it back to water.

Some of the vultures had tried to salt the meat, by rolling it in the caked dry salt on the floor of the crater, only to spit it out when their poor sense of taste could still pick up an intolerable saltiness to the meat.

Dennis stuck his head in deep, getting rotting juices over his paws and back. But his head and mouth more importantly savaged, ripped, and tore at the fresher meat below. After several bites, he was full, and drew himself out. He then realised a layer of blood and slimy, rotting juices coated him. Backing back into the desert, he hacked his throat from the horrid scent of putrid flesh, which was completely overpowering him.

The bushbaby scampered over the carcass, grabbing at flies and carrion beetles, ripping the small insects to pieces.

Suddenly, something caught Dennis's attention. He barked loudly at the little bushbaby. 'Get down! Now!'

Felicia leapt off the carcass, hitting the sand and rolling several times before jumping to her feet.

The shadow of a massive flying creature had temporally blocked out the sun. It turned and swooped down, landing on its four long limbs with a thud. This strange beast was the one that Dennis had seen during the dingo chase. Four and a half metres tall at the top of the head, its bill was larger than its entire torso. The wings seemed like a cape around its hairy body, the long arms and legs framed the hairless membrane structure. The last finger on its wing was turned upward to support the long strut-like wing bone. Two others joined the huge, billed creature.

They flapped and squawked among themselves arguing backwards and forwards as one of them simply drove his bill into the carcass and began tearing. Behind them, smaller birds came flying in, including a pair of wedge-tailed eagles and more vultures. A multitude of smaller birds, black kites, crows, magpies, ravens, and smaller leathery skinned bats followed them. Some of the bats also had long necks and short tails like the big ones, however some had teeth. Others had more rounded heads, long tails and resembled nothing like the larger ones.

The dog raised his hackles in alarm as he began to slink away from the carcass, the bushbaby clinging to his underside. 'What the hell are those big bird-bat things?' Dennis asked the condor.

'Doom storks, I like to call them. Some call them doom bats, flight hazards, giraffe storks, pterosaurs, and other names, but I prefer to call them doom storks. They speak like the other animals, though they have never lived on earth, or at least before that theme park tried creating them and got surprised when they flew out into the wild. They are one of the many genetic projects of the past, one of the more ambitious ones.

'I have heard that they are a genetic splice freak project of a marabou stork, a shoebill stork, a vampire bat, a giraffe, a vulture, and who knows what else. Perhaps they even got the real things genes in there as well. They wanted dinosaurs in their creation, so they made them and other prehistoric creatures like the Columbian mammoth that died here.

'This is nowhere near the strangest thing they have let loose here. Some of the things I have seen have made me wonder if they accidentally let demons into the world.'

'Wait… what demons?' Dennis asked with a hint of curiosity and confusion.

'You have yet to see so much. Anyway, we have places to go, dingo, we should be out of this stinking hot wasteland. Your friend wants to get to the Principalities, which is good because I can guide you there.'

The vulture took off; his massive wings flapping a few times as he became airborne.

Dennis cocked his head in confusion. *How did the vulture know where they wanted to go?*

Several long and weary days later, they found a dry riverbed some miles to the east. They had left the desert behind. Surface water was available in small ponds that they could dig into. They had to pass by the river again, ironically heading back towards the mountains and the plains beyond. Dennis hated to stay long due to the risk of competitors.

The dry riverbed seemed to be in a strange way when the trio arrived. The vulture was scouting ahead, hovering high above the pair as they came heavy-stepping down the loose sand. The riverbed was made of hardened mud and sandstone, broken by an occasional pile of sand blown in from the desert. The dry season had stripped almost all the life from here. Only death remained in many places. The dormant trees were awaiting the rains. The cactus was the only remaining greenery.

'Dry as bones, and not another creature in sight,' Dennis grumbled to Felicia. The bushbaby was perched on his back at this point, which was fine until he needed to hunt.

'You evidently were not looking hard enough,' she said pointing at a group of horns visible above the dune further downriver from them.

'Get down and hide!' Dennis said sternly.

She made herself sparse in the bushes; it could be days until they ate again. For the next few days, he would have to stalk this herd of addax that could provide a much-needed meal.

Chapter 14

Logger's Lunch

Natashia

The tigress continued her journey through the forest. The first few days had done much to shake up her view of the world she now lived in; silly girlhood dreams in turmoil within her head. After she briefly roamed to the coast and met Ryan and Melissa, she had wandered back inland. Days had passed since meeting the puma on the coast.

The predator had trouble finding enough food for herself as her white fur made stealth almost impossible. Every time she tried, the potential prey just kept running away. The large aggressive tapir was her big break. Of course, bad people had to get what they deserved. But she had done something far worse. He could had been a friend, someone who, had he been human, she would have said, "Good day, Sir," and passed.

Her hunger was well and truly sated. At least his death had served as a meal to many others. Those Kingdom goons had frightened her, but she had steeled herself to continue, still wanting to train herself at hunting. These and similar thoughts were battling in turmoil inside her head. The tigress continued to plod along the cleared tracks in the forest. The dull, dark brown of the forest floor was alive with fungi and understory forest plants around the bases of trees, but any prey animals fled upon seeing her.

Over a week later, she needed to make another kill. Her stomach began to growl slightly, indicating that she would need to hunt, though she dreaded what she would have to kill next.

Several hours later, she came to the edge – or what appeared to be the edge of the jungle. The trees came to an abrupt stop. Peering out from their shelter, she spotted an opportunity.

Sunlight was pouring in from a hole in the canopy ahead and onto the grassland that wound its way up to the top of a hill, split by a ravine.

The grasslands were near a massive wooden palisade. She stared at the wall, having never seen anything like it before. She shook her fur with an uncomfortable shudder. Who would build such a wall? *Someone who wanted to keep out beasts like me*, she guessed.

Her ears flecked back apprehensively when she realised that she had most likely bumped into those civilised creatures that others had talked about – like the ones who came to the river. Maybe there really were humans running the biosphere? There was no sign of a territorial marker in this area so she concluded that she could be on the edge of a possible new home.

The open grassland waved its millions of green shoots in the wind. In the distance, she could see herds of grazing hoofed animals near the wall. Further out, the land was less crowded than the area near the fence. The tigress slinked through the grass to investigate the ravine, trying not to be seen. Her white coat would make her stand out and would alert anyone from nearby. An ugly brown patch surrounded by the fence, cut into the forest's edge, looked interesting.

The timber yard inside the fence was alien to her. The cleared land stood out like a gaping wound in the greenery. Here massive piles of logs lay on a primitive sledge and were tied with enormous ropes. Further in was a wooden shack; a large thing made of crudely nailed together logs. Its shape indicated that it was composed of a series of connected rooms. This was the closest thing to a house she had yet seen here. There was an office of sorts built into the jungle, the tiny shack dwarfed by the trees beyond. She slunk between the log piles, edging closer to the shack. This building was a two-story log construction with barred windows and a garden of tropical flowers at the front.

The hairs on her back stood to attention as the tigress suddenly realised that coming into this area was foolhardy. She had started to leave the yard when she noticed the owner of the logging group. A goat-like Sumatran serow came out of the building. He turned to investigate an unfamiliar scent. He walked closer and closer to the edge of the log pile where the tiger was hiding.

100

The forest-edge patrol came to the timber yard and interrupted his search. They walked towards the serow in the middle of the courtyard. The group consisted of two water buffalo, a tamaraw, which is a kind of dwarf buffalo, a chimpanzee, and a pair of duiker scouts. The buffalos were armoured, and all wore the symbols of their nation and of their rank.

Natashia noticed they were different from those of the deer seen back at the estuary. More soldier animals came behind them. A large black furred sable antelope, a rare sight here, led them, with a pair of tree kangaroos on his back. The roos were armed with crossbows and rode on a wooden platform held in place with straps. The bows were built into the platforms.

The tree kangaroos used their claws, wrapped around hooks, to draw the bowstring between shots. Their feet were thrust under the straps to help them hold onto the antelope's platform, but the straps were loose enough to allow for a quick exit. Other deer and buffalo came behind it, mounted with monkeys of several species, some armed with crossbows and others with spears and swords. One buffalo had a female gorilla on his back, armed with a large sword. They approached the serow.

The small antelope scrambled up the log pile, and spotted Natashia. She turned and alerted the others. Natashia gasped in fear realising what she had just gotten herself into, before propelling herself into action.

She ran up the log pile, taking a leaping tackle to pull the antelope off her feet and ripped its throat out in one bite. As a buffalo charged, she ducked. The chimp on the buffalo's back barely had time to react before the giant furry paws of the tiger grabbed him and swiped him from the saddle, dodging the sweeping hand motion of the chimpanzee's obsidian chipped sword as she did so.

The ape's cry rang out over the forest and plains. Another guard, an immense buffalo, came barging into the yard nearly ripping the door off its hinges. His task was to make sure things like this didn't happen under his watch. He came running around the bend.

Natashia attempted to drag the carcass back into the jungle before the ox noticed her. When he did, she dropped the antelope's carcass and turned to run, but came face to face with the leader of the group.

The sable antelope was built like a fine black stallion. Unlike a horse however, a huge set of curved horns adorned his head's crown. A pair of steel knives were tied to the tips of his horns. On his back saddle were the two tree kangaroo crossbow archers. The antelope bellowed and charged towards Natashia.

She snarled and roared, and leapt into the air, teeth bared, and fangs out. One of the tree kangaroo riders fired a crossbow bolt. It missed her neck narrowly before becoming embedded in timber behind her.

Another buffalo had charged in from the side to intercept her. It caught her in mid-air, and she tumbled onto the ground. The rider fired a crossbow bolt, striking her shoulder.

Getting up, the tigress hissed in pain before accepting that she was severely outmatched. She now had a crossbow bolt sticking out of her hide, which spread pain through her body. She ran to the best of her ability given the wound.

The tigress yowled as she tumbled over the ground, just missing the hooves of her pursuers. She picked herself up, roaring in pain before continuing to run. Now she only cared about her own survival. The tiger broke into a sprint, adrenaline racing through her veins. She tore back into the jungle, the buffalo barging after her.

She raced through the ferns and underbrush, twisting, and turning as she ran towards the canyon. Fear lent her speed. They chased her – the buffalo's bellow reverberating through the jungle. The apes and tree kangaroos readied their shots. There was only one way out for her.

She remembered passing a small cavern opening under the roots of a massive fig tree on her way there. It seemed to connect to a deeper channel below. When she reached the place, she raced to the right side of the canyon and leapt up the trunk of a banyan fig. She yowled in pain as branches tugged the arrow. She leapt down to the deep dark cave under the tree trunk. She tumbled and rolled through shade growing ferns that grew in rotting rainforest soil.

The arrow caught on a hollow log and was ripped out, dragging fur, skin, and blood with it. She almost screamed in agony but struggled to stay quiet to avoid detection. At last, she came to a splashing stop in an underground muddy stagnant pool.

Her white and brown striped coat was now filthy, covered in her blood and the mud of the cavern. Up above, she saw the buffalo looking around in confusion. The chimp came to the hole but after looking in, decided it was not worth searching. Natashia quickly dived back into the water as he let fly several bolts just in case. She swam like mad, splashing wildly into the dark, paddling through the foul water until she could no longer see the entrance.

She waited until she heard the faint sounds of her pursuers leaving before she attempted to leave the water. She hauled the front half of herself up onto the guano covered rocks. Her paws grasped at the bat faeces.

The open wound seethed angrily, the pain worse than anything she had experienced in her previous life, prior to her illness. Back then she would have called out for her mum, dad, anyone.

The memories of the cardiac monitor came back, beep, beep, beep, vision fading. Then there was pressure and pain on her bones as the sweet release of her first death occurred. She remembered the sobbing of despair of her father as death released her from pain. These confused memories came back to her as she lay on the rocks breathing heavily in barely restrained panic.

She mewled waiting there. Her mind remembered that she always liked the tiger the most out of the animals in the nature documentaries. Those filmed in the Martian biosphere were her favourite. The films were taken many years ago when the tropics were still an icy wasteland. The tigers lived in giant domed glass cages back then. The option to live again came up temptingly. With her mother's and father's permission, she selected to come to Mars. She knew she would never see her parents again but thirteen was too young to die.

Her motivation to live came back. Those tigers were no pussies. They didn't let an empty stomach and a single wound keep them down. She was indeed a fearsome beast, a queen of the jungle. She was going to take life by the jaws. Her enemies would tremble before her roars. Her prey would fall to her cunning and brute savage strength. She crawled back out of the cavern, growling with a new sense of determination, and kicking her legs regardless of her pain. She was not going to let her parents down by being a coward. She needed to show them who she was. Her inner strength took a new form. She was not a sickly little girl, but a fearsome beast.

When she left the cave, she let her knowledge of her new-found strength be known. She emitted a massive, brave, fearless, feral roar that reverberated through the canyon. She shuddered afterwards as tiredness and pain clawed at her. She needed rest but her wound would heal quickly, and she would set out with a new-found sense of confidence and bravery.

The next day, the cat limped out of the cavern. Her pain would not go away, but she was determined to ignore it. She decided to begin by exploring the ravine where she was hiding. She climbed the side and looked at the gate across the meadow. It could barely be seen, but it looked like the land behind the gate stretched for some distance. A brownish lump suggested a town might lay further inland. Her enemies probably lived there, those that killed other carnivores arbitrarily – the same group that tried to kill her.

The ravine was about twenty metres deep, filled with thick trees that had not been cleared during the logging. Before entering, she checked to be sure that no more guards were near her. Her muscles rippled when she sensed movement. But it was not her enemy. It was just a herd of elephants moving towards the logging camp. She slipped silently into the ravine navigating down to the lush gully below.

Down here, the trees partly blocked out the sun, creating shade where she could rest. She prowled the base of the cliff looking for a possible den. Mosses, lichens, and other jungle plants, like ferns that gripped the cracks in the rock, covered the sides of the ravine. They dripped with the moisture brought on by humidity. Further along the cliff, she came across a small indentation in the rock, just big enough to keep out of the rain. Here she slouched down, lying on her side and went to sleep.

When she awoke, she heard movement in her cave. The tigress rolled onto her side. She saw a small group of tiny furry mammals, no bigger that a rabbit. They spoke nervously as they darted into the hollow and around her.

She studied them as they moved close. 'Who and what are you guys? You're adorable.' Potential friends would be good to keep her spirits up. Even though she was hungry, she didn't want to hunt some of the only animals that showed her any positive interest since arriving here – aside from Ryan and Melissa of course – and these seemed cute and friendly.

'We're bush dogs. We prefer to keep to ourselves, and like you, we want to keep out of the Kingdom's way. We don't think you're a spy,' said one.

'The vultures have told us of your presence here and Suleiman doesn't employ tigers. He knows you're here. His goons will try to kill us all,' said another.

'Anyway, it is great that you are not trying to kill us. Is there anything that you want of us,' asked a third. 'We do not like being pets or servants, but we will not be food. If you kill anything, may we have the scraps?'

'Of course,' she said., 'You guys are just too cute to say no to.'

She turned over and allowed the smaller dogs to come near enough to sniff her paws.

'Just one thing. Do you guys have anything to help with this pain in my side? I had an arrow ripped out of me yesterday and got run over by a charging buffalo, so my ribs feel awful.'

Chapter 15

Bernard the Bear

Ryan and Melissa

Back on the coast, Melissa and Ryan were relaxing by the edge of the woods near the sea. In their shelters, they enjoyed the last rays of the sunlight as it set in the west after another day in the wild. Ryan was resting in his shelter in the tree. The tiger claw marks were still healing from his earlier encounter, the first of many scars that he would have.

'Another beautiful sunset. We could spend our days here, so long as that weird bunch of herbivores don't come back in their boat.' Ryan looked off into the distance through the coconut palms and casuarina leaves.

'I'm not so sure. The herbivores will probably come back to catch us. I think we should get going further along the coast away from them, or maybe far inland to the desert where there are few creatures claiming territories,' she said. She pulled herself into a furry heap to prepare for sleep.

'Sure, but that's a long way to go. They may not come down here. We could be perfectly safe moving just a bit further into the jungle,' Ryan said.

'No. That flag says this area will be eventually settled; in which case, we will surely be hunted out. The mountains and desert on the other side of the plains are out of their reach. If they go that far they have to deal with the Citadel, one of their enemies,' Melissa said before she closed her eyes.

They had slept for over an hour when someone prodded Ryan awake. The puma snarled, hissed, and jumped back, sweeping his paws, before falling out of the tree and landing on the sharp casuarina nuts. 'Ouch!" he yowled.

The bear that had woken him raised himself onto his hind legs, roaring in surprise. Melissa scrambled to her feet quickly when she saw the bear.

'A bear? What are you doing here?' Ryan hissed in surprise.

Melissa came out of her den to inspect the intruder. A shaggy, black sloth bear stood looking at them.

'Oh, it's you, Bernard. I haven't seen you in such a long time. What's happening?' said Melissa excitedly. She ran up licking Bernard's white muzzle. The bear threw his massive arms around her and hugged her.

'I'm glad you and your new friend are still alive. I saw what happened to the crocodiles. There is very bad news tonight. The animals of the Kingdom are going to build on this very spot soon. Those animals you saw come from the boat a few days ago were scouts looking for the best place to set up their camp. Tonight, another hunting party is preparing to go on a carnivore hunt. They will eventually destroy this stretch of jungle. The carnivores are fleeing inland to the savanna, or east to the sixth sun empire or to the west ahead of the purge. We have friends there.

'Go inland to the savanna and avoid the walls and fields of the Kingdom at all costs. The hunting party will pass through the area near here and into the jungle beyond. Their spies are spreading out to find the predators wherever they are.'

Melissa slipped out from his arms and shrank back in anxiety. 'How do you know all of this and why did you come here?' Melissa asked.

'Messenger birds intercepted the nightjars and hornbills loyal to the Kingdom. I'm going with you and the fifty or so animals I have already contacted. Others are coming with me further inland. If you don't want to face a battle, it is best you don't come with us. I had to come to this side of the river to avoid the city. Just head to the savanna inland for your own sake and avoid the civilised animals of the forest. We will eventually regroup in the tropical dry forest at the junction of the plain-splitting river and the headwaters of the Mother of the Kingdom's river.

'This threat is so serious that even the vultures are leaving. The crocs are heading out to sea and up the rivers and the big cats are leaving their territory behind. This river mouth is the next spot for

107

them to build their base, they want to control this area as well. In only a few days they will send their ships to settle here.' Ryan left the base of the tree and nervously approached the dingo. 'If this bear is speaking the truth, we must leave now and head inland.'

They watched as the bear turned to head in that direction. 'See you on the savanna if you make it,' the sloth bear finished as he left for the open grasslands beyond the Kingdom's reach. Bernard roared as he retreated into the jungle beyond.

Something caused the cat to look towards the river. Bright flames flared from several torches that were attached to parts of a larger ship, one of several coming down the river. Soldiers and supplies from the Kingdom crammed the ships – enough to begin setting up a camp.

'Let's get out of here quickly. We'll head inland as fast as we can,' Ryan said.

Melissa turned and started off. 'We need to go. Now!'

'They couldn't reach us from here, right?' Ryan asked with concern in his voice.

'They most certainly can. We need to move faster before they find us!'

Ryan and Melissa sprinted into the jungle along an exposed sandy trail. Birds descended from the sky. The macaws and white cockatoos could still make them out in the dark. The poorwill birds flying through the canopy kept an eye on the retreating predators.

Bernard had split off into a deeper more tree-covered route. The parrots swooped down and found exactly where the predators were retreating. Calling shrilly and with claws at the ready, they attacked Ryan who was behind Melissa. The cockatoos followed with their talons extended. The carefully tied on steel knives on their talons were exposed. The cat ducked as one took a swipe at his neck. The steel knives scrapped over the puma's fur before the second cockatoo, a red and black one caught up with Melissa. This one landed on her shoulders, clamping on tightly and causing the dingo to whelp and falter.

A black cockatoo made it to Ryan. Its claws latched onto his neck as the cat jumped. One heavy paw swipe was strong enough to shatter the black cockatoo's hold and send it smashing into a tree. Ryan had to stop for a second. The white cockatoo latched on to the top of his neck, embedding razor sharp claws from one foot, and trying to reach around for the jugular vein. Ryan spun with great force and swiped the bird as it spiralled off. He managed to collect the one on Melissa's shoulder with a second swipe of his paw, buying Melissa time to escape.

Blood trickled down the back of the puma's neck as they sprinted for the cover of the trees. Ryan and Melissa disappeared into the darkness of the forest and the birds finally stopped their pursuit.

The attacking birds had also caught up with the bear. Several attacked at the same time and tried to sever his spinal cord, something not possible on his thick neck. The attackers then headed for his head instead. Bernard swiped at the birds with his large claws, and they flew off. He lowered himself, roaring at the retreating cockatoos.

A sulphur crested cockatoo flushed a roosting vulture out of the trees in front of Ryan. He could only watch in horror as the cockatoo overpowered the bird and bit viciously at its throat. The two flapped and fumbled until the parrot's beak snapped shut around the turkey vultures' neck, and with a massive tug, the head was ripped messily off the body. The corpse dropped bloodily onto the ground as the cockatoos continued to harry more of the nearby roosting vultures.

The normally diurnal birds squawked loudly. Their shouts were carried through the night air as they mass-vacated the area. The cockatoos gave pursuit as some of the vultures fought back. The parrots had the advantages of sharper claws with the tied-on weapons and stronger beaks.

By the time the ship was unloaded, the area had been cleared of carnivores and the birds had returned.

Chapter 16

A Clash with The Kingdom

Ryan, Mellissa and Natashia

Earlier that evening, the tigress walked down to the river for a drink, cautiously checking for more guards whilst doing so. She scanned the water for crocodiles or fish for food. Lapping the muddy but cool river water, she kept her eyes peeled for any signs of trouble. She grimaced from the wounds she had gained the previous day. Turning upstream, she saw a medium boat loaded with animals. Some seemed to be armed. Realising the danger she was in, she backed into the jungle to avoid detection.

More boats appeared, enough to make up a small fleet. A massive set of crossbows were attached to the largest ship, looking something like a medieval caravel. The huge sailing ship was proceeding at the back of the fleet. They were obviously not just going down for more resources from the forest. Other ships were loaded with goods like tools, and more unarmed creatures. Whatever purpose they had, she must avoid them. She slunk back into the jungle but continued to watch.

Two gorillas pulled open the massive front gate of their enclosure at the edge of the fields, by winching the rope that held a counterweight. The weight was essential when they needed to close the gate quickly. Through the gates came a party led by a mammoth. In the centre of the group walked a trio of war elephants. Around the edge were the stags and buffalos. Some had riders. Other shorter figures moved around the sides of the war party. Once through the gate, they marched past the wooden palisade into the open lands beyond. At the edge of the group was a messy, unorganised passel of giant wild hogs with steel knives tied-on their tusks.

The elephants had massive crossbows on their back, set with nets to trap prey. A group of macaques in their howdah staffed the bows. As the party left the walls, the doors were closed by letting the stone counterweights fall. They trotted off across the grasslands into the darkness. Bright torches illuminated their path.

The lights were dimly visible across the field by Natashia as she watched from high in the trees within the canyon.

***

The journey inland went quickly for Ryan and Melissa. There was no time to investigate all the new scents of the jungle. The noise of insects was almost deafening. Dark shadows covered the floor obscuring all beneath them. The cartwheel ruts indicated that the Kingdom had used this route before. The bear had joined them, and the trio travelled together with Melissa at the front.

Excessive harvesting had chopped the undergrowth back here. They kept their eyes peeled looking for any danger and sniffed for any suspicious scents blowing on the wind.

This was a dangerous route to travel, but they took it because it meant they would not get lost in this tangle of trees. Uneasy, Ryan looked around. 'This is not the most trustworthy of routes,' he said looking at the wheel ruts.

'You're right, I think we should leave this road for a safer route. They will probably see us here. Bernard will direct us if we veer off course,' Melissa said checking with the bear. Bernard agreed and Ryan nodded and turned to leave the path. The trio continued through the safety of the forest.

A couple of hours later the trees ended.

'It looks like we may have come to the end of the forest. Is this the savanna you were talking about, Bernard?' the cat said optimistically. He ran out, dodging the fallen trees to land on the soft grass. He looked up to the sky, breathing in the beauty of the band of the silver Milky Way. Melissa came out and stopped in shock.

'Wrong way, Shit! We are so screwed! We've come the wrong way, Ryan!' Melissa yelped in fear.

'Apologies, but I agree with you, Melissa. We have indeed made a wrong turn,' Bernard said with a deal of concern.

'What?' Ryan backed off a little.

Bernard stood looking around. 'This isn't the savanna. It's a lot of cleared land alright, but it all used to be jungle. This is the Kingdom common where they graze. We are less than a couple of kilometres from the gates. We have gone the completely wrong way. We need to turn around.'

'We are almost at the Kingdom's outer walls! We will all be killed if they see us! We must turn around and follow the edge of the woods so that we don't become lost again,' Melissa said turning back towards the trees.

'Wait, who is that over there? It's the white tiger!' Ryan exclaimed upon seeing the feline in the low branch of a durian tree.

Ryan's disappointment quickly turned to excitement seeing their brown and white striped ally was still alive. The puma and the dingo headed towards the canyon to meet her. Bernard waited, thinking of alternative safe routes.

Ryan dashed up to Natashia, glad to see her, and trying not to express anything that could be seen as a threat.

She clambered down from the tree, chuffed to meet them. She stood, staring out into the plains with a degree of worry. 'Happy to see you, but why are you guys here? You should be back in your territories.'

Melissa was quick to say, 'There is a death warrant on all of our heads. The animals of the Kingdom are out hunting tonight. If they catch us, they will either kill us immediately or execute and then skin us in the fort. You need to come with us out of here.'

Startled and remembering her last encounter, Natashia said, 'I need to warn my friends. Quick, come.' The tigress turned to run to the ravine. The dingo, and puma followed. Bernard saw them head off and quickly headed after them.

As they approached the ravine, Melissa heard someone following. She paused and sniffed the familiar scent in the night-time air. The scent of sloth bear. 'Bernard! Is that you?' she yipped.

The bear caught up. 'Sure is, though I would stay quiet if I were you. We don't know how close the Kingdom's troops are. We need to get out of here and head around the commons.'

The little bush dogs came out of their holes to investigate the newcomers. Before Natashia could properly introduce her friends, they heard a series of hoots, bellows, and thundering yells come from both sides of the canyon.

Quickly realising that they had gotten themselves into a terrible situation, Bernard readied himself and looked both ways, looking for an escape route. He saw a narrow ledge on the side of the canyon that might do.

The tiger was staring at the ends of the ravine. Bright torches were visible at both ends. Much to their horror, they saw lights coming from between the trees less than a hundred metres away. The other half of the attack came from the other end. On the ridge of the ravine, the chimps appeared, pointing their crossbows down at them.

The bush dogs clambered out from the undergrowth to see what was brewing. 'What's going on? What are all… oh, this is a lot worse than I thought,' one of the bush dogs gasped, seeing the angry crowd surrounding them.

'Get down into the burrows, they won't find you there,' Natashia snarled.

'We're trapped! I thought you three knew better than this,' the bear cynically scolded.

'You said you knew the way. We wouldn't be here if it wasn't for you,' Ryan snarled.

'That just leaves us four to fight our way out of this mess,' Natashia cursed.

When the crowd filled both ends of the ravine, a chital stag herald spoke, 'You're under orders to be captured and executed for murder of a citizen of the Kingdom, being an illegal species and trespassing on lands belonging to the Kingdom, by order of Suleiman the Royal Chief. You, Bernard, are already wanted on charges of being an enemy of the state from working with the insurgency. Your bounty will be claimed by the end of tonight. We will either arrest you now and kill you all later or kill you now.'

Near the front of the group of foes, on the back of the Indian rhinoceros, was Andrew, a high-ranking gorilla, his iron armour glistened in the moonlight. Only a handful of their attackers wore this armour. His hoofed herbivore's plate-like skin, an inbuilt suit of armour of its own, was moving as the rhino flexed, ready to charge.

113

Planks of timber and hides tied together in the correct pattern were attached as additional thick armour. The rhinoceros snorted in challenge at the four carnivores.

'What do we do now?' Ryan asked Melissa, the only one with experience with these civilised beasts.

'We escape or die trying. I have a crazy and probably stupidly suicidal idea that may work. The chimps won't shoot their own and most of the deer cannot attack upwards. So, there is one way out; on their backs.'

'That's insane, it would get us killed!' Ryan snarled at the apparent suicidal bravery and stupidity needed to undertake such a plan.

'No time to complain. If you want to go up the trees and run over the open ground above, try it. The tiger and I will go across their backs. You climb up and get past the crossbows. As for the bush dogs and the bear, I don't know. See you if you survive. Now we go, ***run***!' she barked.

All of them were snarling except for Natashia. Standing off to their right-hand side, she opened her massive jaws letting out a thunderous, primal, low-pitched roar of challenge. Bernard stood on his hind legs roaring before dashing for the trees and an upwards exit.

The dingo ducked as the chimps fired. The arrows missed. Branches of the foliage or the rocky cliff blocked most. Ryan flung himself up a tree, hugging into the trunk and propelling himself upwards with all his strength. He reached the top before the chimps could reload. Bernard was not far behind him. The bear had his own strategy for escaping. A group of bush dogs decided to take their chances and follow him.

Bernard was heading for the narrow ledge covered in epiphytic ferns and cliff clambering foliage. He barged his way upwards, swiping and slamming his paws into the enemy who came down the ledge to meet him. A number of macaque monkeys were smacked aside and at least one fell through the tree. It was then an unexpected animal came to challenge him.

The wooden-armoured spectacled bear working for the Kingdom roared as he came sprinting down the cliff side ledge. The sloth bear roared a challenge as he ascended the ledge. The two bears engaged in battle. The orange chested spectacled bear pushed down. Bernard

114

stood his ground, raised a paw, and slapped the spectacled bear in the head. From the force of his swipe, Bernard nearly lost his footing and slid back onto the vegetation.

The spectacled bear staggered, blood coming from one side of his face, where the helmet did not cover the short muzzle. Other animals raced down, climbing up on enemy the bear's back.

Just then, an arrow sped towards Bernard. He flinched sideways and it passed through his long fur and just scratched the skin on his underbelly.

Bernard swiped at the bear's head again. His swipe flung the spectacled bear backwards. He regained his footing and thundered forward, rearing, and swinging his paws where Bernard's head had been just a second ago. As Bernard ducked, a tamaraw came hurtling down from the top of the ledge. The small buffalo's hooves barely missed the bear's back. Bernard turned and jumped, landing on the bull's head, neck and scrambling onto his back. Trying to escape, the buffalo charged up to the jungle beyond. Bernard held on, keeping his claws around the panicking bovines' neck. A small number of the bush dogs also scrambled on to his back during the fight.

Whilst the bear was forcing his way out of the gully, the tiger and dingo were racing towards the main attack near the edge of the ravine, getting closer to the incoming herd of angry beasts. The pigs came barrelling and weaving between the trees. A small group of the bush dogs' pack members had come back from a hunt. They wheeled away from the pigs, scampering for their lives or to their deaths. About eight came running down in a single file along a tiny grass track. They quickly scampered into the burrow. The giant forest hogs continued leading part of the charge. Behind them, charged the deer. Natashia ran towards the pigs, dodging their tusks.

Some of the deer were beginning to pull back in fear as they realised that an incredibly angry tiger was chasing them. Their riders were nervous as well, trying to convince their mounts to face the incoming feline. They fired arrows, but most missed their mark because the deer were squirming wildly. A group of African giant forest hogs charged forward. Attached to the pig's saddle and held by macaques were massive swivel lances. They headed straight for the tiger.

115

Coming underneath them, some of the remaining bush dogs tore at either the pig's boar parts or their undersides. The hogs wheeled and bucked in panic, trying to disrupt the dogs. As they did, they either thrust the blade into the crowd, or into the cliffs or trees. When the hogs tried to squash the dogs, the canines jumped out of the way and began to run under the main horde.

One of the boars reached Natashia almost head on. From his right, a saddled Indian rhinoceros came to finish the cat. The boar was going to spear the feline, the rhinoceros intended pummelling her into the ground. Melissa was close by. They had only milliseconds to react. Natashia ducked under the rhino as it charged at Melissa. She dodged and ducked under the blade held by its gorilla rider. It raked her ears, cutting them slightly. The canine leapt onto a visayan stag, then sideways onto the backs of the sambars further back, avoiding their riders in the process.

Natashia changed direction. The gorilla swung around and threw his spear, embedding it into another rhino's hard plates of natural armour. Snarling and exposing her still white teeth, the tigress leapt onto the spear, spring-boarding off the wooden-handled weapon onto the back of a sambar in the second row. Torchlight illuminated the white pelt as she came crashing down on a deer. She leapt to the next deer and the next – until they deliberately left a huge gap.

One stag reared to send his antlers deep into her chest. She leapt at his throat, pivoting herself to the left to swing around. During the twisting motion, she pulled the stag off his feet as she ripped his throat out with her teeth. Arterial blood sprayed hot over the leaf litter below before he fell to the ground dead. She flew spiralling onto another stag before turning around.

Up ahead was an elephant with one of the crossbows, and near to it, the mammoth. As the stag came close to the elephant's rear, she leapt from the stag onto the elephant's back.

The dingo was running on the backs of the deer, too quick for most of their riders to target her. Suddenly, one reared at her. She dodged to the right, hitting an elephant. She swung her legs to hook into the elephant's hide and harness, to climb to the animal's back.

A macaque jumped on her. It grappled at her fur, aiming its jaws at her neck. The extra weight made her miss her jump, tumbling backwards onto the mammoth's face. He reached for her, but she

116

tugged away as the macaque formed its hands into a choke hold, choosing not to bite.

The elephant coiled its trunk reaching for her but missed the dingo and got the monkey instead. He tossed it towards the front. Melissa leapt onto the back of another deer and continued to leap from one to the other, getting desperate to find a way out.

Further forward, the ranks were in disarray from ankle biting bush dogs and panicked pigs. One pig accidentally gutted a visayan deer with its iron knives.

On the elephant's back was the scorpion crossbow, an immense piece of siege equipment, a metre long with an eighty-centimetre bolt. Natashia quickly spun it to face the mammoth. A chimp jumped up from the crowd, intent on disarming her. The tigress fired, sending the bolt through the chimp, knocking it backwards. She quickly reloaded and aimed it again at the mammoth.

A stag, in those fleeting seconds, saw his monarch in danger of an eighty-centimetre-long, fifteen-centimetre-wide crossbow bolt. Knowing how much damage his death would do to the society, he leapt up to take the missile. It skewered him in the ribs. The two critically wounded animals fell at the mammoth's feet. The tiger roared in exasperation that she hadn't killed the leader.

Suleiman's expression showed his horror at his subjects' sacrifices.

Natashia let her guard down just long enough for the gorilla, Andrew, to leap from the nearest buffalo onto the elephant's back. He swung his arm into a choke hold, tearing her off the crossbow and thrusting her over the elephant's side. Yowling, the cat fell onto the ground below. The elephant grabbed her tail with her trunk and swung the tiger high off the ground.

She roared in confusion as the elephant hauled her tail-first high into the air, and then slammed her downwards, smashing her onto the grass with a thud so hard, her computer brain was knocked out. The other animals quickly disembarked to restrain the unconscious tiger.

Ryan waited just long enough for the chimps to turn their mounts around before bursting out of the trees. He jumped down onto a chimp, swatting him off his sambar deer mount by grabbing him with both paws and throwing the ape aside. He clamped his jaws very close to his mount's neck and dug in his claws.

'If you try to get me off, I will sever your spine, *run now!*' The cat yowled. The sambar deer, preferring life to death, bounded off down the hills, jumping over boulders as it ran. The chimps fired again, one hitting the deer in the rump, but he was too panicked and pumped full of adrenaline to feel it. The deer continued to run, jumping, and dodging the various obstacles. It was not long before they made it to the tiny grove of acacia trees at the base of the hills, the leafy branches brushed his head. It was hard to hold on to the deer as it ducked and weaved, forcing him to dig his claws in harder.

Another mounted deer came alongside. The rider fired his crossbow. The chimp's arrow missed the cat as he slid over to the side. The missile hit the stag's hindquarters instead. The stag faltered in his stride. With two crossbows in him, he decided to try and buck the cat off.

Ryan snapped his jaws shut but missed the deer's neck when the animal ducked his head. The other deer was now directing its iron knife-tipped antler spikes at his face. Some of the thrusts hit him. The cat realised that the opportunity to ride this deer was over.

Just as he jumped, one of the chimps sprinting down the hill into the grove of acacia, tossed a lasso in his direction, hooking the puma's head. With a tug, the rope pulled him backwards, swiping his arms in vain as he fell. A second lasso caught the cat's hind legs whilst the puma struggled to right himself. Ryan writhed around, clawing at the ropes, his heart pounding in fear.

One of the deer who had captured him charged ahead. His mounted macaque tied the other end of the rope to the antlers. The two ends of the rope were pulled far enough to lift him off the ground. A third rope captured his left foreleg. Suspended above the ground, the puma snarled, yowled, and spat in anger, writhing with fury. He came to the realisation that struggling was in vain. It would just get him into a bigger tangle. He relaxed and let them carry him.

***

Melissa had also fallen on bad luck. Struggling to get near the back of the herd, she was dogpiled by macaques and other monkeys atop an Alfred's deer. Another macaque fired a blow dart in her direction, hitting her on the rump. The mild poison in it was an immobilizer; not strong enough to kill but enough to cause vomiting and agony.

118

She barely got another metre before dropping, spasming in agony. Vomiting quickly followed. She was still shaking when the chimps collected her.

The sick animal spasmed all the way to town, falling in and out of consciousness, and staring down at the ground and the fur of the sambar that carried her. He tossed her into one of the many wooden cages of the Zoo. Around her were other such constructions, both on the inside of the large wooden wall and outside of it. In cages around her, others languished. Many were already thin, or had evidence of disease such as ring worm, mange, or ticks. Others had open and infected wounds.

Delirious, she barely cared now. Her computer mind struggled to make sense of the broken and distorted physical signals. She drifted in and out of consciousness. When awake, nostalgic memories filled her vision.

She remembered warm days out in the savanna, back in the youth of this life; she remembered playing with her packmates; listening to stories from the parents she was given when she was reborn; practising hunting of various game animals on the savanna; she remembered her first love in this life. The sorrow of this life came back, and so did the good and bad from previous lives, but from her pleasant dreams, one thing was clear, she just wanted to get back home; her original home in this life, that is, if she could escape.

She awoke trembling. Rather than retaliating, she just lay there still feeling ill, unable to eat. She noticed a puma in the cell next to hers and stared at it to see if it was Ryan. She didn't see his familiar markings and relaxed, hoping he had escaped.

In the cage on the outside of the fort's wall was another cell where the restrained, now conscious, Natashia was placed. The tiger was unable to free herself, yet she was still breathing. The cut on her head had begun to heal, but not the one on her shoulder where the crossbow bolt was pulled out.

In this situation, the animals could do nothing to fix the main horrible problem. They were on death row.

Melissa was finally beginning to return to her senses. The other dingoes in her cell stared at her in concern while she struggled to get up. The dog was still shaking. She began to howl, long, loud, and eerily.

One of the guards banged her cage. '*Shut up*, you're making too much of a racket!'

As the guard, a female gorilla, backed off, the howl continued. The other dingoes in the same cage began a haunting chorus of howls. Several kilometres away, ears were listening.

As Melissa tried to rouse herself, Natashia was struggling to undo her bonds, biting at the tough hempen ropes and gradually unweaving the fibres. She swore she would personally destroy whoever made these borderline indestructible ropes. Her incisors were beginning to hurt from the tugging and pulling when a familiar face came past the cage.

A now injured spectacled bear, who was chewing on an orange before spitting out the seeds, followed the sable antelope. The antelope looked in and sneered at the struggling tiger.

'Now, was it such a good idea to come near the edge of the woods? Regretting it yet?' he sneered as he came closer to the cage.

'Why? Why go to all the trouble of bringing me here? Just killing me back out there would have proven your point. Why were so many sent after us?'

She managed to get closer to the gate. She felt her bonds coming looser on her forepaws.

'You're a murderer and an insurgency sympathiser who doesn't even know that your friend Bernard is one of the most wanted animals in the entire Kingdom. He is one of the top three highest ranking members of that group of terrorists. You carnivores are dumber than we thought,' the antelope said with obvious contempt.

'Why can't you and your friends leave us in peace? Okay, I killed one guy before you came for me. To be exact, I killed one of your soldiers when he alerted you to my cover. I could have just slunk away but you guys had to chase me down. Why is that so?' she asked in an annoyed yet confused tone.

'You and the rest of your kind are nothing but murderers. Slaughters of animals that are far more noble and kind-hearted than you thugs. If we had let you go, you would never make amends and would just keep killing again and again. Serial killers, the lot of you.'

'But we only hunt to survive and to protect ourselves and those important to us. Your kind hunt far beyond where you normally go, and don't even eat those you kill. All species have a right to exist, your species and mine included. Are we not meant to be able to hunt to feed ourselves and our families? How does reincarnation fit into this? For all I know you may have been a predator like me in previous lives.'

'Fuck you and your family. For all I care, go off and starve to death. Your agony and torment from doing so would be vengeance for all those you have killed or would kill. Every time I see a dead carnivore, it pleases me. If I could rid this world of all carnivorous animals and genocide every one of them off the surface of this planet, it would be a dream come true. I and others like me would be far better off if those Terraformers never recreated you guys.

'You all should have remained extinct. The tigers, the crocodiles, the vultures, the sharks, and every damn cat and dog between here and the southern tundra should be completely and utterly dead on this planet. Add the unmodified humans on earth to that list as well. The humanity we used to be sure messed up that planet and triggered the biggest mass extinction ever. I'm sure they're behind the annihilation.'

'Wait. What happened to make you hate humans so much? You used to be one. Besides, Earth was getting better when I left. Regardless of that, what happens back on earth is irrelevant here on Mars. Why do you believe that being a predator is the worst thing you can do? There are far worse creatures out there than both of us!'

At that point, the bindings around her front paws finally came loose. She shot her forelimb between the bars, scratching the antelope before the gorilla shoved his spear at her to force her back into the cage, snarling in the process.

'So foolish, but it doesn't matter, you will be dead soon, you won't even see dawn.'

Not far away, guards untied Ryan in his cage – the ropes loosened and quickly cut away. First the one around the head and neck, then

121

the one around the front leg, and finally the back leg binding was torn away.

The guards rolled the prisoner into the cage before he could turn around and lash at them. They rapidly slammed the cage roof door shut and quickly tied the bamboo gate. The rest of the cage was stronger with wooden bars. Outside, the captors peered in and jeered at the prisoners in this cage and the others beside it.

'Disgusting murderers. We're going to kill you tonight,' one voice jeered. Another yelled, 'You should be ashamed of what you did.'

Melissa raised her head at the commotion and snarled as she realised it was Ryan they were taunting. She slumped down defeated. If they had captured Ryan, there was no one to rescue them.

A vulgar voice hurled further hateful insults, 'Your kind should be hunted and killed to the end of the world.'

The puma snarled back as he turned around in the cage, his long fangs were bared in anger.

He looked around and saw that he had joined another puma, also a prisoner in the cell. The newcomer looked at the surrounding crowd with anger, fear, and disappointment. The other prisoner was far more relaxed about the whole ordeal.

The first prisoner pulled himself up off the ground and walked towards the newcomer, who righted himself until his four feet were on the floor. 'Well, you're new. What are you here for – what crime did you commit?'

Ryan shook his head in disgust. 'I was just in the wrong place at the wrong time. I tried running like a coward, but they chased me down and lassoed me. My friends, if they have not been killed yet, are probably nearby.

'Ah, I've been here for a few weeks. The confinement is starting to drive me crazy. It's nice to have another of my kind to talk to. I would have preferred someone of the opposite sex, however. I would have preferred a cute puma, but you'll have to do. I was put in here for murder – or what they called murder. My old home was being torn up by a logging crew. I had to defend myself. I killed a chital deer, a few monkeys, and a peacock. I guess eating one of them really did not make me seem innocent. I ripped out that deer's throat with my teeth before daring the rest to have a piece of me. The gorilla pounded the stuffing out of me though with a stone club.'

Ryan stared at the facial scars on the puma's face from that battle. 'You put up more of a fight than me. What's your name?'

'My name is Zhang. Yours is?'

'Mine is Ryan. Pretty plain name, I know. I've only been running around in the wilderness for a couple of weeks. This is the first town I've visited here.'

'Shame we won't get a chance to go sightseeing. I guess there is always another lifetime,' Zhang responded.

Ryan turned his head and focused on him. 'My first time on the planet as well. Dying and living again is going to be tough.' Nervousness wavered in his voice.

'Yeah, this kind of sucks, locked up and waiting for execution. Maybe we will be reborn sooner than we think.' Zhang turned as the roof top door opened. 'Wait, something is going on at the top of the cell.'

Through the roof hole, the mangled carcass of a spotted cat was dropped. Its innards had been sliced out. The young cat, scarcely over a year old, hit the floor.

'Dinner time,' Zhang chirped. Rising to his feet, he moved to the carcass. He sat down and ripped and tore into the raw cat flesh. He swallowed chucks, slicing them against his premolars. 'Looks like Pantanal cat is on the menu,' Zhang said whilst chewing the cat's limbs. He stopped suddenly and stared at the carcass.

'No black feet, they are meant to have black feet... wrong spot combination for clouded leopard... tail is too long for lynx... spots not consistent with lions or tiger cubs...' As Zhang spoke, gradually more and more dread crept into his voice. He crept back, his ears flattened, staring at the carcass, spitting out bloodied chinks of fur, and mewling in fear and shock.

A still set of blue eyes were open when the tiny corpse was flicked over to reveal the characteristic line of spots near the back.

'No, no, no, what have they done!' Zhang backed away with growing horror in his voice.

'Is it cannibalism – they tricked you into?' said the fearful Ryan, watching from a short distance away. 'I knew we would throw away our humanity out here, but cannibalising children of your own species is kind of messed up.'

'Yes, he very well could have been my son. These monsters think forcing a father to eat his son is acceptable!' The puma rose up onto his haunches, snarling as he faced the bars. Outside, one of the guards, a gorilla, and a sambar stag walked past. The stag was wearing wooden and flax armour. The gorilla had a strange black material for a breast plate and other smaller plates on his limbs and back. The sambar deer leered at the horrified cat.

The puma bounded across the cage, throwing himself against the bars. His clawed paw flew through the bars, slicing the deer's hide on its hind leg, drawing blood.

'You sick monsters murdered my son and tried to feed him to me!' he yowled defiantly at the edge of the cage. A long sharp spear was shoved between the bars. He jumped back from the cage bar, hissing at this aggravator. He slinked back into the cage, glaring out into the crowd leering at him.

'If it was my son I just ate, I am not going to be in a good mood for a long time. As we probably won't have long, I forgot to ask you how your friends ended up here. I assume your friends are that white tigress and the dingo who looked like it was having a fit. They came in with you, didn't they?'

Ryan snarled in disgust at Zhang's lack of empathy for Melissa, before replying. 'They were with me when I was captured. Like I said, wrong place at the wrong time.'

***

By the end of the night's hunt, the Zoo had its cages stocked. It was more of a mockery of a Zoo, where they tossed the carnivores of the same species in the same pen. But Natashia, the tiger remained alone in hers. A bear cub had also been captured and put into another cage on the other side of the path, along with two other bears and three cubs. Bernard was nowhere to be seen.

The male cub was mewling and meekly begging for the mother he had been given to when he was reborn.

A small group of nocturnal baby animals came wandering through the zoo. This was one of the night classes for their gaoler's young animals. They came up to the bars, peering in curiously at the cats and talking amongst themselves about what they were seeing.

Melissa stood and walked to the bars and called out, 'Ryan, we're in a terrible situation here. We're probably going to die.' She was still frothing from the poison.

'Oh, Melissa. I didn't see you there. Yes, we're not in the best possible situation. I never thought I was going to be caged again. I suppose they'll have spectacular public executions of some sort,' said Ryan.

Zhang, the other puma in Ryan's cage said, 'This is kind of like death row for us. Where is the insurgency when you need them?'

'Zhang, you are only the second puma I have seen. Ryan was the only puma I had seen in this world until I saw you in the cage before Ryan was brought in,' said Melissa.

Zhang nodded and said to Ryan, 'She a friend of yours?'

'Yes, she was teaching me the ways of this world and how to hunt for food."

'She would be a nice mouthful,' Zhang said.

Ryan glared at him and then turned to look around the cages nearby. In the dim light of the torches, he could see that a trio of fossa and a large python occupied one. Only a few plants grew in the dirt-floored pen – some patches of miserable grasses and a few ferns to create the illusion of it being an actual zoo.

One animal cage caught his interest. Next to the python cage was a lynx. Why a lynx was this close to the equator perplexed him, though anything could be expected considering the bizarre assortment of animals. The cat had a brown coat with many small spots on its pelt; so many that they nearly formed stripes. He also had a beard of sorts.

The lynx was angry, prowling back and forwards. He shouted angry expletives at those that passed by his cage. 'You coward! You pick on anyone who could oppose you. If you just joined the Six Sunners then this whole stupid war would be over. Doesn't mean much to you blind idiots, but we are all going to be dead soon.'

During his several minutes of ramblings, Ryan heard something about a liger queen, a cat born to a lion and a tiger, in another tribe or civilisation. The lynx suggested Suleiman may have been threatening to invade their civilisation; or something along the lines of that. It was hard to make sense of his ramblings.

***

Numerous animals passed by the cages to see the carnivores that had tormented them. Animals they had feared when they still roamed free. Yet most of them did not express hate; though a few angry individuals pounded on the bars demanding to know what happened to their family members or friends.

One group of animals walking back and forwards, were students from a nearby school. They had come on a night-time excursion. A larger male long-tailed monkey carried the load of eight baby animals including a tamarin, two opossums, a peacock, and several rodents. One of the group – a baby tamarin – clambered onto the bars to look inside. The mangabey urged the baby monkey back to him, so it clambered onto his tail. The monkey proceeded to Ryan's pen.

The puma stopped pacing and moved to the back of the cage when the baby animals started gawking.

'It's a puma!' one of the baby monkeys exclaimed.

'So that is what they look like,' the opossum said peering in.

'Did you eat my dad?' the baby peafowl asked sombrely as he also peered in.

The last comment caused Ryan to flinch, pulling his ears back with guilt. The cat hunched over with his head hanging. He had yet to harden himself to hunting. He was consoled by the knowledge that the baby peacock could never know which of the many males was his dad. Neither did his siblings, such was the curious nature of fertilisation of the eggs.

He was a murderer, plain and simple. The cat knew that. They all did; but what choice did they have. Kill or be killed was the lore. Without eating, he would starve. The population ultimately needed to be kept in check, though that was a pragmatic way of looking at it.

However, unlike on earth, if you had the cybernetic brain and died here, you could simply live again as another animal. Here, death was not the end of all things. Sure, you never got to see your loved ones

126

again. You had to leave your entire life behind, but at least there was always going to be a new life. Many of these herbivores were killers in their last lives. They had faced the same dilemmas and had chosen the only logical option. The entire wild system ran on a carousel of life, death and suffering known as the food web.

These thoughts were running through Ryan's head as he tried to justify his killing. His human morals still fought with the need to kill.

Outside, beyond the Zoo, an execution ceremony area was being set up. A crowd was already gathering to watch the events unfold. For Ryan and the others, it was evident something bad was going to happen tonight. Most likely, it would involve their death.

The voice of one of the apes came over the broadcasting system, 'The executions will begin shortly.'

At that point, the tamaraw came around the corner, with two chimpanzees hanging in the harnesses. They were armed with iron tipped spears to help subdue any unruly prisoners. They went to each of the cages, inspecting the prisoners inside.

They opened some of the cages carefully, prodding the occupants and dragging out the ones who were too scared to fight. The animals screamed, snarled, and struggled as the guards dragged them to the execution area. When they came to Melissa's small cage, she tried to pull herself together and got to her feet, snarling.

By this point, several other animals had been executed. Their corpses were dropped carelessly by the side of the killing stone.

Melissa prepared herself for the worst.

***

Natashia's cage was outside the fence and a little way away from the killing stone. As she listened through a tiny hole in one of the walls to the screams and snarls of those dragged to the killing area, something caught her attention. The guard chimp standing near her cage suddenly raised his hand and opened his mouth to call out. A blow dart hit his eye. As he clutched his face and groaned in pain, a large group of small animals scampered across the ground from the wall. The partly blinded chimp lashed out, grabbing one of the small animals by the torso, and trying to crush it.

Many more of these small creatures ran to the cages. Squirrels came with stolen keys. They clambered to the top of the cages and slotted the keys into the doors. The opossum that blew the blow pipe helped open each of them.

While this was happening, the group of bush dogs that Natashia had met earlier leapt onto the guard chimp and tore out his throat. They scurried around the area, quickly silencing a potential witness in the form of a fleeing bush turkey, tearing the hapless bird down and devouring it alive. They needed to maintain stealth.

Keys were turned and cages undone. A macaw landed on a cage and tried to sound the alarm, but a trio of orange-headed turkey vultures quickly jumped on him and brought him down. Natashia's cage door was quickly opened. A group of rats ran inside and gnawed at her hind leg restraints, which soon snapped. She padded out just in time to see another witness, this time a chital, turn and run. With a low-pitched growl, she bounded past the other cage, leaping up and wrestling the stag to the ground. She snapped his neck quickly. Normally this would be a meal for her, but there would be no time for feasting now. Soon other animals joined her.

The ringleader of the rescue, the king vulture, appeared on top of the last cage as the animal inside walked out quietly.

Natashia turned around from the kill and looked at the bird. 'Thank you, you saved us. What's the plan now? There are others contained further in.'

'I have an idea but need a distraction.'

***

Melissa was too sick to fight. A chimp grabbed her by the scruff of the neck, his knobbly fingers finding little resistance in the sick dog. As he dragged her out of the cage door, the other animals made a massive racket, screeching, roaring, bellowing, and banging the bars. This unnerved the captors but not enough to distract them just yet.

The chimp dragged her across the sand and threw her up onto the altar. The head stone was slick with blood that flowed through the stencils carved into it. She whimpered as they hauled her onto the execution rock. With a nod of approval, the execution preparations began. The chimp lifted the steel sacrificial knife and aimed carefully at her throat. As it swung down, she closed her eyes … only to open them three seconds later, amazed at still being alive.

The knife had missed her and hit the stone. She had only a second to wonder why he missed before the chimp fell to the ground with a crossbow bolt stuck in his back. Surprise and confusion rippled through the crowd before someone on the gatehouse of the prison yard yelled, 'Enemies at the gate!' Suddenly the fort's gate exploded.

Giant, angry, red flames roared from the gatehouse and a pillar of smoke rose into the air. The hot flames ripped into the courtyard. The walls of the building caught fire as the flames raced into the fortress yard. Several guard animals on the wall were set alight and immediately dropped to the ground in an attempt to extinguish themselves. The angry wall of orange and red was broken when the wooden righthand gate leaned over and collapsed onto the flames, briefly smothering them.

The flames quickly engulfed the gatehouse. The exploding timber sent flaming splinters flying into the crowd. Animals screamed and yelped as sharp fragments of timber found their way into the flesh of hapless victims who were standing too close to the gate. They ran as they were injured or flailed about as they bled.

It was then the attackers swarmed into the enclosure in the most brazen of attacks. Across the burning buildings they came. Several tamaraw emerged, barging out of the flames. Their black silk-like body armour had fire resistant plates of a hardened version of the same material blocking the heat. Panels of the large wooden walls were thrown over the fire. They dampened it just long enough for attackers to run over the temporary firebreak.

Horned heads of the insurgents swept from side to side as they engaged the deer and antelope cavalry that came to oppose them. On the backs of the attacking antelopes, rode clouded leopards, chimps, coatis, and monkeys. They clung to crude saddles firing their bows into the crowd gathered for the execution or swiping with spears and paws in the melee.

Behind them came the tigers, Anthia being among them, wearing armour of the same material as the tamaraws. Further back, the gigantic ground sloth lumbered across as the flames came up behind her. She wore a wooden saddle on her back with many metal loops for tying ropes. The female sloth roared as she plodded towards the wooden cages. One of the chimps charged her with a spear. She reared, swiped, and flattened the chimp, sending the corpse flying into the burning section of the wall.

Some of the bears had come through the burning gateway. The other animals in the rescue operation were now barging through the other gate. The elephants ramming, trampling, and throwing the defenders out of the way. Others began to fall from their injuries. The remaining elephants threw grappling anchors over the wall with their trunks, hooking the gate frame, and pulling the entire building down. The crowd panicked and moved quickly away from the entrance gate in an attempt to flee by the back entrance.

The immense fireball engulfing the gatehouse area continued to burn fiercely. The elephants dropped a chunk of the wooden wall onto the flames. The wood would take several seconds to catch, enough time for the next wave of attackers to run across.

It was difficult to see exactly what was going on, but the captives knew it was someone coming to save them and wreak havoc. At least Ryan, Melissa and the other prisoners hoped it would be. Melissa finally found enough strength to lift herself to her feet. Confused animals were panicking and looking for weapons.

The outside guards rushed over the chunk of wall after the attackers to help protect those inside, as the big cats and chimps made their way into the courtyard. The attackers headed more for the prisoners than the guards, but they were still mauling anyone who got in their way. The insurgents rear guard now came in, including a rhinoceros and tapirs, with possums, tree kangaroos and coati for riders.

Several bears appeared including Bernard. He rushed into combat, long fur trailing behind him. He reared and leapt from the final step, flying straight into the face of one of the female gorilla soldiers. He flung his massive paw across her face.

The gorilla fell back, clutching her bleeding and mangled face. She recovered swiftly and lifted her hand and whirled a heavy weapon – part axe, part club, part war hammer. Bernard ducked away from it, but a heavy blow unexpectedly knocked him off his feet. He jumped up, banging into Andrew, the head of the Kingdom's military. The gorilla came at him with his shark tooth studded sword. Swinging the weapon, the ape forced the bear into retreat; until a jaguar pounced on Andrew.

130

Both the ape and the feline were now flailing around on the ground in an angry pile of muscle and fur. Andrew's metal breastplate and his neck guard, made from the silk-like material, protected him from the jaguar's claws.

Bernard returned quickly to the rest of the group just as the sloth demolished the gate to the inner prison and the elephants stormed in.

The elephants and the sloth barged through the cages. The tapirs were trying their best to help. One ploughed into a few serows that had come to fight. The odd-looking mammal tore their throats out with their sharp horns. One of the tapirs swung itself around, smacking another of the deer into a post, with the dying animal still attached to its horn. The elephants tore the wooden bars of the cages out, releasing their occupants.

The noise of battle had attracted attention from Kingdom reinforcements who had just returned from patrol. Between a gap in the flames, the ground force of the defenders poured in to deal with the insurgents. The dwarf buffalo, also called tamaraws, led the charge for the Kingdom's troops. Three came running over the fallen section of wall, ramming into the rhino, the bears, the tapirs, and tigers.

Both sides threw themselves into the battle.

The noise increased as the fighting grew more violent. The dingoes ran as a multi-coloured pack, leaping and dodging the tamaraws and aiming straight for the back gate. The others that had shared Melissa's cage were now running for the hills.

One of the larger sambar stags charged into the pack heading for the gate, kicking several aside and sweeping his enormous antlers around until he caught one. He rammed his antlers into the white dingo, shoving it around like a rag doll, as he drove his weapon deeper into the yelping dingo's guts.

At this point, Suleiman entered the battle. When most of the Kingdom fighters were fleeing or losing their battles, the Mammoth thundered into the fight.

He grabbed one of the dingoes, shaking it like a limp puppet, slamming it into the ground several times before sending it flying high into the air over his back. The dingo came crashing down a good thirty metres away in the attic of a house. His high-pitched yelp was interrupted by the cracking of the roof and the falling timber that killed him.

Suleiman continued his bloody rampage, grabbing a weapon from his saddle with his trunk. He caught one of the buffalos with his tusk. The sharpened metal caps placed over the tips pierced its armour. The mammoth wielded an enormous version of the gorilla's weapon with his trunk. He slammed the club end down on the buffalo's skull, imploding it, sending the bovine tumbling down with sparks flying from its smashed brain computer.

A jaguar leapt from the burning buildings onto Sulieman's side. The mammoth urged his riders, a group of chimps, to attack the cat. They jabbed at the jaguar with their spears. One managed to cut the jaguar's back. The feline beat a hasty retreat, but Sulieman wheeled around, bowling the cat over. Rearing one leg up, he brought it smashing down on the jaguar's ribcage, crushing it into a bloody mess of armour and gore. Still the mammoth fought on.

Now it was time for the bears and the tigers to flee. Natashia ran along the fallen section of wall as it begun to catch fire from a dropped torch and entered the fray. She leapt over a buffalo as she ploughed her way past the crowd, focused on Andrew.

Nearby, a sambar stag was being ravaged by a female armoured-jaguar who clung to the panicking beast's throat and chest, tearing bloody flesh from the bucking animal until it fell over and died, showering the feline with blood.

The gorilla saw Natashia approach, drew his sword, and began to swing it around. Only a quick skid prevented her from being slashed across the face – a potentially fatal injury. The tiger roared and turned to fight a stag rushing into the carnage. She slammed into his side so hard that he lost balance.

The tiger clung to the deer's head, shoving her paws and torso between its antlers as it bucked. She raked bloody claw marks across its hide before sinking her teeth into its neck, snapping the neck in the ensuing battle.

The archers had climbed onto the roof of one of the buildings. They aimed down at the melee but were afraid to fire in case they hit their own fighters. As they stood, unable to release their arrows, the bears came at them. Their black shaggy forms clambered up the building and attacked the chimp guards. Other bears on the ground pushed their way through the crowd, battling the enemy. Those not fighting went to check for any remaining captives, but their friend's cages were open, and the prisoners gone.

Most of the defenders scattered or fell back to protect the fleeing civilians. The few remaining off-duty soldiers engaged the bears. Bernard slashed with his claws at one deer, causing it to reel away with blood pouring from a lethal neck wound. The doe collapsed, jerking around as she died.

A Kingdom elephant, coming in to help those who were fleeing the chaos, tossed, and stomped on some of the dingoes as it came into the fray searching for its prey. The sloth bear that the elephant was aiming at jumped aside. Bernard sent it back into the crowds with a vicious swipe at its trunk, as one of the tamaraws, aiming at Bernard, barged into the elephant, drawing blood with its sharp horns.

Natashia leapt onto the buffalo's back, her claws raking its side. She briefly rode on the tamaraw until the elephant came barging in their direction. Sensing her chance, she twisted and leapt off the back of the bovine. The tiger clambered onto the back of the elephant, shredding the huge ears, and scratching the face; only just missing the eyes.

The elephant panicked and tried to shake the tiger off.

As the elephant wheeled around, Natashia grabbed a torch from the wall with her jaws. She used the flames, pressed dangerously close to the elephant's head, to direct the panicking pachyderm straight into the cages at the Zoo, colliding with the bars and smashing them to pieces.

The now inflamed elephant ploughed into more cages, cracking wooden bars in some and shattering bamboo bars in others. The numerous panicking eagles, hawks, and vultures that streamed from a broken aviary worsened her fear and injuries. When she ripped the bamboo poles out, the binturongs and coati, those that were suspected spies from the Sixth Sun Empire and carnivore supporters, were let loose. Those still loyal to the Kingdom came to fight with them.

Kingdom warriors on top of the cages, used their spears to try to swipe Natashia off the back of the elephant. The tiger leapt back as the first wide bamboo pole swung into the space she had been occupying. At this point, she left the elephant, whose head was now burning.

It barged through several internal walls in a panic, spreading flames further throughout the compound.

The tigress landed onto the roof of the cages. She fought monkeys there, swatting and slashing them with ease. She had reached a state of berserk bloodlust from the thrill of battle. Many of the monkeys fled as the tigress let loose all restraint. She knocked their weapons aside in a savage fury. Moving from a chimp to a monkey, and then to another, she ripped the smaller primates apart with her jaws and paws throwing the corpses off the roof.

The giant sloth now came in through the edge of the cages at long last. The lumbering behemoth had collected injured and wounded attackers, tying them to her saddle. The wounded creatures almost covered her body as she formed a crude ambulance. The sloth clawed at those that got in her way.

Natashia had cleared the cages of monkeys. She jumped down and bounded through the sparse and isolated fighting. The battle had dissolved into one-on-one duels that others occasionally joined.

At the base of the altar, Melissa was still frothing from the poison, but was well enough for the sloth to lift and sling her onto its back as it lumbered through. The sloth's massive claws disembowelled a foolish, small visayan deer whose rider had tried to charge the large animal with a spear in its paw. An archer hit the mammal with a crossbow bolt, but its thick pebbly hide under the coat formed natural armour.

Monkeys on the sloth's back tied ropes around Melissa as quickly as they could, leaving her hanging upside down and unconscious. They also tied on other wounded animals from their side. The insurgents seized a struggling cuscus from the Kingdom and tied him on securely. They captured him because he had potentially valuable information.

The sloth moved as fast as she could towards the exit. Melissa woke up because of the bouncing, just in time to warn her rescuer about a buffalo barrelling towards her side of the animal. The sloth spun, and with a mighty bellow, reared up and brought his claw down on the charging buffalo. The attacker's horns drew blood from the sloth's belly. But the buffalo had his neck raked by the enormous claws. He fled back to the remaining Kingdom fighters. The serious wounds on the side of his neck bled profusely and left a red stripe along his shoulder.

The massive mammals went their own way as the battle continued in the streets. The few animals left in the rescuers' force acted as a rear-guard.

The behemoth lumbered to the last few cages where Ryan was located. She had to open them fast as the invaders needed to leave soon. The Kingdom's fighters had flung one of the bears back out of the gate and at least one of the jaguars was dead from an attack by a gorilla and the mammoth. Wounded and dead from both sides, lay around the battlefield. The insurgent animals tied their wounded onto the ropes around the sloth and the buffalos with difficulty. The giant behemoth and the elephant set to work to finish breaking open the cages.

The timber cracked and splintered under the force of the paws and trunks ripping the bars out and tossing them aside, tearing the cages open for the animals inside to leave. They moved to each of the cages to free those inside. Not long remained to get them out before the reinforcements arrived. Already parrots were swooping and swarming overhead, harrying at the various attacking carnivores.

Soon the caged animals began to stream out as they continued to crack open more of the enclosures. Ryan waited impatiently for them to reach his cage. As the sloth lumbered over, a chimp leapt from the cage tops, armed with a steel-tipped spear, aiming it at the sloth's back.

Spinning around, the large mammal dislodged the chimp and immediately after, ripped the bamboo bars clean out of the puma cage.

The chimp scrambled back up the bars and passed through the gap.

The other puma, Zhang, who was in Ryan's cage, seized his chance. Running the length of the cage, he leapt out through the gap, grabbing the chimp in the entryway, and pinning him against the sloth.

The pair slipped onto the ground. After a struggle, Zhang drove his massive canine teeth into the chimp's throat. Zhang then proceeded to chew on the ripped-out throat. Ryan had not learnt this behaviour before. He watched Zhang, before following the sloth. The massive mammal moved along, quickly vandalising the remaining cages. More and more creatures came out to join the fray.

Then as everything seemed to be going well, one of the hawks landed on the cage top and shouted, 'The reinforcements are here!'

Sure enough, the outer gate began to flood with a herd of armed deer cavalry. The sloth broke into the fastest pace he could muster. The others of the raiding party were leaving through the back gate.

'Thanks for saving me, walking ball of furious fluff. Now we need to swipe a few faces on the way out and get to our destination, wherever the hell that is,' said Ryan.

The sloth looked over his shoulder to see the monkeys on the deer searching the empty cage.

'We need to get out of here *now!*' The sloth roared as he thundered towards the gate.

Within seconds, one of the sambars came galloping down the lane after them. Ryan snarled, revealing his white canines, before bounding to the widest wooden plank he could find. He leapt off the ground, and pivoting quickly, turned so that his hind legs made contact with the beam. Then, leaping at the stag, he knocked him off balance. His teeth curled around its neck, and bit hard, severing the spinal cord. He let go and the deer fell to the ground. He then swatted the mangabey monkey archer in the head, sending her wheeling back with huge claw marks across her shoulder. The two pumas bolted for the exit.

Ryan again thanked the sloth for helping to save him before bounding out into the battle.

Andrew was furious as he charged in, tackling one of the jaguars, and sweeping it over as he began to stab at it with the sacrificial knife. Suleiman was amongst the fray. Several riders on his back manned the ballista turret on his shoulders. The mammoth swept animals left and right, tossing a bear right out the gate with his trunk. All the animals that had been locked up were now free and assisting in clearing the guard. However, they needed to get out soon, so they began to fall back to the back gate.

The wooden back wall was at the end of the cages. The pair of pumas had a flying start. They leapt halfway up the wall, then, gripping the bark of the logs with their claws, quickly climbed to the top. Ryan swatted a small deer in the guard tower that would have called in more reinforcements. The doe fell, thumping onto the dirt five metres below. The two pumas leapt from the wall, realising that they had to move quickly to avoid the next wave of reinforcements.

The last of the captive animals streamed out of the walled area. The sloth rampaged down the street swatting aside those that got in his way. The large mammal was the last to leave, the wounded tied to its back. Her black shaggy fur had become increasingly red from the blood she drew from those who tried to stop the sloth ambulance.

The fort itself was now ablaze. The fire alerted every single animal within kilometres of it. The group formed a long line as they raced through the streets of the town next to the fort, Fortown. The buildings here were at serious risk of catching fire.

The town stretched as far as the nearby cliff, which was higher than the fort walls, and too high to be used as an easy exit or entrance. Evacuation of the residents had already begun. Animals streamed out through the streets as the group came pounding down, smashing, and damaging the marketplace they charged through.

They flipped stalls, sending produce over the ground. Dirty paws and hooves trod it into the soil. The stampede turned over signs and small pieces of furniture as it thundered by.

Some of the citizens were still around, waking up, and confused to see the group running. A dusky pademelon – a tiny kangaroo – hopped far ahead to warn of their escape. Birds erupted from the higher levels fleeing from their approach.

Many of those fleeing saw guards between the buildings and turned left to avoid them, spilling out through the streets. The sloth and a few others took a more direct route to the exit, smashing through the fragile walls that got in their way. Natashia stayed with this group because of her injury from the crossbow bolt and other minor fresh wounds from earlier fighting during the escape.

The main group was within sight of the avenue at the end of town. The chimps had stolen crossbows from the guards to use to shoot any other guards that dared challenge them. But before they could escape from the town, they ran into another courtyard. Behind them, the guards finally became visible. Two Indian rhinos charged through the street leading towards them. They took refuge in the recently emptied barracks, where the soldiers slept, and stored weapons.

One of the stampeding animals had trampled a bird. The rhino crushed it when he ran over it. The cats had already leapt up onto the roofs to continue their escape. The chimps busted into the armoury, and dragged out a wheeled scorpion crossbow, the same type of bow that had impaled two animals earlier that evening. The bolt they found had a small keg of gunpowder attached to it, designed to be used against ships. They had the bow loaded by the time the rhinos came in.

They slammed the wheeled scorpion into one of the tamaraws, hitting it side-on as it wrestled with one of the gorillas. They cracked the cow's ribs before trampling over it, crushing the ribcage in the process, and killing it quickly. Then the bow fired. The barracks wall exploded in a blazing inferno. They knew it would be less than a minute before the rest of the gun powder ignited.

The remaining animals made their way onto the roofs or bashed their way through the wall until they were in the building next door – a crèche full of frightened baby animals. One of the fossa snatched a baby monkey before continuing onto the roof. The group trashed the beautiful painted interior and fragile, delicate toys and play areas as they rampaged through.

Ryan paused for a moment to warn the cowering binturong, a medium sized, black-furred, raccoon-like creature, which he thought might have been the crèche nanny. 'Go, now! There will be more explosions. I won't hurt you!'

The Binturong hesitantly nodded then called three dozen baby animals out from the various nooks and crannies and told them to rush outside. Ryan sprinted out and just launched himself onto a roof of a nearby building before the entire block exploded in the inferno. He checked for a moment to see the Binturong with a small crowd of the babies running down the street. Then he proceeded along the roofs to bring up the rear.

The main part of their group had already travelled some distance ahead by the time Ryan got himself out of that street. He had to run and jump along the rooftops, accidently collapsing some. The group was still bashing its way through the streets and across the roofs. The edge of town was already visible.

The roof tiles slipped under his feet as Ryan scrabbled up. He jumped to the next roof, his paws crashing through thatching. He pulled himself out and clambered over to another landing on another weak roof. This time he crashed directly into a curtain shop, much to the horror of the possums and rats that owned the stall. A lizard customer ran under the table as the cat leapt out of the window after pulling a curtain off himself.

Wooden beams ran between the buildings. Along them came armed monkeys. A fossa was caught off-guard and shot down with a small crossbow.

Clambering out onto the stronger beams, the puma continued to run. He found stronger roofed wooden houses to run along. One was a block of flats, with tiny boxes for rodent and bird rooms. The occupants screeched in terror as the cat clambered up the structure to avoid the monkeys coming after him. The rest of the group had reached the edge of the walled area and fled into the fields beyond.

Ryan clawed his way down ladders then sprinted along another wooden plank roof before leaping down to street level. He came barging through a busy market stall street sending produce flying. Rosella fruits, a durian, berries, cassowary plums, oranges, wild bananas, and other fruit were sent flying as he barged through a fruit stall.

A hide stall was next. Ryan recoiled in disgust and horror when he brushed against the skinned pelt of another of his kind. He slipped out and sent the tree kangaroo merchant scampering. Flimsy wooden structures tumbled to the ground as he swatted away a pair of macaques that chased him.

He re-joined the main group as they ran past the last of the houses and down an avenue of trees. The heliconia plants around their base helped hide some of what was happening on the road, but they needed to keep moving. The Kingdom guards still chased them.

The group ran through the boulevard of trees, before emerging into an open field.

Across the field, the edge of the town came into view. A tall, wooden, log wall sat on top of a levee. More wooden houses were built up the sides. Their traditional wooden and thatch construction –

some with normal sloped roofs, others more slanted – resembled houses that were built in the islands of Indonesia in past millennia.

Ryan's focus continued. Other animals scrambled out of his way. His paws slipped in the mud, but he continued to charge. A boulevard of trees including figs, lily pilly, nutmeg and other jungle trees led to the levee bank and the gate that the sloth barged through. Ryan leapt up the wall. His claws grabbed the wet timbers still covered in bark. Passing the surprised chimps in a flash, he leapt down into the long grass on the other side of the levy bank taking a tumble as he did so. He righted himself, just as the gate exploded outwards. Two elephants had barged the gate, flinging it open, as the escaping animals reached it.

The group of animals dashed through the corn fields. Melissa was still tied onto the back of the giant sloth, which was one of the slowest of the animals. Although, this large mammal was a bit faster than the average tree sloth, moving at a speedy seventeen kilometres an hour, an amazing speed with so much weight on its back. But she was tiring from the abnormal fast retreat. A group of animals stayed behind to help protect her and bring up the rear. The group paused to allow other animals, including the remaining tamaraws and an elephant to transfer some of the wounded to their backs to give her some relief.

Up ahead, some of the chimps rode on the tamaraws, the big cats kept pace along with the bears and surviving dingoes.

The snake rode on the sloth. The front group was aiming for the fence on the far side of the Kingdom. It would take hours to get there.

It was at that point that things started to go from bad to worse. More of the animal soldiers were after them, heading up the main road. The cornfield quickly came to an end and changed to a fruit orchard that grew both fruit trees and shade loving crops. The latter were being trampled into the ground. The soldier animals stayed behind, watching the group of fleeing animals. They were making sure that they kept track of the main party until their reinforcements arrived from downriver, which would happen soon.

The pursuing group was small, but when it looked like the fleeing animals would escape, they charged in anyway. They dashed in-between the trees and ran over the crops. The big cats turned to attack the buffalo and pigs behind them.

140

Bounding quickly between the trees, Natashia leapt and locked onto the buffalo's horns. She began to wrestle with it, dragging the animal's head to the ground. The pigs soon ran off when the dingoes harried them. The buffalo struggled free and ran out of the orchard. Behind the fleeing crowd, the fugitive owls had stolen torches and set fire to the crops to create a firebreak. The crops of sugar cane were soon ablaze creating a far bigger distraction than the fleeing animals. This bought time for the others to quietly and silently slip into the orchard to continue their journey.

'What was that for?' Ryan asked Bernard. 'Why set fire to viable food crops?'

'Fire breaks. They will be so busy putting the fire out to save their crops they will lose interest in chasing us. We must leave this area for our safety. The deep drainage channel ahead leads underground and is prone to flooding, but we must divert any parties sent to look for us. By some of us following the ditch, we can split their cavalry, which would chase us down on open ground. You should go down there to help.'

Ryan nodded and disappeared, bounding past the burning cane field towards the channel.

The ditch had been unseen to most until they almost fell into it. Dirt crumbled inwards as the miniature buffalo stopped, staring into the hole. It was wide and deep enough for the cats, the sloth, and the smaller animals to travel in without being seen. The chimps and cats immediately began scrambling down and the sloth eased herself in to continue her escape through the trench.

The cavalry of deer, antelopes, and zebra mounted by chimps, more monkeys and tree kangaroos came to the sides. Coati rode in on some of these mounts as well.

To confuse their pursuers, one-half of the group headed towards the partly submerged trench. The faster group broke into a charge across the open meadow. The faster moving animals included the elephants who barged through a corn crop, flattening the growing stalks in the process.

A flock of parrots guided the pursuers who were organised into three groups. They came to the sides of the trench, some running over and back across bridges. The black sable bull led these groups.

It was difficult and rather noisy to fit so many animals into the tight space of the drainage ditch that connected to the fertiliser yards and the public privies, but the rescuers and rescued pressed onwards through the muddy trench, which reeked of manure. Parts of the route was submerged into leafy vine filled tunnels of lantana, jasmine, morning glory and similar vines. They were careful to keep quiet to avoid making themselves easier for their pursuers to find and attack them. Parts of it had thick mud, which was often mixed with animal dung. In many places, they had to clear thick growths of lantana vines, which helped to hide the fleeing animals but made travel difficult. The water in the ditch was foul, stinking of dung, sewage, and mud. It was so polluted that not even the frogs would dare swim here, yet it was the only way out without being seen.

The group continued to plod down the channel, churning up the filth. The sloth was panting heavily as she began to lag. As for Ryan, if he did not get the filth into his mouth, he could live with it, even though he was turning his nose up at it. He sprinted down the channel with the tamaraws behind him. The sloth continued to amble through, keeping the injured animals clean and safe.

Part way through someone shouted, '*Attack!*'

Before they knew it, monkeys, apes, and squirrels jumped down from the sides of the pit. Nightjars flew overhead, having spotted their procession. Ryan, Natashia, and the other remaining tiger, Anthia, readied themselves for a fight.

Bernard caught a chimp that had leapt down with an obsidian blade. The bear roared as the chimp lacerated his arm muscle at the bicep. He smacked his one good arm over the chimp's face, his claws raking the skin, ending in its eyeballs. The bear pinned down the blade with his wounded arm and mauled the chimp, driving his teeth into its face.

The next foes to come his way would have made Ryan chuckle had it not been for their furious assault. Squirrels and rats came armed with tiny toothpick size knives tied to their tiny paws. They poured into the pits in a horde, savagely attacking the creatures behind the sloth. A dingo fell into the water as a squirrel sliced its pelt with sharpened, poisoned, bone knives, while another knife was shoved straight into the dingo's eye.

142

A hawk who had attempted to gore a stag's eye out, was now under the wrath of the deer's riders. It was trying to fly away but several squirrels from the deer's back were biting into it. The sharp talons of the bird clutched one, but another ripped out the bird's throat with its incisors.

Just behind the sloth, tamaraws were carrying a few of the patients. One tamaraw was not lucky. Owls came after it, trying to grab squirrels off its back. They butchered its patients while they were still tied on it. The buffalo hurtled into the dark in a panic. It was too late for some. But a number of these squirrels were now gliding into the ditch and assaulting the attacking creatures within. At least one goanna that had been freed resorted to swimming through the waste to avoid them. Up above, the deer who had been ridden by squirrels lost his riders as another hawk attacked. More animals were pursuing them as the enemy's reinforcement joined the chase.

Ryan ran along the sides of the trench, jumping up the banks to pass other groups. An enemy squirrel leapt onto his back, drawing a poisoned bone shard, attempting to stab and cut him. He tumbled inwards, landing in the mud with a splash. The knife narrowly missed him, instead burying itself in the mud. As he righted himself, several of them latched on like rodent clamps.

An eagle owl snatched one of the larger squirrels off his back. The squirrel stabbed the owl with the now un-poisoned dagger. The mud had washed off the toxin. Other squirrels and rats wallowed in the sewage after the owl had ripped them off.

The sloth stopped, exhausted, unable to carry her load any further. She stood, panting, and looking around in fear at the group catching up to them. She tiredly moaned. 'Get these patients off me. Go on without me. I'll stop them and give you time to get away. I'm only slowing down the ones behind me.' She looked back at the approaching soldiers.

Ryan, pulling himself out of the muck, looked back in horror as many more animals came thundering along the side.

Dozens of deer and sable antelope came with bow-wielding monkey riders. Zebras that had not been in the initial group, arrived. The chimp riders with crossbows were aiming down.

Without thinking, Ryan ran to the sloth, quickly clawing through the bonds, allowing fossa, a goanna, and a clouded leopard to escape. Partway through untying the leopard, a volley of arrows rained down. One of the missiles hit the leopard. It rolled off with a yowl before limping away with an arrow in its back.

Ryan had to dodge an arrow aimed at his neck. It hit the sloth instead and pinned a fossa to the large mammal. Ryan shielded Melissa under him as he clawed at her ropes. As she came off, they both rolled from the back of the sloth. The thick hide of the giant animal helped to block the arrows. Longer spears were now being hurled into the pit.

Melissa splashed into the wastewater with Ryan, making sure none of the foul water landed in her wounds. She was still in somewhat of a daze. Owls fought the gliding squirrels trying to fly into the pit. An eagle owl grabbed a sable cow, driving her claws into the brown antelope's face.

Ryan walked beside Melissa, shielding her from more arrows. More bolts rained down on them. One would have hit Ryan in the back, but a massive hairy arm blocked the bolt. The sloth bellowed out in pain when the bolt hit her. Ryan dodged a spear thrown down, moving Melissa out of the way with his forepaws. It grazed his coat, drawing blood as the obsidian tipped weapon shot past into the mud below.

'We need to run, Melissa. We need to run *now*!'

He nudged her from behind. She caught herself from falling over and began to run. The dingo sprinted ahead, splashing through the mud, her tail tucked far under her behind.

As they left, the last of the tamaraw ran around under the wounded sloth's arms. The animal yelled, 'I'll fight them off. Get the wounded to safety! Save yourselves!' as the buffalo dragged several wounded creatures with it.

Ryan looked back at the sloth. A zebra had got too close, and it hauled it into the pit. It screamed as the sloth hurled it against the other wall. She slammed it with her clawed limbs with enough force to shatter the zebra's bones. Its guts were still wrapped around the sloths' paws as she brought her fists down.

Another attacker, a beast of unknown species, covered in the pelts of many animals, leapt onto the sloth's back, wielding a pair of

144

obsidian knives. This beast clambered onto the giant mammal's head, driving a knife into each eye. Bellowing in pain, she hooked an ape with both arms, ripping the ape in half as she fell.

The beast moved around, thrusting the knife down her throat, stabbing the bottom of her mouth, and then ripping the knife around. It roared in triumph as the sloth fell.

Tearing away a baby possum still tied onto the sloth's back, he ripped into it, tearing out its guts with his teeth as he ate the squirming animal alive. He embedded his knives in two other wounded animals still tied up – a snake and a fossa. He was laughing maniacally between bites. The nearby Kingdom troops turned away in disgust at the butchery.

Another animal caught behind the sloth was the last dingo, the one with white fur. Several arrows shot it down. It yelped as it fell into the waste.

As Ryan fled, something seemed to be creeping into the back of his mind, a stifling uncomfortable feeling, a voice that was in his head and yet not his own. 'Run little cat, hide if you like, but one day I will come, and the whole world will pay for what they have done. I will enjoy my painful fun with you all. I so look forward to getting to know what hurts you, even from afar.'

He could not pick who spoke those words. Surprisingly, the Kingdom's beasts all turned to look at him as he ran, but he did not turn back.

The survivors continued for kilometres using this system of channels. The other group carved a trail through the crop field and around the rice paddies to the wall. Eventually, they found a hole in the outer wall. The channel underneath it had eroded the soil so that part of the structure had collapsed. Rocks were strewn and tumbled everywhere. This could have happened from a recent flood, or heavy rain. The animals were relieved to see a way out. The crumbled wall showed a meadow outside and possible safety. Across another stretch of open grassland was the forest.

Chapter 17

After the Escape

Upon reaching the edge of the fence, Ryan ran onto the grassland. The river marked a long path inland to the savanna and safety and freedom in the Citadel. Melissa loped up to Ryan. She had recovered from the poison, enough to be able to walk a long way again without tiring. After checking for crocodiles by bashing a large stick held in his jaws on the water, Ryan and Melissa washed the filth off by jumping into a hyacinth filled pond. The dingo padded over to Ryan and, with his permission, began to lick his wounds.

'I'm glad that we're alive. I thought we were going to die back there,' said Melissa. 'We do need to go ahead quickly. We have to go away from here and further into the jungle to reach the savanna. This is a lesson for us. Don't screw with the Kingdom. If you do, they will turn you into a fur rug, or worse as we have already learned.' She spoke as she licked his and her wounds.

Ryan returned the favour by licking the top of her head, with one big slobbery lick while she wagged her tail. Of course, this did not have the same meaning as a kiss but was the way felines and dogs show platonic affection. It was a sign that Ryan really did have a friend that he would be unlikely to meet again in another life, one to savour a moment with. The pair spent time at the edge of the plains.

The sun was beginning to rise over the grasses. Relieved that they were both alive, they began to move.

One of the elephants caught up to the other animals. A chimp climbed from his back into a tree as they entered the jungle. Many of the other creatures followed them to the wilderness beyond. The small herd included tigers, jaguars, chimps, buffalo, and deer. Some veered to the east and the others walked to the south. They were determined to scatter so the Kingdom would not find them again.

The dingo and puma walked into the dawn light at the east end of the bend in the river.

The rest of the group blended back into the jungle. Ryan had not counted how many animals came to their rescue. It was a large group. They separated, heading in different directions but would eventually regroup further in the forest.

'We need to travel some distance into the jungle to avoid any more hunters coming after us,' Melissa said.

Ryan and Melissa continued together through the rainforest. They stuck to the dense sections of jungle, staying on the game trails to avoid the possibility of enemy spies sighting them. Occasionally they peered out to see parts of the river, but they continued with their plan of hanging back to avoid being seen.

An hour or so later, Ryan saw a dam, built of stone; an advanced construction that was best avoided in case it was close to another town.

As they passed, Ryan looked at the dam. An immense stone wall spanned the entire gully. As he suspected, it was next to a town of sorts; not a place they should be near. Smoke rose from chimneys and an odd little tower could be seen above the town. They continued, keeping themselves hidden but glimpsing the dam one last time before it vanished into the black, brown, and dark green of the forest floor and undergrowth.

The late evening wore on. They travelled further along the top of the riverbank. Upstream of the weir created by the animals of the Kingdom, the river had spilled out over its normal bank to fill an entire gully. The bank was a grassy verge on the edge of the dam.

The fugitives had to keep a close look out in case there was a guard manning a post on the other side of the river. There was none, but the splash created by a crocodile-like black caiman on the surface of the water caught their attention. The jungle stretched high above the stream, the tall trees partly obscuring their path. There was little they could see other than the golden reflection of dawn on the water. Insect and bird song created a pleasant background of sound. Swift's captured small insects off the water surface with rapid dives.

The first of the morning's rays glowed orange. Yet amidst this beauty, there were signs of Kingdom's work. A badly worn stream bank was devoid of trees on the other side and that had killed the pond plants over there.

More trees would be gone if it weren't for the fact that Suleiman was careful with his water catchment. None of the waste from the city could be spread up here.

But even here Ryan and Melissa were not truly safe. They both limped along, half-hearted from the previous night, wincing in pain from the numerous injuries they had picked up since their time on the coast. Melissa scanned the forest ahead for anywhere that could make a suitable temporary den.

Partway through the journey, she found a midyim berry patch in the jungle undergrowth. Ryan watched, with a puzzled face as Melissa began to nip off and chew several of the small white berries.

'I thought you were a carnivore?' Ryan said.

'Not entirely. I am omnivorous, though meat still forms most of my diet. If I were to go vegetarian, I would have to compete with every other herbivore, and I would still have nutritional deficiencies. Unfortunately for you, all felines, unlike canines are obligate carnivores. This means that you cannot live off plants at all. You simply would not be able to handle large amounts of plant fibre. Neither can I, for that matter, hence I stick to softer plant matter like fruit.'

Ryan nodded.

Melissa began scanning the forest floor again. 'We'll need somewhere to sleep. How about here?' She gestured to the base of a large kapok tree. Its roots created an immense set of buttresses, dozens of metres from the river.

Ryan nodded and climbed high up the tree to find a suitable place to sleep. The fork at the top of the tree had bromeliads, lichens and other epiphytes that created a soft green bed. It was in an awkward spot between branches, but here he fell asleep for hours, not minding the small animals that nervously made their way around him.

***

That evening Natashia left the group. She didn't really know why but she wanted to live free of the recent series of hassles and chaos. Everything seemed to have escalated so fast. Never had she been in so much danger in such a short time. She hung her head, regretting getting so involved. Nearly getting herself killed had made her aware of the comfortable life she had made for herself. She wondered what happened to those little bush dogs that lived back in the canyon. She had last seen them when they unlocked her gate. Their reappearance when they freed her was a comforting sign.

Their likelihood of survival would have been low. They may not have made it out after that. So many questions have plagued her since being freed and escaping.

Was it ethical to murder for sustenance? Why did she pick an impractical colouration of her fur? Was her hunting for meat justified for survival, or would they all be better off if she rolled over and died? Was it truly worth even coming here to Mars? What plans did she have for the future, what hopes, dreams, or aspirations?

What was important at this moment was finding a new territory and friends or allies. Perhaps these creatures that were leaving for the savanna would be good company. Better, at least than those who tried to hunt her. She realised though that she would do better in the concealing jungle than in the open savanna where there is nowhere to hide. And she was still in no shape to trek to the savanna.

The last several days' injuries had taken their toll on her. The arrow wound still pained horribly. Her head ached from many other injuries. Her limbs felt raw from continual running as adrenaline drained out of her system. Other injuries were slowly chipping away at her strength. Somehow, she had run for many miles. *Better to break up the sprinting with some trotting,* she thought. But now, she needed rest and sleep. She found a hollowed cavity below a partly toppled buttressed jungle tree. She settled into the hollow, sighing in exhaustion and pain, and trying to avoid lying on any of her injuries before drifting off to sleep.

When the tigress woke, she left the area around the top of the dam, beginning in an easterly direction, but where it would lead, she didn't care. She did know she needed to eventually catch something to eat. Most of her earlier hunts had been more luck than good tactics. They had failed due to her lack of camouflage. Her attempts at hunting since escaping had been unsuccessful. The first, a bush turkey, saw her even before she had seen the prey. Many more attempts failed for the same reason. She was too obvious. Her gift of a striking white coat was now acting more as a curse. Even on the dark nights, it still stood out. If this continued, she would starve. Perhaps more easily caught prey could be found to the east of here.

***

The sun had already dipped below the horizon when Ryan awoke. Stretching, he slunk his way down the tree before waking up the sleeping Melissa. The forest floor was already beginning to darken from the lack of light. The dingo hopped out of the buttress roots, shaking sand off her coat. They crept quietly back towards the river. Finding it in the dark posed a problem.

The Mother of The Kingdom River was about fifty metres wide but had a slow current. They proceeded down a slope to glimpse it through the branches. They pushed between the bent stalks of a bamboo clump. Many had been cut for building materials. They walked onto the red sand and padded down to the water. The pair would have to swim across this river without attracting the attention of the crocodiles or caimans or the alligator gar fish. They checked both sides of the river, looking for any boats, before setting out without making a splash, paddling further into the brown stream.

Part way across the river, something popped up through the surface of the water, creating multiple splashes and startling Ryan. A hippopotamus appeared beside them. Melissa became nervous while doggy-paddling, emphasising her frailty with an unsure whine. One of the hippos passed beneath her, giving her another scare.

'What is so wrong with a hippo?' Ryan asked her as they continued to swim.

'If you anger one by accident, they will almost certainly kill you. Just don't upset them, for both our sakes!' As Melissa spoke, she looked around to see more hippos appear out of the water. They turned their heads to watch the swimmers. Ryan and Melissa slowed down to look at the hippos more closely.

'What are you doing so close to my herd?' the bull hippopotamus asked, opening his immense mouth as a warning not to try their luck eating any of his calves.

'We're just crossing the river, trying to escape the creatures of the Kingdom who are chasing us,' said Ryan.

'Alright then. Just don't touch any of my family, or we will rip you in half,' replied the bull.

The pair finally reached the other side of the river and pulled themselves up onto the shore. Ryan checked to see if Melissa was out, then they both shook the water from their pelts.

The sand on this side was just as red as the first side, in which they had left their footprints. They ran up the riverbank, clambering over the slope and into the forest beyond. The puma and dingo continued into the trees, careful to keep a low profile.

Ryan and Melissa walked for two days through more rainforest, keeping track of the river as they went. Meals had consisted of an unfortunate macaque Ryan had caught up in an Australian red cedar canopy. A monitor lizard was the other half of the meal. They made sure their catch was not allied to the insurgency first.

The pair went slowly through the jungle, the trees hiding their position but making navigating more difficult. The terrain remained monotonous rainforest for several kilometres. It was only as they climbed to the top of the highest ridge that they could see what was ahead. Ryan had to scramble up the slippery leaf litter to the summit.

At the top, was the last kapok tree he would see on his journey. It was an immense structure thirty metres high. Ryan scaled it with ease, climbing up to a high branch in under a minute. Gripping at the bark, he stared at the landscape around him.

Ahead, on the other side of the river, thick green rainforest stretched beyond the horizon in an unbroken bumpy green covering. Back the way they had come, it was broken by the clearing of the Kingdom. He could see the dam they had passed days before.

He turned to check the way they were going. Beyond here, the forest changed dramatically. Something was fundamentally different. The durians and other fruiting trees thinned dramatically beyond this point. The next section of forest had massive Indian sacred figs, many kinds of tall hardwoods, eucalyptus, and vine thickets. Palms, acacias, and baobabs also joined the new variety of trees. Beyond the bottom of the hill, the new forest continued to another horizon. The savannah was beyond there in the foothills of a distant but visible conical volcano. The river could be seen taking the low ground through the new forest.

Looking out over the forest, he saw white cockatoos flying above and below the canopy. Turkey vultures circled above, and something far stranger caught his eye. From his position high in the canopy of this tree, Ryan watched the strangest animals he had ever seen float by.

They resembled cuttlefish – if cuttlefish flew like birds. Their mantle-like wings propelled them along. On their backs was a large sac of hydrogen gas that kept them floating. The creatures made a thrumming bellowing noise.

The whitish animals had flushing pink along their backs and black lines along their bodies. The strange flock of about eighteen flew towards him, landing on a nearby fruiting fig.

Lorikeets scattered as the Teuthidoplanes, bizarre alien creatures who were introduced to the planet centuries ago, hung on the trees using their tentacles. Some of their seven tentacles gripped the tree, and the others were delicately picking the fruit and placing it inside their mouths between the front tentacles.

'Are you seeing this, Melissa? What the hell are these things?' Ryan yelled downwards.

Melissa gave a dog like smile and her tail began to wag. 'We earth borne animals are not the only animals here. The terraforms have an entire alien ecosystem elsewhere in the world. The squid things are just one of the many alien species they imported here. A few of those strange critters fly by sometimes.'

'They're non-sapient right, then why don't we hunt them instead?' Ryan yelled back down the tree.

'Because if we did, they would have disappeared already. That's why they're so rare.'

As soon as Melissa said this, a Philippine eagle swooped down from dozens of metres up. The squids turned bright pink in alarm. Their eyes, both on the end of their torso and the tip of their ears, watched the eagle coming.

They all ducked below the tree, dodging, and weaving between the lower branches. The eagle flew up unsatisfied.

'There are many others. We may see some in our trek, though they are far more common on the west coast of the Thrassian uplands, along with the other alien critters. If you think they're amazing, wait until you see the other creatures running about,' Melissa said as Ryan slid down the tree.

Landing with a slight thud on the ground, Ryan looked at Melissa, eyes wide in shock. She nodded, and they proceeded into this strange new forest.

He noticed that this was a much dryer forest than the one he had been in before. Less flora meant it was harder to blend into the brown leafy undergrowth. However, his brown pelt made camouflage possible. They proceeded down the leafy path cleared out between the trees, listening to the strange birdcalls in this part of the forest.

This new forest seemed to blend gradually out to a brown understory. Large tree branches covered the sky. The trees still had green leaves while the wet season lasted. Many new animals lived in the forest – strange creatures that Ryan had not seen before. In the distance between the trees, he could make out a giraffe moving through the forest.

Melissa continued down a narrow track that was hard to follow. Ryan was close behind. They followed the path as it snaked through the trees and over the crunchy leaf litter, keeping their ears peeled. Melissa paused part way through to look up at the sky. Through the gaps of the leaves, they could see the outline of a parrot flying overhead. It was looking down at them.

'We're being watched,' Melissa said, with her head towards the sky. Sure enough, the parrot landed a short distance away, and kept watching them. Its presence seemed suspicious, as it stayed close and continually watched.

They walked for several more hours, until the thick rainforest trees began to thin out. The canopy was opening slightly. There were still many trees; however, their species composition was one that would tolerate more seasonal rainfall.

The time taken walking through the dry forest was difficult to guess. Grey clouds hung overhead. Sadly, they did not bring any rain. The heat continued to scorch the forest floor turning the track to dust. The trail began to lead downhill. Through the canopy, they could see the river snaking through the gap between two ridges. At the bend in the stream was a bare rocky patch of shore. The pair decided to turn towards it by following the trail down.

The forest ended at the start of the basalt rocks that the erosion of the river had exposed. The water was a turbid greenish-brown flow that trickled near the bottom of the rocky headland.

Ryan padded to the edge to get a drink. He leaned his head over the flow, lapping the water as it passed his mouth. After finishing, he backed away, only to jump back in surprise. Directly next to him was a black caiman lying on the rocks. The brown-headed crocodilian had been watching them. Ryan turned towards the caiman to address him.

'We are lost. Do you know if the savanna around here is a good habitat for us? Have you seen any large groups of animals with many carnivores, moving through here recently?' he asked.

'I've heard that there is a mass emigration towards the savanna. Some guys from the insurgency or something. Bad idea for all of them, and you too. Dumb plan really. You should be going to the mountain. It has lush cloud forests with plenty of prey. The plains are dry, open, and full of predators, I've heard. Not to mention that the Citadel tramps over everything east of the boulder field. Your choice. But to get to the mountains, you have to get through the marshes. The river is still very low around here, but the mud retains much water below the surface. Walking through it will be a literal slog.'

'Okay, you seem to know a lot. Thank you for your advice. So, you are saying we should head to the mountain summit to find safety, right?' Ryan said nervously. He turned to Melissa. She nodded. When he turned back, the crocodilian had disappeared back into the green water.

The pair turned away from the rock to continue following the bank inland in the direction of the swamp. 'The swamp way it is then; I guess?' Ryan said as he followed Melissa away from the bank.

A flock of strange birds were circling in the distance in the direction they were headed. Ryan watched them with interest. The orange flickering coming from them made him suspicious of their presence. They turned to follow the flock into the forest. As they continued, the trees seemed to gradually change again. Some fresh sap-leaking stumps were present, and several were bruised heavily or had limbs sawn off.

The cat was peering ahead when he spied something. 'Get down,' Ryan said quietly.

They crouched in the leaf litter and underbrush. He had heard a group of animals in a clearing up ahead. They snuck forward to investigate.

The trees thinned. In the clearing, dozens of animals moved around in confusion. Ryan realised that the insurgency was setting up camp here. The group had erected tents and were building lean-to structures. Entire trees had been felled to clear the space. The branches provided fodder for numerous herbivores, including a pair of giraffes. Temporary dens were set up for others – some were dug, and some were hastily made lean-to shelters. Armed herbivores were on patrol, with a few diurnal animals manning their weaponised saddles.

Ryan looked around the group. Most were carnivores. Dingoes, big cats, and a bear were among them. The bush dogs were in one area and a pair of giraffes supervised other animals while chewing their food.

Some of the animals had killed and skinned a chital deer. They were in the process of devouring it. Several dingoes and a striped canine-like animal that Ryan didn't recognise tore at it.

'I think we have found the rest of the insurgency,' Ryan commented as he rose off his haunches to walk into the camp. The dog-like animal turned to look at him. The other creatures paid little attention to them at first.

Melissa turned to see an injured animal being treated in an infirmary tent. Someone was sterilizing an infected arrow wound. Improvised tents had been built to tend to the wounded. Others had been taken inside for treatment. Some cubs of varying species were playing in one corner.

Several animals look strangely at them as they approached the centre of the group. Then a familiar face appeared between two sable antelope bodyguards. Ryan immediately recognised the sloth bear.

'Great to see you again, Bernard!' Ryan said, his relief at seeing the bear alive and well was obvious by his relaxed expression, his head held high, and ears pointed forwards.

'Glad to see you too have made it. I had faith in you two – the odd duo,' Bernard replied with an air of warmth and friendliness. They had, for now, found a place of comparative safety to rest from their long journey for a couple of days.

155

The camp was well organised. Animals were milling about busily, and herbivores were systematically stripping each tree for food. Their medics used the few Citadel-supplied medicines they had to treat the many wounded animals that were still unwell. A few temporary shelters, a latrine outside the camp, and another spot where different animals slept together under the shade of the trees, made up the rest of the camp. A larger tent had been erected at one end: Bernard's tent, evidently.

Melissa turned to Ryan. 'We have walked far, but we may need to help out. We should get some sleep tonight and help with the hunt tomorrow.'

'Hunt? Well, I will, at least,' Ryan said.

A monkey scribbled with a goose feathered quill onto a clipboard to allow them access. If Bernard had not vouched for them, they would have been suspected as possible spies.

'I say we should have a chat with the other animals, then go to sleep,' Melissa said as the afternoon heat increased.

Ryan helped with the construction of shelters. His strength and dexterous paws made moving narrow, strong logs into place easier – even though, at one time, he hit the wrong part of a shelter causing it to fall. Other animals like lemurs and fossa, normally natural enemies, were working together tying the shelters together.

Melissa, meanwhile, helped round up stragglers from the forest. She joined the tracking team that was also acting as scouts to look out for the Kingdom's presence in these woods.

Before long, it was nearing sunset. It was time to settle down and rest. Melissa snuggled up to Ryan, finding his pelt more comfortable than the bare ground. Before going to sleep, she turned her head to look up at the countless stars. A brilliant silver belt stretched across the sky. The clouds of the previous day had receded. The faint reflection from one of the off-planet space stations could be seen in the vast open space, separate from the other lit up parts of the night sky.

Chapter 18

A Fiery Escape

The next morning the sun was rising when Ryan began to stir. The dawn chorus echoed through the trees. The heat soon began extracting moisture out of the ground again. The dry season was still slogging on.

The vultures, led by their king, circled over the forest, taking advantage of the early morning thermals. The hammering and sawing noises of boats being built near the river echoed inland. They would assist in the crossing.

Stragglers were still drifting into the camp. The puma decided to make himself useful today by accompanying several carnivores out on a hunt. They wanted to catch some more deer to feed the increasing number of refugees.

Ryan slinked through the tall grass with his nose focused on finding the scent of a deer. A group of tawny frogmouths decided to help scout around. He saw one in a nearby tree, though this was an odd time for it to be awake. Ryan could still barely see anything beyond the tall grass and dry bushes. Then the scent of his prey wafted his way. Peering over a conkerberry patch he spotted the deer. The herd was large, possibly up to one hundred strong. Extra care had to be taken to avoid the grey langur monkeys that were perched in the trees in the middle of the group. They could alert the herd and ruin the element of surprise.

Ryan was slinking towards the trees when he came close to one of the deer. He could see the spotted pelt of the chital deer. He hadn't encountered this species many times yet; though it looked like the visayan deer he had seen earlier. He froze to avoid detection. An odd bleat-like clicking sound came from deeper within the herd. Concerned voices came from further in.

At that moment, a cockatoo flew overhead with a torch held in its claws. It brushed passed a dry branch of eucalyptus leaves directly above the herd, setting it immediately alight.

A blazing branch fell off the tree into the middle of the herd, causing the entire deer herd to panic. They stampeded in Ryan's direction.

The first doe saw him and ran sideways to avoid him. As the rest of the herd approached, Ryan ran to a nearby eucalypt tree to climb. The tree would ensure a better vantage point for the scene and a way to pounce on a suitable prey animal. Only a metre up, he could see the entire herd stampeding past the base of the tree. He launched himself, claws extended, limbs out, and teeth bared. He landed on the shoulders of one of the does, forcing her to stumble.

'Please, no… you bastard. I don't want to die!' The doe begged. He dug his claws into her shoulder, trying not to listen and wrestled her to the ground.

Then, to his surprise, a massive animal head-butted him off the deer. Twisting into the dirt, he caught a glimpse of the large beast running off. It was an antelope. More of the big animals came around the deer. They were giant eland, majestic beasts with long twisting horns and an immense flap of skin on their necks.

He looked up to see that the canopy had started to burn. There was no way to stop the fire and there was still a hunt to complete. Nearby, the strange striped canine had caught another deer by gripping onto its leg. Ryan raced over to help him put the struggling animal down. Then he turned and saw the deer herd was funnelled into a forest of octopus cacti that formed an impenetrable wall. The front of the deer herd hit the cacti, which impaled their hides. They pulled away with numerous cactus spike wounds. This clump of cacti was burning. A group of deer continued to weave their way further into the forest of thorns. Others had seen the flames and turned back.

From the trees above, he could hear the sounds of angry birds whirling back and forwards.

The puma helped finish off the wounded deer, gripping its neck and delivering the killer bite. He looked around in horror. Hot ashes drifted through the air carried by scorching winds. The undergrowth glowed shades of reds, oranges, and yellows. The red fire beast encircled its hungry arms around the clearing. The wildfire was spreading and searching for fuel.

Ryan looked above the clearing into the sky. Birds were fighting. Vultures, eagles, hawks, peregrine falcons, barn and eagle owls were trying to defend the camp.

Parrots, crows, and hornbills were already among them, twirling and circling in a carnival of death. They were tearing and ripping at each other. Birds fell from the sky, some without their wings. Other birds carried burning branches. They dropped them into the forest in a deliberate attempt to ignite the tinderbox.

The situation had become dangerous for those on the ground. The forest was already alight, and the encampment was a raging inferno. The smaller birds of prey were decisively losing, having their wings snapped off from their bodies and sent tumbling.

The cat's first thoughts were, *I need to climb one of the trees that is not burning.*

Seeing the flames spreading around on the ground, the hyena darted out the last available escape route. Ryan looked around in panic, he knew he would have to go above ground to escape. He darted up a eucalyptus tree that was not burning. The top of the massive boxwood was high above the flames. His plan of escaping the fire was to leap from tree to tree, providing the fire did not reach the crowns.

His claws had trouble gripping to the smooth white timber that was devoid of bark except at the base. He moved quickly to give himself enough momentum to make the leap to the next branch. He continued down that limb of the tree, searching for the next possible escape. Looking ahead, he saw that the next tree was a foxtail palm tree. The puma knew that would be much harder to land on. The base was aflame and already starting to give way. With nowhere else to go, he flung himself at the palm, cracking its trunk. Gripping tightly, the cat rode the burning tree down before leaping off to the next tree. By this stage much of the forest floor was ablaze, anyone down there now had no chance to survive.

A yellow-bellied glider, a nocturnal gliding possum, flew past him to another tree, continuing its escape flight. Ryan continued outwards, crossing a leopard tree next, as flames crept up its trunk. However, the next tree was a mesquite; a tangle of branches and thorns that could easily injure him. The puma turned and leapt onto a wattle, landing on one side, and breaking the branches. This tree was too weak to hold his weight, and the golden pollen from its flowers brushed his coat as he passed through. He didn't know if he was heading in the right direction. He needed a better vantage point.

An immense Madagascan baobab seemed ideal. With all his strength, he flung himself onto the smooth bark of the tree, digging his claws in deep to give him enough grip. Heaving and panting as he raced up the immense tree's trunk, he used his upwards momentum to keep going until he reached the top.

***

The camp was turning into a barbeque. The attacking birds had come as a complete surprise, flying under the canopy of the trees to avoid detection by the vultures. Now the vultures were eagerly tearing them apart, lost in a blood lust.

Melissa stood in the centre of the burning clearing whimpering, her ears pulled back, hyperventilating, with her tail tucked far between her legs. Trees were beginning to fall.

Branches came crashing down into the flames. The parrots flew off. A disastrous inferno encircled the camp. The medical tent was set aflame, and the lean-tos were now campfires. Other animals were dragging out those unable to escape. One coati was screaming in agony as other animals extinguished the flames on his fur.

The tigress, Anthia, was dragging an injured tamaraw out of the tent and helping her to her feet. The buffalo was limping as he tried to follow Bernard who barrelled out of the camp, roaring defiantly at the flames. Many animals following him, including a pair of giraffes were harried by the birds flying overhead. Other smaller animals followed in panic.

Melissa was panting in the heat, still wide-eyed. Fighting down the impending panic attack, she fought to calm her mind and find a way to escape the flames. Smoke was starting to obscure the campsite and the way out.

The flames spread rapidly through the camp. Animals tried to climb up trees, only to fall back down alight with flame. Others more successfully scampered from branch to branch.

The birds that hadn't joined in the fight, had all left.

As she turned to leave, Melissa saw a kitten, sitting on a log by itself, mewling loudly for his mother. Motherly instincts stirred in her mind. She had to save it. She ran over and grabbed the small feline in her mouth, trying not to break the skin. She sprinted to find a way out.

Animals ran back and forth, some on fire, others in a general state of panic.

The two giraffes barged their way through the undergrowth, forming a temporary way out, which several of the animals gladly followed. The dingo whined desperately when surrounded by the intense orange flames. She sprang to take advantage of the temporary exit. She had flames on both sides, but she focused on running towards the river. Behind her, a burning branch fell, spelling the doom of those close behind.

***

From the top of the baobab tree, Ryan turned back to see the inferno. His lack of ability to see red and green meant that the red of the fire became a golden shimmering glow, and the greens of the dense forest were muted to browns, yellows, and blues. The fire now reached the base of the baobab. The pyromaniac parrots had disappeared. He watched as birds of prey caught small animals that were outrunning the flames. The massive Philippine eagle landed with a different yellow-bellied glider to the one he had seen earlier. This one had a more orange belly. The eagle viciously tugged the adorable small mammal apart with great enthusiasm.

Ryan looked for a way out of the tree. He noted an immense eucalyptus with acacias near the base in front of him. He leapt off the massive baobab falling and slipping on the smooth trunk of the eucalyptus tree. He crashed into the thick twiggy branches of the acacia. The impact knocked the wind out of him, and the branches scratched his pelt. He snarled in regret. Leaning over the branch, he found he was at the edge of the burning forest. He left the trees and looked around for other survivors. Dozens of animals, including many carnivores, didn't make it out of the flames. Others who had done nothing to wrong the Kingdom were still caught up in the crossfire.

He loped back to the edge of the forest, calling out Melissa's name. He paced back and forwards along the fire front. The flames were creeping towards the grass. Lower down the hill he could see the beginning of a swamp, with thick green reeds, rushes, and bulrushes. That would be safe from the fire. He hoped that Melissa had made it out.

The grassy verge was now catching fire. Giraffes ran along the edge of the forest looking for more animals leaving the woods. Everyone who had escaped the flames fled into the water. One last unhurt figure came running out of the woods as another flaming eucalypt log tumbled down, spraying hot cinders. Injured animals continued to tumble out of the woods, shrieking and moaning in agony as they flailed at flames on their bodies.

Ryan jumped back as deer fell burning to the ground. He turned to the river to see the crowd of animals standing in the shallow edges and swamps. They all watched in horror as the flames feasted upon the forest they had left.

Ryan sighed with relief when he saw Melissa bolting down the hill towards the swamp with a small animal in her mouth. Her terror was evident. Her tail was tucked in behind her and her ears flattened against her skull. She barrelled down the hill in seconds, eventually launching herself into the cold water. She tried to make sure the kitten didn't go under, though he was dunked anyway. She briefly submerged her head before lifting it above the water in triumph and paddling upstream towards the shore.

The dingo pulled herself out of the river, with the kitten still in her mouth, carefully shaking her coat. She put the kitten down for a second and looked back. She scanned the water for a feline shape and lowered her posture in relief when she saw Ryan pacing near the fire front.

In the nearby grass was a worried adult Pantanal cat. Putting one and one together, Melissa silently went back up and gave the kitten gently to her. The mother mewled to her kitten as she groomed her.

'Thank you so much for saving my precious little girl,' she said with a relieved smile on her face.

Melissa weaved her way between other relieved animals. She focussed now on getting to Ryan. He was further west than the other animals, so she had to leave the crowd of survivors. She walked towards Ryan who was staring back in disbelief at the hillside behind him. The flames had turned it from a heavy forest into an immense inferno that had devoured so many creatures.

Melissa looked at the sky to see desperate flocks of birds flying away. No more animals came from the forest. The survivors were calming down as the cool waters of the river and swamp caressed them. Small grass fires continued to burn. The whole riverside was on fire or had been burned out. *This massive destruction*, she thought, *was the work of the Kingdom. How could these people be so cruel?*

She made her way to Ryan, who was licking a scalded paw. He turned his head. When he saw who it was, he let out a playful chirp. The two ran up to each other to snuggle. They rubbed against each other in total relief, overjoyed they had both survived.

'You're alive!' Ryan finally said, mewling as he hugged his great big paws over Melissa. He stayed there for a time, wrapping his huge limbs around the dingo, who gave him affectionate licks to the face. He loosened his grip and turned back to the flames. The pair watched the woodland disappear as the last sticks fell in flames.

Chapter 19

Can't Hide; Can't Hunt

Natashia arrived at the edge of the swamp valley. After several days of wandering, hunger was gnawing at her stomach. Half a catfish was her last decent meal. *Why does everything have to be so hard?* she wondered regretfully. The apex predator had expected a far easier life here, more kindness, less violence and far less moral unease. Had she been more naïve, her hopes and dreams would have shattered in this new world. Luckily, she had found the resilience to pull herself back together and push on.

The valley was a huge stretch of land with a cliff along one side and a smoother slope on the other. Kingdom's troops didn't patrol this area, so it had become a haven for misfits and throw outs from civilisation. On the far sides of the valley, the jungle gave way to a large mangrove swamp that stretched almost a kilometre.

Natashia could see a taller grove of trees further away. She decided that this was worth a visit, so she detoured from her original plan to go straight to the savanna. Instead, she headed through the jungle in an easterly direction.

The mangrove forest had not been there long. It appeared after mass seed releases, sent from the open oceans by the terraforming machines. A recent phenomenon of tidal change created the forest. She asked a small dove about why tides existed in a planet with no moon. According to the emerald dove, the tides had not flowed for long and only appeared recently, much to everyone's surprise. The dove told her this information came from a red-tailed tropic bird that claimed to have witnessed the phenomenon years ago. At least two other animals passed the information on before the dove heard it.

When asked, the Terraformers had refused to comment, but many suspected that it might have been a symptom of a far bigger problem with the planet. Never-the-less, the daily ebb and flow of the oceans over the last few decades made the formation of proper mangroves possible. They grew on the coast and out to sea for at least ten metres, sometimes further in places. A large number of creatures had moved into the mangrove swamp. Some came from the surrounding jungle and ocean, and Terraformers put others there.

Further around, she saw something strangely familiar. It was the Terraformers' drop off point. The white building, a few kilometres from her current position, was the point where she had been released.

The clearing between the trees was visible. In the distance beyond the shore, strange flying shapes followed what looked like an irregular shaped cloud. One moved its limbs through the air and floated along, slowly sinking towards the ocean. Natashia could see a patch of trees below it as it descended. Other boat-like machines swam far beyond the shore, leaving a trail of plankton and nutrients. The tigress slowly scratched her way down the eight-metre-tall tree on the hilltop and walked between the banyan's massive roots on her way to the mangrove forest.

Chapter 20

The Boulder fields

Ryan, Melissa and Natashia

The sun set over the blackened forest. The ashes blanketed the surrounding area in black and white. Logs still glowed a brilliant orange as they continued to burn, smoke and sizzle. The field beyond was empty of fleeing animals. They had spread in different directions, but many continued inland towards the Citadel.

Others decided they should go back to the jungle, so they headed for the tropical dry forest that the fire had not reached. Another group decided to set out west and east to other parts of the coastal rainforest stretch. These animals were rainforest animals who could not survive in the open savannas beyond. They needed the safety and food from the trees to provide a home and habitat. These herbivores also knew about the various predators that roamed the open plains.

Other creatures decided this was exactly where they needed to be. They crossed the massive river to avoid the inevitable pursuit.

Whichever way they were going, they all knew that they were likely to be hunted down, killed, or recaptured.

Suleiman would not rest while they evaded him. If they stuck together, they made an easy target. Ryan and Melissa decided it would be safer to leave the insurgency fighters who were heading towards the Citadel. The burnt forest gave way to open grassland. Now from horizon to horizon the mountain range that they were heading for was visible.

Between them and their destination, the marshland barred their passage. Flooded marsh covered two thirds of the distance. The rest was overland walking, and a fifty-metre stretch of open water.

The remaining survivors of the fire were terrified of the parrots' potential to begin another fire, so they headed across or along the river in a large crowd.

They came barging through the reeds and churning up the mud. Eland and buffalo headed the group. Smaller animals rode on the backs of the larger ones. The birds travelled on the giraffes.

Crossing the swamp ahead was a formidable task. Those that swam across the channel risked crocodile attack. Most of the swamp was very muddy, and deep enough to require them to swim across the open water.

Melissa and Ryan walked down the burnt grassy slope towards the swamp. A slight difference in the types of grass they passed through showed. It changed from thinner blade grass on the slopes to the thick papyrus and bulrushes nearer to the water. The real challenge now would be crossing the murky river. The mud devoured their paws as they slogged through the maze of outer reeds on the bank.

Animals like the lechwe antelope that lived most of their time here, were not so badly affected by the mud. These swamp dwelling antelopes did not sink so deeply as the heavier antelopes. At least one wallaby got stuck in the mud and had to be rescued. The agile wallaby now hung onto the neck and horns of a Nile lechwe that had now reached the start of the water. Flushed out of their homes by the fire, the wildlife from the forest joined in the river crossing. Upstream, the remaining chital deer came across as a tightly packed herd. An American crocodile splashed violently as it attempted to drag one of them down into the water.

Three nearby sambar deer from the forest came near Ryan and Melissa, staring at the predators as they passed. The puma could see they were dismissing Ryan's capacity for danger as he passed them in the reeds.

This mud was going to be particularly hard to wash out of their fur, as it stuck to the predators' pelts and seeped through to the skin. Birds, including various species of ducks, rails, a jacana, and other water birds, flew through the reeds. So much prey was out of reach and Ryan snarled in annoyance.

The sun belted down on them, making their journey less comfortable. The two slogged through the mud to a large patch of papyrus that was so tall the top shoots created a shady spot. They rested their undersides on the mud in the shade. Ryan tried to pull himself up onto shallower mud but fell asleep from exhaustion.

Traversing the swamp that night was easier with less heat from the sun. The sounds of frogs and insects filled the air. Ducks left tracks on the undisturbed mud. The swarm of mosquitoes over his head was annoying enough to prompt Ryan to retreat further into the marsh.

By now the rest of the animals had left them behind, many heading towards the Citadel.

Ryan and Melissa came to the edge of the extremely swampy ground. Here the water covered the mud deeply enough for them to move faster. They pushed themselves into a kind of swim to cross the remaining portion of the marsh. They crawled past Macquarie turtles that swam out of their way. Melissa was now watching for any crocodilians, though they were probably underneath the water, out of view. Other creatures inhabited this part of the marsh. A water mongoose swam in front of them across the water, pulling itself into a matted mass of bulrushes on the other side.

The river surprised them by suddenly opening at the edge of the bulrushes. They could now see further downstream to where other animals were crossing. They were slower and had become separated from the main group. The colder water was fresher than in the marsh. Looking back, Ryan could see the burnt black hills they had come from.

The slog through the marsh on the other side was less challenging. The muddy part was nowhere near as wide, allowing the pair to pull themselves onto dry land much faster, avoiding exhausting themselves again.

They pushed the tangle of reeds out of the way and saw a small copse of galley forest they had yet to traverse. The dry forest trees were sucking the marsh water through their roots. The dingo had more difficulty pushing through these trees than the cat did. Elsewhere, the migrating herds ahead of them had knocked down or bent the trees out of the way.

After leaving the galley forest, they came to dry savanna grasses. Melissa checked the grass at her feet before looking up at the broad sweeping plain.

She stopped and shook herself dry, sending muddy water into Ryan's flinching face.

'What was that for?' he asked with amusement.

Pleased to be able to move freely again, Melissa dropped onto her elbows into a playful pose, wagging her tail. 'What are you waiting for?' she said, daring him to chase, before running off. Ryan took off after her. They played chase for some time. This tested Ryan's ground pursuit and agility. They dodged, weaved, and raced through the grass in play. Tension and stress evaporated as their bodies relaxed into the joy of running freely.

The plain was vast, with scattered trees and numerous small hills and gullies creating a slight difference in elevation and structure.

The dry, long grasses coloured the land orange and yellow. Those grasses swayed gently in the breeze, like a furry pelt. In the distance, they could see herds of antelope, including sable, lechwe and gazelles moving and grazing, frolicking in the open spaces.

Between them and the mountains, frequent gullies carved a series of channels into the surrounding earth. Further away, strange beasts, larger than any birds, flew above the landscape. What appeared to be strange machines wandered across the distant savanna. In the middle of this tangled landscape was a rocky outcrop, with trees at its top.

Melissa and Ryan crossed a creek linked to the river that they had crossed earlier. Pulling themselves out of the mud and muck of the creek bed, Melissa rubbed her fur into the dry grasses. Ryan copied, rubbing his legs and paws to get rid of the mud. Other animals came out of the water about a hundred and fifty metres further downstream. Once clean, the pair set off into the hot grasslands beyond.

The hot Martian sun hung high in the sky, beating down on the pair as they weaved and brushed through metre tall grasses. They were out of sight of other animals in this long grass. There would be no prey stalking by them. They couldn't even see their quarry. Overhead the welcome shadow of a vulture followed them.

The grass had been well used. Cane rats, porcupines, foxes, and other creatures had left crisscross tracks. Bird song carried over the grassland and swifts circled in the skies. Further along, the grasses grew higher and higher. The pair was well-hidden.

Out on the plains, in a gully near a mesquite tree, lay a ruined cart. Its front right wheel had fallen off the broken axle. To Melissa and Ryan, the wagon looked more like a modified stagecoach than a simple cart. They circled the wagon checking out the scene.

The cart was about five metres long and two metres wide. 'The two buffalos who would have been pulling it have obviously been killed by something huge,' Melissa said.

They examined the massive three-toed footprints that surrounded the wagon. Smaller canine-like paw prints littered the mud.

Scattered remains of the smaller occupants from the wagon; monkeys, cuscuses, unidentified birds, and a giant forest hog littered the ground. All that was left of one of the buffalo was a severed horn.

Ryan glanced around nervously, his ears flattened, while Melissa cautiously went over to sniff the wagon's contents.

'What killed these creatures? I mean the smaller footprints could be dingos... but those massive three-toed tracks...' Ryan asked anxiously while he gazed at the scene of devastation, placing his paw on the sun-bleached giant forest hog skull.

'The kingdom has done well to eliminate the larger predators within their territory. Out here, bears and tigers are still technically mesopredators, on a high level in the food web, but not on top. There are far worse things out there than lions, bears and tigers. Like dinosaurs. This was probably one of them. Maybe a tyrannosaur from the prints.'

Ryan continued to look around, noticing more sun-bleached bones, and other parts strewn around the area. It was then he found paw prints of the canine-like feet both above and under the massive three toed footprints.

Melissa pried open the side of the carriage to see if there was anything inside. The interior of the cart contained smashed pottery and glassware, ruined linen, and to her surprise, a startled pack of coyotes. A mother coyote stood snarling over her pups, her hackles raised, tail tucked beneath her. The pups were cowering beneath their growling, terrified mother. Melissa assured her that they were in no danger, and she relaxed a little but still stood protectively over her pups.

The dingo also noted that a box that had contained a black silk shipment had been smashed and the contents removed and stolen, along with weapons from an open weapons' crate.

Pulling out of the wagon Melissa called out to Ryan, who was still prowling the perimeter, 'The inside has been ransacked, evidently the victim of a robbery of some kind. From the tracks here, this had happened sometime before this mud dried out. A family of coyotes is living in there. I assured the mother that we were no threat.' As she spoke, Ryan kicked up the dried cracked pieces of mud. 'Hungry as I am, I'm not eating the coyotes in there. It's a little close to cannibalism for my tastes. Time to get moving,' Melissa said turning away.

Ryan stood looking at the paw prints. 'I noticed something interesting, however, those paw prints look familiar. I wonder who looted the cart after the initial attack?'

'That I do not know. There is nothing else of interest for us here.' Melissa noted the sigil on the side as she walked away from the cart.

They continued to move until Ryan noticed a strange scent on the breeze. The vaguely familiar scent was coming through the grass ahead. He pushed his way through the one and half metre-high grass and then froze in his tracks. He met the eyes of an unmistakeable black and white large Grevey's zebra mare. Just behind her, a foal was curled up in the grass.

'Apologies. I mean no harm. I should be going,' Ryan said meekly. He quickly turned to move away with great speed.

Before he had finished apologising, both zebras rose to their feet. The mother swung her head down towards him. As the puma turned, she grabbed his tail in her teeth, not hard enough to break bones but enough to hold him. She dragged him back, reared, lifted the feline, and with a head shake, flung Ryan into the air. He landed chest first with a thud, jumped up and turned to strike back at the zebra. But when he flew back at where she had been, they had both gone. They were tearing across the savannah, away from something else. A familiar roar echoed through the air.

'Lions!' Melissa yelped as she turned her head and reared up in a twirl to see better, briefly lifting above the grass. She could see the lone outline of the male lion charging towards her through the tall grass.

Spinning around, Ryan saw more lions charging over the small hill. Their approach sent the zebras into a panic, neighing noisily as they turned and leapt into a gallop.

The zebra attack had Ryan on edge. He turned and ran in the same direction as the zebras. Melissa tore after him, quickly sprinting through the grass. An incorrect turn caused her to run in amongst a fleeing herd of zebras. The giant striped equines, easily one and a half metres tall, kept pace either side of her, moving at great speed. Melissa had to dodge and leap to avoid the hooves of the zebras around her. Then, as a horrifying scream filled the air, the equines dug their hooves into the ground, screeching to a halt, flattening grass in the process, and kicking up dust.

One zebra crashed into Melissa, sending her rolling forwards under the legs of the zebra in front of her. She then fell a short distance, hitting and slipping on the smooth basalt boulders before coming to rest in a grass tussock. She looked up after raising herself off the ground to find that the zebras had run into a field of boulders with deep leg-snapping gaps. One of the equines jumped and landed on the rocks, gruesomely snapping his leg. The bone was sticking out of the mangled limb. Screaming, he tried to drag himself up with his one good front leg.

A lion flew off the rock's edge, landing hard on her paws before slowing down to confront the zebra that was screaming. More lions came around the zebra herd. Two more lionesses leapt down from the rocks. One ignored Melissa, sinking her claws into the neck of the struggling equine. Finally, the male, a young one with a bright red mane, parted the remaining zebras to get his share. He leapt onto the rocks. On closer inspection, it was clear that the birds of prey overhead had acted as scouts.

Langur monkeys came out of the rocks, having hidden there waiting for something like this. Their small cart was parked on the far side of the boulder field.

Soon the lions were hauling the dead zebra between the rocks. It became apparent that a few antelope and a buffalo were with this hunting group as well, as they were milling around the edge of the boulder field. The hunters had killed two other zebras, but the rest of the herd had broken free.

Ryan walked to the edge to see what was happening. He looked over the rocks; a tangle of boulders leading back to another tributary of the river. Caves, hollows, and a creek that ran through crevices and cracks appeared before him. Between the boulders, patches of scraggly grass bushes and trees grew from the areas with limited soil. Melissa saw Ryan on the rocks. Behind him, immense billowing storm clouds filled the sky. Suddenly, an eight-foot-tall bird lunged for him.

Melissa couldn't speak. She could only let out a crude bark, giving away her position by warning Ryan. The terror bird swung its beak at him, gripping his shoulder skin and throwing the terrified cat into the air.

Ryan tumbled into the grass again as Melissa clambered up the boulder to try and distract his attacker.

The lions, hesitant to let their kill go, roared defiantly at the bird.

The terror bird ran after the cat. But he never made it. An immense black creature barrelled out of the tall grass, leapt over Ryan, and swung his horns aggressively at the bird. The terror bird shrieked and turned. She had just invoked the wrath of an African buffalo bull – a species infamous for hot-bloodedness and vengeance.

'These were with our allies, the insurgency, remember, idiot!' the buffalo bellowed. The terror bird backed off.

'Why did you do that?' an astonished Ryan asked the buffalo as he watched the bird run off into the grass.

The buffalo replied, 'You are not the targeted prey. I recognise you as one of the group that was saved by the insurgency and people of the Citadel. If you explain where you are from, they may accept you. If you want to go there, the Citadels are over the boulders and river in that direction,' he said pointing, 'Apologies about that. We are one of the hunting parties going out to catch meat for the others.'

Ryan and Melissa listened but had other ideas about where they should go. Melissa eventually scrambled out of the pit as the Langur monkeys loaded the dead zebras into the cart. An annoyed and wounded Ryan said, 'I don't want to get thrown around like a rag doll again.'

***

173

Natashia was growing hungry. Days had passed since a kill. The foes slain during the flight from the Kingdom did not consist of a proper meal, as there was not time to eat them. She had to keep moving to save herself. She did not have much more success with her hunting in the woods, since she had decided not to follow the group. In the wild, she knew tigers like her would often go for days without a good-sized meal, but even by tiger standards, she was struggling.

All the prey was simply scattering too fast. The cassowaries, the deer, and the monkeys, all ran back for the safety of the trees or undergrowth when she came near. She had attempted to chase the prey. She was fast and strong enough, but not fit enough to keep up a long pursuit. If this continued, it would cause her severe problems. Now though it was not so bad. In the last month or so, she had lost several kilograms simply from not finding enough food. This day her luck changed in an unexpected direction.

Ahead of her at the foot of a hillside, was a village. It had fortifications built around it. The fort set into the mountain protected the small village below.

Past the mountain, closer to the river, another town was visible. The mangrove swamps were close to the nearby village. Around the foot of the mountains were trails of open paths leading back to the Kingdom, further west. Whilst still technically part of the Kingdom, this was a different province. The inhabitants preferred to keep the sanctuary away from the prying eyes of outsiders.

The river here was a catchment area separated from the main watercourse. Boats came in and out through the channel that connected to the ocean and went further inland. She had observed all of this from the low branches of a giant fig that was overlying a cliff edge. This tree's roots clung to a tall precipice of basalt overlooking this valley. Vines, crow's nest ferns, elkhorn ferns, and mosses covered the black and green cliffs below. The richly vegetated rock face disappeared into thick jungle below. Orchids occasionally broke the dark green with their coloured blossoms.

After clambering down, she continued along one of the trails that led down the cliff edge and headed close to the outskirts of one of the towns. A good two hundred metres still separated her from the civilisation, which she could see beyond a fallow field beginning to be colonised by weeds. There were plenty of places to hide. A group of animals stood, not particularly worried about anything, least of all her – the enormous white shape moving between the trees.

This tiny group could be a much-needed meal or perhaps a much-needed group of friends. She was getting lonely and would love to join other animals for dinner – eating alongside them, rather than eating them. That may not have been such a well-thought-out idea considering the proximity.

Something, however, seemed unusual about them. They should not be on the open ground. The animals were all young, except for one sub-adult, pig-like mammal, the peccary. They included young bush turkeys, three baby coati raccoons, a flying squirrel, a pademelon, and a baby tegu lizard, only one hundred and fifty centimetres long.

The tigress watched the group with increased interest. The baby animals were playing, racing around, and shoving each other up and down.

They reminded Natashia of when she used to play with other young, a long time ago. It appeared as if the peccary was on babysitting duty for the other little young animals. The younger creatures were occasionally running off into the undergrowth and back out again.

'So cute, so innocent,' she muttered under her breath.

She would look like a monster doing this, but she was starving and needed food. Creeping closer, she tried to keep to the undergrowth, hiding behind the taro plants to keep out of sight. The near base of another tree provided more cover. The animals were too busy playing to notice her approach. The peccary was looking the other way at the juvenile animals playing and frolicking in the undergrowth. Somehow, the baby-sitter failed to notice her near the taro filled puddle. It was then Natashia noticed two more creatures.

They blended into the shadows, but she could sense their presence. They were strange, feathered creatures; one in the undergrowth, the other in the trees. They were both watching their prey. The one on the ground moved closer until it could get to the group in a single bound. These unfamiliar animals were hunting. They held their long rodlike tails stiff as they stalked. The black feathers on their backs were raised slightly. The one and a quarter metre high beast came closer to the group of baby animals. Natashia was most concerned about the one directly over her in the same buttress root tree that she had just passed. It watched her pass with intent in its dark yellow eyes.

The one on the ground came brushing through the undergrowth, within two metres of the other animals. When the peccary let out a warning squeal, the animal leapt at the group with long powerful hind legs. The sharp teeth and hand-clawed wings came at the peccary.

The smaller animals scampered for the nearest tree, only to find another waiting up there for them. They dashed down again and headed for a hollow log.

The hind feet of one of the toothy feathered predators pinned down the peccary. A switchblade claw pierced the writhing flesh.

The tigress sprang into action, flying out of the undergrowth straight at the first avian beast. It had just enough time to turn a yellow eye in her direction, widening its pupils in surprise. But he didn't have time to react to the massive tiger smashing into him, sending him tumbling to the forest floor.

The creature's wings flapped into the ground trying to reposition the sickle claws on his hind legs to the tigress's underside.

Natashia slammed her paw onto his clawed wing and then sent her fangs directly into the throat of the animal, attempting to reach the arteries and veins. It tried to wound her with its large, clawed hands, which raked across her shoulders and neck. She bit hard and then pulled with such force that she ripped out his throat mid-shriek. Natashia immediately turned for the other one.

The young coati and some of the other animals had fled into the hollow log. The pursuer from the tree attempted to catch the creatures that ran into the undergrowth, leaping down, flapping, and landing with a thud. She hadn't yet realised her mate's demise. She stuck her head into the log. The feline charged. The animal turned and screeched, baring its serrated teeth.

The tiger leapt at her, slamming the beast with her paws. The feline's claws scraped through the feathers, not able to get her claws into the flesh beneath.

The raptor leapt out of her grip. It ascended the tree with a massive vertical leap before bounding down onto the surprised tiger.

The tigress reared and fell back onto the tree, attempting to shake the raptor off. She roared in pain and anger while snapping at the air. Suddenly, an arrow hit the raptor on the tiger's back. The animal tried to jump off. Two more bolts pierced the dinosaur's air sacs, partly flooding the lungs in the process.

Natashia shook the dying raptor off her back and tumbled to the ground. Something about the dinosaurs caught her attention. Their feet had bands that were similar to the bands used on birds' feet in the Kingdom's military. She questioned the allegiance of these raptors.

She turned in surprise as the dinosaur spasmed on the ground. She then turned to the archer, who, much to her surprise, was human. This was the first human she had seen in a very long time. A flash of recognition went through her mind. The woman wore a brown and green leather and cloth shirt with brown leather pants. Her dark hair hung over her shoulders and a breathable scarf partly covered her face. The leather quiver was visible over her back. She still pointed her bow menacingly at her.

Natasha stared. *Why hadn't she seen any more of them earlier? Was she one of the modified animals as well?* Her thoughts raced. *How can I get out of this situation?*

'I'm sorry, really, I wasn't trying to hunt the young ones!' she lied. 'I was after these bird things that were trying to kill them. I saved the children's lives.' She hyperventilated as she spoke, stuck between fighting or fleeing.

The baby coati came running up to her with several other animals, including some deer with monkey archers and, most strangely, a bear that reared up upon seeing her.

The black-furred bear with a golden-furred face stood down when the coati exclaimed, 'Don't shoot her, she saved our lives. Dad will want to hear of this,' the baby explained.

The woman lowered her bow, and without moving her mouth spoke, 'You have shown yourself to be a capable fighter. The boss may consider using your services if you agree; that is if you are not a spy or saboteur. Come with us. If you join us more permanently, there may be a way to make a real difference. And yes, we know of your connection to the insurgency. We will discuss this with the patriarch.'

Natashia realised the woman had the same brain computer as all the other intelligent animals. *Why were humans added to the other species of this planet in the same way, and why had she not seen more of them before?* she wondered.

Chapter 21

Not unlike Cats and Dogs

Ryan and Melissa

That night, Ryan and Melissa continued across the grasslands, observing the scenery while looking out for prey. They avoided a zebra carcass because of the lion and terror bird that were tugging at it, trying to haul it back to town to share it. There would only be dirty scraps by the time they were done. Those scavengers they met – Natashia, and the insurgency – had been the only friendly groups encountered so far on this side of the river. They were now crossing the tall grasses, brushing the ground over behind them as they walked. They had only the light of the stars and the reflection of Phobos to guide them through the darkness.

Small creatures moved in the grass as they passed. Finches burst into the air like tiny feathery butterflies, flapping out of the way of the pair. A spring hare and a kangaroo-like rodent noticed the pair and hopped off into the grass, long fluffy tail trailing behind him.

Melissa cocked her head and ears in the general direction of the springhare, sniffing the air.

'It's a shame that most of the animals we passed have fled from us in terror before we saw them,' Ryan noted as he watched the large rodent disappearing into the dark.

Melissa, still looking on, responded, 'It's perfectly understandable for the prey to do that. Most of them know that's the way it is around here. We only hunt to defend ourselves against those that threaten the things we love, our enemies, and those that we need to kill as prey. The prey killing part is what shocks most people when they come here, as it did you. Having to murder to keep yourself alive is a moral conundrum. Should someone else have to die to keep you alive?'

Ryan was surprised by Melissa's insightful response. He had many questions he wanted answered as they travelled further into the night. Her comments might very well help fill some moral holes in his computer mind. He had to know more. 'What makes you want to keep going even though you have to do such terrible things? Would it be more ethical to not exist as a carnivore?'

Melissa had to think of her answer to this difficult question. 'Most creatures are selfish enough to say "yes," myself included. But the Terraformers heavily discourage suicide. Some say that those who suicide, end up reincarnated in the open sea, a bizarre empty hell where they have a huge nothingness around. They say it plays havoc with their minds. Many go mad in the biosphere as the toll of their memories and guilt mounts over their repeated lives. It's a vicious cycle that can hardly be fixed. Moving on is often the best solution.

'This means that the wild is littered with broken animals – physically fine but broken mentally. They let their instincts guide them more than their own conscience; or worse still, there are those who embrace their madness and let it twist them into angry cruelty. Some pretend to be your friend, then kill you for themselves. Others take out their anger on those that they should love, their mates, friends, or family. A few more optimistic ones begin to work together within new civilisations like those of their old world – like that mammoth and his Kingdom and the creatures of the Citadel.'

Melissa's mind filled with painful memories. Ryan's ears turned back. He paused wide-eyed. 'You can stop if you want. You seem distressed; I don't like seeing you upset,' Ryan said.

'No, it's alright. I have to remind myself sometimes to remember the events of past lives, so that I don't forget the lessons. Some of us are selfless and try not to hurt anybody. However, the selfless carnivorous starve, only eating scraps and never harming a living creature. Starvation or other carnivores take their lives. Other flesh-eaters kill more than they need. The tribes on the southern tundra often mass slaughter prey when the first snow falls, freezing the meat in the permafrost. I met my end once in one of those bloodbaths, driven off a cliff while on fire. Not a nice way to go,' she continued.

'Isn't that a bit wasteful?' Ryan had to ask as they continued to pass through the long grass together.

'You're right, though you have to do things like that when the darkness lasts for up to eighteen months. You need all the frozen meat you can get. A quick death by a carnivore's killing bite is better than starving or having parasites munching on you. Some animals die covered in hundreds of ticks that drain them dry. Others have strange creatures consume their organs from the inside out while they are still alive. Plagues are worse. Entire settlements have been wiped out when unknown diseases occur, or if the plague jumps species. Infections and broken bones that cause long slow painful death also strike down many. In those situations, sometimes killing them is a mercy.'

'That sounds terrible when you put it like that. Is there anything to hope for here without going through an eternity of torment?' He mewled, now with concern.

'Even among this story of pain and misery, there is hope. Some have risen above the wild rabble and rebuilt societies; however, we have no place in that Kingdom of the mammoth. Carnivores simply cannot coexist peacefully. We must exile ourselves to live the best lives we can. I don't know how those at the Citadel manage themselves in that regard.

'My goal for life is simple, enjoy what you can and treasure those who are close to you. For every creature I harm, I try to help one other creature – you are one example. It gives me moral justification to continue. However, in all honesty, there are upsides to living here in the biosphere. We have the freedom to shape our fate, travel where we like, do what we want to do, form the relationships we can, and have some of the best friends and family we may ever find, and of course, immortality of sorts. In actual truth, it is still worth living here in this hell,' she concluded.

Ryan sighed in relief.

'To alleviate our negative emotions, I should tell you what we are doing. We are heading to the cloud forests on the mountain, a safer area than these open plains. We may well stay on the mountain side. However, we will see if we can see the Citadel from there. If something terrible were to happen to the cloud forest, we could make our way to the Citadel to escape it. Either on the mountain side or at the Citadel we may very well be able to find a better life for ourselves.'

She stopped walking to look around nervously. Ryan did the same. They had walked through the tall grass for several hours that evening.

Though they were still heading in the right direction, they had lost their sense of place. This however was not the biggest of their concerns. Melissa sniffed the night air and noticed a familiar scent, something like a dog, mixed with a terrible bad breath.

'We're being followed. Several animals are around our flanks,' Melissa commented.

Ryan peered around with his ears locked back. He snarled and raised his hackles.

The two of them looked around nervously in the darkness, unable to pinpoint the source of a new fresh scent that came around and through the area where they had just walked.

Ryan was about to rear for a better look, when a figure exploded out of the darkness, tumbling him over. He screeched and yowled as he tried to fight off his attacker. Melissa turned and launched herself at the aggressor before it could break Ryan's ribs with its teeth.

The assailant held Ryan to the ground. It lost its footing for a second when Melissa jumped onto its back. Ryan rolled onto his feet. The creature was about the same height as Melissa but much more solidly built.

The attacker backed onto his feet, letting out a distinctive loud whooping laugh. Ryan suddenly realised what Melissa already knew. A clan of spotted hyenas had found them. More were waiting just metres away, slinking out of the tall grass, hanging their heads down, and whooping with their tails high or horizontal. They came out of hiding to join the hunt. No need for a chase when their prey was already cornered. If the outmatched pair stayed, their death would follow, slowly and painfully. If they fled, which was almost impossible, the hyenas would run them down and kill them. They were in a situation that would result in their death either way.

'Nowhere to go. Such a short hunt, poor guys. You walked right into our territory. In fact, you will make a nice meal for us. Ironic considering the topic of your previous conversation that we overheard. Girls, it's time for you to teach these intruders what we do to trespassers and prey,' one of the larger female hyenas said, gloating, as others surrounded the dingo and puma from all sides.

Another voice announced the attack. Others began to grunt in challenge as they approached.

Acting on impulse, Ryan sank his teeth into Melissa's neck scruff. He launched himself over the hyenas, soaring over three metres into the air in a panicked leap. He dropped the dingo onto her feet. Melissa tumbled when let go. As she righted herself, she whined slightly in pain from the ripped skin on the scuff of her neck. Within three seconds, they were both sprinting away with their attackers in pursuit.

The hyenas soon caught up and were trailing them to the side, running in to take bites at them. Ryan desperately searched for the one place they would be safe. Then he saw it. Outlined against the grey of the Milky Way was a lonely acacia's branches. *At last, a possible escape route.*

'The tree!' Ryan shouted to Melissa, both were running flat out with the hyenas behind them, laughing loudly, their distinctive war cry echoing through the night. They heard his direction, and some left the chase to reach the tree first.

Ryan could now see the base of the tree. A stretch of short grass, and a hyena were between it and them. He sped up, launching himself off the ground and hurtling towards the hyena. He smashed the wind out of the animal. The smaller animal tumbled, snapping angrily. The rest of the clan raced towards the fight to help. Melissa took the opportunity of the distraction to continue her efforts to reach the tree.

Ryan focussed on his goal and sped towards it. It was only fifty metres, but this disappeared within seconds as all the animals hurtled towards his goal.

His heart was racing, and his mind was focused on getting there and helping Melissa get away. He jumped up, grabbing the tree trunk, and running up to the first fork. Three metres above the ground, he turned to help Melissa, who was closing the last few metres. A hyena came between her and the tree, but she had already leapt. Her momentum slammed him against the tree trunk. She landed thudding on the ground and then leapt again, digging her claws into the tree. She slammed into the trunk desperately trying to climb. Her claws were not sharp enough to pull her up.

Ryan reached down; his paw found its mark painfully in her shoulder. He grabbed the dog and backed up, pulling the yelping dingo, causing deep bleeding scratches on her shoulder. She was still yelping as Ryan lodged her in a fork. The terrified Ryan looked down and hissed at their pursuers.

The hyena that Melissa slammed into recovered his breath. He stood against the tree, looking at them hungrily, his mouth drooling. He whooped in anticipation as he strained to get at them.

The rest of the hyenas had arrived at the tree as Ryan hauled Melissa up into the fork.

One of the female hyenas took a run up and charged at the tree. She tried to leap up at them, but the pair were too high. The hyena fell, landing on the ground with a thud. She yelped and groaned.

Melissa caught her breath. Scarlet blood ran from the marks on her shoulder. The hyenas continued whooping and grunting, rounding the tree in frustration.

Out from the darkness slinked the matriarch of the hyena clan, shaking her head in shame of her clan's failure. 'Cole, you incompetent idiot, why did you attack before I sent the signal, you nearly got yourself killed.'

The leading hyena angrily bared her teeth at the subdominant male. He slinked back to the others.

'What will we do with you two? I certainly do not recognise the cat. Why did you stray into our territory?' The matriarch asked the pair.

Ryan responded to this question. 'We were fleeing the Kingdom to the north and trying to find a new home on the slopes of the mountain. We had to pass through your territory to get there. We're sorry for this. We only ate one prey animal in your territory and were just passing through, please spare us.'

'Wait. Melissa, is that you?' The matriarch hyena, Cassandra, spoke with a great deal of surprise in her voice.

Melissa stared at the hyena. Her eyes lit up as she recognised her. 'Mum, it's great to see you again,' Melissa replied much to Ryan's confusion. 'I am not pleased about the circumstances though. You all tried to eat me! But hello to all the extended family as well. I've haven't seen any of you in so long!' Melissa yapped out excitedly while breaking it up with pained whines.

Ryan looked backwards and forwards in utter confusion. 'What's going on? This is your family? But they're not your species. You never told me about this; and they just tried to kill us!'

'I was adopted… long story. This is the Mountain's foot clan, my old family. We need to get out of this tree,' she replied.

The hyena pondered before responding. 'So, this is what those birds meant by those fleeing from the Kingdom. Girls and guys; don't eat these two. They are welcome to be our guests for the night. Let's all head back to the den and call it a night. We can hunt for prey in the morning, maybe with these guys' help. You two can come down now. My name is Cassandra.'

'Let's get down. Can you help me please, Ryan?' Melissa asked. Ryan seemed to snicker when he pushed her out of the tree. She gave a confused, frightened yelp as she hit the ground, followed by whining. She rolled to her feet, shaking dust out of her fur.

Ryan leapt down far more elegantly, landing softly on the ground on forepaws first, then on his hind paws with a thud. The clan turned back into the grass. Various strange comments were made as they continued to the den site with the others in tow.

The path to the den was worn from the hyenas passing by many times before. Their scent was heavy in the air. The group entered a patch of tall grass, cutting off their view of the land around them for a time. The pair travelled in the middle as the spotted hyenas moved around them, escorting them to the den.

The site was a large circle of bare soil within a ring of dirt mounds. One mound had a cliff around one side and a burrow dug underneath. It had two entrances. They had dug tunnels into the ground under all the mounds, providing their shelter. Pups that were playing in the centre of the circle stopped to look. The adults that had stayed behind were initially happy to see their clan return but were confused by the presence of Ryan and Melissa.

A dead tree was the roosting spot for a pair of vultures. They turned their heads to look at the pair.

'Who are these two? Is that Melissa? Didn't she leave years ago vowing not to return? And now she is coming into our camp like this?' Brenda, one of the female hyenas that stayed behind asked Cassandra.

The hyena responded. 'These two are our guests for the night and morning. They have come all the way from the jungle to the north, fleeing Suleiman's Kingdom. Nobody here hurts them, okay!'

Melissa paused, looking around the camp. She pictured her previous time here – sunny days chasing and playing with the hyena cubs, learning stories from her adopted family.

She recalled playing tug of war with pieces of rawhide and splashing around in mud puddles. She remembered when she was still small enough for her mother to carry her in her mouth.

Later recollections came back; her meeting with her first love of this life, Lerato. The days they spent together in their adolescence. She recalled when they learnt to hunt together and them snuggling, even when listening to instructions from their trainer.

The romantic nights with her under the moonlight. But it was after this that a more negative memory came back. This broke her nostalgic daydreaming and bought her back to the present.

The clearing was a bare patch of grass in a slight hollow. The burrows dug into the mounds were large and deep, leading metres underground and linked up with different entrances. The hyenas had turned from their various jobs, staring at both the newcomers and the returning hunting party. Some of the hyenas groaned and softly squealed excitedly when meeting the newcomers. They had to kill anything that they ate, and scavenging opportunities were sparse. The clan numbered at least thirty. Many were inside the burrows.

Most of the members were female, though only a trained eye could pick that out. A small number of males watched the incoming group, along with their female superiors. Pups were moving and others resting around the camp. Others were whining while chasing their mothers and aunts around the campsite. One of the males stood in the entrance to the burrows with the pups beside him. They stared sleepily at the pair.

Another hyena came trotting into the camp, looking around in surprise at the unexpected situation playing out in front of her. 'What's going on?' the hyena asked. Then she answered her own question when she saw Melissa. She was not the only hyena in the camp who remembered her from years ago.

The rest of the clan came out of their burrows to view the returning group. Melissa looked to see if she knew them. The pups that had been playing earlier included a striped hyena pup – a different species. The clearing was kept clean. One of the males was disposing of food scraps, crunching the bones, and swallowing them, shards, and all.

She went off to reunite with her old family, while Ryan wandered in a different direction to explore the area.

Sometime later, Ryan sat next to Cassandra, talking to her, and looking over the camp on the savannah. Melissa was playing around with the hyena pups, including the odd one out.

'Just how and why do you have that stripy pup. It's a different species, isn't it?' Ryan asked.

'Well, it's incredibly hard for a pup to survive on their own without their parents. If they can be a useful part of the clan, we try to help them fit in. We offer to adopt them and raise them as part of the clan if they help when they grow up. Most are grateful. Melissa joined us that way. However, she found out the truth and left; her mate Lerato left after her. This is the first time we've seen her for years,' she coolly and calmly explained.

Ryan tensed and raised his front legs off the ground. 'And what happened to her biological parents?'

'Her parents for this life were eaten by us when we were clearing the territory of rivals. Her mother died, backed into the wall of the den, putting herself between her pups and us. We adopted the four pups.'

Ryan stared at the hyena with furious disbelief, flicking his ears back, narrowing his eyes, and snarling and hissing. 'How dare you. First, you killed the parents, and then you lied to their children, by not telling them that they were being raised by their parent's murderers. Explain why!' Ryan spat the words of hot anger and sympathy with revulsion.

'Out of mercy, I decided to take her pups into our care. There were four, Melissa, two sisters, Mary and Jane and a brother, Max, who was eaten by the other pups when the babysitter wasn't paying attention.'

Cassandra was going to continue but Ryan sat there slack jawed. 'Your pack killed the parents and one of the adopted babies!' Ryan said in exasperated horror.

Cassandra continued, 'Sometimes the kids are horrid little things. One of my sisters, Millie, devoured my brother ten minutes after he was born. We were in the same litter. I admit we are terrible, but we are just following our instincts. Some weaker pups get eaten. The fittest survive, grow strong, and dominate weaker ones. The females are always bigger than the males. We keep males near the bottom of the pecking order.

'However, we do have civilised traditions, like picking our leaders by popular vote, as opposed to the nepotism normal for our species. We treat other members of the same gender nicely and try not to kill more than we need. We hyenas are flawed, but not the complete monsters our enemies believe, especially lions. They're pricks. As for your reaction – I understand the concern for your friend and her upbringing, but I would advise watching your temper whilst you are our guests. My family and I will be trying to be hospitable enough to ensure your safety during your stay.'

Ryan changed the topic. 'Do you know about the current situation in the Kingdom; how Suleiman tried to kill so many carnivores before the insurgency intervened?'

'That's old news. Suleiman has now left the Kingdom in the hands of either Ronda or Andrew.'

The puma's eyes opened wide in surprise. *What does this mean for the Kingdom?* he thought.

Cassandra continued, 'The mammoth is in musth and roaming the grassland around here chasing females and taking a break from ruling. He's too horny and testosterone influenced to rule now. Tiffany saw him with a herd of female mammoths today. Poor guy, his hormones get the better of him at this time of year. His wives are somewhere in that herd. I've heard that things may not be going so well back at the Kingdom.'

'Why does no one try to kill Suleiman when he's alone, to destabilise the Kingdom?' Ryan asked.

'Several problems with that. One: attempting to kill or harm him will bring the anger of both the Principalities and the Kingdom upon those who are foolish enough to try. The other thing is that without powerful guns, you would need a small army of smaller animals to even stand a chance of killing him. Poisoning the water is forbidden. Everyone else who drank from Suleiman's water hole would die as well and their loved ones would hunt down the perpetrator. I have another thing I would like to ask you, Ryan.'

'Sure, and that is?' he asked.

'With your permission, when you do go to the mountains, one of the vultures will go with you to protect you on the way, and return with information about what it is like over there? I've never been, and it could make for interesting hunting opportunities. You can head there when you feel like it.'

"Yes, we will be pleased to have a vulture accompany us. It can act as scout for us and warn us of any danger along the way,' replied Ryan.

A different group of hunting hyenas came back from their nocturnal hunt. They brought the remnants of a partly consumed duiker. Their offering still had meat holding the spine together, and on the shoulders and legs. The head and feet were the only furred parts left. The newly arrived hyenas gathered around Ryan and Melissa, curious to know who they were and why they were allowed into the camp. Cassandra filled them in and warned them about hurting their guests.

The kill was placed into the dimly lit den area. Excited cubs whined as they bounded up to the adult hyenas. The hyenas exchanged greetings, but the pups were impatient. They had already tried to grab a piece of antelope leg. The male cubs were more nervous than their boisterous sisters and stood back to wait their turn.

Once feeding was done, the hyenas lay around, playing with the cubs, or starting to fall asleep. The hyena clan settled down for the morning. One lay with his hind legs up in the air. Others retreated to the dark of the burrows to escape the increasing heat of the day.

'So, what is happening now? It seems to be that everyone is going to sleep in the shade of the dens,' asked Melissa as she sat near Cassandra and groomed one of her forepaws.

'Your stay would normally be over, however you two are exhausted from your long night's trek across the plains. You need sleep before leaving for the mountains. You can use our spare burrow if you want to sleep in the cool underground chambers. It would be cruel to leave you outside.

'Thank you so much. It's so incredibly kind of you to do that. I was expecting to have to trek another two hours until we could find a good resting spot.'

Ryan was still playing with the hyena cubs, letting them delicately nibble his toes. One of the females tried to nip at the puma's flicking tail. A male pup was leaping up to touch Ryan's raised paw as he rolled over.

'Hey, big cat, we have some accommodation for you and your friend,' Cassandra shouted.

He stood up and shook the dust from his coat then walked away leaving the pups to play among themselves.

'Thank you for the hole to sleep in. I have never slept in a deep den. My kind are not exactly the best of burrow diggers,' said Ryan.

He and Melissa moved down a deep tunnel into the burrow. It was deeper than he expected. His back fur brushed the roof. The passage narrowed until he reached the musky smelling chamber that was comfortably out of the sun.

The cubs had placed dry grass near the entrance of the darkest section. The little hyenas continued to come in and out, carrying bundles of hay to make a soft bed for the pair.

Ryan tried to stop them. 'Thank you all very much. We didn't ask for the grassy bedding but thank you very much. Seriously, you don't have to do this.'

The pile of hay now blocked the other entrance to the inner chamber. He pulled the dry grass into the den. Before long, there was a soft comfortable bed of grass for the pair to lie on.

Melissa had been outside chatting with other hyenas. She came squeezing her way into the deep chamber to curl up beside Ryan before falling asleep. The puma let sleep take him, drifting into a peaceful slumber. He was pleased to be out of the hot sun that continued to beat down on the earth above their heads.

The male cubs snuggled up in the patch of grass left in the doorway and fell asleep. The faint sound of mole rats burrowing through the dirt echoed in the burrow. A mole rat burrowed into the side of the chamber, only to make a hasty retreat when he saw who was lying there.

Ryan didn't hear him. It was one of the best sleeps he had in ages.

Chapter 22

Didn't Think This Through

Dennis

Many days had passed, since Dennis, Felicia, and Akash started their journey from the crater. They trekked through the desert, eventually reaching the foot of the mountain again. They had headed east since leaving the conifer forests on the western side of the mountain. When the Kingdom captured the cougar and dingo, Dennis was still in a riverbed, several miles east of the mountain's base. He continued to wander for miles. This was the day he would try to hunt. His prey so far had been scraps; a few gerbils, some grass seeds, and the peccary eaten ruins of a melon. He wanted to score a big kill, enough to feed both he and his vulture friend who was still guiding him over the desert.

Today he found a suitable prey, an addax antelope calf among a herd of antelopes. With the help of Akash, he formulated a hunting plan. Dennis found tussocks of green grass in the muddy shallows of a drying section of riverbed. The condor helped scout the antelope herd while carrying the grass tussock. Felicia, the bushbaby, and Dennis helped partly bury the plants roots near the herd. Then they retreated to a safe distance. The dingo crouched, blending into the reddish coloured sand of the riverbed.

The desert antelopes came over the ridge into the dune. Other addaxes followed the mother and baby. They moved around browsing on the short shrubs that dotted the dry riverbank as Dennis watched. The adults could easily kill a dingo, as their horns were long and sharp. The little calf on the other hand would provide the meal Dennis needed so much.

The five other addaxes browsed on stunted acacia bushes as the mother and calf came to a tiny depression in the sandy riverbed. They approached the muddy hole where Dennis had removed the grass.

His plan was working, but a bit too well. The presence of the mother addax could foil his plans. He needed to separate the antelope from the calf to have any chance of success. Dennis waited for his opportunity.

A simple gesture from one of the bulls temporarily gained the female's attention. She wandered away from the young animal, towards the bull. When the calf looked back at his mother would be the time to strike. He only needed to shred the prey's throat and let bleeding do the rest.

Dennis darted out from the bushes, broke into a flying sprint, and launched himself at the baby antelope. He let out a terrified bleat as the dog attacked. The dingo savaged the baby antelope's neck. His canines and premolars missed the jugular and the arteries. This was a grave mistake.

'*Help mum – save me!*' the calf shouted.

Dennis had missed his chance. The mother spun around and thundered across the dune, her long keratinous spears lowered. Her horns caught Dennis by the side, scraping his ribcage, but not penetrating. He let go of the young calf and yelped. He felt himself hoisted up into the air and tossed over the furious mother's white-furred back.

As he hit the ground with a thump, he rolled over and recovered his footing. Blood oozed out of his side. He gave a loud vicious bark and tried to refocus. Desperate for food, he thought a second attack could still work if he caught the calf and got out quickly.

He leapt again at the startled baby antelope, gripping his neck this time. But of course, his mother walloped him in the ribs again. If he had killed the calf, he might have been able to retreat and eat later, but now the antelope rammed him into the ground, pawing him with its wide hooves, and tossing him around with its long horns. His pelt ripped, and the injuries were mounting. He yelped loudly until a large black flapping shape seized the horns and dragged them off Dennis. The pacifist condor had finally intervened.

The huge black bird had launched himself off a branch of a nearby tree, beating his massive wings low over the herd. They scattered as he swung his talons forward to grab the antelope by the horns. Akash had flapped hard to pull the antelope away from Dennis.

The dingo quickly righted himself and pelted out of danger with his tail between his legs. He ran along the riverbed leaving a trail of hot blood behind him.

A little later, the dingo limped away from the riverbed, still losing droplets of blood. He came up the rocky slope to a small outcrop of bushes at the top of the hill. He retreated through the clumps of mesquite shrubs to a sandstone overhang.

The angry antelopes were still watching the side of the river in case he attacked again. His only thoughts were how to escape and not bleed to death. The shallow overhang surrounded by creosote bushes protected him from the worst of the sun's heat. The shade would make a good resting spot. He flopped down panting and wincing from the pain of his wounds. It would take a long time to heal from this fight. To add insult to injury, he did not have any food. He would need food to heal and to keep up his energy. Already he had lost several hundred grams of weight from the energy he had expended in the first fortnight here.

He lay in the cave, keeping his wounded side facing upwards. Felicia hitched a ride up from the riverbed on Akash's back. The vulture perched himself in the bushy mesquite and stared at Dennis.

'Thank you for saving my life back there. Too bad… I'm probably going to die anyway. But why did you help; you are normally a pacifist, right?' Dennis asked.

'When it became apparent there was no hope of you making a kill and the antelope was in the process of impaling you, I decided to intervene without hurting anybody. I saved you because you are someone in need of my help. But if you die, I will eat your corpse, since we don't want your death to be wasted, and you would be nothing but food by that point.'

Dennis took a second to take in the condor's word. 'Okay, you're a bit stranger than I initially realised, though I owe you for saving me after my foolish and reckless behaviour. Thank you.'

The condor ruffled his feathers and continued to sit on his perch.

Felicia had run off after inspecting Dennis's wounds. It was at that moment the little bushbaby came bounding back across the sand, carrying a twig with some leaves in her mouth and a small strip of a herb branch in her right hand.

'You all right, Dennis? You are hurt so I need to heal you. I know a few useful herbs that can ease the pain and reduce the infection. I just need to get the tea tree leaves and the snake vine ready. You do look to be in a lot of pain, and you have lost a significant amount of blood. You need to rest.'

'Thank you. Healing me might be the most useful thing you have done in my presence. Go right ahead. But try not to kill me in the process.'

The concerned little primate pulled the leaves into the cave. 'We need to clean that wound. Possibly a god-awful infection could break out from the bacteria on that antelope's horns.'

'Could you please get the herbs ready before I sleep?' Dennis politely asked the helpful little primate.

'Yes, of course. This is a great spot to camp for the night. You need some rest.' Felicia ripped the leaves into smaller pieces with her tiny paws and mouth.

Dennis merely smiled in the way that dogs do, his tail thumping slightly as it wagged. His ears pricked in the small primate's direction.

The dingo watched the bushbaby take more herbs from the bag she had been carrying when they met and grind them to make a crude antibiotic from the various plant sap. He had noticed the small pack she had been carrying had been transferred to the condor's body, tied between his wings on his back.

'So that is what was in the bag, healing herbs. I was worried about what was in it and why we were carrying it to the principalities. As he is carrying the bag now, why didn't you get Akash to carry you all the way to the principalities when he joined us, instead of continuing on the ground with me?'

'Well, I didn't want to leave you behind. Besides, I would need a backup if something happened to Akash. I lost my last ride. A spur-winged goose named Langley was carrying me, but a Spanish lynx ate him when he was getting a drink at a pond on the mountainside. I had tried to get further but I knew I could never make it across the desert on my own and then I met up with you.

'Also, there is more than herbs in there. And the more samples and data that I collect may become too much for Akash to carry while flying. I may need to carry another bag. I'm helping with research into volcanic eruptions in the area for the mines. From my readings, the eruption of the volcano is not yet possible, the spectrometer up at the mines have yet to show any earthquake prior to the one that opened that cave. There has however been a bulge slowly building beneath the caldera lake, changes in the water around the mountain streams, and occasional gas releases. This is not the only location that is at risk, there are others.

'Thanks to your help, we are making progress in getting across. We should be able to make it over within the next week, though I know our pace has been slow. Point being, I needed to get these heavy samples over to the principalities and Akash cannot carry both me and the heavy samples. So, I needed both of you to help. Alone you would not have the endurance to carry me and the weight all the way over either.'

'Why would a bushbaby like you know what to do with a bunch of volcanic rocks, polluted water and scientific equipment,' Dennis replied sceptically.

'I used to be a volcanologist before coming to Mars. I died during a volcanic eruption in Mexico. We had the soul capture for the town set up on a nearby hill. The entire town I was in was vaporised; flattened by a pyroclastic flow of rocks, and ash that was intensely hot; several hundred degrees Celsius. When I came here, I wanted to continue my mission of helping people any way that I can and protecting them from disasters such as that volcanic eruption. There is tectonic activity on the planet that is gradually increasing. I must do something bigger than myself.

'I failed those people back on earth. The only way I can make it up is stopping the same disaster again. That is why I came all the way from the university in the opal empire to here and onwards to the principalities to collaborate with the scientists on a way to monitor the volcano. It's a shame the Terraformers are not helping us with this. They simply don't care about us. Had I not taken you over to here and beyond you may not have survived the inevitable volcanic eruption. I don't know anything about you before you came here, Dennis, would you like to tell us about yourself?'

Felicia and Akash listened silently as Dennis began to speak.

'I was not a good person before I came here. If I hadn't died the way I did, I would have faced the death penalty.' Felicia gasped slightly when Dennis mentioned this.

'I have thirty-five homicides to my name – five of them police – twenty-five vehicle thefts, numerous drug related crimes, charges of assault – three of them sexual – and as for violent ones, there were more than I can count – and I forget how many traffic offences. I have served at least five years in prison. I was killed and my soul taken and sent here after a bank armoured vehicle theft went wrong, resulting in ten deaths, three million in property damage, and three broken police cars. I died when the stolen truck veered over a cliff after I was shot in the chest.

'I would rather that this life amounted to a different path than a path of crime down the gang route. This is my chance to change my course and hopefully become a better person for it. The struggle for survival and the assorted vicious cycle that is the food web is something that doesn't seem to affect me very much. I guess I kind of got used to death and killing.'

Felicia audibly gasped. Akash took interest in his struggles. 'I see that you have had a tumultuous path in your past. If you need help with anything, I can try to help find people who can assist you, either by taking you to one of the therapists in the principalities, or to one of the churches, mosques, or Buddhist temples at the principalities, if you are religious.' Akash offered.

'Thank you. But a sinner like me has got to do a lot to get redemption. Had I not come here, I would surely have gone on a path to hell. Haven't been to church in years.' Dennis laid down with a huff as Felicia got to work on the wound on his side.

'You have been through a lot, Dennis. I'm not sure if I can help, should help or should be afraid of you. At least this medicine ought to heal your wounds. Thanks for helping me get this far and for continuing to get us where we need to go,' the small primate nervously replied.

The dingo then lay down to go to sleep, closing his heavy eyelids.

The day was ending. Akash needed to roost at night, but Felicia was at her most efficient under the cover of darkness. Being nocturnal, twilight was the most efficient time for her and the dingo to be operating.

Sleep did not come easily to Dennis. He awoke and yelped painfully at several points when Felicia used strong, stinging, bitter fermented ethanol from cactus fruit to disinfect the wound. The cactus thorn needle she used to sow the skin back together was likewise painful. She put a stick in his mouth to stop him biting his own tongue. His breathing normalised as he fell into a light sleep.

The next day, the group continued to travel together. Dennis's wounds were healing slowly, and he forced himself to keep moving. The three creatures soon reached another part of a dry riverbed. This was a different creek to the one where the antelope disaster occurred. Water became a problem as angry black clouds passing over the mountain released a deluge of rain.

'Surely most of this would have missed the desert,' said Felicia. She was sceptical of the help the rains could provide them. An old striped hyena den provided shelter by the fallen base of a gidgee tree.

It rained for hours. When they awoke inside the abandoned burrow it was still raining. The dingo darted painfully between gidgee trees on their way to the riverbed.

Once there, the bushbaby sat upon a rock, looking up at the mountains through the rain. The condor soared high above, watching something coming down the mountain. A torrent of dark, borderline black water was sloshing through the last of the inland jungle. It poured over the pine forests on the southern side of the foothills. The forest's floor was slowly becoming water-logged as more water rushed down tributaries leading to the river. The condor decided it was time to warn the other two.

Dennis was panting in the dawn's rain from the exertion of continually running and trying not to get too wet. He stood under a corpse of mesquite trees, watching over the desert plain below. The huge open expanse of desert stretched to the horizon in the southern and southwestern directions.

Strange metallic shapes roamed the plains beyond, partly obscured by the heavy desert rains. These metallic forms were visible in the light from the west, their deep rumblings echoing through the night. The massive terraforming machines wandered these deserts astride huge limbs that distributed their weight over the sand. The legs held the chaises about ten metres above the shifting dunes. The machines belched water vapour and breathable gases as they plodded along. Further towards the horizon, a heat mirage was visible beyond the edge of the rain cloud. Above them, the stranger looking pterosaurs flew on their annual migration.

The condor swept downwards his huge wings fanning out over the dead tree where he landed. He spoke to the dingo urgently, 'We need to move. A flash flood is coming. It will cut off our access to the Principalities and to the swamp you want to reach. Make your choice, the mountain, or the Principalities in the swamp beyond.'

Akash showed his decision by pointing his head to the southeast. Here they could see the Principalities; the spot where many river systems turned inland.

'Are the towns where you wanted to go?' Dennis asked the bushbaby.

'Exactly,' she responded looking to where they indicated. 'Is that where it is? We are so close! Let's go!'

The bushbaby crawled onto Dennis's back, and he turned and trotted out of the riverbed and up the dunes. As they crossed the bed quickly, the first of the flood waters flowed under his feet. A barrage of broken sticks, twigs and branches came with the water. Debris carried at the front of the flood, partly obscuring the dirty water beneath. The flood waters toppled Conifer trunks further upstream. The flow wet the sand, then passed over it, pushing a raft of pine needles with it. Soon the rocks had water flooding over them.

'Forwards it is then, I guess,' said Dennis as he scrambled up the hill side on the far bank of the river.

The water continued to flow, and more was coming. In places, the rocks seemed to sizzle with white frothing bubbles. After giving his warning, the condor had turned to fly high up above the top of the mountain again, leaving them alone on the open sands.

As the days passed, Dennis grew hungry again, running so low on food for so long resulted in him attempting increasingly desperate sources of sustenance. Mice, gerbils, spiders, frogs, dung beetles, and scorpions gave him meagre sustenance. He attempted, without success, to catch a desert monitor even a rattlesnake and a black footed cat.

He decided it was not worth the risk of being bitten by the rattlesnake or the angry monitor lizard and the cat had fled well before he could cover the fifty metres to reach her.

He even attempted to eat fallen dates, desert quandong fruits, aloe, and prickly pear fruit out of desperation. The cactus fruits hurt his mouth and the rest lacked the nutrients he truly needed to keep going. He was barely putting in more energy than he was expending at this rate.

The bushbaby occasionally hunted the night-time insects that flew near the trees to provide her with sustenance, but she was still hungry. They reached the shrub-covered land of palms, eucalyptus, cacti, and mesquite. They were nearing the woods surrounding the swamp when they descended into the underbrush. Already the first signs of new life were appearing. Mushrooms were emerging in the wet dust between the dead grass stems. The river was flowing. It was a narrow stream where frogs and toads came out of the sand to enjoy the bounty as flying insects like mayflies whirled over the water.

Dennis's injuries had undergone much of their healing. He stalked through the creosote bush. He had come across peccaries. Around them in the recently wetted down shrub-covered land, hopped ring-tailed lemurs.

The lemurs were gathering fruits. Dennis prepared to grab one of the lemurs. He dashed out. The lemur screeched and leapt over his head. The dingo quickly grabbed the primate in his jaw, crunching down on the prey animal. He skidded on the sand, snarling. He was determined to finally get another chance to eat. He turned back, still carrying the screeching dying animal in his jaws.

Suddenly, from the corner of his right eye, he saw something charging. The peccaries ran off, leaving their cactus fruit behind. He had only a second to watch the last peccary piglet pull itself out of a dust scraping before an armoured lioness hit him hard from behind. As he rolled and bounded to his feet, he saw the sigil engraved upon her armour. It indicated allegiance to the principalities, the nation whose land they were now trespassing.

The dingo turned and ran with the captured prey and sprinted up the other side of the river. The lioness took pursuit. Dennis ran back out into the open between the bushes and grasses. The commotion had attracted a second male lion. Together, the two were trying to catch Dennis. The dingo kept swerving, dodging, and crossing back over his track to try and confuse his pursuers.

Akash was watching. Suddenly he had to dive to avoid an unexpected additional pursuer. The vulture had been watching Dennis and had paid little attention to the other flying creatures. He was more concerned with Dennis's situation on the ground; until large flying creatures turned in his direction. He plummeted to take evasive action as a giant pterosaur missed his feathers with his beak.

The vulture tried to find Dennis again and quickly spotted more pursuers. It was evident that a small patrol of soldiers had followed the dingo for some time. The riparian vegetation where Dennis had been hunting obscured their position. It was a strange repeat of what had happened to Natashia back in the coastal jungles. Two diprotodon with langur riders armed with spears came barging through the grasses after the dog. More birds pursued him as well.

Dennis's wound screamed in pain as he found himself darting, ducking, and attempting to shake off his pursuers. He sprinted through another acacia bush. He had to cross a stretch of short grasses before the desert began. The pair of lions barged through the trees. The normally clever Dennis was quickly finding himself out of options as the lions pursued him up the dune. Their heavy feet sank deeper into the sand than the lighter and nimbler dingo.

The diprotodons thundered over the dunes behind them. The roller bird scouts fluttered their bright blue wings over the dunes as they kept track of the fugitive. The dog leapt and began to tumble down the other side of the dune into the gully as the lions came over. It was now that the pterosaur plummeted over the dunes. The massive wings of the brown furred beast tucked behind it as the beast dived.

The male lion had cut ahead. He reached the bottom of the dune before Dennis.

The lion's paws bowled him over instantly. Dennis was twisting as he was pushed along. He opened his mouth, letting the dying lemur fly out. She tumbled onto the sand. Dennis rolled over the corpse. As he rose to run again, the pterosaur came down. It was buzzing the lions that roared in support. He opened his beak, came right up behind the canine, snapped its beak closed and lifted the yelping canine off the desert sand.

The dingo squirmed and snapped furiously as the massive set of jaws clamped around his torso.

As the pterosaur dropped him, the lemur pack arrived and threw ropes around his kicking legs. The primates hog-tied him to a tree trunk and then let his head drop underneath. The bushbaby had tried to follow the group of lemurs but was quickly left behind.

'What the hell is going to happen to me now?' Dennis wondered as they carried him away.

Chapter 23

Thicker than Blood

Ryan

Ryan and Mellissa spent another day and night with the hyenas before Cassandra invited the pair to hunt with them. Melissa had been catching up with members of her foster family she hadn't seen for a long time. Ryan had been acquainting himself with Melissa's family.

As the sun set the night before the hunt, the leader of the clan was sitting atop the dirt mound looking over the rest of the clan. The hyenas were milling about. Among them were two dingos. Beside her, Ryan watched with interest. "I'll wager that those dingoes are Melissa's sisters, Mary and Jane. Am I right?'

'Yep, Melissa's two sisters. She's already met with them again. It was a happy reunion. They, unlike her, chose to stay after hearing the truth about their biological parents. It was a tough time on all of them when they found out. They took it a bit better, probably because they didn't get to hear of their parent's deaths in the same way. We broke it to them more carefully. Melissa found out in a more dramatic way. It was my sister Carrie's fault. She was… let's just say she lacks my love and compassion.

'Melissa may have mentioned the night she walked in on Carrie with her mate. If it had simply been love-making it would have been awkward, but not as bad as what she found. Kevin, I think was the poor dude's name. As is the clan tradition, he had already made his way around the rest of the clan before he got to Carrie. She forced herself on him and when he tried to get away, she simply ripped him up; tearing off some of his skin and then started to eat it.

'Melissa was drawn down by the noise. She attacked Carrie to defend Kevin. They fought. Carrie won, but before she could kill Melissa, she gloated about how her birthmother struggled and yelped as she ate her alive. She rubbed in the truth in the worst way possible. I barged in to see what the commotion was about. Carrie and I fought, and she was exiled. My sister ran off into the night and we have not seen her since. Melissa, Mary, and Jane all asked if that was true and found out it was. Well, Melissa did not take it well and left us behind, running off to the north. I still love her, of course, but I understand our relationship will never be the same. I'm surprised she's even willing to come back to us for a while.'

***

Dawn broke over the hyena clan camp as the sun pulled itself up into the air high above the clouds. The low angled sun poorly lit the den site and left the interior of the hollow in shadow. Further away, the bustard bird ran across the grassy hillock to observe the gradually lighting up savanna, only to realise that heavy rains were pouring over the grassland. It boomed out a deep haunting melody as part of the morning birdsong choruses. Frogs croaked in joy at the arrival of the wet season. The whydah birds sang as the dawn chorus begun. The last of the nocturnal curlew screaming died down as they hid from the oncoming hyenas that parted the grass.

The vultures awoke from their roosts in the acacia trees by the deep rutted gullies and soared on the morning thermals. They quickly discovered scraps of meat left from a distant tyrannosaur kill – a decapitated and eviscerated buffalo carcass that the seemly out of place coyotes chewed. Their appearance jarred with the African sunrise.

Ryan awoke in the morning before dawn, bumping his head against the roof of the burrow. His moaning soft mew woke Melissa. Both pulled themselves up from their straw bed and climbed towards the surface. Outside, the dawn's light slowly rose over the horizon. Heavy clouds released dense rain that soaked the savanna. The roof of the burrow angled so that they would not be flooded in the case of downpours like the one that occurred over night. Ryan yawned, showing his large canine teeth. Melissa asked the other hyenas about the day's hunt.

The lack of prey caught the previous night necessitated a hunt this day. A smaller group of hyenas conducted the last successful hunt, but only a small duiker antelope had been caught, enough to sate some but not all the hyenas. Unlike canines like Melissa, the hyenas did not eat the same food they were preparing for the cubs to try their teeth on.

The food was not regurgitated, half-digested, already broken-down meat. Here, baby food was a nigh-inedible hoofed foot, snapped off at the midpoint of the tibia – more bones, hooves, sinews than actual edible meat. The milk from their mothers was still the primary nourishment at this teething stage, though the cubs had their canine teeth already. Cassandra watched the cubs come to the edge of the group, lining up behind the rest of the hyenas.

Their leader addressed the clan members as they gathered around. 'We're going on a hunt this morning. We're aiming for gnu or a tsessebe antelope, though they can be way too fast for us. Zebra even, if we have to. A wallaby would not be fulfilling enough, and the elands and buffalo are far too big.'

The hyena turned to Melissa. 'Come with us. We can hunt together again, just like when we were young.'

Melissa turned to Ryan. 'You're coming too, Ryan. If we chase them your way, you can help spring the trap.'

Ryan purred. 'Sounds good.'

Some of the hyenas nodded in agreement as their leader, Cassandra, laid out the plan with the rest of the clan. Then they set out, saying goodbye to the puppies on the way.

When they reached the hunt area, as decided, Ryan hauled himself up an acacia tree and set himself into position to wait for the prey to come to him. African daisy bushes broke up the grass around the dirt game trail below his position. The savanna gullies were filled with short, grazed grass, the longer grasses around the base of the acacia that held Ryan had not yet been grazed.

The other hyenas set up their positions around the prey. Melissa had gone off with them at the beginning of the hunt. In a short while, deep whooping and the sound of hooves alerted Ryan to what was coming.

Around the corner ran four animals. The leading animals were a pair of tsessebe antelopes. The brown and black hartebeest relatives sprinted along with a bird-like creature that had a long tail, neck, and legs. The legs ended in dangerous claws. The white bird-like beast leapt up the side of the gully, scampering up the slope and bounding over the top. It sprinted away, hissing as one of the hyenas pursued it.

The other beast was a bipedal furry lizard-like animal; a small ornithopod-looking animal with a scaly tail. It ran down the gully so fast that Ryan missed the chance to jump for it. The first tsessebe was also sprinting too fast for Ryan to have a chance of leaping onto its back, but the second had already been nipped at the ankles. The pain and muscle damage slowed it down.

Ryan leapt. Its horns hit his underside. The puma yowled as he rolled over, dragging the antelope down with him. He sank his teeth into the neck for a quick killing bite.

The second antelope's death was not as clean. The pack hemmed it into the wall of a gully. Quickly outsmarting the animal, the lead hyenas pounced on it and bit into its legs and haunches. Others followed and pulled at its flank, ripping skin off his belly. They tore him down with their immense jaw and upper body strength.

They began tearing the beast while it was still struggling to escape, ripping the abdominal muscles away. The antelope, running on adrenaline, screamed as the hyenas dragged its intestines out and ate them outside of its abdominal cavity. Eventually shock set in and the poor beast keeled over, before dying in a final spasm of the front legs.

Ryan had simply dropped his kill in horror and disgust. Melissa began to nibble at Ryan's kill, cringing at the other antelope's death. They both growled in disgust as the corpse was ripped apart in a noisy commotion of snapping bones, tearing flesh, growls, and whoops.

'This is the reason I have ethics and why I encourage a quick and merciful death to the prey,' said Melissa after wolfing down a mouthful of meat. Ryan could only nod in agreement. His ears were still tucked back in shock and disgust. They twitched while feasting on the fallen antelope – instinct made him on edge. His hackles raised as he turned from the dead antelope.

'What's wrong are you still in disgust over the kill?' Melissa asked as Cole and Brenda, two of the hyenas continued to wolf down their meat. Ryan stood peering into the distance. 'Something is coming this way.'

Three large black-feathered beasts came over the grassy ridge, several deer came behind them. Overhead, a flock of birds came flying. All the animals had black armour or parts of armour. Some of the hyenas watched the weird procession until their destination became clear; the suspected Kingdom soldiers were heading straight for the den site.

'Enemies are heading to the camp!'' Ryan yowled.

The rest of the hyenas immediately noticed the intruders, who began to pick up the pace. Cassandra came running up to Ryan and then quickly turned to run straight back to camp. Melissa bolted after her.

Ryan and the other hyenas came thundering down. Already a small part of the intruders' group had broken away and now headed for them.

'We have to warn the others!' Ryan yowled as the dozen or so hyenas sprinted to the campsite. A second group of attackers came running. The sable antelopes thundered across the savanna, leaping down into the trenches. Ryan turned around to cover the hyenas' retreat. He yowled and leapt at the four sable antelope cows.

They curved their horns downwards ready for him to leap at them, so instead he swerved to the right, leaping onto a tree trunk, and onto the sable's back. The horns of the antelope came rearing back.

Ryan leapt backwards to avoid the rear facing horns. The other antelope turned to gore him. The macaques on its back had blank expressions and horrid scars; some even had weeping or infected wounds. The horns from the antelope aimed at him, the feline jumped onto the back of the macaque's antelope, smacking the head down with his hind legs so that the horns went downwards, impaling the other antelope's side.

He quickly discovered that the black covering over their backs was skinned hides. A serow skin was over the back of the one he had jumped onto. The antelope had something like cords or cables coming out of its skull.

Ryan swatted the knife-wielding monkey aside. One tried to get a noose over Ryan's neck, only to lose his balance and get yanked off his mount by the feline. The puma leapt back onto the ground. He snarled as he dived at the antelope, gripping its throat before its horns could come down. He launched himself at the much larger antelope, seizing its neck with his forelimbs. His canines sunk into the brown antelope's neck. With a massive heave, he ripped the throat of the antelope. It staggered for a second, then collapsed, blood streaming around the carcass, as the dying antelope twitched. The other two antelopes had run off towards the campsite. Ryan chased after them.

***

The den site was in absolute chaos. A group of visayan deer, two sambars, about six raptors and several other animals were in battle with the hyenas. The hyenas tore into the attacking macaques, tearing the armed monkeys limb from limb treating them, like the meat they were to the canines. One monkey was manically stabbing a hyena while the hyena was tearing out his guts. Nets were fired from the saddles of the sambar and the two-remaining sable, capturing hyenas within them. They dragged three members of the clan away from the group. They snarled and snapped while the nets hauled them away into the long grass.

Melissa's two sisters were fighting one sword-wielding raptor. One was hanging from the tail, the other leaping at the arm. A second raptor tackled a hyena down and sank a deep toe claw into its gut, eviscerating it before snapping with his jaws and mauling the moaning hyena in the throat. More raptors were trying to get to the den site. Cassandra was sitting on her behind defiantly; the posture hyenas take to prevent their behinds from being bitten.

Cole was on the back of another raptor, ripping at its neck while the beast bucked and used its clawed wings in an attempt to rip the hyena off. The enraged hyena snapped and tore at the black cables in the raptors head and neck, until it toppled down with a snapped neck.

Melissa ripped into action, jumping at one of the three visayan deer, ripping into its buttocks, tearing at the ham strings. The deer fell. It turned over before someone else leapt onto its back, wrestling the doe down to the ground.

Ryan tackled a mounted deer, throwing the opossum riders off, smashing their skulls and exposing their cybernetics.

The puma wrestled the deer down. Her riders had fired a net onto one of the hyena cubs. It was thrashing in the net. Ryan sank his teeth hard into the back of the deer's skull, ripping the bone and part of the cybernetic brain out of the back of its head. Blood and sparks flew as the greenish black computer brain flashed sparks and then went out. The deer toppled over.

Melissa ripped the two knife-wielding opossums apart, managing to reopen Ryan's claw wounds on her back as she fought. She barked in rage after throwing half a possum out of her mouth.

Ryan immediately sprang into action, rocketing across the campsite to block the attackers. One of the raptors pounced to intercept him head on.

The feline looked up as the dinosaur came bearing down on him, claws ready to strike his flesh. The puma rose on his hind legs, digging his claws into the ground for balance. The raptor landed where the cat had been only seconds ago. The feline used his strong hind legs to leap over the raptor and drive his fangs into the raptor's spine. As the raptor pulled away and turned, Ryan's claws raked its underbelly. The two fell, continuing to brawl in the middle of the camp.

Melissa stood panting examining the scene. The pack had killed most of the invaders, but at least five hyenas had been dragged away, and another six lay dead or wounded around the camp, amongst the bodies of their enemies. The remaining three raptors were fighting the surviving hyenas, but most of the other animals had fled by this point.

She spun as a deep thunderous roar announced the arrival of the final two combatants on the enemy side. A series of pained yelps followed the roar, as Melissa's sisters dodged out of the way of a massive orange furred paw. The large male tiger directing this attack, came thundering into the clearing, immediately pouncing on a group of three hyenas, ripping one of the hyenas' head off with a deep bite and a thrash. The other two hyenas bit into him. The tiger yowled in pain before slapping one of them with such a strong backhand that he tumbled into the dirt. The third backed off.

It was the next combatant that came running behind the tiger that took Melissa by surprise and caused her to recoil in horror. Her exiled aunt, Carrie, joined the fray; the same crazy aunt that had killed her parents and her own mate years ago and tried to kill her, was now entering the fight on the clan's foe's side.

The tiger and hyena together came running to the entrance of the den.

Melissa gasped, whining slightly while trying to figure out what to do.

Cassandra stood her ground while her sister and the tiger were closing in.

'Get out of the way or we will take you like the others, or simply rip you to shreds,' the tiger said with an audible growl.

Carrie stopped in front of her sister. 'I've been enjoying my vengeance, sister. Sanjay, leave her to me. We will soon have lovely tender cubs to eat.'

Cassandra bared her teeth in a vicious snarl. 'You will be having the cubs over my dead body!' Cassandra leapt at her sister. The two hyenas began to fight, snapping at each other. Melissa sprinted in to protect her adoptive mother, leaping onto Carrie's behind, snapping at the fur on her back. Cassandra attacked again but Sanjay the tiger went after her and slapped her aside.

Melissa's two sisters came in to help her. 'This is for our mother and father, bitch!' Melissa barked as she leapt onto her crazed aunt, toppling her over. Carrie snapped into her neck fur. An injured Cassandra ran down into the burrow entrance to stand guard over the cubs.

The older hyena continued to squirm, clamping Melissa's younger sister, and throwing her aside, ripping her skin and shoulder muscle in the process. The hyena leapt away. The two dingo sisters gave chase. Melissa headed for the burrow.

Cassandra let Mellissa slip past into the burrow then followed. The dingo climbed down to the interior of the den to find that her aunt was entering by the other entrance. As the exiled hyena arrived, she pounced on one of the striped hyena cubs.

The rest of the cubs cowered in the corner, trembling, watching in horror as their relative ripped their sibling apart and ate her guts. Mellissa flew into a rage wanting to do the same to Cassie but her first thought was to protect the rest of the cubs. 'Get behind my mum and me. We will protect you.'

The pups scampered in behind the pair.

The intruder chuckled and said, 'Oh, you sound just like your mother – your real mother. The one who put herself in front of you and your siblings while your father distracted Cassandra. I cornered your mum and enjoyed doing this ...' she lunged at Melissa. They met head on. The dingo didn't dodge as she knew the crazed hyena would land on the pups if she did.

The hyena rolled and tore at the dingo's back, trying to find a way to snap her neck. Blood spurted into the air as her back skin was ripped. Melissa turned her head to the side, trying to snap at her opponent's belly. She missed and latched onto her front leg. The hyena yelped and let go. Blood flowed down Melissa's back as she squirmed out from the hyena's underside. The larger attacker pulled back as the dingo ripped into her leg. The hyena lunged downwards and latched onto Melissa's left ear and tore. She yelped as the cartilage of her left ear was ripped and torn into shreds.

Cassandra flew into the fight. 'Get off my daughter!!' she yelled in rage as she latched onto her sister. They rolled around in fury, tumbling into the cub group. Melissa leapt to the cub's defence, wincing as her back and ear ran with blood. A massive orange paw slammed into her, taking her by surprise.

The tiger hooked the dingo with his claws and began to pull her out of the den. Melissa yelped and tried to bite him.

He soon made it above ground. He released his hold. She turned around snapping in defiance. She went to lunge, but Sanjay's massive paw simply slapped her to the ground. Then Sanjay went in for the kill.

She squirmed just far enough away for the tiger's jaws to grab on to her back, his fangs going around the vertebra instead of through it. His premolars further lacerated Melissa's back. Then he let go and sank his fangs into her abdomen and started to shake her.

An enraged yowl came from the top of the dirt ridge on the burrow. Ryan leapt down straight onto the tiger's head, aiming for the back of the neck. The tiger moved and he landed on his back. He sank his paws in, yowling furiously. The tiger immediately let Melissa go and reached his paws around to tried to knock him off. The puma hung on as the tiger rolled. Then the tiger threw himself backwards and slammed Ryan into the wall of the dirt rise, dislodging the furious puma.

Ryan leapt in front of the injured Melissa, snarling defiantly, locking eye-contact with the tiger that was staring him down. 'Get away from my friend!' Ryan growled before both felines launched themselves at each other. For someone who fled for his life from a tiger only months ago, Ryan fought with as much bravery as he could muster.

Sanjay staggered back on impact. Both felines were slapping and clawing at each other. The two embraced standing on their hind leg. Sanjay easily overpowered Ryan in the vertical wrestling match as neither animal was used to standing bipedally. They fell to their four paws and swiped at each other. Ryan dodged the paw the size of his own head and lunged at the tiger's throat.

The tiger forced Ryan down, snapping at him from above. Ryan fought to squirm his way out. The tiger pushed back, eventually toppling the puma. Sanjay swatted Ryan's head aside and reached down with his mouth, grasping him around the throat. He started to squeeze, slowly suffocating the puma.

Ryan looked at the wounded Melissa bleeding out into the dirt, her chest rising and falling slowly. He was struggling to breathe as the grasp got tighter.

'Oh, I am enjoying this so much, shame you are not female, then I would have an even better time.' Sanjay gloated.

Cassandra came out of the burrow behind Carrie as the hyena sprinted away into the grass followed by the dingo sisters.

A second group of reinforcements for their enemy came bounding in. The deer and sables returned with more monkeys. An elephant who had a disgusting, bloody, infected wound on its head lumbered into the clearing.

One of the reinforcements, a visayan deer whose skull was showing between augmentations, came over to the tiger. 'Mr Hyde may well prefer the puma alive for his experiments, to add to his collection that you have been destroying,' he said in a distorted voice.

Ryan was gasping for air as the tiger squeezed his throat. Three tree kangaroos now held down his paws. They reeked of infection. Others fetched ropes to tie his limbs. The last of the sable antelopes came back as well, carrying more hyenas tied up in nets upon their backs.

Just as they tied the rope around Ryan's paws, a deafening roar thundered over the clearing. Sanjay winced, then ducked as a white vulture swooped his head with claws out. Over three dozen more followed this vulture. They began to swoop and harry the new arrivals, killing corrupted birds, chasing some of the animals away, and killing others.

The source of the roar was now thundering towards the camp; heavy footsteps sending vibrations that were shaking the hyena camp.

Sanjay leapt back, releasing Ryan, as a giant feathered creature leapt into the trench in front of the den. Ryan staggered to his feet, gasping for breath. He moved as quickly as possible to shield Melissa as the titanis terror birds, the same two-metre-tall bird who had tried to kill the puma several days ago, came at the tiger.

The tiger roared and reared back, dodging the massive beak of the long-legged flightless bird. The bird started to chase the tiger out into the clearing where the backup was fighting for their lives. The zebras and African buffalos came thundering around the den site. The deer and corrupted antelope fled. The raptors that had returned to the fight stood atop the carcasses of the slain, staring around in genuine fear.

A raptor went to lunge for the terror bird, getting a sprinting start. As he ran up, the second of the three remaining raptors had already leapt onto the dirt mount above the terror bird, pivoting ready to leap onto it, only to redirect at the last second.

The tyrannosaur came barging into the scene, snapping the first raptor out of the air. The larger dinosaur's jaws slammed shut and crunched the terrified raptor's body in his jaws, shaking the feathered beast around like a piece of short rope. Then he opened his mouth, sending the crushed carcass tumbling onto the ground.

The second raptor leapt onto the four-meter-tall tyrannosaur's side. The thirteen-meter-long reptile could not turn to his attacker, instead he spun ninety degrees towards the cliff side in frustration. It was then that his rider became apparent.

The lion, dressed in steel plate armour that covered his body, spun around to face the black raptor who was climbing up to meet him. The raptor stabbed at the chain mail-covered mane with the knives on his hind claws, as the lion leapt at the raptor. The dinosaur bird's head struck the spiked chest plate of the lion, cutting it on the blades as he tumbled off the back of the tyrannosaur. The larger dinosaur turned to chase after the retreating sable antelopes. The zebras, ridden by langur monkeys, raced behind them.

The lion leapt down on the raptor. The raptor's knives on its hind claws scraped against the lion's belly armour.

The lion stared the raptor in the eyes through his armoured faceplate, before pinning the raptor's snarling head down and biting its muzzle, breaking the nose bones with his jaws. He repositioned to grab at the throat, ripping it out in a mouthful of flesh, blood, and feathers.

After jerking a couple of times, the black dinosaur bird stopped moving. The limp carcass was added to the increasingly large pile.

A pair of langur monkeys came over to Melissa with a stretcher, as more of his kind moved to the other injured hyenas laying around the clearing. 'Exactly who are the lot of you?' Ryan asked the lion with concern as the medic monkeys lifted the injured Melissa onto the stretcher. The ambulance, a modified all-terrain four-wheel drive vehicle was parked nearby, looking very out of place.

'I am Prince Bartholomew, heir to the Savanna Citadel. My soldiers have come to your aid due to sharing a common foe in these tortured and corrupted pawns of the mentally disturbed creature named Mr Hyde,' the lion spoke proudly.

Ryan was still confused and concerned. 'Uh, thanks, but where are you taking Melissa? Don't we already have a stash of medicine in one of the burrows?' Ryan asked whilst looking at Casandra who had come to see what was happening.

She nodded and responded, 'Yeah, but there are too many wounded for us to treat. This help is greatly appreciated. I am still amazed that you guys turned up though. Ryan, you may be able to head to the Citadel with Melissa if you wish. We should probably be greeting our other friends that came to help; the vultures.' Prince Bartholomew ordered the other medics to help the wounded hyenas. Some of the attacker's carcasses were being loaded onto the tyrannosaur's back to be taken back for study. One that had its guts ripped out was still struggling as it was hog tied, as if it were a reanimated corpse.

Several members of the clan were wandering around in great distress at the sight of the bodies of their family members that lay between the corpses of their attackers. Others, including Cassandra, had decided to feast on the carcasses of their enemy.

The medics checked Ryan's wounds and invited him to travel in the ambulance car with Melissa. The presence of such a machine out here in the hands of the Citadel seemed strange. He noticed the massive flock of vultures that had helped in the battle were now coming down to feast on the fallen carcasses, including those of the slain hyenas. Some were squabbling over the remains. The turkey vultures made up the majority. Two condors had joined the flock and even a wandering lappet-faced vulture was there.

A familiar face appeared among the scavenging birds. The king of the vultures flew down, white wings flapping to a stop as he landed on the ground. He grabbed a piece of offal. 'I'm going to take this little piece right here,' he said as he dragged it away. 'Hey, it's you two again, the puma and the dingo. I can see there has been quite the disaster here. I am deeply sorry for your loss. It's great to see those who have survived though.' The king vulture looked around at the group, his brightly coloured head sticking above his white layer of feathers.

Cassandra came out from her meal, licking blood off her chops, leaving the rest of the head drenched in gore. 'Hello again, old friend. I'm sorry for not really being in a talkative mood, things went really bad here.'

The king vulture nodded grimly. 'So, I see.'

'Thank you very much for your hospitality, Cassandra,' said Ryan, 'But we have to go. Melissa needs to get medical attention, along with the other wounded survivors. Can we come back again if we need to?'

'Of course. You and Melissa are always welcome,' Cassandra said walking over to say goodbye to her daughter.

As she parted with her extended foster family, Melissa and the hyenas snuggled and sniffed each other goodbye.

The ambulance turned to leave for the Citadel several minutes later, having gathered all the wounded. The puma rode on top of the car, the nervous flick of his tail expressed worry for his friend riding in the back. He looked over the grasslands, taking in the scenery as the four-wheel drive vehicle drove ahead of the other animals following them back to the Citadel.

The massive volcano now loomed over them. But the rainforest up the slopes was not yet visible. He could see the first of the jungle

215

birds and he noticed light from the fires of a small village on top of a set of cliffs to the east of the grand central valley. Up at the higher points above the canyon, jungle trees gave way to conifer forests, with alpine tundra above that. Even the first small layers of snow were visible near the top of the mountain.

The wydah birds were out, and blue and red butterflies came fluttering over the wet long grass that was waving in the breeze. To the west, many miles away, massive metal and concrete pillars hung over the savanna and desert. Near them were small hills composed of the rubble from other towers.

Ryan took time to look ahead to where the vehicle was now heading – the area above the savanna grasslands. They drove over another ridge. Beyond this ridge were large, marked fields, which were growing different crops, both cereals and vegetables. Fruit orchards of citrus, marula, date palm and sausage fruit trees could also be seen.

Beyond these, there was a moat like river and what looked to be suburbs around a massive stone wall.

The buildings inside the wall towered over them. The identity of two of them immediately became obvious; the giant cathedral steeple, over a hundred metres tall, and the enormous castle-like construction that covered most of the interior of the wall's space. They had finally reached the Citadel.

Chapter 24

I Fought the Law

Dennis

The huge, strong lioness that had her jaws clamped around his neck dragged Dennis into the black basalt hallways, paws tied up. Any attempt to squirm too much or escape would be met by certain death in this situation. She dragged him over a set of antelope fur rugs that had been sewn together.

The lioness dropped him at the foot of a throne in the centre of the room on a softer long rug that lay the length of the room. This one was made from dyed wool, shorn from dozens of guanacos, llama-like creatures, several years before and imported from the Opal Empire over three hundred kilometres to the west. The walls were draped in tapestries of battle, hunting, work, and history of the Principalities and others. The figures in tapestries were carefully woven into the wool. Some of the tapestries also doubled as curtains over the large windows.

Many other creatures surrounded him in the black hall, some of which were familiar. Others were new to Dennis. And of course, there was the throne.

This was a magnificent construct, two and a half metres tall. It was carved from a solid basalt block and finely decorated. The arms on the throne had a lion head on each side; not carvings but the taxidermy remains of lions. Their glass eyes stared out across the hall. The fur from their manes blended with the chair as manes of many other lions covered the sides and the base. Atop of this fluffy base was a single large beige cushion. Behind it was the engraved back of the throne. At its top was a wreath of horns and antlers from various hooved animals. Eland, buffalo, Mountain nyala, Oryx, Nile lechwe, elephant tusks, sambar, elks, deer, and even dropped reindeer antlers.

A smaller ornately carved wooden throne was next to it. This throne was carved from fine rainforest hardwoods, partly made of mahogany and ebony. Its top held several plant pots, filled with brilliant tall white, red, and purple flowering orchids. A light green cushion was on the base of this chair.

Carefully manicured vines also cascaded down from the constructions. Yet for all the splendour of the thrones, lit up in the afternoon light through the western window, the occupants of the seats were very small.

The bodyguard lioness dwarfed the tiny head that peered over the end of the cushion. Another smaller head was on the wooden throne to the left. The creature upon it was a lizard, covered in uneven black and white splotches. The king of the Principalities and his partner were black and white tegus, a large omnivorous South American lizard species.

'All hail the High Principal King Gerald and his mate, Queen Ellaine. All please bow before your monarch.'

The entire court bowed to their ruler. Dennis merely slumped onto the floor, bowing his head out of respect and out of a dislike of having his head ripped from his shoulders. He tried to pull himself up before everyone rose.

'Thank you for your attendance. I see that today I have some issues relating to carnivores, trespassers, criminals and captured Sixth Sunners. All will need to be dealt with in this session. First to come is... who is it? A pitiful dog?' The king gestured to the wounded animal staring up from the floor.

'My name is Dennis. I am a dingo and a carnivore. I killed one of your citizens for food out of hunger before your soldiers caught me. I understand that you would rather see me dead, and probably my pelt added to someone's rug around here. Is this what you want to do with me? Flay my sorry hide to add to your throne? I know I murdered her, but unless your lions are vegans, they too also need to hunt for flesh like I did. This was my first meal in days. Are you going to kill me or are you going to enslave me to do menial tasks?' Dennis did not plead for mercy, guessing his first life on this planet would end quickly.

'If this were peace time, I guess I would, but not now. War beckons and we need warriors to defend our borders. Perhaps our military can knock some sense into your foolish head and make you a fine warrior one day. Perhaps they will even use you for breeding stock, though that depends on whether you will be allowed a mate. If you prove yourself worthy, that might happen.

'However, now I decree that you will be taken out of my throne room and begin your training upon the morrow with our allies in the kingdom; that is providing you survive the initiation rites. They are starting to experiment with carnivores in their ranks; quite different from their previous policy of exterminating the carnivores. After a two-week period, you will be transferred back to the mountain town to continue your training there. You will be far from the current theatre of war up on the mountain, however.'

'Not so far away from the war as you might think,' Dennis replied sternly, staring the lizard in the eye, and drawing his eyes back to him.

'Careful what you say, dog. What did you see?' the lizard asked.

'I was up on the mountainside a few weeks ago, before I decided to cross the desert. There was an earthquake, which shook the side of the mountain. After a large landslide, the slipped rocks revealed a passage into the mountain. It had clean halls of steel and white painted concrete,' Dennis said.

'This we already know about. Anything else before I have you dragged out of this room,' the tegu asked sternly.

Felicia, who was also present in the room spoke up. 'Wait, Dennis is a good man, he has been roped into things far bigger than he knows. He has made only one mission-jeopardising mistake. He could provide some information on exactly what was seen at the mountain before the sunlight drove the remaining alien wildlife down into the tunnels below. Plus, there is plenty more he can help with; perhaps going to help the kingdom with their spider silk situation.'

Dennis stared at her as she spoke. He had no idea she was there. Grateful for her intervention, Dennis spoke confidently, looking at the lizard who was staring at him. 'I saw one last thing, which you may not know about. The lake at the base of the landslide is connected to another tunnel, one not covered in steel. It was deep and mysterious. The water that poured out was glowing in a pale blue colour. Strange creatures were swimming in the water. I tried to catch them. They did not speak, but they were fish-like things with pale blue skin, and four big black eyes, two on each side. Weird crab-like creatures also crawled in that pool along with something that looked like a huge millipede with armoured flanges.'

'Strange you speak of such creatures. We did not see them on our investigation after the landslide, but perhaps they simply hate the light. There would be much to learn if we could get a closer look at what lives up there. We would be most interested in finding a passage into the great underground tunnels of the planet, the tunnels that some creatures claim, stretch the circumference of our world.' Before Dennis could respond, he started again, 'I have already consulted the scientist who has a great deal of knowledge of plate tectonics, xenobiology and had once worked for the Terraformers.' The tegu gestured for Felicia to come out.

'Thanks, Dennis, for getting me here. I would have never made it otherwise. Akash has confirmed that the pool was covered up after the cave partly caved in. Had you not caught that lemur we could have just walked in,' the bushbaby spoke calmly.

Dennis glowered at her the entire time she was speaking. Behind her, Akash sat upon a perch.

'Traitors, the pair of you. Why didn't you tell me you were working for them?' Dennis snarled.

'I told you I had a very important mission. I needed to transmit classified information and scientific equipment and samples from the volcano and the Opal Empire relating to tectonic instability on this planet. I needed to cross the desert. Akash was originally meant to pick me up, but you got us lost. I have come a long way. That cactus forest was not my original home. I used to live in the Opal Empire and had been catching a spur-winged goose over, but as I told you, he died. I was stranded so I needed help completing the journey. You provided the help I needed.

'Akash would have carried me and the bag of samples, but we needed your personal testimony since we did not see the fish or the entrance to the tunnel. I do wish you the best of luck in your future endeavours, friend.' The primate stared at him, her eyes wide and black and her pointed ears pricked in his direction.

The dog still growled. The wallaby judge hammered loudly with his wooden mallet from his podium to gain quiet in the throne room.

Denis thought the action was a mockery of an actual court proceeding back on earth.

'In the meanwhile,' said the King, 'you will be taken to the mining camp on the side of the mountain to begin training as a soldier for our cause. We need to get that wound in your side healed first. You will be drafted into our military, complete with a tracking microchip to prevent your desertion.'

The lizard's expression conveyed his interest in Dennis's welfare. The lioness took the dingo out of the room. She put him into a cart that would take him to the vet hospital. Dennis's free roaming had ended.

***

'Who watches the guards?' asked the buffalo guarding the other side of the entrance to the room where a meeting was taking place. More animals waited to enter the room.

Getting the guard job was good for Natashia, but she knew that it meant she still needed to be watched lest she be a spy or saboteur. Right now, she was posted outside the meeting room with one ear to the door, listening keenly to what was being said within. Occasionally she would peer through a tiny hole in the wall and look for anything interesting.

The coati sat in his chair, upright like a cat. The door opened and Natashia and the guards posted at the door let the rest of the animals through. The door guard was to prevent any unwanted individuals venturing in. She reviewed each invitation and checked the animal against the woodblock print of the faces of invited guests. A wallaby had forgotten his invitation, so she removed him from the queue. He was pinned down and dragged away. By the time she got back, it was her job to close the door. She shoved it back into place.

Exactly how she had gained such privilege was a surprise. She inquired about a job, and they promised her one on the understanding that she had to maintain secrecy about the position. She signed the contract with a great feeling of unease and potential regret. She had not considered closely what she had got herself into. It was arguably the most confidential and serious contract she had ever signed. Before it had been just her life at risk, but this contract could put her in the position where her actions could endanger the lives of many others.

221

Now she was guarding the hall under the wood-covered hill. The torch illuminated room was entirely underground. The assembled crowd of hand-picked potential recruits and other more trusted creatures was waiting for the coati lord's speech to begin.

'Welcome, ladies and gentlemen. I have something I need to tell you. A select number of us have been invited to be involved in this project. By the time it is completed, it is likely that everyone will have heard of it. Now all those here must know that there is no going back out of this. Anyone who stays must keep the utmost secrecy about what I am about to say.'

Natashia was beginning to regret guarding this meeting, let alone being employed by this lord.

The coati lord continued his speech, 'There is something very wrong in the Kingdom. Since our chief, Suleiman left, everything has become worse, as we have seen. Before, the only executions were for carnivores, traitors, and the worst of criminals. Now they rip apart and kill creatures daily in the most depraved ways. Teams moving in the opposite direction rip some apart. Others have boiling sugar poured over them. There are crucifixions, public torture, live devouring, vivisection, forced self-cannibalisation, flaying. Atrocity after atrocity has been going on since Suleiman left for musth.

'After Ronda was disposed of, either by coup or by assassination, Andrew took the position of leader. However, his behaviour is beyond the normal blood lust he had back when Suleiman was still around. Why this is happening is apparent to some of us. A figure known as Mr Hyde sneaked his way into the hierarchy of power before Suleiman left. These atrocities are mostly happening in the company of that wretched creature, Mr Hyde. He walks around covered in rotting hides, occasionally adding small animals to his mask. Judging from the lack of reaction to his atrocities, I have deep suspicions that he is in fact an admin creature abusing his powers.'

There was a stunned silence in the room. Natashia, who was listening through the wall scowled in confusion.

'It will be only a matter of time before they destroy all those he wants to torture, torment, and kill. Then he will encourage them to increase their efforts against us. I have an idea how we could help stop this tyranny. Many of the animals still in the Kingdom want out and will resort to extreme methods to escape. More now get shot than make it out. There are hundred toiling to their deaths in the factories and quarries. So many are dying that this sustains their carnivores. Rumours have been going around that they have been recruiting more carnivores. Any criticism of that makes me hypocritical. I recently hired a white tigress.'

The coati took a sip from a small water bowl before continuing, 'A group of birds led by a hornbill left three weeks ago to find an admin creature who could remove the brainwashing inflicted by Mr Hyde. Well good luck to them if they succeed, since the potential candidates for admins between here and the Citadel are non-existent. I, however, have a far more cunning and dangerous plan, operation "Cloth doll" we've called it.

'It may surprise you, but some members of their government have fallen into corruption. This is great as one member of their council has agreed to collaborate with us for our profit and to save hundreds of their citizens' lives. Desperate times have called for desperate measures. We are going to buy them out with certain products that are in high demand for trading purposes. The Sixth Sunners have much demand for hemp, lumber, and certain other chemical substances. The emperor of the Sixth Sun Empire has banned these chemicals in his domain, or more precisely, the growing of drugs, but there is a black-market demand,' the coati proclaimed.

Natashia did a double-take. She looked in disbelief at the buffalo standing at the other door. *What had she gotten herself into?*

'Seriously, are you going to release slaves by trading with drugs?' an animal in the crowd said after raising his paw.

Natashia knew of these drugs. One, cannabis, had been legalised years ago back home but she never tried it. As far as she was concerned, all illicit drugs had a horrible effect on health and mind. She did well to stay away from them.

'Yes, drugs, like marijuana, catnip, cocaine, angel trumpet and magic mushrooms. There is a hemp factory where the slaves are making hempen cloths and fabrics. However, their soils do not support hemp as well as ours does over here. We can grow more with higher quality. Hempen fabric is legal in the Sixth Sun Empire. However, we can ship our products back west to the Opal Empire or south to the Principalities, the Citadel, or even the desert land Pirate Raiders. The quarter masters of the factories will accept enough hemp and other such products if it equals the price of some of their slaves. Also, we will have others making slave escapes easier for those working in the factories. So many rat holes can be enlarged and exploited for our purposes. We will need to negotiate the deal correctly. They already have a hemp trade agreement. The river can sometimes be used to distribute materials to us.

'That is another thing that could make rebellion easier or win over more affection from the factory supervisors. The trade with the Sixth Sunners would normally never happen under Suleiman's rule, but he is not there, and the mad beast's torture factory needs a legitimate front, despite the fact we are still technically at war with Sixth Sunners. Perhaps the Principalities or the other eastern civilisations will be their victims this year. This we can use against him.

'However, to smuggle other objects into the Sixth Sun Empire, we need some way to hide them. We will cover the suspicious stuff in hemp smell! They will be thinking that it is just another hemp shipment or the shipments of recreational drugs to them, but instead we will be smuggling weapons and high-tech gadgetry to assist in their rebellion. We will take something out, perhaps bags of manure fertiliser, and between the sacks, dozens of fleeing refugees hiding between the overwhelming scent of manure or drugs.

'The damn guards will be misled trying to sniff the stuff. It's not glorious or pretty but it would be hilarious if we can smuggle out refugees and contraband right under the noses of the border guards. We can even work without this if done correctly. We need to discuss this in more depth at a later point.'

His words captivated Natashia. She nodded in agreement. Finally, she would be part of something like the insurgency. She would now be able to genuinely help people, even if less honourable methods had to be employed to do so.

The coati continued, 'To carry out this plan, we need to gain support of someone from the inside.'

The racoon gestured to the door.

Natashia moved out of the way as a pair of gorillas turning a large wheel pulled the door locking rocks from the ground.

Juliet, the saola, one of the inner circle of Andrew's administration, walked into the room. The brown furred bovid walked through the door under the surprised stare of Natashia. Two tamaraw guards with capuchin riders came after her as her bodyguards.

'Surprise seeing you here!' the coati said. It was no surprise at all to him. He, of course, had planned it to happen.

Natashia gaped in shock. She had not expected one of the most respected members of the chief's council to be corrupt enough to work with the coati lord in his scheme. She had only previously heard of her by name. This person had not been a combatant in the previous fighting at the Kingdom's fort.

'Hello, I believe we have important business to discuss. I would not normally associate with such creatures as you, nor your drug dealing industry, but the situation is sufficiently severe to allow this to happen. I did not consider this lightly. However, what Mr Hyde is doing to the nation I love and want the best for, leaves me with no other reasonable option. If we do nothing, then Mr Hyde will slowly torture and kill increasingly more of us, causing irreversible damage to the Kingdom. So, I need to help save my people, even if it means working with some of our enemies, metaphorical devils and traitors.'

Many of the people within the room were angry and displeased with her presence and her words.

'I want more than to just evacuate the factory workers. Disposing of Andrew and Mr Hyde is a goal, although that will be a long way off unless Suleiman comes back with an army of pagan nut-jobs chasing him down or following him from the east or an army of escaped members of my nation. I want to get this done before the Empire of the Sixth Sun does it to us and kills us all in the process. I am not yet ready to hand over our nation to them, preferring to preserve our sovereignty. If this continues, I will not want to stay and watch the nation fall into more and more severe oppression of everyone.

'That gorilla broke his promise to the mammoth of being subservient to his appointed ruler, Ronda, the spectacled bear, letting the monster, Mr Hyde into our town. This is our chance to make Andrew less capable of fighting the next army that comes after him. We need to be the ones that finish him off. If we succeed, this will get rid of both Mr Hyde's and Andrew's reign and restore the rule of Suleiman.'

'Wait, does this make you kind of corrupt?' a member of the crowd rudely called out.

'You do have a point. I am also technically committing treason by associating with you. Sometimes the legally wrong thing can be the morally right thing against a tyrannical regime,' she said as she looked at Natashia who was standing in the doorway.

'Do I recognise you? You've had history with us, haven't you?' the bovid asked the tiger.

'Yes, I was once seized on one of your hunts, but I escaped and made my way here.'

The coati considered her for a moment. 'I believe we have already registered you and hired you into the army. I have a little project for you. I could have handed you in for that time you tried to kill Sulieman and for being a known insurgency member. Good thing that they are now in cahoots with us. I will be visiting the textile factories in a few days to gain some of the black spider silk that is as strong as Kevlar. We need the help of animals like you to gather the silk. It makes bullet proof armour that we will need to make ourselves resistant to their weapons. To the swamp we must go. You, Natashia are dismissed.' The coati finished speaking before putting the cigarette back into his mouth and continuing with his paperwork.

Hopefully, the entire idea was not thought up under the influence, she thought. The tigress was left giddy with excitement. She would help to save other creatures from what sounded like a terrible fate. Thoughts whirled through Natashia's head as she left the room following a parade of the other animals.

***

Filtered sunlight filled the dingy armoury room. Natashia came into the chamber to be armoured. She strode up to the dressing table. Several monkeys, cuscuses, coatis, and opossums were assembling the black silk armour. They draped the silk-like material over her back. The squirrels that had come to help with this stage were quickly tying the under-layer on. Parts of her head, underbelly, and lower legs were left unarmoured.

Then the coati hoisted the wooden plates on, and attached metal pieces along the back, the shoulder plates, and her helmet. The armour was complete with a studded chain-link scarf-like part that they placed over her neck. The squirrels were pulling the hempen ties tight to hold the armour pieces in place, tying it delicately into knots.

Natashia waited impatiently while they finished her armour. She looked towards the entrance of the room; several other animals were sufficiently armoured. The coati was now bringing the crossbow platform to her, the base of which was already built into her back armour. Other animals came into the room to be armoured. Possums, cuscuses, and tree kangaroos were getting their various tools ready for harvesting the silk. A long-haired striped hyena was one of the animals going over to get outfitted. Behind him came a dingo, his ears flattened, and tail tucked in fear. He relaxed a bit upon seeing that they were armouring up for battle.

'Well, hello there, fellow comrades… oh I guess, that didn't come out right,' Natashia said.

The dingo looked up at the armoured tigress and spoke. 'Natashia, is that you?!' he spoke softly while still expressing surprise.

Natashia was still confused until she remembered back to the drop ship. 'Dennis, is that really you! But you were released miles from here,' Natashia said wrapping a large foreleg around Dennis.

The dingo froze before calming down. 'Sorry, I'm a bit on edge. Had a bad incident with some lions back south, got myself arrested and sent here as part of my punishment. Though this is more of a promotion than a punishment, I guess.' Dennis spoke looking at Natashia's facial armour, which left wide holes for the eyes.

'Why were you arrested?' Natashia asked, curiosity piquing her voice.

'Ate a civilian. It was a bad way for the prey to die. It's not the worst thing I have ever done by a long shot, but it's the one that got me caught,' Dennis admitted.

'I did too. I got shot with a crossbow for that. Then the rest of the Kingdom came after me. Got myself arrested but I escaped with help from the insurgency,' she replied with a sense of confidence in her voice.

Dennis stared at the suit of armour that moved easily as Natashia walked around the room. 'Good for you. That armour of yours looks good. From what I have seen, it looks like it's from the Principalities. The lionesses that chased me wore similar armour.'

227

The hyena was already getting his armour fitted. Dennis was about to go over to the waiting team of cuscuses and squirrels when he asked one last question. 'How old were you when you died as a human? Just wondering, as I was about 36 at the time of my first and so far, only death.' Dennis flinched slightly as the cuscuses started to move his black silk vest over his body.

'I was only 14. I died of leukaemia. Honestly, while this life has been dangerous and scary, I am still enjoying myself; when I am not too badly hurt that is. I'm still uncomfortable with killing animals who have done nothing against me,' she replied.

'I'm so sorry for you, to have to go through this so young. Trust me, kid, this world doesn't give two shits about you unless you make it. We must look out for ourselves and each other. You especially,' Dennis commented.

'How about we be friends. We can help each other learn the ropes,' Natashia said.

Dennis replied, 'Sadly, I'm down here for only a few days. After the initiation with the spiders, I'm being posted up on the mountain, but we can definitely be comrades in the meanwhile.' As he spoke, his iron helmet was fitted over his head, blades coming up the middle of the muzzle.

It was at that point the door swung open and two strange figures walked into the room, one small and the other enormous. Both figures moved bipedally. Natashia adjusted her eyes and stared at the larger figure.

Dennis was still gaping at them both. 'So, a human and a dinosaur just walked in. I mean, I knew about the pterosaurs out on the deserts, but humans? Why are there humans here? I thought this was mostly for the animals, right?' Dennis spluttered in surprise as Natashia continued to study the pair.

'I have not seen you two before. You don't look like you are from around here,' Natashia said.

'We are mercenaries from Arabia terra,' the larger animal, a scaly therapod dinosaur began.

'No, we're the hunters of glory! Great and mighty mercenaries searching for fame, money, glory and the glorious ascension to

Valhalla!' the human warrior boasted, holding both axes out from his body.

'Please ignore him, he's over the top like this a lot. The chap is more than half mad,' the spinosaurid dinosaur spoke, the conical teeth visible along his elongated snout as he gestured with his arms to the enthusiastic human.

'And exactly who is this mad man?' Dennis had to ask.

'Me, oh, I'm Sigbjorn Ragnarson, I am searching for the most epic of dooms; a demise so grand and awe inspiring that the gods shall notice and approve; finally making me worthy of entering Valhalla after so many lives.'

Dennis shook his head. 'Okay, so you are mad, fanatically religious, a mercenary, have a British accented dinosaur as your friend and are suicidal, anything else you want to tell us in a normal voice.'

'He used to be an office working accountant named Steve. He once lived in England and was a strict protestant, emphasis on used to be. Despite both of us being Englishmen, he is truly the madder of us two,' the dinosaur continued.

'Still, we need to armour up and prepare ourselves. The boat will soon be leaving for the spider colony. We will need to be ready for the upcoming battle. Though I suspect I may be swimming or fighting on the ground and not in the trees like you. Also, are the possum riders kind of prone to, you know, involuntarily playing possum under heavy stress or fear?' the dinosaurs said.

The opossums that were attaching the hyenas armour looked firstly as if they were insulted, then with more understanding.

'We usually try not to end up on the front lines for that reason. Still, we will give our best to help our side in battle, especially while riding upon the back of our mounts,' the opossum spoke as the hyena finally came out and joined the others.

Meanwhile, Sigbjorn unpacked the spinosaur's armour pieces and moved them over the larger dinosaurs back as they prepared to head out on the hunt. 'When were done, we will be meeting by the docks.'

Several hours later, Natashia was ready for the spider silk hunt; the test to see her worthiness as a soldier. In the evening, she headed down through the loud and raucous town, gaining many stares and some fearful reactions as she walked along.

When she reached the rickety mangrove docks, she trotted across the planks. Other animals were moving backwards and forwards loading and unloading ships. She saw a massive barge tied to the end of the harbour. Animals were taking supplies, including pullies aboard. They mounted weapons on the boat. She noted cannons and pickle guns amongst them. Elsewhere muskets were attached to rotatable posts along with scorpion bows at other points in the ship.

Natashia paused for a moment, realising that she had not seen firearms anywhere else so far; not even the kingdom used them normally.

More animals loaded and restocked the immense steamboat's charcoal engine room. The entry was visible through a small room off to the side. It was two stories tall with a massive engine in the centre made from a destroyed terraforming machine. Small animals worked as the crew with their dexterous paws. The captain's cabin was high up near the top of the vessel.

In the line-up, she spotted familiar faces in the boarding crowd. Dennis and that hyena Audie were ahead, climbing up the ramp together, talking to each other. Behind them came several more animals.

The dinosaur made a large splash as he leapt off to the side of the dock, wearing his armour. He quickly resurfaced with a gasp before diving again.

Natashia spotted the familiar human watching his friend swim around in the water. Sigbjorn saw her and walked over. 'Oh, hello there, nice to see you again, Natashia. Are you excited for today's hunt?' He gestured to his friend in the water. 'Bentley can swim just fine. He's going to be more use in the water than on the ship. The others are still back on the coast. They should be coming through after that coati finally signs the mercenary contract. They are then going to have to do another hunt.'

A bear joined them and Sigbjorn said, 'Another member of our crew is also having an induction today. Natashia, this is Asuka, Asuka, this is Natashia.' He gestured to the two of them.

Natashia tried to shake paws with the ill-fitting paw of the Asian black bear. She said, "Nice to meet you. I love your armour, by the way.'

The bear shied her head a bit from Natashia's retort, her dark red and black amour moved, different plates sliding over each other. A large set of metal horns came up from her armour's head piece. A red tattoo of a sigil on her paw flashed briefly. Behind that on her arm, was a mechanical contraption that held a folded-up sword, a set of metal talons was on her other foreleg.

'It looks like we are boarding soon. Say, I do wonder if we will have to contend with crocodiles and bull sharks as well on our hunt,' Asuka asked nervously.

Sigbjorn boasted, 'Pah sharks, I've killed at least a dozen of them in my time with my axes alone. I remember hearing from a visayan deer a while ago about a puma that had a tug-of-war with a nurse shark over a hunk of venison; and their teeth are not even designed for meat. I'm not worried. I do really want to see these giant spiders though. Have not seen them yet.' By the time he finished, the bear and tiger had already walked up the gangplank and onto the boat.

'Hey, wait for me!' The axe wielder spoke as the ship's whistle blew. Moments after boarding, the step ladder was rolled away, and the ropes taken back.

A team of manatees tied to the boat helped pulled the ships away from the docks without engines.

As the steamboat left harbour, Natashia sat on the second floor, watching other parts of this town passing by. Beyond the crop fields, she could see that tied vines, cut branches and wooden gangplanks linked the tops of trees together. These walkways led to crude huts that were small basket like structures placed into the trees' branches. Many mammals inhabited the trees. Monkeys, cuscus, possums, and rats all made their way along the mangrove walkways with opossums and monkeys. Lizards and birds moved through the mangrove district as well.

In more sheltered spots, high enough not to be inundated daily, a patch of huge cotton trees stood, their lower trunks disappearing into a messy conglomerate of shacks and buildings. Several floors of these buildings had a height of only a few metres. Each floor was far shorter than her. The buildings continued among the mangroves that grew in the water. These were shared common spaces and shops, worked in shifts based on the tides. During the low tide, mammals worked in this area. During the high tide, fish took over the tasks.

This town was hidden in the depths of the eastern river delta, in the pocket of land separating the Kingdom from the Sixth Sunners further to the east. It was a sanctuary for those pushed out by both factions.

Mangrove town was in contact with the Burrows fortress and the Citadel much further inland. Between the borders of the Sixth Sunners and the Kingdom was the swamp.

The village preferred to keep to itself away from the prying eyes of outsiders. This river was separated from the main river, except for an inlet to the west where the boats came in and out as they travelled up the main channel that connected with the ocean.

Chapter 25

Into the Spider's Parlour ...

Natashia and Dennis

The massive trees of the swamp hung over the lagoon below. They began after the ship had sailed through a channel between two huge concrete walls of stone. The remnants of a surrounding wall from centuries ago appeared. Massive bull pines shadowed the parts of the forest floor not underwater. Travelling through here on foot would be more like swimming since this area was a swamp forest. Here, the swamp and jungle merged into a tangled underwater jungle.

Various inundation-tolerant dipterocarp trees, common in regular parts of the rainforest grew as well. As the water deepened, normal looking trees disappeared. Below them shrubs and bushes such as tall tree ferns reached up. In other parts, horsetails and saw grass cut off the channels. Pandanus grew, rooted on the few small islands.

The smell from the swamp was abhorrent. The pungent stench of rotting plants mixed with the rotten eggs smell from the occasional animal carcass. In these waters, other creatures lived. Crocodiles revealed themselves along the route. Giant otters appeared occasionally near the cattails on the shore. Catfish swam under the boat as they travelled along. The large swamp boat did not include any water creatures. Their business was a land animal's job, or to be more accurate, a climbing animal's job.

The normal loud swamp chorus of bird song gave way to a more sinister silence. Even the drone of the mosquitos and the cicadas seemed to drop off as they approached their destination. When they came across a leaning kauri pine, it became apparent that this was no ordinary foe. A huge black silken cable, as wide as Natashia's paw, was attached to a part of the trunk. Other cables were wrapped around the other parts of the trunk.

The widest she saw was a whole metre wide, attached to other trees and keeping the trunks upright. This kauri pine and the others in this grove were far larger than the norm of their species. They were closer in size and scale to the American sequoias at the base and not normal height for a mature specimen of their species.

The black web spreading through the trees was the treasure they sought. This web continued for some distance through the forest. It seemed like a black abyss formed of tens of thousands of black threads. Hanging from one of them was a crocodile carcass wrapped up in the silk. There were other blobs, birds and monkeys snagged in the webs.

An elephant carcass was halfway out of the water and only partly wrapped in the webs. The carcass was rotting. Putrid flesh was leaking from one of the big holes in its side. Some of the animals diverted their eyes in disgust. Even the vultures would not touch such a carcass, as it stood there unmoving in the water. From the boat, they could smell the unpleasant odour. Natashia scrunched up her nose in disgust and her ears betrayed her horror as they flattened back against her skull; but this was a situation where she had to be brave.

Dennis came up to the deck where Natashia was sitting. Noticing the smaller animals on her back harness, he said, 'Well doesn't that look intimidating.'

The opossum, one of the four operators of the crossbow on her back, greeted the dingo. 'Err, hello, Sir, my name is Bonnie.' Two of the riders were hutia, which resembled large rats, and there was another opossum.

One of the hutias said, 'We're named Hanzel, Bruce and Kim. None of us are sure what today's initiation is going to be like. I mean, we only got onto this tiger's back today. It's a bit different from firing from the training dummies.'

The engineers stopped shoving peat into the furnace and the ship turned and stopped. The manatees assisted by pushing the ship so it could rest. Bales of water hyacinth were tossed over to feed them. They would get their monetary payment back at the dock.

The crew lowered the first gangplank for getting onto the webs. The various soldiers preparing to help were readying themselves. Dennis, Audie, Asuka, and Sigbjorn were all waiting for the command to begin the assault.

The ship's captain pointed at the partly fallen tree on the edge of the clearing. 'This is far enough; we will be cutting the strands attached to that tree over there.' The crew threw ropes from the boat's roof and tied it to other trees near the base of the kauri pine. The drop bridge was released from the deck and was hooked into the decomposing part of the tree. Climbing animals moved onto the bridge as they began to disembark. Natashia joined her new-found friends as they ran out onto the tree trunk.

'Is this the best possible way of doing it?' Natashia asked the opossum and the hutia on her back.

'Yes, and this is the best place for the black web. Any closer and we would be in more danger. Now get on with it. Please get us to the tree branch,' the hutia named Bruce urged.

She leapt off the boat and swiftly climbed the tree to reach the location of the black webs. When she reached the place, she sat down on the leaning tree trunk. The webs held it up. Most of the tree's base had decomposed.

The animals clambered up onto the tree to find the best pieces of webs that they could cut swiftly, without whatever might be hiding in the black mass attacking them.

Shark tooth saws, obsidian and even iron saws and axes were pulled out from the boat and hauled up the trunks towards the various anchor points. Incredibly strong adhesive chemicals that had soaked through the tree's bark attached the black silk to the tree. Those daring enough to do so could climb the webs.

The other initiates were also cutting. Asuka's sword was already extended, hacking into one stretch of silk. Sigbjorn slammed his axes repeatedly into the other end. The immense force released from the snapping silk, breaking like a suspension cable, and making a thunderous crack as it did so, almost threw him off the branch.

A group of monkeys climbed out onto the black webs, carrying the giant saw with them. They were carefully treading to avoid causing vibrations that could awaken the spiders. They manoeuvred the saw onto the web, about thirty metres out. Near the black mass, they begun to saw – ripping the thousands of small threads with the shark's teeth. As threads were cut, the remaining strands had to hold more and more weight. This could easily backfire with horrible consequences.

Dennis rushed along with the hyena onto the trees. 'We probably would not be of any help cutting, so instead let's focus on killing as many spiders as we can.' He was searching for any attackers when he saw the precarious nature of the silk collection.

The other animals were sawing on different strands. When they began to snap, creatures held onto the remaining strands as the sections of cut web contracted instantaneously like rubber bands, hitting the logs with audible cracks akin to those of a whip. A few animals forgot to let go properly and were suddenly launched into the air and flung into the canopy, the water, or worse still deeper into the mass of webs. Those on the web would have to vacate quickly. A cuscus among those flung, wheeled through the air for at least fifty metres before splashing into the dark water below.

It was then the first of the spiders turned up. They were enormous; a bit over a metre from their pedipalps to the curve of their scorpion like abdomens. They cast the black silk from spinnerets on the end of the abdomen. Some spiders were swinging on silk, like trapeze artists, their silvery bodies glistening in the canopy light. Other spiders, a different caste from the first lot, jumped out on webbed legs, gliding downward, and aiming for the ship. Bigger spiders came rumbling through the webs. Thousands of smaller, younger spiders came teeming out of the webs and the waterlogged carcasses. These smaller spiders were darker than their silvery parents.

The dingo barked as he set off into battle, the hyena following him. Their purpose was to clear every spider between where they were and the other unlucky group of web-gatherers further up. Three spiders, larger than they had seemed came clambering down.

The hyena jumped at the first one, which was coming straight at them. He crushed the spider's brain and eyes with a single bone crushing snap. The dingo leapt over him, dodging the tail before leaping and biting the raised tail of the spider behind them. He dragged it down and snapped at the three legs, cracking the exoskeleton in three limbs on the right-hand side in quick succession. He then leapt off as Audie dove underneath and rapidly stood up, dislodging the spider above him.

The dingo raced ahead, clambering up along the surprisingly easy to grip black silk. He looked up and saw in horror that the small group

236

of working animals had at least 20 spiders bearing down on them, jumping, leaping, and clawing their way down from the treetops.

He paused for just a second. He could just head down, continue helping those below him and leaving the group of animals to die. He thought they all would probably die anyway, so he could just run back to the safer part of the webs. Hanging his head in frustration, he decided that would not be what he would do. If he did, he would be condemning his colleagues to die. Audie was busy getting another spider off his back, defending several creatures lower down.

Dennis leaped, grabbing a hanging section of silk with his teeth. Swinging along the line, until he could grab the log with his claws, he rapidly dragged himself up onto the log. He was almost too late for the ten animals working there.

An opossum that had been flung into the web was suddenly grabbed by a spider that poured silk out of its spinnerets to tie the creature up. The spider's fangs sunk into the animal's flesh. It fainted even before the fangs reached it. The spider devoured it.

Dennis leapt into action, throwing some of the hutias off into the water with his mouth with enough force to cut their skin. He yelled, 'We have to get out of here now, we're about to be ambushed!'

He barked the warning just as the spiders arrived. One landed directly on top of him, pinning him to the tree trunk, the fangs glancing off his armour as it tried to stab him. The dingo yelped and squirmed. Another spider began feasting on a black and white cuscus that failed to leap in time. Most of the others were about to leap.

It was then something jumped on to the back of the spider atop of Dennis, almost crushing him under the combined weight. A roar filled by splitting, cracking, squealing and a shriek followed. Asuka's sword missed Dennis by centimetres. She threw the dead spider off, helping the dog to his feet.

Dennis turned to the bear. 'Thank you for saving my life. We need to get out of here.'

The black bear in the red armour had come tearing up the webs, shredding the still hardening silk with her claws and blades. The bear and the dingo grabbed the animals and threw them down near a floating log in the water. Asuka grabbed a silk-throwing spider with her paws and bit down hard, crushing a weak patch of the exoskeleton with her teeth. Another spider came bounding along a fraying section

237

of web up behind the Asiatic black bear and proceeded towards the remaining cuscus. The strands finally gave way and that section of web flung inwards towards the log, with a thunderous crack.

The spider moved off the strand in time, narrowly avoiding being flung. Dennis pounced on it, ripping one of its fanged mouthparts off, then slamming his head towards the mouth. The knife attached to his helmet sliced the spider until it slashed its arteries.

The animals still on the web fell off, taking the saw with them as they plunged into the black water. More and more spiders streamed from different parts of the web, climbing onto the strands that were still attached. The animals on them jumped into the water for their own safety.

Dennis's jaws crushed another smaller spider and he ripped it back and forward, shaking the creature to death. In under a minute the log was almost clear.

Only Dennis and Asuka remained on the hanging log. Asuka drew her sword, stood upon her hind legs and roared in challenge, 'Who wants to die first! Come and get me!' The spiders came from both ends.

She dropped back onto four legs as the first came, slicing its two legs off with her paws. As she slammed her legs down, Dennis leapt over her back and lunged downward onto the spider, biting into its cluster of eyes. The bear then spun around as another spider came up behind her, slashing her blade at its throat. She then pounced on this spider, using the metal claws on her right paw to rip into it, tearing open its visceral cavity. She halted as a third spider came along. Its fang swung downwards on the bear's back, bluntly hitting the armour plating.

The bear then head-butted the spider with her knife horns, impaling the giant creature on them. She then moved her hind legs up and rolled herself forward.

Dennis had killed another three smaller spiders and as another came towards the bear, he leapt at it, shoving it off Asuka.

She suddenly stopped as a spider sank its fangs into her hind legs. She roared in pain, mewling briefly before she rolled, taking the non-venomous fang out. She threw her metal claws on her right paw straight into the spider's multiple eyes. Her left paw then sliced off its tail. The bear turned tail and leapt, plummeting twenty metres into the dark swamp water beneath. Dennis, noticing her disappearance and three more spiders coming towards him, also decided that leaping was the best option and took off after the bear.

***

Natashia

The harvested silk, kilograms of it was falling into the water as the spiders scrambled along the partly cut lines that had yet to snap, straight towards the animals still cutting the webs.

Seeing two spiders the size of leopards clambering along the web, the captain yelled, 'Back, *now!*'

Scorpion bolts and a hail of bullets fired from the multiple guns attached to the ship targeted the gliding spiders. Some were shot dead with bullets. Others were set alight by flaming arrows. At least a dozen of them were swinging down towards the remaining animals. An unlucky cuscus failed to leap in time and hooked spider legs dug deep into its fur and abdomen. The struggling squirming animal shrieked as the fangs swung down on her.

This horrified the animals still on the log that the remaining strands were now struggling to support. The guns were fired after being reloaded for another volley, when a spider made its way onto the rotting timber. Multiple impacts knocked it into the water. However, many more spiders were streaming along the remaining strands. Bullets continued to fly. As they reloaded, the monstrous creatures made their way onto the log.

The soldiers, including Natashia, a few far-off chimps and clouded leopards were also fighting off spiders elsewhere on the webs. Natashia roared in encouragement as she readied herself to fight more of the spiders. Her howdah was a wooden platform with paw-holds and a loaded crossbow with ammo. This was her time to protect the other animals. Justified fear and anger tempered her enthusiasm.

Two other animals that had just pulled themselves out from the water came sprinting up the log and scrambled along the web to join the tiger.

Natashia snarled, ears tucked back, contemplating how she ended up being separated from the rest of the group, beside these two. The bear and dingo came running back up. Natashia could see that they still had some distance to climb before they could get to her.

The tiger leapt up the trunk and collided paws-first with one of the spiders. The smaller animals on her back were temporally pinned to the trunk, struggling to get loose. The spider screeched when Natashia quickly sunk her fangs into the black joint between the thorax and abdomen. A crossbow bolt to the face of the spider from the animals on her back followed. A second spider came to help the other, leaping high into the air. The riders on Natashia's back scrambled when they realised that they could very well be squashed. The opossum named Bonnie aimed one of the arrows upwards at the falling spider. It writhed as its own weight completed the impaling. Natashia fell backwards onto the trunk, wincing as the unloaded crossbow on her back dug in. Her back legs swung forward. She caught the giant spider, and her front legs hammered its face. Her left paw's claws aimed at its eyes. The spider pulled back its fang in pain. The arrow that it fell on impaled its underside.

Elsewhere, Sigbjorn was screaming in fury, wielding his twin hatchets. He spun from one spider to the next, axing them in the face, severing limbs after multiple blows. He sheathed the hatchets when he noticed that spiders were approaching the workers. He pulled out his much larger axe and charged towards the threatened animals.

The spiders kept coming as the remaining animals sawed off many more pieces of web. They gathered the webs and threw them down from the log. The silk disappeared in swamp water, which seemed to consume it. However, catfish caught the web, wound it around their bodies, and hauled the clumps to the boat. As they were being hauled over the deck of the boat, the log was attracting more and more web gatherers. The final supporting webs were being sawn. The shark tooth saws cut the web with surprising ease, but it still took thirty seconds for a pair of cuscuses to cut through the sheet-like sections of webs. Some were sawing closer to the tree, but others were sawing webs in the higher branches of a tall pine.

The cuscuses hung from a branch upside down, another thirty metres above the tree trunk. They hung by their tails, supporting themselves with their hind legs. They moved the saw back and forwards between them in synchrony. The black web thinned and pulled more on the branch.

It was at this point that one of the spiders jumped out from the greater web on its own safety line of silk and landed on the same branch where the cuscuses worked. The cuscuses noticed the spider immediately. They shouted an alarm as they deliberately sawed faster. The spider came closer as it scampered along the branches and up the silken web, closing the gap very quickly. Just then the branch gave way taking the spider with it.

The branch was the final thing holding up the massive rotting log. The cuscus's branch was at such an angle that they would hit the water hard after falling from such a great height. The crocodiles below were already scaring off any opportunistic aquatic predators that were ready to ferry any falling animal back up into the trees.

The tiger continued fighting as another wave of spiders swung over the gap between the logs like trapeze artists. They launched themselves from the inner parts of the web and swung over an already established tangle. As they leapt off the branches, they used their inertia to swing downwards. They cut their own webs with their legs as they came up. They flew, their large legs catching the webs they had aimed at.

The tigress reared up and caught one of the spiders in her paw. She quickly crunched her canines through the spider's exoskeleton. More spiders scuttled out after the retreating small mammals. At this moment, Natashia saw the tree kangaroo. The female macropod took a bundle of the black silk in her arms and leapt from the top of the trunk. The untied silk would not break her fall. Realising the danger, Natashia leapt to the rapidly unravelling pile of silk, landing upon it, and anchoring it with her paws.

The archers on her back fired another shot as the tigress spun around, swatting at the various spiders on the high webs. The tree kangaroo was yanked partway down, clutching the web as the other mammals fell into the water. Those from lower positions were much better off as they had less distance to fall. However, those paddling along the surface could see numerous shapes emerge from the depths, darting quickly at them.

The tigress turned, before she could leap, another seven spiders came at her from various directions. She jumped at one, pining and crushing its face. Her archers shot another spider. Two more came gliding in from the sides, another three from behind her. She roared and ripped, stabbing one with the head knife on her helmet, throwing it to the side.

Still they kept coming, they pressed against her armour holding her in place. Their fanged mouths were trying to find any hole in the armour. The plates and other armour accessories that she had put on before the battle were saving her life.

She roared, squirmed, snapped, and snarled as the fangs finally found a gap in the armour.

Dennis leapt at the spider pile, ripping one of the spiders off her back. He toppled a second one off in the process. He snapped and squirmed as it moved him towards the upside-down arachnid's mouth. Asuka came in next, leaping onto another spider, dragging it off Natashia.

However, the spiders outnumbered the tiger and her friends, and they rapidly pinned her down. One spider ripped Bruce off her back, impaled him and then ate the unfortunate rodent alive. His squeaks terrified the other riders. Bonnie then promptly fainted, playing possum, something that put her at greater risk.

The bear slashed at the spiders. The tiger finally freed herself and jumped out of the pile, rocketing straight up in the air. She then aimed to come down onto the last two spiders. But the bear had cleared them.

Natasha heard a screaming man splashing the water. She quickly realised that the commotion was attracting more spiders and crocodiles. She looked down at the ship, where the crew was now fighting the gliding spiders that had boarded. She could see that dozens of kilograms of the silk had been collected already. More spiders were extending their webs down to get to the water. Those animals that survived the spiders and catfish were now at the mercy of the rogue crocodiles.

Natashia, Dennis and Asuka jumped to the massive log hanging near the ship. The tiger looked up to see it was about to give way. Fighting on the already cracking timber, the three carnivores fought side by side, cutting down another six spiders. Natashia ripped one spider off Dennis after he had evaded the grasp of another.

Then the bear slammed her paws down on a spider and they heard the audible crack as the log finally gave way under their weight and the weight of the branch pulling it down. Natashia watched as the few

242

remaining animals let the silk go from their grasp. The tree kangaroo turned, and begun to hop down the trunk, dragging a long silken road behind her. She was leaping along as the log snapped and carried her downwards. The vines and webs attached to the log pulled tight and snapped.

The log began breaking into a great pile of splinters. This pile formed a dense cloud as the dead rotting timbers split in two. The dirt from the decomposing wood scattered as the other massive end of the log hit the water with an enormous splash, spraying mud everywhere. The timber slowly sank. The rotten soil inside spilled in a dark reddish-brown cloud through the water.

The three fell together. Dennis tumbled as he fell. Natashia turned so that her feet faced down. Asuka hit the water first, plunging below the surface, hitting a bull shark attracted to the massacre. Her swords impaled the shark as she fell several metres under water.

Temporarily submerged, Natashia avoided the second shark that swam right past her. The shark lunged for the struggling dingo, who was paddling furiously.

It was then that a massive shape thundered out of the gloom, snapping the shark up in his jaws, quickly ripping into it and tearing it apart. Natashia broke the surface just as Bentley reared his head above the water. The dinosaur dismembered and swallowed the back half of the shark, letting the front half fall back into the water to bleed out.

Bentley stood upon the wedged broken section of the log, before plunging and swimming straight towards a shoal of toothed catfish.

The African, toothed catfish were quickly becoming a bigger danger than the spiders for the swimming creatures. Already one of the fish latched onto the leg of a monkey and dragged it down. The crocodiles had seen this threat and quickly sprang into action.

Many mammals were being bitten and dragged down by the catfish. The crocodiles quickly brought those with catfish injuries back to the surface, scattering the thrashing fish back into the swamp. Some of the crocodiles, however, were completely wild and were contributing to the frenzy by eating both the drowning mammals and fish alike. Even a spider that had fallen into the water was suddenly grabbed and pulled under by a crocodile. The reptile's tail whipped above the surface as it pulled the spider into a death roll. The screeching alien creature already had one of its limbs twisted off and consumed.

Bentley arrived, grabbing a rogue crocodile, eviscerating it with his claws before snapping at the catfish. He accidentally bit into a tree kangaroo in the process. Realising his error, he focused on the crocodiles, plunging again to grab another.

In the water, Natashia watched the small animals go towards the ship and the wild crocodiles head in their direction. Some of the crocs carrying animals offloaded their charges onto the ship before engaging the wild crocodiles, who were now focussing on Natashia. One friendly crocodile had picked up Kim carrying her to the ship. Bonnie had regained consciousness and was frantically paddling towards Natashia.

She had just noticed Sigbjorn clambering back onto the ship, using his hatchets as climbing picks when something else caught her eye.

A pair of American crocodiles came at her, one from behind, and the other from the front.

She hissed in fear as she swam. Her remaining crew member clung to her saddle. She loaded another arrow and fired at the crocodile coming head on.

The tiger dived and rolled to evade the croc. On her back, Hazel swore as she scrambled out of the way. The crocodile snapped at the wooden construction where she had just been, ripping it from her back. The tigress clawed at the crocodile, cutting its belly scales. The reptile dived and turned around before emerging again. The hutia on her head alerted the tigress to the second crocodile that was rapidly gaining from behind. She flicked her tail out of the way and turned in the water to make that croc miss. The first crocodile collided with something under the water then turned and charged the tigress. The second crocodile, missing her tail, charged unexpectedly from the side. Its huge jaws snapped shut. They hit white fur.

The tigress moaned in pain and then tore away. Some skin between the legs, also known as the primordial pouch, saved her life. The loose skin was torn. Blood soaked out of the wound. The tigress pivoted as the first crocodile came in front of her, erupting out of the water with a defiant snap of his jaws. He landed sideways in the water again with a massive splash. The tigress kept swimming. The ship was getting closer as she swam.

The ship's crew pulled animals into the boat as they clambered up the precious black silk. More catfish and piranhas streamed from the swamp depths to assault those still in the water.

The remaining monkeys not on crocodile's backs, were yanked below as the piranhas begun to nip and bite the swimming animals, leaving the crocodiles alone. The catfish swam near the surface of the water looking for other animals that were paddling about. Not even the spiders were safe. Those that fell into the water were now floundering as piranhas chewed at their exoskeletons. A catfish caught another opossum and devoured it. The predatory fish now made a beeline for the animal clinging to Natashia's back.

The tigress scrambled up and over the sunken log, roaring and focusing on getting back to the ship. The two wild crocodiles came back for her, diving under the log. As she paddled closer to the ship, they accelerated, one aimed directly at her face. As it breached, another larger set of jaws came hammering in from the side, clamped shut and abruptly impaled the crocodile.

The crocodile gasped underwater as the hippopotamus ripped its body with massive jaw strength. Another hippo came to drive the other crocodile away.

Nearby, the manatees were pushing to turn the boat around even though there were still live spiders aboard. The tiger moaned as her paws clung to the sides of the ship. More hippos came splashing up from the depths. One mother and calf, a bull and three others swam around, keeping the crocodiles away.

The tigress finally reached her destination, clawing her way up onto the ship by a rope that both Sigbjorn and Asuka were holding. Dennis and Audie helped pull her on board.

As the ship began its journey home, Natashia looked back. On the fallen tree was a terrible sight, a much larger spider than the ones that attacked her earlier. It was easily three metres tall at the top of the silvery abdomen, and four metres in length. It was a female carrying a large number of eggs on her underside. All the other spiders were the males or juvenile females.

245

The giant spider was fishing out the remaining strands of black webs from the water. A few fish were entangled in the web, along with the remains of the spiders that had fallen in the water. The giant spider turned to see the boat leaving. She emitted a screeching hiss as she watched the boat disappear into the gloom of the swamp, the boat's cabin brushing through the undergrowth.

The tigress was still soaked, even after shaking the water out of her fur. Natashia watched a crocodile pick up the spluttering, drenched surviving mammals and head for shore. Catfish finished off the ten drowned mammals.

She had just begun to relax when a spider leapt from the roof. She turned and pounced, grabbing the spider's underside with her paws, and sinking her fangs into its face. She flung the arachnid aside and ran to the ship's cabin. The other animals fought more spiders there.

A spider had one of the tree kangaroos pinned down and was ripping it to shreds. It was too late for him, but Natashia leapt at this spider, gripping, and tearing it apart. As she killed it, three others attacked. They aimed their fangs at her. Asuka came to her aid. She smashed a spider through the control room's window, knocking the ship's throttle to full, driving the ship into full steam in the process. A snarling, striped hyena came running up with his mane raised, and leapt at the second spider, pulling it off.

The hyena snapped a leg straight off, pulling the spider back and continuing to savage the legs. Up on the roof another spider came crawling along. The tigress thundered over the bow, leaping up onto the second deck in front of the control room. She winced from the broken glass but jumped onto the roof, growling at the arachnid as it leapt off. A gun blast shot another gliding spider out of the air as it retreated.

Seeing a spider in the engine room stabbing and dismembering the cuscus operating the coal feeder, Natashia leapt down off the balcony. Flaming coal rolled onto the floor setting it alight. She saw a wooden barrel at the far end of the room, which she knew contained cool water. She had to extinguish the fire before the entire ship went up in flame.

The tigress leapt into the room, barrelling the spider over in the process. She dug her claws into the barrel. The flames continued to smoke the room out. She managed to get the barrel open and splashed water all over the floor, smothering the flames there. She called for help as flames flared up in adjoining rooms.

Within a minute, the remaining crew managed to extinguish the fires on the ship. The broken boat glided into harbour with over 300 kilograms of priceless black silk.

Natashia sat licking her wounds near the front of the boat as it came into dock. Next to her was the striped hyena who was still bedraggled from swimming back. He was eating spider flesh.

'Thank you so much for saving my life,' the tigress said.

'I believe we, the survivors that is, have passed the initiation test. Congratulations to us,' he answered, 'Perhaps we could be friends.'

Chapter 26

Psychotic Cruelty

Natashia and Dennis

Several days later, and after one vet hospital visit where she was treated by a talented lemur by the name of Dr Dianna, Natashia was finally let out. She had received stitches in her belly wound made by the crocodile bite. The tigress was lucky that the bite missed all the important organs and only hit loose skin. It was the day after leaving the hospital that she was called for her next assignment; one which could have been her undoing.

Natashia walked through the yard of the textile factory in the outer suburbs of the capital of the Kingdom, in the same general area as the swamp. She had creatures sitting on her back. Behind them, dragged in a cart, were a group of captured animals, criminals supposably, who were to become slaves. Her ears turned back, and she leaned away from the cart at the sight of the chained animals. It seemed wrong to her to deny the freedom, rights, and welfare of another living creature like that. It ruffled her fur in all the wrong ways.

'Slaves are not something the Kingdom ever dealt in previously. What has Andrew and that thing done to this place?' Bonnie the opossum on Natashia's back said.

'I'd stay quiet if I were you,' Kim, who was also on her back retorted. The tiger flicked her ears backwards to hear the two mammals better. At the front of the line was the coati boss. The tigress had since learned that his name was Fernando. She had not heard his surname, but then again surnames were not something she had heard spoken in this world.

The doors to the factory opened and a group of animals came out and invited them in. The individual leading the procession was particularly striking. This enigmatic individual was draped in animal skins. Others referred to him as Mr Hyde. His real name was unknown as was his species. According to the rumours, he never took those skins off. She briefly thought back to the still itching stitches on her belly.

Other more normally dressed animals in the entourage walked alongside Fernando. In the group was a duiker who somehow had survived the risks of working with Mr Hyde. He seemed to own and run the factory, though Natashia suspected that he could be mentally affected. *Could Mr Hyde read her mind?* she wondered.

It amazed her that, despite being unable to write or weave, and not being too dexterous because he was hooved, the duiker had still risen to a high position in the textile factory.

As they entered, they saw many animals scuttling around down on the factory floor, moving over numerous massive weaving machines, ten in all, that helped enormously with the weaving. The looms were on the ground floor.

The coati took them on a tour of the factory. 'These older wooden constructions are used for some of the more delicate or coarser fibres. They are far easier to make and can replace the industrial weaving machines when they break down. They are based on 19th century designs and weigh roughly one metric ton.

'The smaller mammals and birds are much more efficient in using them than the children who had originally worked them back on earth. The hemp is mostly processed through these machines, then loaded up high and split apart as it slides down a chute. A belt spins, pulling another part of the machine around. Dozens of square metres can be made in a day. The fibres are processed before they were properly spun.'

Natashia watched with interest. Elsewhere on the floor, spinning wheels were used on other fibres – such as the small amount of finer silk that was beginning to be produced since the arrival of silkworms and mulberry trees from the western Opal Empire.

The animals worked efficiently together. The fibres were moved back and forwards across the floor, being spun and then woven in the different machines. In one corner an animal was spinning an unusual black fibre on a wooden wheel.

'What is that black stuff they're spinning over there, by the wall?' Devan asked Fernando.

'That's the black spider silk. The same stuff we collected earlier. The last hunt was much more successful than I had hoped. The weaving is the easiest part in the process. Hunting the spiders and stealing the silk comes with a higher chance of death as some of our workers and soldiers have previously found out. The silk makes a tough fabric capable of withstanding bullets of significant calibre. Attempts at domestication led to problems, due to their... eating habits.' The older coati gestured to a large bamboo barred cell, mostly made of wood that contained the giant spiders.

'That's where the worker's union ringleaders go; or those hapless creatures that get ripped apart by the sewing machine; or anyone that sufficiently annoys me; or anybody in here I don't like. Except that guy on the wall, he badly annoyed Mr Hyde,' Fernando said grimacing.

Natashia wanted to be furious with the strange creature but could not get sufficiently angry. Her mind fought against the metaphorical chains being slung around it, as if there was a stop-gate on her mind.

She looked over at the supposably annoying creature that the older coati had earlier referred to. He was impaled on the wall eight metres above the working floor. The clouded leopard on the wall had already had its skin removed, revealing red and black rotting flesh that stained the wall and floor below. One of the eyes was missing. Fernando said it had been gouged out with the two wooden stakes that secured the body to the wall.

Below, written in black rusted blood and rotted fluid were the words, 'KEEP WORKING OR YOU WILL BE NEXT! RESISTANCE SHALL BE CRUSHED PAINFULLY!

Much to her horror, Natashia noticed that the wall had many similar stakes impaled on different sections. The carcasses they originally held were missing. Another carcass was impaled above them – a chimp this time. The skin was still on, and the eyes not impaled. But the eyelids had been removed. This one was shackled to the wall near an overhead walkway. Even worse was the realisation this tortured soul was still alive. He started shrieking again as Mr

Hyde walked past – agonising screams that made the already nervous workers more unnerved.

The tigress ducked her head, fearful of staring at the carcasses. *This is the worst thing I have ever seen,* she thought. *This is wrong, sick, evil, disgusting and despicable.* It was an absolute outrage that had to be fixed, but how could she act? For the time being she wore shackles on her mind.

Mr Hyde glanced at the shrieking chimp. 'Don't worry, those ones on the wall actively tried defying me. The bad workers go to the spiders though, such is my compassion, a rarity for me. My little antelope friend manages most of the business and fabric weaving side of things. I just keep the workers in line and use them to amuse myself.

'Anyway, the deal is that for this hemp you keep giving us, I will give you the bad workers that I normally feed to the spiders. I don't kill them. They prefer fresh prey but will keep sucking rotting corpses dry as they decompose if they are hungry enough. The digestive juices they inject in the dead carcasses from the fangs further down their throat, helps break down rotting bodies by dissolving the internal organs of the victim. They are happy if the dead meat has gone off a bit, but I sometimes give them live food for their entertainment, and mine also.

'Enough with the morbid talk. I do like your deal, but if we are to have more of these brilliant bullet proof vests, we need more silk; preferably wild-harvested. I've heard that you helped in the retrieval of several hundred kilograms of the stuff out of the swamp. A big haul. That will be useful.' Mr Hyde's conversation put several of the animals at unease.

His cruelty was confirmed when they passed the thatching machines. A small opossum had an accident. Her paw had become trapped and was completely stuck. Mr Hyde walked calmly over to the stuck possum. He grabbed the animal and ripped it free, severing the paw in the process. He then bit a chunk out of its abdomen before throwing the dying, screeching animal to some of the more carnivorous workers. A pair of dingoes tucked in, ripping her in half and wolfing down the arterial squirting blood. The mad beast grabbed the young-adult possum, the son of the one just killed, who was staring in a wide-eyed shock. He threw him to the dingoes too.

A dingo caught the animal in his mouth. Other nearby carnivores set to work eating the innocent creature. Even though, in her own way she was brutal when hunting, Natashia would never sink to that level. Willingly harming and eating your fellow employees is illogical and needlessly cruel in any workplace. Even she had to move her eyes away from this animal's squeaks and hisses of agony and ignore the snapping and snarling.

They watched the machines weaving the fibres and flattening them into ropes and strings. The hemp had already been spun into fibres. As the machines moved their smaller parts back and forwards, it weaved the material into a sheet of coarse fabric. In another place the mats were being hung. Some were being woven together through a loom, moved by some very tired primates, chained to their station.

One of the overseers walked past, whipping them with a thorned vine, causing squeals of pain.

Natashia scrunched her face away in disgust. Glancing up, she noticed something horrifying. Dozens of birds, bustards, cockatoos, vultures, albatrosses, pelicans, flamingos, one of those strange bird beasts and many others were nailed into the wall or hung from the wall. *How did Mr Hyde collect so many exotic birds from far off lands?* Natashia wondered. A few were even suspended from the ceiling with hooks pushed through them. They were more victims of the mad monster's handiwork. Even what looked like a pterosaur was hanging dead and rotting from the ceiling. Many of the birds were recently killed. Some still squirmed in agony.

She crouched to snarl, lagging behind the group. *What kind of monster did this? What the hell had happened to the Kingdom?* This must have been what Fernando was warning about. Sure, Suleiman was merciless on carnivores. There was good reason for that, but this was just cruel, torturous butchery. It was then Mr Hyde turned around from the start of the group and noticed her. He carefully and slowly walked over to her and then proceeded to yell.

'What do you think? That I'm the monster here? I do whatever the fuck I like! They're all my playthings. You are all created to experience misery repeatedly. I can read all your minds like a book if I choose to do so? Your entire purpose is being the Terraformers' playthings. You need to be reminded, painfully!' the beast yelled.

Before Natashia could swipe his head off his shoulders, a massive shaking, sharp, continuous agony hit her. She felt as if she had been hit by an epileptic fit or electrocuted. The tigress fell to the floor writhing before the beast pulled out several hooks and chains. She was temporally paralysed as the meat hooks pieced her skin.

Dirty stinking meat hooks, corrupted with the blood of previous victims, hung in her skin. By the time she stopped writhing in agony, she was tied to the wall of chain link over the planks.

During this time, her mind briefly flashed to a vision of herself back when she was still human, only, in the vision she was being pulled tight by similar chains, blood seeping over the hospital gown. She quickly flashed back out, wondering what on earth the mad beast had done to her body and mind.

She was in a desperate situation.

Hours of agony followed. The improvised torture device painfully pulled the skin on her back. The longer she spent tied up, the more painful any attempt to move became. As she tried to move, she pulled at multiple chains that were attached to the wall. She wondered what would kill her first, thirst or infection. She listened to the agonised cries of others, including the mournful sounds of a pinned-down giant otter. After dark, the otter stopped making any noise. *Perhaps he finally succumbed?* she thought.

Her mind begged for such an end. If she just died, she could reincarnate anew and begin again elsewhere, though she would probably never get to be a tigress again. She swivelled her head to where the otter was hanging, only to notice movement on the floor, something ducking behind a section of partition. She strained against the ropes that were holding her to the wall, trying to get free. A familiar voice stopped her.

'Don't struggle too much, you will only attract more attention and make the injuries worse.'

She sighed with relief.

Dennis had snuck back into the factory after dark. Work continued on the nocturnal shift elsewhere in the factory, however.

Behind Dennis came a small group of brown shapes. The otter had freed himself and was limping along, bleeding onto the floorboards. But the other brown shapes bought back fond memories. The eight bush dogs quickly set to work digging the hooks out from her legs. She suppressed the urge to growl in pain while this was being done.

After them came the last figure. The human awkwardly crouched as he came into the room. He was shuffling over the floorboards behind the weaving machines. Sigbjorn came crawling in, quickly reaching, and unhooking the meat hooks tied to Natashia's back. The man shushed her when she went to speak.

'Were busting you out, along with anyone else we can get. We need to get out before we are found.' The man spoke the quietest she had heard from him. She noticed that he had his hand around his hatchet, listening. A small figure came around the corner with a bright torchlight. The group of animal rescuers ducked, though Natashia's white pelt was spotted. The dingo guard, who had a strange oozing black mask-like contraption on his head was about to bark when Sigbjorn rapidly stood up and threw the hatchet as hard as he could at the dingo.

The dog whimpered when the axe split his head open. Blood and sparks flew from the hole. The man then dived, grabbed the dog's foot, pulled him under a table and struck the axe down into the throat severing the neck vertebra.

The guard dingo lay still, bleeding out onto the floor, its head horrifically mangled. Crudely attached cybernetics were surrounded by badly formed scar tissue that oozed infection in some locations.

Natashia looked at the dead canine, surprised to see the metal inside what should have been the braincase. She had not eaten that part of the animal before.

'Are there any other prisoners in this part of the factory?' one of the bush dogs asked. Natashia tried to smell out any unfamiliar scents from the blood.

'Not that I can see or smell; except that poor guy on the roof.' She gestured upwards, grunting in pain as she did so, looking at the bloody hanging entrails of some poor antelope that had been flayed and half gutted before somehow being hoisted up and nailed to the roof. The reek of decay filled the air.

'What's with this place and the random acts of torture? At least those Six Sunners kill you before they do strange things with your corpse.'

'The factory is run by some madman who can take control of people's minds. He tortures them for his amusement,' Natashia replied, still grunting in pain.

Another minute passed as they began to sneak their way through the factory towards the exit. Terrified factory workers on the night shift fled further into the mill when they saw them, scuttling around the wooden instruments. On the way, they rescued a black and white tegu lizard with a leg chopped off. They had to use a crude tourniquet to stop the flow of blood.

Another opossum who had a hole torn in the scruff of its neck by an iron stake and had been hung, was released.

Natashia felt dreadful. Had she still been human she knew she would have been sobbing. Her white and black pelt was striped red with her blood. Some of the meat hooks had hit muscle, forcing her pace down to a limp.

They were making their way out when they heard a voice. 'They have escaped, boss!' one of the guards, a duiker called out.

Immediately panic set into the group. Natashia started to limp as fast as she could, holding the front leg where a meat hook had pieced her shoulder.

The duiker ran back to Mr Hyde. Looking over the area, he saw the missing prisoners and the trail of blood, along with the butchered carcass of the guard dingo. Two more dingos came behind him.

The two dingos bounded over the wooden floorboards, sniffing vigorously as they quickly followed the blood trail.

The escapees moved as quickly as possible. The bush dogs and otter were racing ahead. Dennis was helping carry the injured tegu and opossum. They found an open doorway and dashed inside. Sigbjorn tried to board the entry to stop any pursuit. Natashia stared at the entrance, growling silently as the dingoes' scratching could be heard at the door.

The tiger turned to continue to limp along to a side door that Dennis was currently attempting to unlock. Then, something terrible seemed to take over her mind.

Outside the door, the voice of Mr Hyde said, 'I know you are all in there. I will get you out.'

As he spoke, Natashia suddenly collapsed. She roared in agony as every nerve in her body seemed to be firing off at once. Her nerves felt like they were on fire. The part of her computer brain meant to sense pain was having a seizure.

She spasmed, unable to concentrate on anything other than the pain. But it was not enough for her to pass out, of course. Mr Hyde was not going to spoil his fun. She sensed movement coming towards her. She glanced out the corner of her eye. She tried to leap to the side, but her body did not respond. Painfully, she ducked her head. Sigbjorn's hatchet missed her by inches, the twirling blade slicing fur and a nick of skin off her back.

She realised Mr Hyde controlled the Viking's mind too. Her friend was now mad, howling in a berserker fury, as he came running straight for her. He wielded his final, much larger axe, easily large enough to sever her neck in one swing. Now though, she noticed Mr Hyde was splitting his attention between the two of them, just enough to allow her to move. Instead of pain all she felt was adrenaline. She turned to her friend.

The man came screaming at her with the axe. Natashia went to dodge, swinging her lame paw painfully to slap the man over. He tumbled, only to flip and prepare to strike again.

***

At the back of the room, Dennis heard the roars. 'Something seems to be holding Natashia and Sigbjorn up. The roars can only mean one thing; they have been discovered. Hopefully, they are fighting Mr Hyde and his goons off.' He turned to go back and help then stopped. 'Get the otter and the others out of here. I'll go back for the tiger and the human. Go now!'

He went through another door that led to the factory floor. He stared around in the dark and then spotted something that might help. There was a crane with a rope holding what looked to be an extremely heavy crate over where Mr Hyde was standing outside the door. *If I can cut the rope and take him by surprise, then the crate would crush him.*

He broke into a sprint, running up the ladder, clambering up and up, leaping up the steps as fast as he could to get to the top of the crane. He needed a knife and knew where to get it.

On the upper section near the factory roof, he found what he needed. A chimpanzee was impaled on a wall not too far from him. He dashed along trying to get to the ape. The blades he was impaled with were what Dennis was after. As he reached the end of the platform, he swung his paws around a rope, carefully making his way to the mutilated corpse. Below him, also impaled on the wall he could see the corpse of a leopard. The dingo went for the knife in the ape's eye socket, gripping the blade with his teeth, gradually dragging it out slowly and quietly. As soon as the knife was out, he almost dropped it in surprise.

The chimp's left arm suddenly jerked back to life. The seemingly dead limb suddenly reached out and grabbed the rope. It then reached for him. The dingo, focused on not dropping the knife, accidentally urinated below him from the shock. He swung back to the platform and rolled onto the floor – his ears flat against his skull. To his shock, the impaled leopard corpse below him also started to move. It detached from the wall, then started climbing towards the platform below, red bloody muscles plainly exposed.

Mr Hyde focused, and the two newest puppets that he brought back to life came thundering after the dingo. The chimp Dennis had taken the knife from ran along the rafter, leaping up. The clouded leopard, however, came pacing along the bottom. Dennis stared in disbelief.

Her entire face had been previously ripped out except for one whole eye, one damaged eye and the jaw muscles. The cat leapt to the underside of the walkways and started to stalk the canine above her.

The chimp however was proving to be easier to evade. Blindly running down the walkway after Dennis, the ape overshot its target as the dog side-stepped onto the box poised above Mr Hyde. *At least now there is a chance to get to work,* Dennis thought. He quickly positioned the knife and started cutting.

***

Sigbjorn was not a match for the wounded Natashia without his axes. The man, still screaming incomprehensibly, dodged, ducked, and weaved with a surprising amount of skill as Natashia lashed out. Eventually the Viking got to his larger axe and began swinging.

The tigress bobbed and darted, relieved that the pain was going back to normal levels. *Evidently Mr Hyde's attention is elsewhere*, she thought. Distracted by this thought, she yowled when the axe hit her hind leg. She roared out in pain, twisting before finally grabbing Sigbjorn and pinning the screaming man down with her leg. She held him down, hoping that he would just snap out of his mania now that Mr Hyde was distracted by something else.

***

Dennis franticly shifted his neck back and forwards, cutting at the rope. It gradually frayed. The tightly packed metal components for another threshing machine sagged more and more on the pulley attached to the ceiling.

Then a movement behind him caused him to stop. Turning around, he dropped the knife. He exposed his teeth into a vicious snarl.

The clouded leopard leapt onto the box. The movements seemed almost robotic or pre-planned. The feline swished her bare red arms as the canine dodged and ducked. One paw slipped over the edge. The box swayed and he launched at the feline, managing to get onto the cat's back. He buried his teeth in her flesh. She roared and squirmed, the bare muscles convulsing as she did so. Dennis bit harder, desperately trying to get to her spine. No other mortal injuries were having any effect on the feline.

He struggled to get through the vertebrae. He snapped more and more desperately.

The chimp finally found its way onto the box, now clutching the knife. It snarled, exposing blood-covered teeth from the ruins of its face, and then joined in the attack.

***

Sigbjorn fainted, which was somewhat of a relief. He was still breathing. However, the toto hand claw marks where her claws dug

258

in were bleeding. Natashia mewled softly to see the injury she had caused. She had tried not to kill him in that fight.

That's when Mr Hyde's dingoes finally opened the door and came into the room.

The tiger cowered as a bright orange fiery torchlight filtered into the room. The mad beast outside was highlighted by the torch's flames above him. He wielded two short steel knives. His mask shadowed his head against the dark; this version was without the spike. The mass of flayed skins was draped over his back like a cape.

'Oh, this is getting to be wonderful. I'm going to enjoy breaking you. I shall invite you, young girl, to dance with me.'

Natashia hesitated, as behind him the torch was dropped by one of his dingoes.

The dingo jumped to one side, then in the dark pivoted again, leaping off the wall at the tigress and forcing her towards the doorway. She ducked, wincing as she put weight onto her injured legs. She then spun and swung at the smaller animal. He dodged and spun out of the way. The dingo then leapt up to the roof spinning around and leaping down again. The feline dodged.

The mad beast started taunting her. 'Oh, I know who you are, Natashia! I know everything about you from when I read your mind.' He lunged at her with his knives. The feline dodged and skidded back, snarling defiantly near the torch.

'Your parents are definitely dead by now. Daddy may well have killed himself in grief.' He swung over again with the knife, only to stick his blade into a cloth sack beside her that rapidly started spilling grain. 'Mummy was driven to bankruptcy, wasn't she? For nothing! You died anyway, you miserable piece of shit!' he lunged again. The tiger dodged hissing defiantly.

Natashia lunged at the beast, who dodged out of the way. 'That is none of your damn business, you were not there, you probably don't even know what it's liked to be loved!'

'I have loved. I do love. I love pain. I love hurting things. I love bringing misery. It's the only thing that seems to work in this hell! Why do they subject us to this unending series of torments if not for torments sake!" he yelled before lunging at her again. 'It's the only source of joy in this world! We will all succumb to it! You have killed dozens already, hundreds more shall die to you throughout your many lives here. Were all monsters here. I just enjoy being so. You are an utter failure, failing to finish school, failing to get a boy, dying young, never achieving anything in your past life and getting sucked into the cartel in this life!' The being screamed as he swung his knives around and leapt onto her back.

'You shall always be a failure, right from the time you were born. And I'm sending you around again.' Now the beast was gripping onto Natashia's back, riding the bleeding feline like a rodeo bull, aiming the blade closer and closer to her nape. 'We have both killed so many, yet you deny it. You chose to oppose me, you chose to help your friends and even strangers, which is all pointless; they are going to die anyway. Everything dies, we live, die, and repeat for all eternity. You have killed innocents, so do I, but I admit it. What gives you the drive to fight me in the face of inevitable death? It's pointless!'

***

Dennis let go of the leopard and barked and yipped as the ape chased him around. The feline also came lunging after him. He was briefly distracted by the noisy argument coming from the floor below. The chimp finally grabbed his hind leg, dragging him closer. The knife was held high. The ape grinned as he was about to plunge it down. Dennis cowered waiting for the blow, but something strange happened; the chimp suddenly went limp. Sparks came from the back of his mouth. The figure then tumbled off to the side. The energy-drained body limply fell over the side of the box, landing onto the floor. Just as it did so, the feline glanced at the rope, to see that the last few strands were thinning out.

***

Natashia spun and flipped painfully, flinging the beast off her back. 'I do the things I do because it's the right thing to do. Sure, I failed in my last life, but that was not my fault. I am trying to make anew. You had every chance to improve but you keep killing and torturing to your heart's content. You are the one that has succumbed to your mental weakness, not me.'

The beast got to his feet and lunged forward, too quickly for Natashia to avoid the blow. She gasped when the knife slammed into her head, cutting her jaw muscles, and scraping her computer brain.

260

She was somehow still conscious after what should have been a mortal wound, but her jaws were out of commission. She could only gasp in pain.

The beast stepped back looking to the fight above him.

Natashia looked up and saw the box swaying. She grabbed Sigbjorn with her paw, moving them both out of the way as quickly as she could. The corpse of the ape hit the floor, startling them all.

Then the massive box plummeted from the ceiling. The undead leopard let go as it fell. Dennis was airborne, tumbling as he fell. He landed on a pile of hemp fabric.

**

The mad beast leaped backwards as the box crashed onto the floorboards where he once stood, smashing them completely with over a ton of weight. Shattered planks from the floor flew through the air. Several landed on Mr Hyde, one pinning him to the ground.

Grunting in pain he realised he was lucky not to have been crushed. He struggled to lift the heavy debris off himself. Eventually he pulled himself out from under the pile, ripping a bloody nail out of his leg. Pushing the logs off, he rose to his feet, shaking the great mask on his head, wincing from the various wounds inflicted by the planks.

He inspected the leg wound; without cleaning it would certainly get infected.

He looked around; several surprised animals were looking in the door. He was so focused on his plight that his mind control on those around him had slipped. The animals looked in horror at the scene. They connected the dots between him, the murders, and his control of the factory. Realising he was in no condition to fight, he focused, projecting his computer mind over Natashia, Dennis and all the nearby animals, reprogramming their computer brains to temporally ignore him. Had it not been for his ability to control the minds of others like this then he would have been killed a long time ago.

He could hear the surprised and panicked sounds of the remaining night shift workers. They screamed when they came out from under his mind control, suddenly realising all the mutilated carcasses that were hung over the factory were down to him. Such a break in his control was, for him, simply unacceptable.

After he returned his attention to himself, he gasped in pain, limping away from the commotion and into a secret tunnel that led to his safe house, over a kilometre away in the jungle. Reaching it was going to be painful.

***

The mad beast's concentration broken, the human awoke in surprise and some degree of pain in Natashia's grasp. She was stunned that he came back so quickly, almost ignoring the knife in her head.

Dennis whined when he came down. He inspected the devastation caused by the fall of the heavy crate. He looked for Mr Hyde but when he didn't see him, he assumed he had been crushed. He could see parts of the leopard sticking out from under the box where it must have slipped during the descent. Most of the debris from the smashed floorboards had gone the other way. As he brushed the small splinters off Natashia, he stared in horror at the massive knife sticking out of her head.

He turned to the human struggling to his feet beside her. 'We need to get her medical attention immediately; she will bleed to death unless we do. Look at the knife in her head!' Dennis barked.

Sigbjorn immediately replied. 'I know the way to a hospital, less than a kilometre from here. We need to get going. A cart is going to be needed for Natashia, send someone to get one.' Dennis hurried to the exit and told a bush dog to find a cart.

***

The walk out of the room was painful. Blood trailed behind Natashia. She was already feeling faint from loss of blood. Dennis and Sigbjorn were with her, helping guide her towards the exit. But she felt she was not going to make it. She could feel the life seeping out of her.

Her mind swirled with thoughts as her subconscious mind fought to control her body. '*I can't make it.* No, you must, everything he said will be true if you don't. *But I am a failure, I have accomplished nothing in this life. He probably already knows about the coati's plan.*'

'No, you must not think that way, that kind of thinking is giving up. You cannot give up. You must push on. You will die if you stay here.' Then she could see the doors opening and a wagon less than fifty metres away. The bush dogs had run ahead for help and returned.

I can just stop now, lie down, and everything will be alright, she thought as she slumped to the floor. But her mind fought back, 'No you cannot, you will die if you do that. You must get to the wagon. Your friends are counting on you to get through this.'

I can't make it. Nobody cares if I live or die. 'Do not think that way, you must persevere!' She was starting to audibly yell. Dennis watched in concern. Just then her vision came back into focus. She stumbled drearily the last couple of metres before collapsing into the wagon. The occupants of the transport immediately got to work. A half a dozen different nurses started bandaging the bleeding. A blood bag was prepared, the sterility questionable, as the aye-aye doctor got the needle into position. She was also injected with an anaesthetic needle.

Dennis stared in horror and worry at his friend's state. 'What can I do to help?'

"Nothing you can do, except perhaps pray. This patient is another of those atrocities Mr Hyde keeps committing. We need to go NOW!' The doctor shouted the last command to the drivers of the open wagon. The pair of buffalo pulling obliged and started their way towards the hospital. It was on top of a grassy knoll surrounded by rainforest trees, only a few hundred metres away. Dennis could only look at his still breathing friend in concern. The human was running alongside the wagon now. The otter was already in the hospital being treated.

There was no guarantee the tiger would even survive the night, but she had tried with all the strength she had, that was the best she could do.

***

Mr Hyde limped through the dimly lit tunnel. From the scrambled bits of extra information, he was able to get from Natashia's mind, he had gathered small bits about plans being made against him. Evidently, his control had not been anywhere near as total as he previously thought. This whole incident, plus the multiple injuries required him to seriously reconsider everything.

First, he had to regain control over the current situation, not die from his injuries and perhaps take a less obvious route to his degree of control and infiltration.

For what he wanted to do, he had to wait until just the right time, to have the right equipment and enough creatures in the right place. Then and only then could he undertake the full-scale destruction he intended. That is if he lived long enough.

He limped down the tunnels, determined to get out of there and plan. Grabbing an unlit torch off the wall, he lit it from the remains of the torch he had previously used against the tiger.

He shook his head in disbelief. That determined bitch somehow walked off after being stabbed through the head. Few creatures had the tenacity or the will power to keep fighting him after he used control over them. If they were to meet again, he was going to make her pay for her defiance. At his hand or at least that of one of his underlings.

What he planned would bring the kingdom to its knees. If he did not die first. He grunted again as he continued to limp, holding the torch in one hand, making his way to an exit passage of the tunnel.

Bestiary

A list of the vertebrate animals seen in this book after the release. This is not a complete list of all species found in this area. Is not indicative of all animals in this region of the planet. Some species are vagrant species from further east or west. Alien fauna and reconstructed dinosaurs included.

Mammals

Marsupials

Agile Wallaby *Macropus agilis:* Orange and white savanna living wallaby.

Allied rock wallaby *Petrogale assimilis* East Australian grey coloured rock wallaby.

Dusky Pademelon *Thylogale brunii* Small brown wallaby from Papua.

Bennet's tree kangaroo *Dendrolagus bennettianus* Brown and black coloured, arboreal quadrupedal Australian tree kangaroo.

Herbert's river Ringtailed possum *Pseudochirulus herbertensis* Brown and white rainforest living prehensile tailed possum from North Queensland.

Yellow bellied glider *Petaurus australis:* Yellow and brown Australian gliding possum from dry forests.

Sulawesi bear Cuscus *Ailurops ursinus:* Grey furred Asian possum.

Common Spotted cuscus *Spilocuscus maculatus*: Piebald Papuan possum.

White eared Opossum *Didelphis albiventris* Omnivorous south American Opossum.

Grey short-tailed *Opossum Monodelphis domestica:* Small shrew like grey furred opossum.

Afrotherians

Elephants and kin

Columbian mammoth *Mammuthus Columbi*: Subtropical climate living Coarsely haired Pleistocene era North American mammoth.

Asian elephant *Elephas Maximus*: Grey and pink rainforest elephant species.

Manatees

West African manatee Trichechus senegalensis: Freshwater round tailed aquatic herbivorous mammal.

Hyraxes

Rock hyrax *Procavia capensis*: Small herbivorous tailless gregarious mammal.

Other afrotheres.

Grant's golden mole *Eremitalpa granti*: Mole like eyeless desert living small mammal.

Euarchontoglires

Polisimians

Ring tailed lemur *Catta:* Adaptable banded tailed social primate.

Mongoose lemur *Eulemur mongoz:* Dog snouted brown furred lemur.

Senegal Bushbaby *senegalens*is: Solitary large eyed small grey furred nocturnal primate.

Monkeys

Diana monkey *Cercopithecus diana*: Tricoloured African monkey

Uganda mangabey *Lophocebus ugandae*: African brown furred social monkey.

Rhesus Macaque Macaca *mulatta*: Grey furred pink faced short tailed gregarious monkey.

Brown Mantled Tamarin Saguinus *fuscicollis*: Small south American monkey.

Tufted Gray Langur (Semnopithecus priam) Grey dry forest living monkey.

Apes

Eastern lowland gorilla *beringei graueri:* Strong heavy set black furred ape.

Chimpanzee *Pan troglodytes:* Wiry pink skin black furred ape

Modern Human *Homo sapiens*: Mostly hairless ape, make all this possible.

Lagomorphs

Volcano rabbit *Romerolagus diazi:* Small grey rabbit.

<u>Rodents</u>

Murid Rodents

Common Mole rat *Cryptomys hottentotus:* African Subterranean rodent

Polynesian Rat *Rattus exulans:* Asiatic rat

Greater Egyptian Jerboa *Jaculus orientalis:* long eared and legged desert rodent.

Pale gerbil *Gerbillus perpallidus*: Mouse like desert rodent.

Porcupines and cavimorph rodents.

African bush porcupine *Atherurus africanus:* Small rat like procupine.

Malaysian Porcupine *Hystrix brachyura:* Rainforest living Large black and white porcupine.

Desmarest's hutia *Capromys pilorides*: Cuban rat like rodent.

Squirrels and relatives

Large black flying squirrel *Aeromys tephromela*: Asian rainforest living squirrel.

Plantain squirrel *Callosciurus notatus:* Brown furred Asian squirrel.

Prevost's Squirrel *Callosciurus prevostii:* Tricoloured Asian squirrel.

Springhare *Pedetes capensis* Bipedal hopping rodent

Xenathrotheria

Anteaters

Northern tamudua *Tamandua Mexicana:* Central American black and tan arboreal anteater.

Sloths

Harlan's ground sloth *Paramylodon harlani:* Large Californian Pleistocene era ground sloth.

Laurasiatheria

Bats and others

Spectacled flying fox *Pteropus conspicillatus*: gold and black Australian fruit bat.

Lesser forest shrew *Sylvisorex oriundus*: Small rainforest shrew.

Carnivorans

Bears

Asian black bear *Ursus thibetanus:* White chest patched bear

Sloth bear *Melursus ursinus:* Shaggy fur big lipped omnivorous Asian bear

Spectacled bear Tremarctos *ornatus* Herbivorous south American bear species.

Canids

Dingo *Canis lupus dingo:* Carnivorous Australasian large canine.

Coyote *Canis latrans:* Small adaptable grey canine.

Bengal fox *Vulpes bengalensis:* Grey furred Indian fox.

Bush dog *Speothos venaticus:* Small pack living south American canid.

Mustelids

Ratel *Mellivora capensis:* White backed afro-asiatic badger

Giant otter *Pteronura brasiliensis:* Large pack living south American otter.

Raccoon relatives

Coati *Nasua nasua:* Pack living raccoon relative.

Felines

Lion *Panthera Leo:* Plain patterned plains dwelling large feline

Tiger *Panthera tigis:* Striped forest dwelling large feline.

Jaguar Panthera onca: Rosette spotted large feline from the Americas.

Clouded leopard *Neofelis nebulosa:* Medium sized rosetted Asian feline.

Puma *Puma concolor:* Adaptable solitary plain coloured feline

Spanish lynx *Lynx pardinus:* Short tailed medium sized European feline.

Pantanal cat *Leopardus colocola braccatus:* Small black footed swamp dwelling south American feline

Black footed cat *Felis nigripes* Small black footed desert dwelling African feline.

Hyenas

Spotted hyena *Crocuta Crocuta:* Pack living plains large dog like carnivore.

Striped hyena *Hyaena hyaena:* Back maned black striped dog like omnivore.

Mongooses and relatives

Fossa *Cryptoprocta ferox:* Brown furred Madagascan arboreal carnivore

Binturong *Arctictis binturong:* Omnivorous shaggy black furred civet

Water mongoose *Atilax paludinosus:* Large semiaquatic mongoose.

Odd toed hooved mammals

Grevey's zebra *Equus grevyi:* Narrow striped equine

Brazilian tapir *Tapirus terrestris:* Semi aquatic trunked hoofed mammal.

Indian rhinoceros *Rhinoceros unicornis:* Armoured one horned hoofed mammal.

Cervids

Sambar *Rusa Unicolor*: Large Asian brown furred deer

Chital deer *Axis Axis: Herd* living spotted deer.

Viviasian deer *Rusa alfredi*: Philippine dark brown and white spotted deer.

Bovidiae

Water buffalo *Bubalus bubalis:* Asian Large swamp living bovid.

Tamaraw *Bubalus mindorensis:* Small buffalo like Philippine bovid

African buffalo *Syncerus Caffer* Curled horn herd living black furred bovid.

Saola *Pseudoryx nghetinhensis:* Small rare long horned brown furred bovid.

Giant eland *Taurotagus derbianus*: large orange antelope with white stripes.

Nile lechwe *Kobus megaceros:* Swamp dwelling black and white antelope.

Tssesebe *Damaliscus lunatus lunatus:* Brown and black sloped back antelope.

Blue wildebeest *Connochaetes taurinus:* Striped necked migratory antelope.

Sable antelope *Hippotragus niger:* Large horse like antelope

Arabian oryx Oryx leucoryx: White desert antelope with straight horns.

Addax *Addax nasomaculatus:* White desert antelope with curly horns.

Red forest duiker *Cephalophus natalensis* Small red forest living antelope.

Sumatran serow *Capricornis sumatraensis:* Grey furred small horned wild goat.

Dorcas Gazelle, *Gazella Dorcas:* Desert dwelling gazelle.

Pigs and kin

Giant forest hog *Hylochoerus meinertzhageni*: Large black furred African bony faced pig

Collared peccary Pecari tajacu: Pig like animal with grey and white fur.

Other even toed hooved mammals.

Masai giraffe *Giraffa tippelskirchi:* Dark spotted east African giraffe species.

Okapi *Okapia johnstoni:* Striped short necked giraffe relative

Common hippopotamus *Hippopotamus amphibious* Large hairless semiaquatic herbivore.

Birds

Game birds

Indian peafowl *Pavo cristatus:* Long feathered brightly coloured gamebird.

Waigeo Bush turkey *Aepypodius bruijnii:* Red wattled bare headed black gamebird.

Parrots

Military macaw *Ara militaris:* Mostly green feathered macaw

Sulphur crested cockatoo *Cacatua galerita:* Yellow crested white cockatoo.

Red tailed black cockatoo *Calyptorhynchus banksia:* Large Australian cockatoo

Rainbow lorikeet *Trichoglossus moluccanus:* Bright coloured Australian parrakeet.

Birds of prey

Philippine eagle *Pithecophaga jefferyi:* Large, brown and white rainforest eagle.

Turkey vulture *Cathartes aura:* Black feathered new world vulture

King vulture *Sarcoramphus papa*: white vulture with a multicoloured head.

Californian condor *Gymnogyps californianus:* Massive, red headed black feathered vulture.

Griffon vulture *Gyps fulvus:* Brown and white large old-world vulture

Malay Eagle owl *Bubo sumatranus:* Rainforest dwelling tufted headed owl.

Broad-winged hawk Hawk *Buteo platypterus:* Widespread hawk species.

Peregrine Falcon *Falco peregrinus:* Blueish grey fast flying falcon

Eastern Barn Owl *Tyto javanica:* Australian brown and white owl.

Nightjars and kin

Forest nightjar *Caprimulgus batesi* Small nocturnal insectivieous bird.

Tawny frogmouth *Podargus strigoides* Large sized carnivorous nocturnal nightjar.

Seabirds and kin

Australian Pelican *Pelecanus conspicillatus:* large beaked fish-eating waterbird.

Great Frigate bird *Fregata minor:* Thieving red throated black feathered sea bird

Red billed Tropic bird *Phaethon aethereus:* Red tail feathered White seabird.

African janaca *Actophilornis africanus*: large fotted small waterbird

Spotted Curlew *Burhinus capensis* Long legged ground bird.

Silver gull (Chroicocephalus novaehollandiae) A small red beaked seagull.

Others

Terror bird *Titanis walleri* Huge flightless Pleistocene era carnivorous bird.

Northern cassowary *Casuarius unappendiculatus*: Orange wattled Papuan flightless bird.

Rhinoceros hornbill *Buceros rhinoceros* Huge black head ornamentally horned herbivorous bird.

Pin tailed Sand grouse *Pterocles alchata* Small pigeon like desert bird.

Australian Bustard *Ardeotis australis* Huge ground dwelling white, Black and brown bird.

Buff-banded rail *Gallirallus philippensis* Small ground dwelling water bird.

Black swift (*Cypseloides niger*) Small black flying bird that seldom lands.

Passerines

Torresian Crows *Corvus Orru:* Australian crow

Chihuahuan Raven *Corvus cryptoleucus*: Mexican desert living raven species

Maghreb magpie *Pica mauritanica:* black, white and blue desert living crovid

Eastern paradise whydah *(Vidua paradisaea)* African long tail feathered finch

Black headed grosbeak (*Pheucticus melanocephalus*) Pine forest living finch.

Reptiles and Amphibians

Amphibians

Sonoran Desert toad *Incilius alvarius* Desert living toad

Spencers Burrowing frog, *Opisthodon spenceri* Dry season hibernating frog

Crocodile newt *Tylototriton verrucosus* Poisonous Asian newt

Squamata

Burmese Python *Python bivittatus:* Large Asian python

Mojave rattlesnake *Crotalus scutulatus:* Desert dwelling viper

Argentine Black and white tegu *Tupinambis merianae*: Large omnivorous black and white lizard

Lace monitor Varanus varius: Spotted and striped Australian monitor lizard, is also called the Goanna

Desert monitor *Varanus griseus* Desert living monitor lizard

Marine iguana *Amblyrhynchus cristatus* Black scale seaweed eating iguana

Common Chuckwalla *Sauromalus ater* Desert living iguana

Australian Tree Skink *Egernia striolata* an arboreal skink.

Burtons Legless lizard *'Lialis burtonis'* A snake like lizard.

Non avian archosaurs

Crocodilians

American crocodile *Crocodylus acutus:* Large crocodile species from the Caribbean

Black caiman *Melanosuchus niger:* Large black alligator like crocdillian

Gharial *Gavialis gangeticus:* Crocodilian with bulbous tip to elongated snout.

Reconstructed dinosaurs

Tyrannosaur: closely resembles tyrannosaurus rex, but wit ha coat of non pennaceous feathers.

Spinosaurid: Resembling suchomimus , this large primarly fish eating semiaqutic therapod is the apex predator of the swamps.

Oviraptorid 'Psittaraptor Albus' Reconstructed dinosaur made from various bird species genes including parrots and bustards.

Black raptor 'Dromeoraptor Foxxi' Reconstructed dinosaur made form bird genes including eagles and hawks.

Ontihiopod *'Hydrochoerusaurus Alfredi'* Generic looking ornithopod reconstructed from reptile, mammal, and bird DNA.

Other reptiles

Red footed tortoise *Chelonoidis carbonarius* Small south American tortoise

Macquarie turtle *Emydura macquarii* Small freshwater turtle

'Reconstructed pterosaurs' two species of pterosaurs reconstructed form many animal genes, one is large, the other small.

Cartilaginous fish

Sharks and kin

Tawny nurse shark *Nebrius ferrugineus* Slow swimming large nurse shark.

Bull shark (*Carcharhinus leucas*) large shark found in marine, brackish and freshwater environments

Rays

Torpedo ray *Torpedo marmorata* Electric marine stingray.

Bony fish

Teleost fish

African toothed catfish *Clarias gariepinus* Swamp living carnivorous catfish.

Yaqui catfish *Ictalurus pricei*: Desert living catfish.

French angelfish *Pomacanthus paru*: large blue and grey reef fish

Seychelles butterflyfish: *Chaetodon madagaskariensis*: Small striped reef fish.

Potato cod *Epinephelus tukula:* Large spotted grouper

Red Belied Piranha *Pygocentrus nattereri* shoal living carnivorous fish.

Alien fauna

Teuthidoplanes '*Archeomantellis sp*' Strange squid like flying aliens.

Black silk giant psuedoarachnid '*Araneokevlaris Negro*' large spider like aliens that produce the valuable black silk.

Wyrm '*Wyrm Gigas*' Strange huge burrowing aliens.

Crab things??? '*Xenodromia Obsurus*' strange subterranean crab like aliens.

Millipede things '*Gigascutigera Horridus*' Strange many legged subterranean aliens

Blue fish thing '*Parapisces Azure*' Strange fish like aliens that live underground.

About the author

Matthew Anderson developed his unique concept for this book based on his YouTube video game movies (machinima) that he created as a teenager.

After tens of thousands of views and a considerable following requesting more episodes, Matthew decided to commit this creativity to this novel.

He is a lover of Natural Sciences and has a Bachelor of Science in Animal Ecology. He has an exceptionally creative mind, especially when he blends his boundless knowledge of animals with his gift for speculative fiction.

When he is not writing, studying, and working as an Animal Ecologist, he is travelling widely to experience all the animal wonders of the world.